The Second Wind

Samantha Benson

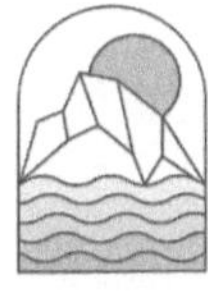

www.samanthabensonauthor.com

ISBN: 978-1-961611-01-6

Editors: Brent Burchett; Lisa Hollett, Silently Correcting Your Grammar
Formatting: Stacey Blake, Champagne Book Design
Cover: Sarah Hansen, Okay Creations

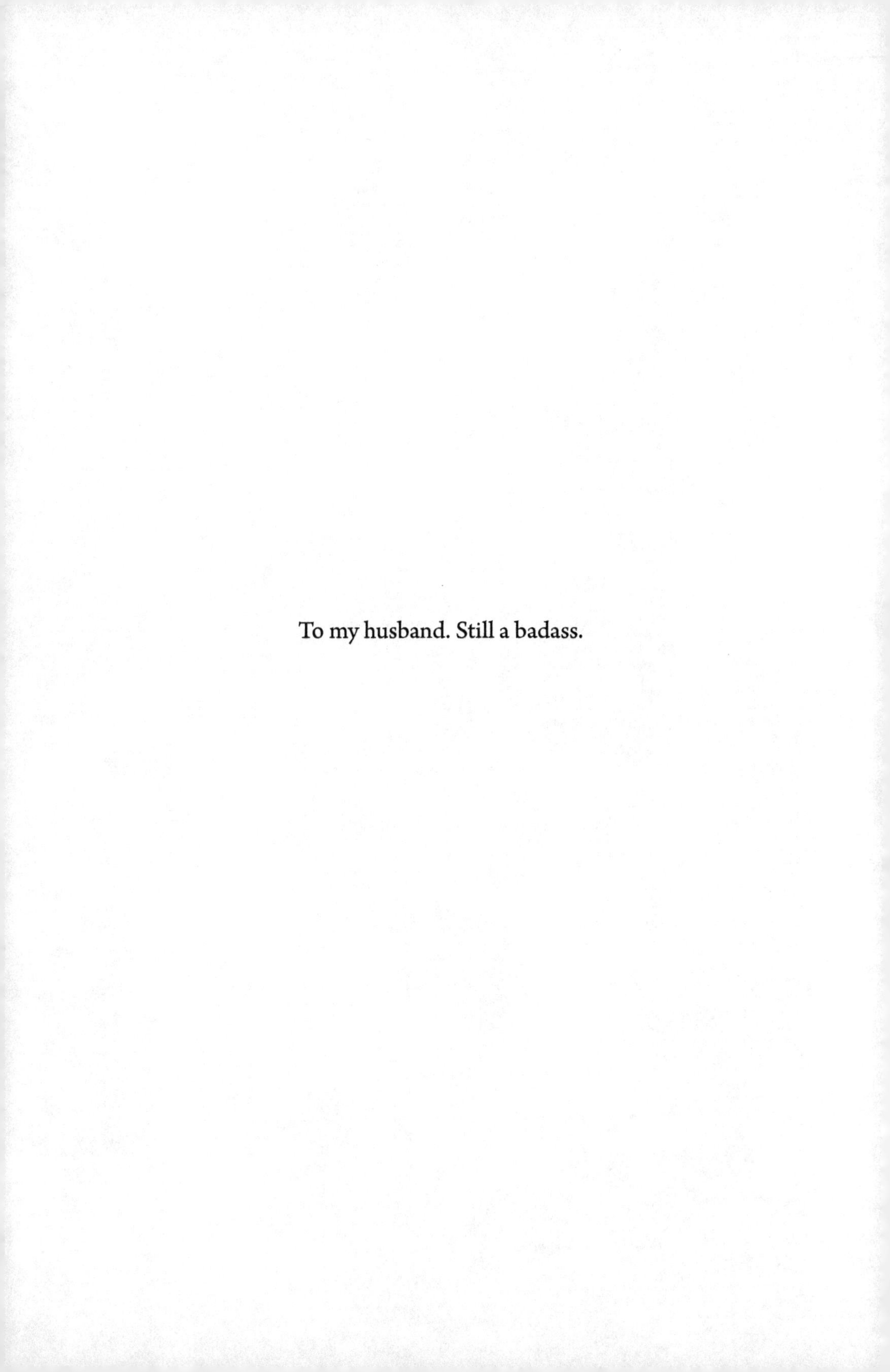

To my husband. Still a badass.

The Second Wind

Chapter One

SMACK. SMACK. SMACK.

One foot in front of the other.

The cliché pops into my head during my morning run.

Just keep putting one foot in front of the other.

Do I enjoy running? Not particularly.

Am I an adrenaline junkie?

I suppose I used to be.

I suppose anyone who plays football at the professional level—which, up until a little over a year ago, I did for a living—has to be somewhat of an adrenaline junkie.

But right now, I just run to feel *something*. Anything.

Sweat drips down my brow, and I wipe my forehead with the bottom of my shirt. It's a foggy morning on the Central California coast, which is par for the course. The increased humidity and salty air make everything heavier than normal, and my shirt hangs on me like a damp rag.

The fog greeted me today, as it does most mornings, with a stillness and a challenge.

Get up and get moving.

My father used to greet me every day with a cheesy saying. "Let's go, Nicky! Today is another day you are alive!"

He's been dead for twenty-five years, but I still remember the twinkle in his eyes and the smile in his voice.

Smack. Smack. Smack.

To my left is Highway 1, quiet this Saturday morning. To my right is the Pacific. The ocean thunders, the gray water rolling in along the wet sand as I run. The air is thick with salt, and the sea gulls bark overhead in a gun-metal sky.

I run between the two small beach towns along the pristine coast, towns that have looked nearly the same for the past fifty years. After spending so much time around the country in my former life, I am still amazed at this wide swath of coastland that has remained undeveloped in California. It's far different from San Diego, my home in my former life, an area developed within an inch of its life.

A couple mega-builds loom ahead as I run back into town, but homes like those are few and far between. It's too much of a hassle to deal with all the permitting and rules, I imagine, to build the McMansions of San Diego in Estero Bay.

I used to live in one such McMansion. A 15,000-square-foot monstrosity up in the hills. On a clear day, you could practically reach out and touch the Pacific. A custom-built palace, complete with Venetian columns along the circular driveway and a water fountain in the giant foyer that constantly made me want to take a piss every time I heard it.

Thinking of that place now creates a pit in the deep part of my stomach.

It does *not* make me feel alive.

So I keep running.

I run back toward home—Estero Bay, my hometown, a small beach and fishing community. I came back here after my football career ended suddenly and without notice. That's not to say it was a surprise to me. I was the only one who wasn't surprised. I made the decision to end it.

I made the decision to return to my hometown alone.

Only, now I'm not alone.

I have my black Labrador running alongside me—Layne Staley, my constant companion and, currently, the love of my life.

Layne looks happy. Although to be fair, he usually looks happy. He'd run forever if I let him. He pants heavily, his tongue lolling out of his mouth, content to run alongside me as long as I want. He also knows there are treats waiting for him at the end of the journey, so that's an incentive.

I wipe my brow again as we creep closer to the bay. As the fog tapers off, I look for the giant rock, the centerpiece of the Bay, and the reason this man-made harbor was built over a hundred years ago.

Each morning is a battle between the fog and the sun. Some days, particularly in the foggy season, the Rock isn't visible but for an hour or two. Other days, the sun wins out and beats back the fog, leaving the nearly six-hundred-foot-tall rock naked for everyone to see.

On this day, I can't see the Rock. I can barely see twenty feet in front of me. But I know it's there.

It might sound strange, but the Rock—really a volcanic plug that made its way out of the ocean over twenty million years ago, and yes, all the local kids are taught that in elementary school—is a comfort, a standby. I feel a tinge of relief every time I see the Rock. It's a stalwart of this town, of the coast. No matter what happens on the outside, the Rock is still here.

I don't have a McMansion. My football career is over.

My personal life…well.

The less said about that, the better.

But the Rock is still here. If this damn Rock that serves no purpose other than to offer me comfort can survive for twenty million years, I should be able to survive whatever I'm going through right now.

Smack. Smack. Smack.

Layne Staley and I run closer to the town proper, past the high school, a beachside park, a couple motels. No one is out. The Embarcadero—the main drag through town, full of shops and restaurants—will likely be more crowded with folks walking their dogs, getting coffee. The fishermen will be there, getting ready to head out for the day, if they haven't left already. They rise earlier than I do.

My grandfather, a second-generation Basque immigrant, was a fisherman, catching salmon in the summer, crab in the winter, and operating an oyster farm year-round. It's hard work, the kind that doesn't stop just because of a holiday, a football game, or an illness. Pops is retired now, but he often walks the Embarcadero early in the morning with his buddies, catching up on the gossip and drinking hot coffee.

I turn past a seafood restaurant and slow to a walk, making my way to the steps down to the docks. I stretch and catch my breath before continuing down the footpath, Layne Staley trotting beside me.

"Hey, Nicky!"

Sure enough, my grandfather sits with a cherubic grin on his face as I approach the bench. He's there with two of his oldest friends—Larry, a former fisherman like him, and Cesar, a retired plumber. All three of these guys were born and raised in Estero Bay and like to hold court out here with fellow locals and tourists alike.

"Hey, Pops." I wheeze out a greeting, still catching my breath from my twelve-mile run. I nod to Larry and Cesar.

"How was the run? How's the leg? And how are you, ya mangy mutt?" Pops speaks this last question to Layne Staley, who attempts to join the men on the benches. I swear this dog thinks he's a lap cat.

As to "the leg," Pops refers to my right one. The leg that ultimately ended my football career. The leg that still pains me, on some days making me feel like I am ninety-two instead of thirty-two.

Again, I feel a discomfort in the pit of my stomach, like a brick has settled in there nicely.

"It's good, Pops," I tell my grandfather a little quietly, leaning down to stretch my hamstrings.

"Good, good," he responds easily, scratching Layne Staley behind the ears.

"What else is going on today?" Larry asks me, setting down the *Estero Times* newspaper he's been holding.

"I've got yoga later this morning," I reply. "Probably go to the Brew later," I continue, referring to the local restaurant in town run by my older sister Julia and her husband.

"Julia and Linc are around this weekend, right?" I ask my grandfather. "I might need Lincoln's help tomorrow."

"Yeah, no sports chauffeur this weekend," my grandfather responds. My sister and her husband have two daughters, ages six and ten. Between the various sporting events they participate in, it's not unheard of for them to be out of town for the weekend, taking their kids to soccer or softball or cheer competitions.

"But I think Tatum already got them lined up to help her," Pops adds.

"Oh yeah? What's going on with Tatum?" Tatum is my little sister, a lawyer, and the most put-together person I know. She's been practicing law since graduating from Pepperdine Law early at twenty-three and will probably be taking over the world here within the next few years.

"Her friend is moving back to the Bay," Pops responds.

"Okay. Who?"

"You know. Summer."

Well...fuck.

"Summer...Mahoney?"

I need to make sure.

"That's the one," my grandfather replies, his eyes twinkling a little.

I did not, in fact, know this information. And I tell my grandfather this, without the profanity.

"Yeah, she's moving back from whatever cold weather big city she was living in with what's-his-name," My grandfather is only too happy to fill me in on the gossip. I notice Larry and Cesar have ceased their own private conversation to observe the two of us.

"And...is what's-his-name returning with...Summer?" I ask nonchalantly.

Pops snorts. "No. She's coming back alone without the idiot."

I see we've moved on from what's-his-name to the name-calling portion of this conversation. But that's fine with me. The less said about Summer's husband—ex-husband?—the better.

But just to confirm...

"So...she's divorced."

"Yup! Just like you!" My grandfather grins, misplaced pride in his voice, like I should be happy to be a card-carrying member of the Divorce Club.

I wince.

"She was always too good for that guy anyway. You know how I know that?"

This is now the pontification portion of the conversation, where my grandfather likes to drop knowledge on Larry, Cesar, and anyone else who happens to be in the vicinity of the benches where they sit alongside the Embarcadero. On this brisk morning, that happens to be me, the sea gulls, and the assorted seals I can hear barking out in the Bay.

And, of course, Layne Staley.

"I know that because of the way he treated those he felt were, you know, *beneath him*," Pops continues without waiting for a response. "He wasn't very friendly to me or your mother, you know. After all, I was just a lowly fisherman." He chuckles along with Larry and Cesar. "Never mind the fact that Summer practically lived with our family for a couple years. She's like my surrogate granddaughter."

I shudder at the thought—not only the thought of another sister. Julia and Tatum are just fine, thank you very much.

But because I damn well never saw Summer as a sister.

"Anyway, Summer needs to come visit with me. We should take her on the boat. Just like old times," Pops continues.

"We…?"

"You, me, Summer, Tatum. Just like old times," Pops repeats.

"Only with two failed marriages between us," I mutter dryly. Pops hears me, though, and glares.

"Now, Nicky," he intones. "Nothing to be ashamed about. You did what you had to do."

Aaaaand it's time to go.

"I'll leave you to it, Pops," I mutter, standing up straight. Layne Staley immediately jumps to my side, eager for our next adventure.

As if he doesn't already know what we do each day.

Wake up. Run until it feels like I am going to pass out or throw up. Shower. Eat. Stare at the Rock. Maybe have a beer or two. Listen to my sisters and mother and grandfather tell me what I should be doing. Do yoga— or "the yoga," as my grandfather calls it. Talk with my therapist. Read. Sleep.

Sometimes, I even go for another run just to shake things up.

"See you later, *gaixo mutikoa*," my grandfather gives me a Basque term of endearment as I pick up my jog to head home along the Embarcadero.

My feet once again pound the pavement, Layne Staley panting happily beside me.

Today is another day I am alive.

Chapter Two

Nick

AFTER A QUICK SHOWER TO WASH THE SALT AND SWEAT OFF ME, I amble into my kitchen. It's quiet—too quiet, even with Layne Staley wrapping himself around my legs, excited as ever about life. The kind of quiet that can allow my thoughts to overtake the rational part of my brain.

I give him a treat, rubbing his ears, and make myself a protein shake before my yoga session.

I would hope we've moved past the issue of whether it's manly or acceptable for men to do yoga in this gender-fluid reality we live in, but just in case we haven't—don't knock it. I look utterly ridiculous doing some of the poses; I am not limber by any stretch of the imagination, and some moves just weren't meant to be done by a six-foot, four-inch, 250-pound man. But the physical and mindfulness benefits of yoga truly saved me. There is no way on God's green earth I would have survived the physical toll on my body after my football career without yoga and some good old-fashioned deep breathing.

My body is still healing, though, and I have limits that are not so visible to the naked eye. That's why I have Luther, a local surfer yogi type, coming to my place to lead me in some vinyasas. Luther is a dude about my age of ambiguous ethnic background, with piercings in his lip, his ears, and his eyebrow, and is ripped as fuck. He lives and lets others live and leads a kick-ass yoga studio here in town.

My doorbell rings, and I lift my head in greeting.

"Howsit, man?" Luther asks as he enters the foyer. His hair is longer, past his shoulders, and tinged with purple on the bottom.

"Not bad. Did a run this morning and my leg is a little sore, but all good otherwise."

Luther follows me into one of the rooms I've turned into a makeshift fitness room, with free weights, a massage table, and a sauna in the far corner.

"How's your headspace, though?" Luther asks me as he comes to sit on the floor with his legs crossed, lotus style.

My headspace is fucked.

I attempt a smile that I don't feel reach my eyes. "As good as can be expected, I guess. Just…figuring out my next act."

Luther watches me craftily. For a guy who embodies the Spicoli-zen-surfer vibe so well, he's more perceptive than all that.

I join him on the floor for lotus, and we get to work. After class, we meander to the wraparound porch on the second floor outside of the fitness room.

"So, listen. I've got some news, brother," Luther tells me after we finish our breathing exercises. We relax in the lounge chairs, me with water, and Luther with some liquid he says is raw coconut water but smells like cleaning solution.

"Someone reached out to me on behalf of Holly Vasquez." Luther references a famous Hollywood actor and singer. "She asked if I would be willing to come to LA for a few months to teach yoga while she films her latest movie."

This is not entirely out of thin air. There are a lot of very nice, very fancy, very expensive resorts here on the Central Coast, from Santa Barbara up to Big Sur, and Luther works at several of them, teaching yoga and mindfulness classes. Some of those resorts attract Hollywood types for retreats and weddings and stuff, given that Los Angeles is a little over three hours away by car without traffic. Which really means a five-hour drive, at least, because there is always fucking traffic.

"Yeah, she was a guest at the Villas a couple weeks ago, and I did a one-on-one with her and some of her people." Luther smirks at the memory, leading me to guess that he did a lot more than downward dog, if you know what I mean. Although, I suppose downward dog could also be incorporated into sex.

I wouldn't know.

It's been a long dry spell for me.

"That's awesome, man," I tell Luther, and I mean it. This is a great opportunity for him.

"So, I am heading down there next week, and I'll be there for at least two months. I am sure I will be back here on some weekends, but I have someone lined up to take on my clients and my resort classes."

"Oh?" I ask. I get a prickly sensation on the back of my neck.

"Yeah…Summer Mahoney."

I exhale, glad he is telling me this after a seriously relaxing yoga session, instead of before. This gives me ample time to really develop a good, strong case of anxiety that won't disrupt my vinyasas and asanas.

"That's the second time I have heard that name today," I mutter.

At Luther's look, I explain. "Saw my grandfather this morning…he mentioned that she's moving back to Estero Bay."

"She's a certified yoga teacher, too. Apparently, she took that up after the dancing thing didn't pan out."

I knew Summer danced all her life—she went to Juilliard on a full-ride scholarship after high school. We'd ended up in New York City at the same time; she was there in school, and I was there for the NFL draft.

A weekend I immediately file into another compartment in my mind, the one labeled "fragile—do not open."

"You know she's getting divorced?"

I grunt. "Does everyone here know all this gossip but me?"

Luther gives me an easy grin. "Hey man, if you weren't such a hermit these days, you'd be up on the gossip too."

"I'm not a hermit. More like…selective about where I want to be and when I want to be there."

"I hear that." Luther takes a sip of his swampwater. "Well, she's covering a bunch of classes at the studio and said she'd also cover my private sessions," he adds.

"She's going to do all that? You have other instructors, though, right?" I ask Luther.

"Well, sure. I have Amber," Luther responds slowly, giving me a knowing look. Amber Bracamonte was my girlfriend in high school. She's nice enough, but a little too peppy for me.

I have no room in my life for pep.

"Other than Amber," Luther continues, "I've got some older teachers who are more into the very low-impact, relaxing-type classes. Not that you couldn't benefit from that too, brother, but I don't really have anyone who's got the background that Summer does. Honestly, man, I think she'll be good for your continued healing. Positive vibes only."

Luther is really big on healing vibes and positivity. I know he means well, and I don't have the heart to tell him that too much positivity can be toxic.

I learned that in therapy, believe it or not.

"All right." I step up off the lounge chair to walk Luther out. "Give her my number, and we can set something up, I suppose."

"Kinda crazy, huh, the two of you being back in town, single after all these years," Luther muses as we walk to the foyer.

"Merely a coincidence," I mutter.

"No such thing, brother," Luther intones.

"I haven't talked to Summer in years, man."

Luther nods thoughtfully. "Didn't she live with your family for a while, anyway?"

"Yeah…after her parents died." I pause at the awful memory of her parents' car accident. "I was already up at Cal, though."

"I'm just saying, brother, sometimes the universe lines things up in just the right pattern."

Luther is also big on making sure I am listening to what the universe is telling me.

"Well, right now, the universe is telling me that it's time for you to beat it, brother." I mimic Luther's nickname and he laughs.

"I'm just putting it out there." Luther pauses at the front door and looks me squarely in the eyes, his goofy surfer persona absent. "Don't ignore the universe, Nick," he says seriously, before turning to go, giving me an absent-minded wave.

"I will not ignore the universe," I mutter to Layne Staley, who barks after Luther in good-bye.

∾∾∾∾∾

Later in the evening, I relax on my balcony with Layne Staley, watching the sunset.

I mean it when I say that I never had the type of brotherly affection—or disaffection, depending on the day—for Summer that I had for Tatum, my annoying little sister, or Julia, my scary older sister. Both of my sisters can be pretty scary, when you think about it. The stereotype about a brother needing to guard and protect his female siblings from the big, bad world has no place in my family history. Julia was kicking ass and taking names well before I could throw long, and my parents joke that Tatum began issuing directives to all us Echeverrias upon her birth. Growing up with strong-willed women was the only thing I knew.

And once my dad died, my mother had no choice but to become even stronger. She had three kids to raise. Four, if you count my grandfather, who always needed a little looking after and was probably like another kid.

Summer was different. She was strong-willed too, but whereas my sisters were likely to arm-wrestle me into submission, Summer did it through the power of persuasion. With my sisters running through the town and our home like tornadoes, Summer was like, well, a ray of sunshine, always with a smile, always making me feel like I hung the moon just for her.

When we were kids, I walked her home to make sure she got there safely. In the summertime, I took her, Tatum, and their friend Lucy to get ice cream. I was a pretty shy kid—and perhaps more so due to my sisters' boisterous natures. It felt almost natural for me to be tagging along with Tatum and Summer rather than having them tag along with me.

My childhood is filled with happy memories, and Summer's in a lot of them.

But of course, kids grow up. And the switch flipped. Ice cream trips and bicycle rides that had been routine eventually became…distracting for a teenager coming of age.

I remember Summer's sun-kissed skin, sprinkled with freckles, as she glided smoothly through the water during our trips to the beach. I remember wanting to reach out and rub my hand over her skin to see if it was as warm and soft as it looked.

I can see her long coppery hair dripping salt water on our towels as she and Tatum lay in the sun to get warm after swimming in the frigid Pacific waters. I felt the urge to comb my fingers through her hair before rubbing the back of her neck and angling her face toward me.

I recall Summer as a teenager in her bikini after lifeguard class, licking her rocky road cone with a vigor that caused a strange tightening in my groin.

And I could never forget her twinkly brown eyes, flecked with gold, looking at me like I was the most important person in her world.

Those same eyes looking at me with disappointment and sadness after the horrible weekend in New York.

I haven't seen her since then. We haven't spoken, haven't texted.

That weekend in New York made me a starting quarterback in the NFL. My life changed overnight, and not just because of my new job.

My new life in the NFL occupied 100% of my time and attention. I gave that job everything I had from day one. But that's not to say that I didn't acutely feel the loss of Summer's friendship.

Since that time, we've both been married, both now divorced. She's also apparently no longer dancing, if her move back to Estero Bay is any indication.

I've consciously avoided discussing Summer with Tatum over the years, and Tatum has certainly never voluntarily updated me.

Coming back to my hometown resurrects a lot of ghosts. The spot by the lifeguard tower on the beach where my dad taught my sisters and me to swim. The high school football field where I led our team to its first state championship. The hills inland, where we hiked and caught fish, and—when we were older—where my buddies and I went to drink and make out with girls. The local dive bar has the same old pirate statue out front, covered in beads; the Embarcadero still smells salty from the bay and sweet from the cinnamon rolls made daily at the bakery.

The damn Rock is still here, mocking me.

But I've changed.

Playing football, at least early in my career, gave me a spark. There's nothing like the adrenaline, the energy, the feeling of performing at an elite level. Nothing compares to pushing your body to its limits week after week with a team of like-minded individuals with the same goal as you.

To win a ring.

But as my playing career progressed, something else came with that spark. It started small, a kernel deep in my chest, a feeling of worry that grew, week after week, month after month, eventually blooming into full-blown anxiety.

That anxiety manifested itself into panic attacks. Not ideal when you are literally the face of a professional sports franchise.

I breathe out, making a point to lower my shoulders and unclench my jaw. Layne Staley rubs his head against my legs before walking around in a circle and popping a squat on the floor next to me.

Several years later, here I am. Back in my hometown, my career over. My marriage over. My anxiety manageable. Not managed, but manageable.

Now I spend my days dealing with the ghosts. Sometimes I feel like I'm in the in-between. I am not who I was before, and I am unsure of who I will become. Unsure if I will ever have the spark again.

Maybe I'll get it back.

But I won't hold my breath.

Chapter Three

I TAKE A DEEP BREATH AND ADMIRE THE VIEW FROM OUTSIDE MY NEW home.

Well, new-to-me anyway.

My new, but not *new* new, home is a two-story condo with weathered brown clapboard along the front, faded blue shutters framing the large windows. Like a lot of houses here, the front door is up the stairs on the second floor. The first floor has a two-car garage with a small laundry area in the back.

I'd only seen pictures of this place before taking the plunge and moving across the country from New York City to Estero Bay. My best friend Tatum inspected the place before I signed the papers. And since she was acting as my agent, she also managed to talk the seller down from the original listing price, given that I was paying cash.

Given that she's not just my agent but my oldest friend, Tatum also voiced her concerns about my making such a big purchase so soon after several months of…upheaval, so to speak.

An unexpected—but perhaps not unwelcome, ultimately—divorce from the man I'd been with since I was nineteen? *Check.*

A career-ending injury leading to my departure from the City Ballet, one of the most lauded, preeminent ballet companies in the world? *Check.*

A move across the country from the City That Never Sleeps to, according to some license plate frames, "The Town That Time Forgot"? *Check.*

"Are you sure you don't want to rent for a while? You can move in with me until you figure shit out," Tatum had said during one of our many phone conversations while I was still on the East Coast.

"I'm sure," I told her. "Honestly, I want to do this. And frankly, I have the money, thanks to my trust. Isn't real estate the best way to invest anyway?"

This topic was one of Tatum's favorites. "Well, the market here is always hot. There's a limited supply and so many regulations that prevent builders from building up a little Miami. But we can also talk about VC—there are some great female-fronted VCs right now—or mutual funds…"

I had tuned out Tatum's voice at that point, letting her pontificate the benefits of high-yield savings accounts versus venture capital versus money market accounts. Finance talk was *not* for me…something that Erik, my ex-husband, used to point out, all while insinuating that I was not as smart or as worldly as him.

"Summer," he'd say with a cool smile. Everything about him was *cool*—not in a hip way. In an understated, dispassionate way. Cool tone of voice. Cool expression. Cool-to-the-touch hands.

"Don't worry yourself about this," he'd say when I expressed interest in his work, in his investments, in anything having to do with his professional life. "You have such a gift for art. Stick to that."

I scoff now, remembering his passive-aggressive tone and the way he could make a compliment sound like an insult.

Erik comes from money. He became rich the old-fashioned way—by inheriting it from his father, who inherited from his father, an East Coast shipping and banking magnate. Erik was only required to do the absolute bare minimum, praised for merely existing as a member of a privileged family, congratulated for deigning to share oxygen with the rest of the world. He was born one step ahead.

The fact that Erik had more money than he knew what to do with didn't stop him from watching every penny I spent like a hawk, and it didn't stop him from engaging in warfare-like tactics during our divorce proceedings to ensure that I didn't take any of those pennies in the divorce.

Not only did we have a prenup where we both walked away with our own earnings, but Erik ignored the obvious: I had, and have, my own money. My father became rich the new-fashioned way—by inventing microchips still used in radiology equipment in hospitals around the world. I haven't really touched my money over the years. And when I was younger, I couldn't touch it anyway, as it was in trust, managed by some faceless trustees working for an equally faceless asset protection company. I received what I needed to keep me comfortable, and for that, I am forever grateful.

Not that I wouldn't trade it all back in a millisecond to have another day with my parents.

Shaking my head of these thoughts, I take a deep breath, unclench my jaw, and push my shoulders down and back, walking up the stairs to the front door. It's painted a bright red, adding a pop of color to the ramshackle aesthetic.

"I should have brought sage or something to cleanse the place," I remark to Tatum over my shoulder.

"I can't help you with the sage, *bruja*, but I *did* bring cleaning supplies, which is really more important." Tatum is fastidious about cleaning—"it's not next to godliness. It's actually above godliness. Who wants a god if there's bacteria on the pearly gates?"—and is carrying a canvas tote of her own supplies with her. "Honestly, you never know what kind of job people do before moving out of a home."

It's really not that bad, though, as we step inside. The tang of lemon is in the air from whatever cleaning solution someone used. The walls are painted bright white, and the ceiling is gray wood, with a long beam running from one side of the room to the other. The front room is open and spacious, with the kitchen at the end behind a big portable butcher block. A loft is visible to the left, accessible by narrow white stairs, and there are two additional bedrooms on the right side of the house, with one bathroom in between.

On the other side of the room opposite the kitchen is the balcony, stretching the entire length of the front of the house. I make a beeline for the sliding doors and open the large glass door, leaving the screen shut, and take a deep breath.

Estero Rock is right outside, beyond the marsh and the bay.

"This is perfect," I murmur. "Honestly, just what I had pictured."

"Good! Good," Tatum says distractedly, running her fingers over the butcher block to assess the dust situation. "Do you want me to start with the kitchen or the bathroom?"

"Ew. Neither." I step away from the balcony and turn toward Tatum. "Let's bring in some of the stuff from my car, and then, if you must, I will permit you to scour the bathroom to your heart's content."

Tatum sighs dramatically. "That might be the sweetest thing you have ever said to me," she says, placing her hands over her heart.

"I mean, obviously, you will owe me big time. Who knows when you will get to clean a bathroom again—one that isn't yours, which I am sure sparkles like a diamond?"

"Truth," Tatum agrees. "When is the big stuff arriving? I roped Lincoln into helping, by the way."

"That's nice, but I paid some college kids to do all that. It would be silly to expect Lincoln to unload all the big furniture by himself anyway."

"In that case, I will gladly join you in objectifying the youth as they engage in their sweaty pursuits. When are they coming?"

"Sometime this afternoon," I reply.

"And anyway," Tatum continues, "I was going to ask my brother if he would help out too." She eyes me cautiously from behind the butcher block.

"Hmmmmm," is my noncommittal response.

"Hmmmmm?" Tatum asks. "That's all I get? A 'hmmmmm'?"

"What were you expecting? And did you actually ask him?"

"Not yet," Tatum concedes. "But I can, if you want?"

"Nah. Tell Lincoln and…Nick—" I pause, testing how his name feels in my mouth "—that I am sure the movers can get it all. I don't have a whole lot."

"You got it. And speaking of, let's get the stuff from your car in before they get here. We should really have them bring the couch in first so we have a comfortable spot from which to ogle them."

I roll my eyes. "Don't objectify them, Ms. Echeverria. And anyway, you know they are college kids, right? I mean, we are practically old enough to be their parents."

Tatum snorts. "I don't know what universe you live in where a thirty-year-old can be the mother of a twenty-year-old. Anyway, age ain't nothing but a number, and I wore a boob shirt just for the viewing."

Tatum shimmies her ample—okay, they are huge—breasts at me.

"They may not be perky as a twenty-year-old's, but they are still real and still fabulous," Tatum tells me.

"Well, Dolly, let's get the stuff in here, so your real and fabulous breasts can relax."

～～～～～

Thwack. Thwack.

"Like, right there?"

"No…a little to the right, I think. A little more…little more…yes! That's the spot."

Tatum grins triumphantly as she steps down from the small ladder and puts aside the hammer she was using to hang a painting in my new living room.

"That looks really good, babe." Tatum gestures toward the painting, which is one I did back when we were in high school. It's definitely abstract and definitely painted by someone who was "in their feelings," as the kids say these days.

"You don't think it's too emo?" It's got purple, my signature color, but interspersed with lots of black and gray and navy. It's dark, literally and figuratively.

"Nah. You've got enough other colors in here so I don't really feel like I am in a goth house or something. Now, if you were going to ask me to hang some My Chemical Romance posters next, we might have a chat."

"Please. Everyone knows the music posters go in the garage."

Tatum snickers and makes her way to the wall, where I've got several other paintings leaning. "I can't believe these were just, like, in storage for so long." She sifts through the canvases, pausing to inspect each one. "They are in pretty good shape, considering."

"When it was clear Erik wouldn't be hanging any of those in our house, *his house,* I put them in a special storage facility." I pause and fiddle with the bun on the top of my head. "Alexis found it, actually. It wasn't cheap. There were, like, temperature controls and stuff…" I let my voice trail off.

Tatum raises her eyebrows at the mention of my older sister. "That was nice of her."

"It was," I tell her firmly. "I know she has her issues, but she comes through when it counts."

Tatum looks skeptical now. "Didn't stop you from marrying *him*, did she?"

"Erik. His name is Erik. It's not like he's Voldemort or something. We can say his name." I make my way over to a chair and plop down, picking up a soft throw pillow and hugging it to my chest.

"I feel like his name shouldn't even take up real estate in my mouth." Tatum joins me on the couch, stretching out her legs.

"Yeah, I hear that." I think about what to say next, then decide to tell her. "She emailed me. Alexis. A few days ago."

"She did?" Tatum looks surprised.

And understandably so. My sister is a certifiable genius, a leader in her field. Her communication skills, however, are pretty atypical. She won't text—I believe her words on the subject were something like "communicating in this fashion will lead to the downfall of humanity as we know it"—and doesn't like to speak on the phone. I think she has to spend a lot of time gathering her thoughts and ensuring they are worded with no room for misinterpretation before sending me an email. And even then, the message will be something benign, like "I saw a swan in Central Park the other day, and it reminded me of you," or "Are you allergic to strawberries?" or "Happy birthday."

"She wanted to know if I had any plans to be back East anytime soon." I didn't and I don't. Between the ballet in New York and the fact that Erik's family owns half of Boston, I'd be happy if I never flew anywhere remotely near the entire eastern seaboard again.

"When I told her no, she mentioned she might be coming to California for a conference. At Stanford, but she mentioned coming here. To the Bay."

If Tatum's eyebrows rise any higher, they are going to join her hairline.

"I mean…" Tatum frowns. "She's come back here, like…never."

"Never," I affirm.

"So…why? Not that, you know, a sister wouldn't want to see her sister after, you know—" she waves her hand around a bit, I assume to generally indicate the state of my life "—but she's not a typical sister."

"She's not," I agree. "But I told her my door is always open and I'd love to see her."

"Damn," Tatum says softly before pausing, like she's considering her words. "She was always too big for this place anyway. Too much going on in her head for her to be content in a small place, maybe."

"Doesn't everyone feel that way about their hometown at one point or another?" I speak in dramatic tones, recalling how Junior High Me felt. "'No one understands me here!' 'No one gets me!' 'When I go away to New York or Paris or London or Tokyo or wherever, that's when I feel like I belong!'"

Tatum laughs. "Yeah, I guess you're right. But you have to admit that this is probably not the best place to conduct research on subatomic particles and how black holes affect them, or whatever she works on for a living."

It's my turn to raise my eyebrows.

Tatum shrugs. "I like to read. Physics is cool, man."

"*Anyway.*"

I move to the island, where we've been grazing all day on snacks Tatum brought over from the restaurant. "Just a few things," she said innocently before setting out Irish nachos, bacon-wrapped dates, and these ridiculously delicious pretzels—soft and warm, with different dipping sauces.

I help myself to a pretzel. "She, Alexis, came to visit me when I was in the hospital with my injury. At a convenient time when Erik wasn't around."

Chapter Four

Summer, before

T HE INCESSANT BEEPING OF THE MACHINES MADE IT SO THAT I rarely slept for an extended period of time. When I saw my older sister—with her lily-white skin and piercing, glacier-like eyes—I thought I was imagining things.

"Oh good, you're awake." Alexis walked into the room and shut the door softly behind her. She strode purposefully to my bed, her stiletto heels clicking, her black pantsuit perfectly tailored to her slim figure. We were built similarly, all limbs and height. Her light-blond hair was pulled back tightly from her face in a severe bun—her signature look, so to speak. I didn't think I'd seen her with her hair down since we were little girls.

She paused at my bedside and looked down at me before lifting her hand slightly, as if to hold mine, before reconsidering and putting her hand back down.

She looked up toward me.

"How are you feeling, Summer?"

"What… How did you get here?" I croaked. I rolled my head toward the side table, where my loyal cup of ice chips waited for me. The IV line impeded my movement; Alexis reached to hand me the cup.

I chewed thoughtfully. I was sure I looked ridiculous. I hadn't had a proper shower in a week. My hair and skin were greasy. I'd have killed for some quality skincare products.

"I had my driver drop me off, obviously, after the flight. I received your email. I wish I had known about this…this thing sooner." Alexis seemed unable to stand in one place, walking toward the window and admiring the view of a brick wall across the hospital concourse, before returning to my bedside, before moving to the various equipment currently attached to my person and performing a brief inspection. She nodded briefly as if in approval and then turned her focus to me. "Your oxygen levels look good," she remarked.

"Thanks…? And…I'm sorry I didn't tell you about what happened," I continued. "I wasn't in the state to reach out, I guess."

"Don't be sorry," Alexis said frostily. "It wasn't your job to tell me that you'd suffered a career-ending injury."

I sucked in a breath. "You don't mince words, do you, sister?"

"It was *your* husband's job," Alexis continued, her eyes flashing.

I tried to laugh. Damn, that hurt. "Yeah, well. Erik's—"

"How is the care here?" Alexis demanded, interrupting me. "Are they treating you well?"

"Yes. Yes, they are. There's a nurse named Yolanda from Puerto Rico who is just lovely, and we talk about dancing. She loves Fosse and—"

"And Erik? Is he treating you well?" Alexis pursed her lips like she sucked on a lemon.

"Does he ever?"

Alexis raised her eyebrows—as much as she could, her Botox looked pretty fresh—at my response.

Apparently whatever medications I was hopped up on made me a little mouthy.

"I just want to ensure you are being taken care of." Alexis spoke slowly, as if the words were foreign to her, as if the concept of expressing concern for her sister's well-being was also foreign.

"I know. I know you do." I took a deep breath. Alexis had some issues in communicating with others, and she would never say anything to hurt me on purpose.

Which was more than I could say for my husband.

"I am being well cared for," I told her patiently, before pausing, unsure how this next piece of news would hit. "And you should know that Erik served me with divorce papers yesterday."

Alexis took a step back, looking like she might topple in those shiny heels. It was clear that whatever she was expecting from my husband, that wasn't it.

"And I am going to sign them or do whatever else I need to in order to get the hell out of here."

I was not referring to the hospital, and I think Alexis knew it.

"Where are the papers?" Alexis asked, all business once more.

"Over there." I pointed to my purple backpack against the window. She moved to take them out. "You're a genius, not a lawyer," I joked, but it fell flat.

Most jokes fell flat with her.

"I'm no lawyer, but that's the thing about being a genius—you hang out with other geniuses, and they all have genius lawyers." Her eyes darted up to mine briefly to confirm that, yes, she'd made a little joke, before moving back down to the papers. She gave another perfunctory nod and placed them in her oversized Chanel quilted bag.

"I'll have them look at these, and we can coordinate next steps." Alexis turned back to me, planning my future like we were negotiating a real estate deal.

"Whatever you say, sister," I slurred. I was getting sleepy again.

"I'll be in touch." Alexis paused as she moved back to my bedside. I knew touch—physical touch—was an issue for her, so I was amazed when she pressed her cold, small hand on top of mine. She squeezed briefly before moving back and turning to leave the room.

"Good-bye, Summer."

The door clicked shut behind her. I was alone again, nothing but the machines to keep me company.

"Good-bye," I said to no one.

A few moments later, the door opened again to reveal Yolanda, my favorite nurse and, currently, my only friend.

"Well, someone had a visitor!" Yolanda beamed at me as she came to my bedside to check my vitals. "Was that the sister you were telling me about?"

I burst into tears.

"Oh, honey. Oh no," Yolanda cooed to me as she grabbed the tissue box, moving the chair over to my bedside, taking my hand in hers. She patted my hand, telling me everything would be okay, not to worry. Her hand was soft, her nails painted a light pink. She smelled sweet, like donuts or cupcakes.

"I miss my mom," I blubbered between my tears. Which was clearly the drugs talking—my mother had been dead for over a decade.

"I know, sweetie. I know." Yolanda continued to pat my hand, calming me, reassuring me. And she sat with me until my tears subsided and I fell into a dreamless, narcotic-induced sleep.

Health care workers do not get paid enough for all they have to do.

～～～～～

I take a deep breath, wondering how Yolanda is doing. We exchanged contact information before I left New York, and I make a mental note to text her.

"Anyway. She certainly expedited my separation from Erik or, at least, found someone who did."

Tatum is unconvinced. "It's the least she could do, Summer. Like, literally. The *least*." She pops a date into her mouth and chews thoughtfully. "Anyway. Of course I'll be nice to her, if and when she comes to see you," she says in a totally unconvincing manner.

"Don't count on it," I mutter.

～～～～～

Later, after we've hung some more pictures—Tatum took one for her house, and I am saving a couple others—I survey my new place. I've gone with eclectic colors in the main living area. Not wanting it to look entirely like a preschool, I've complemented the purple and turquoise with gray and cream accents.

I think it looks nice.

But more importantly, it is *mine*.

Life with Erik was chrome. So much chrome. Our state-of-the-art kitchen resembled an aircraft carrier. And I never understood why we needed such an extravagant, if sterile, kitchen, given that neither of us really cooked, and Erik was fastidious about what we were permitted to eat.

I managed to get some cream and ivory into the mix, but not much. And a purple, a red, even a subtle navy?

Forget about it. Everything with Erik was shiny, like a new coin. But devoid of all color. I ended up feeling that way, especially toward the end, like I'd been buffed and polished within an inch of my life, and even the smallest crack in my veneer would reveal the truth. I had no color, no substance, nothing that was *me*. I was all luster but no life.

I have decided to live in rainbows from now on.

Chapter Five

Nick

"**D**EAR LITTLE BROTHER,**"** MY OLDER SISTER, JULIA, BEGINS AS soon as I sit down at the long bar at the Brew. It's a Saturday night, so the place is crowded with locals and college kids from the university. A Led Zeppelin song plays in the background, occasionally drowned out by a particularly rowdy darts game in the corner.

"Yes, older sister?" I raise my hand in greeting to Lincoln at the other end of the bar and give him a thumbs-up when he points to my favorite IPA on the tap.

"Girl Scout cookies. I have them. You need them."

Julia and Lincoln's youngest daughter is in a troop, as she has told me countless times. "Yeah, I could definitely do with some cookies. Maybe a couple boxes?" I muse. "The minty kind?"

"A couple?! Come on, little brother, I need more from you. Surely an athlete of your caliber can get through a couple boxes a week? You need a lot of calories. At least a case?"

"A case? I am trying to support my niece, not wind up in a diabetic coma. And I think you misunderstand what sort of shape I am in these days. I'm retired, remember?"

Julia rolls her eyes. She's got the same hazel eyes all of us Echeverria siblings have, along with dark hair that she currently has a bandanna wrapped around like a headband. She's got one of her ears pierced all the way up to the top. I count at least seven earrings at the present moment. She has tattoos lining her right arm from shoulder to wrist, and wears a shirt that reads "I'll tap that," with an arrow pointing to a keg with the Brew logo on it.

"Some for your football friends, then." Julia turns away from me to take someone else's order a few spots down the bar. "I am telling you, this cookie business is cutthroat."

Lincoln takes Julia's spot in front of me, patting her on the bottom as he passes her. Gross.

Lincoln is in his late thirties and originally from Los Angeles. Julia met him her first year of college, and they've been together ever since. He's good people, and he worships the ground Julia and their two daughters walk on.

Linc and Julia started the Brew about four years ago, when their youngest daughter Violet was barely a year old. Lincoln is a hell of a cook and usually handles the kitchen side of things. The space they rent is right on the Embarcadero, alongside a souvenir shop on one side and a coffee shop on the other. You can step outside the restaurant and immediately take the stairs down to the floating docks below. And you can smell the restaurant from down the road—garlic, yeast, and other flavors linger in the fog, well before you even see the building.

Something about living on the coast and smelling the salt air has always made me hungry, and today is no exception.

"How's it hanging?" Lincoln hands me my beer.

"Good, man," I reply, nodding my thanks. "What's the special tonight?"

"Oxtail soup, and we should have some fried chicken left too." Lincoln is not Basque like my family. But he's worked alongside my mother in cooking some of what are, in my humble opinion, the best dishes in the world, and oxtail soup is right up there. The meat is so tender after simmering in the soup all day, it falls right off the bone as soon as you put it on the spoon. I am going to need about three bowlfuls to go with my IPA.

"That sounds good. The soup, not the chicken."

"You got it, brother." Lincoln throws a hand towel over his shoulder after wiping down the bar. "Need any Girl Scout cookies to go with it?"

"Ugh, not you too," I reply in mock horror as he smirks a little.

"Hey, man," he replies ruefully, "they say jump, I ask how high."

I shake my head, but I chuckle at his grin as he walks over to the other end of the bar, again passing Julia on his way, again patting her rear. Still gross.

Gross, but I can't lie; I always thought I would have a marriage like theirs. Like my parents. I like the stability that comes with having someone in your corner, without having to worry about where their loyalties lie. This mentality is antithetical to a lot of guys playing professional sports, where the women are a dime a dozen. Anything I wanted, I could have with the snap of my fingers. And a lot of my teammates did a lot of finger-snapping, if you know what I mean, and I mean fucking. Any way you want it, any number of women—or men, although that is kept quiet—it can happen in the League.

There are the stories that are perhaps infamous, the rookie nights where the newly signed players "treat" the esteemed older players to a nice-ass dinner, followed by nice asses of a different variety, usually at a strip club or a rental property.

Then there're the stories that you don't hear about—players with a different woman in every city we play in. Some of the women are just looking for a good time, to be sure, but some of them are looking for something else—any opportunity to snag a player and, more importantly, his check. The myths about bringing your own condoms to make sure a woman doesn't snip a hole in the top of one are not myths at all. Aside from an unwanted pregnancy, there're the health ramifications of sticking your wick in a different spot every night.

For some, "the more, the merrier" is literal, in the bedroom and out of it.

But for me, like I said, I am a one-woman man. I like having a companion, a confidant, and yes, a lot of sex on the regular. A lot of hot, condom-less sex because I am in a stable, safe relationship where I don't have to worry about another man, woman, or any combination thereof. I have no interest in sharing, and during my playing days, I had no interest in living a lavish lifestyle, jet-setting all over the place with a bevy of women.

I like a lot of sex, a lot of different ways, and I like it with one woman.

When I met Gretchen, my ex-wife, I thought she was perfect. She was a middle school teacher, and we met at a country western bar one Thursday night in San Diego. A lot of my football-playing friends from the South loved hitting up this bar on Thursdays, and there were always lots of pretty, jean-clad, fresh-faced women who loved that the players loved the bar.

Gretchen was with a smaller group of women, not the huge packs that flock to a group of professional athletes like ants on molasses. She was gorgeous; tanned, blond, curvy, always quick with a smile. She was smart, and she didn't fawn all over me or any of the other players. She gave as good as she got.

I knew Summer had married Erik. In all the years I'd known her, I hadn't made a move, and by that point, I was too late anyway. Summer had her life on the other side of the country, and I had mine in California. Gretchen was sweet, supportive, and made it clear that she, too, was in the market for a long-term relationship. No field-playing, so to speak.

And for several years, Gretchen was that person. She remained sweet, supportive, and she was always faithful. Of that, I have no doubt.

But after years of injuries, I was tired. The joy of the game, for me, was gone. The thrill of playing a professional sport was still there, to be sure. Anyone who tells you it isn't even a little bit exhilarating to play in a giant stadium with tens of thousands of fans screaming your name is a liar.

But after my injuries—even before the "Leg Incident," as Tatum calls it—I was thinking about my future. My future after football. I wanted somewhere quiet, peaceful, and away from professional sports. A lot of guys go into broadcasting or coaching. If you love the game, it's a good way to continue, and the money is nothing to sniff at.

But I didn't want that.

I didn't know exactly what my future held until Brock Donovan, a six-foot-seven, 290-pound defensive end playing for the Las Vegas expansion team, decided that future the moment he slammed into me, forcing me to the ground and causing a compound fracture. And those things are nasty. Nasty to look at, nasty to heal from.

I was done after that point. I didn't want to play. I wanted to heal my broken body. I wanted to learn to walk and run and do all those things, but I did not want to look at a football for the foreseeable future.

Gretchen did not understand it. Or if she did, she resented it. At first, she was my erstwhile cheerleader. "You can do this, Nick," she'd say, squeezing my hand next to me as I lay in the hospital bed. "I believe in you." "You are going to come back better than before." "You are so strong." It was almost like she was my hype man instead of my wife.

I am not saying the Leg Incident wasn't hard on her. I know it was. The infection nearly killed me. I feel horrible for what I put her through.

But the day I told her I wasn't going to play again was the beginning of the end for our marriage.

Chapter Six

THE LEAD SURGEON DIDN'T SUGARCOAT ANYTHING. THE INFECTION was serious. I was going back under the knife either way. But there was the option of performing another surgery on my leg once they got the infection under control.

In my mind, it wasn't even a question.

"No." I interrupted the doctor in the middle of his speech. I couldn't quite remember what he was saying—something about long-term options, consulting with a plastic surgeon regarding the keloid scars on my thigh. As if I gave a flying fuck about what my leg looked like. I just wanted to keep it.

"Nick?" Gretchen spoke softly, questioningly. "Nick, let's listen to what the doctor has to say."

I was looking down at my lap, where my two large hands were holding on to Gretchen's left hand. Her diamond engagement ring sparkled up at me. Her hands were smooth, her manicure neat, my own hands gnarled with calluses, cuts, and scratches.

"I heard all I need to hear." I looked up at the doctor, who, honestly, was not a bad dude. He looked like he'd walked straight off the set of a scandalous medical drama where everyone was sleeping with everyone else in the on-call room. But he always gave it to me straight, and I appreciated him for that.

"I'm sorry." I remained looking at the doctor. Obviously, I didn't owe him any sort of apology. He looked at me with pity, which I didn't much care for, but also understanding.

"Nick, no matter what you choose, we'll continue to take good care of you." When I didn't respond, he looked at Gretchen for a beat, whom I still hadn't looked at. The doctor cleared his throat.

"I'll give you two a minute to discuss options."

I nodded, and my gaze dropped back to my hands.

"Nick." Gretchen's voice was a little stronger once the doctor shut the door. "Look at me."

I raised my eyes to my right, where she sat, and saw her blue eyes filled with tears. It absolutely gutted me. I hated her being sad. I hated being the cause. I hated disappointing her.

"Nick, you. Can. Do this." Gretchen took a deep breath. "I know you're in pain, I know that everything has been horrible for you. But I believe in you." Gretchen lifted her hand to cradle the side of my face. The tears in her eyes spilled over. "I know you can come back even better than you were before."

I scoffed, realizing that I was choked up too. "To-to what end, Gretch?" I shook my head. "It's not worth it. I've had a good run, I had my time—"

"But Nick, you're just…just giving up?" Gretchen blubbered, disbelief written all over her face. She took her hands away from me to wipe her eyes. "You can't just give up!"

"Gretchen. Please. Listen to me." I raised my voice slightly, looking directly at her, determined not to hide anything I was feeling, determined to let her see the weight and the seriousness of my decision.

"I'm done. I'm at peace with my decision. I know you believe in me, and you have been unbelievable throughout all this. Putting you through this—" My voice cracked a little; I cleared my throat and kept going. "I'm so sorry. So sorry. But I don't need you to be my cheerleader right now. I need you to be my wife."

Gretchen remained standing, her mouth agape. And she stood for a few more minutes, before turning and leaving through the door, shutting it behind her.

She didn't come back to the hospital until after my next surgery, a week later.

ᕲᕲᕲᕲᕲ

After things went south with Gretchen, Julia was pissed. Hell, my whole family was pissed, but I think Julia, in particular. She was, of course, married to Lincoln, and I think she envisioned how she would support her husband if they were in a similar situation. That Gretchen was less than supportive was alarming to her.

❧❧❧❧❧

"Nicky, if you don't want to play, then don't play," she told me during one of her solo visits, before Gretchen had walked out. "And fuck anyone else who tells you otherwise."

"What if my wife is telling me otherwise?"

Julia's hazel eyes widened at that. "Gretchen…she wants you to play again?"

"She hasn't said it in so many words, but I know she wants me to give it another try. Keeps talking about how I am going to amaze everyone when I take the field again, how I am going to come back stronger than ever."

"Well, not that I don't enjoy a good Britney Spears reference as much as the next person, but Gretchen's not the one with a Frankenstein leg. This is your life, Nicky."

❧❧❧❧❧

It was my life then, and it's mine now. I won't deny I am not wild about being alone. I haven't historically done all that well being alone; I've always preferred to be in a relationship. But my therapist keeps trying to convince me that being alone can be rewarding.

"Earth to Nicky." I look up to see Julia in front of me now, motioning to my empty beer.

"Nah, I'm good." I see Lincoln approaching with my oxtail stew, and my stomach rumbles. "I do need about ten rolls to go with this soup, though."

"Consider it done. Oh good, the girls are here." Julia smiles behind me. "Hey, little sister," Julia calls out as she wipes down a spot next to me at the bar. "Hey, Lucy," Julia greets Tatum's best friend Lucy Yashimoto.

I get my spoon ready to take a bite of the stew. It's steaming hot, and I blow a few times for good measure, but I am so damn hungry, I can't wait. I put the spoon in my mouth.

"Hey, Summer," Julia adds, again addressing someone behind me.

Aaaaaand I am choking.

"Oh Jesus Christ," Julia mutters under her breath. "You okay, little brother?" She hands me several napkins as I cough. I cover my mouth to cough into the napkin, because I am not a complete disaster.

"I'm good," I croak to Julia.

So, here's the thing. I am a former professional athlete with a lightning bolt for an arm, or so my high school coach used to tell me. I can run fast—even with my Frankenstein leg, fuck you very much, Julia—touch my toes, and bench-press 300 pounds.

But also?

I am kind of a klutz.

That same high school football coach also commented that it was good I could throw the ball and throw it far, rather than catch the ball after running a route. Some of these tight ends, in my opinion, are the most athletic dudes on the planet. They can run fast as hell, bob and weave like a boxer, and end up at exactly the spot their quarterback needs, catch the football, and hold on with two hands despite the fact that nearly 350 pounds of grown-ass men are tackling them to the ground. Truly a feat of athleticism.

Me, on the other hand? I grew up real tall, real fast, and some days I feel like my brain forgot that I was six-foot-four instead of five and a half feet tall. My feet were size fourteen by the time I was fourteen years old. My mom says I just ate and ate and ate, and kept growing, and kept needing new clothes.

In football, the quarterback is the most recognizable position, but every single one of them will tell you they wouldn't last a single play without five refrigerator-sized offensive linemen providing protection. And in the professional leagues, you have a million guys off the field to help you perform at the top level. Dietitians. Quarterbacks coach. Strength coach. Yoga instructor. Physical therapist, and yes, I had a mental therapist as well.

My klutziness caused anxiety, or maybe I was already anxious and being clumsy increased my anxiety. I don't know. But whatever it was, I was very, very anxious in high school, right around the time that I began to throw the football very, very far.

I am still anxious today, but I know how to handle it. Therapy. Yoga. Time on the beach, in my small town, away from the traffic and noise and media. A total ban on all things social media. This is how I survive.

But today, knowing that Summer is here and near has undoubtedly caused my anxiety to rise a bit. I knew it was inevitable that we would run into each other. And here we are.

I remember what Luther told me earlier. "Don't ignore the universe."

Okay, universe, let's give it a go.

I cough again into my napkin, before glancing up at Julia. She smiles wryly at me and gives me the briefest of nods. "I suppose you don't look like too much of an idiot, Mr. Football," she tells me quietly before moving down the bar to tend to some other customers.

I wipe my mouth and set down my napkin before sliding off the stool and turning to face the newcomers.

My little sister Tatum leads the way, as she often does. All three of us Echeverria siblings look alike—a lot of dark hair, bronzed skin, light hazel eyes. Tatum is a good foot shorter than me, whereas Julia is fairly tall for a woman and lankier.

But even though Tatum is the shortest and the youngest, let there be no doubt that wherever she goes, she's in charge. And she barrels right toward me before giving me a fierce hug.

"Hey—hey," I say, surprised at her greeting. Not that we aren't a touchy-feely family; we are. But I just saw Tatum earlier in the week.

"Hi, big brother. Summer's here and divorced and kind of sad, please don't make it weird," Tatum whispers in a rush before pulling away. I nod briefly and look past her to Lucy. She's about Tatum's height, with glossy black hair currently parted on the far side of her head and flipped over, displaying the other side of her head, which is shaved. Lucy is small, serious, and not to be fucked with. She makes Tatum look docile.

Behind Lucy, I see Summer. She's taller than Tatum and Lucy, which isn't saying much, and while she is slightly built, she has the muscles of a dancer or a gymnast. She has the same long reddish-brown hair I remember and freckles covering every inch of skin not covered by clothing. She's wearing a white T-shirt that shows off her tan nicely, blue jeans, and a brown purse strapped across her body. Her light-brown eyes immediately lock on mine, and I feel it deep in the pit of my stomach.

I am wholly unprepared for the sudden rush of longing that grips me just from Summer's gaze. I take a deep breath and nod to Lucy, now directly in front of me.

Lucy nods back and gives me a wave before going to grab a seat beside Tatum, who's sat immediately to my left. "What's up, Itchy?" Lucy calls me by the nickname that started when she was a kid and unable to pronounce our surname. "I would ask if you remember Summer, but I think that would be a stupid fucking question, right?" Known for her subtlety, she is not.

"Summer," I greet her as she stops in front of me.

Should I hug her? I should hug her, right?

"Hi, Nick." Summer smiles softly and doesn't hesitate—she moves in and wraps her arms around my neck. She smells so good, like coconuts and vanilla. I am momentarily paralyzed as she hugs me, not too hard like Tatum. I remember that I should hug her back and wrap my arms gently around her back. And holy shit, we are hugging and I am smelling her and my breathing picks up and I know I need to get a hold of myself before I do something crazy, like throw her over my shoulder and carry her out of this stupid restaurant in front of all these stupid people.

Summer disrupts that thought when she pulls away before smiling again. "It's really good to see you," she says honestly.

"Hi. I mean, yes." I can feel my face getting hot and know I've got to be blushing. "I mean." I clear my throat and rub the back of my neck with my right hand. "It's really good to see you too."

Summer's smile gets a little bigger, revealing her dimple in her left cheek. I want to kiss her right in that spot. *Fuck.*

I clear my throat again. "How-how are you doing?" Immediately, I realize that's a silly question. I mean, the woman is going through a divorce, right? I wince at my stupidity.

But Summer gives me a knowing smile. "I am good! I am good. It's weird, but I am actually really glad to be back in the Bay." She shakes her head a little in disbelief. "I never thought I would be moving back here, you know? I suppose everyone must think that about their hometown." She nods to the side and gives me a knowing look. "Except for you, though, huh? You always loved it here. I guess it makes sense that you would be back here after—" She stops speaking suddenly. "I didn't mean to bring up anything bad or shitty memories. I'm an idiot."

I shake my head the way she did a moment earlier. "Nothing bad about it. Don't worry." I lean back against my barstool, feeling a little more relaxed now that we are not physically touching.

"You're right, though. It feels really good to be back. It helps that the town hasn't changed all that much. Feels like no matter what happens in the real world, this place will always be the same."

Summer beams at me. "That's exactly right," she says softly. She looks beyond where I'm standing to my dinner. "I don't want to keep you from… whatever that is." She gestures toward the bowl cooling in front of me.

"No worries. I am guessing that I will see you soon anyway—yoga?"

She grins again. "Yoga. You better come prepared, mister," she jokes as she moves to sit next to Lucy.

I try to smile back, knowing there is nothing on earth that can adequately prepare me for a one-on-one yoga session with Summer Mahoney.

Chapter Seven

Nick

I WAS DRAFTED INTO PROFESSIONAL FOOTBALL AFTER FOUR YEARS OF playing at the collegiate level in Northern California. To say that the past twenty years of my life have been devoted to football is not an understatement. I loved the sport, and from a young age, people told me I had a gift—a wicked right arm.

It's also not an understatement to say that the last twenty years have aged me more than the average thirty-two-year-old. I've had too many injuries to count, even as a quarterback, where I am, *usually*, not the one being roughed up on the daily, unless it's a particularly lousy O-line defending me.

I've had strained calves, a pulled groin, bruised kidneys, a dislocated shoulder on my throwing arm, twice. I've had every modality to ease the pain, from massage to meditation to CBD treatments to some gnarly opiates, which I took only as a last resort after my last injury. That they were so easily dispensed in the locker room is an unfortunate reality of the toll the game takes on a body. We're only human, after all.

But that last injury—my right leg injury, a bad break nearly two years ago—is what ultimately solidified my decision to retire, at a time when some said I was in my prime. The break was nasty, a compound fracture of my right tibia and a fractured right fibula. I had fourteen surgeries to fix the break. And the surgeries weren't even the worst part. As anyone who's spent time in a hospital will tell you, it's the danger of postsurgical infection that really fucks you up.

And that holds true for me. I developed sepsis after my ninth surgery. I don't remember much from that time; I was in and out of it, and the doctors kept me sedated as my body fought the infection in my bloodstream.

What I do remember is waking up and being asked whether I would consider amputating the leg in an attempt to stave off the infection and save my life.

That's one moment that will stick with me for the rest of my life—whether to amputate my leg or continue with another surgery to save it. It was at that moment that I knew my career was over. It didn't matter what doctors or experts told me about my chances of playing in the pros was. Seeing my mother's ashen face as the doctor outlined my chances of survival with and without my leg…it just wasn't worth it. And it's no one's fault, not mine, not the guy who tackled me. I knew the risks going into this game, and I knew those risks were no longer acceptable to me, even if I kept my leg and even if there was a chance I could recover and play in the pros again.

My leg now is a gruesome thing to behold. It's full of keloid and colored scars and misshapen. A Frankenstein leg, like Julia says.

But I still have it.

I joke that my sisters are royal pains in my ass. And they totally are; don't get me wrong. But my entire family rallied around me like no one else. They understood that, while playing professional football was one of the greatest privileges of my life, it is not the be-all and end-all of my life. And it certainly was no longer worth the rigor I was putting my body through, for what? To get a ring? To be asked to do it again, knowing the risks I was taking with my body, constantly, day in and day out?

Although I've fully recovered from that injury, it's no exaggeration to say that it dampened my enthusiasm for the game. The pain, the surgeries, the uncertainty, not to mention a potential amputation—I just wasn't living the life I wanted to live. It was *no* life, as far as I was concerned.

My mother, my grandfather, and my siblings understood this.

Gretchen did not.

Chapter Eight

"**O**KAY, AND THEN THOSE BOXES CAN JUST GO IN THE LIVING room." I gesture to one of the movers, who has wheeled up another three big boxes.

"Summer Anne. Jesus Christ. I thought you were downsizing for real." Tatum is huffing and puffing, walking through the front door with another box.

"I did downsize!" I exclaim. "Maybe just not as much as I thought?" I sigh and wipe my forehead.

This moving shit is for the birds.

It's not that I don't love my place now; I do. It is exactly what I need after living with Erik's modern tendencies for so long. I need something smaller, cozier, and not bereft of all human emotion.

But I do, apparently, have a lot of stuff.

"I mean, you have all this kitchen stuff, and I know you are no cook," Tatum says as she sets the box on the floor and flops down on the couch next to me.

"But I could be. Perhaps this is part of the new-and-improved Summer. I will cook, I will eat what I want, when I want, where I want."

"I wasn't aware that the geographic location of where you ate was an issue, but go off."

"It wasn't, not at all. I just." I sigh again. I have got to stop doing that. More inhales, less insufferable sighing. "I don't know. I don't know what this new stage of my life is going to bring, you know? Maybe I cook. Maybe I knit. Maybe I pen Disney fan fiction."

"Hmmm. I would definitely read some hot Flynn Rider fan fic." When

I raise my eyebrows, Tatum rolls her eyes. "Please. I have two nieces. Sometimes, the fan fic is the only thing that gets me through a millionth viewing of those movies."

"Miss Mahoney." We both start at the deep voice behind us. It's one of the movers, whom I have anointed their leader-in-chief. He's gigantic and sweaty, and he's been flirting with Tatum and me all day.

"Yes?" Tatum asks. "What can we help you with?"

"Well, that's a loaded question. I want a good set tomorrow, a breakfast burrito, and her number." He gestures to me, and I can feel my cheeks heating up.

And then he winks at me.

"Um." Is my eloquent response.

Tatum eyes the mover, eyes me, and then breaks into a grin. "Forward! I like it."

"But for my immediate needs," he continues, "I just need to know where you want these pictures."

The guy is, objectively, very good-looking. He's tall and built, with curly, dark hair currently plastered to his head, and a navy T-shirt with the company logo nicely setting off his biceps. He's got a nice smile and manners, and he has referred to me as "Miss Mahoney" all day, which makes me feel a little bit like Mrs. Robinson. I'm thirty, which isn't a huge deal, but this guy is probably in his early twenties. In my view, twenty-two is a big difference from thirty.

"Well." I clear my throat and get a hold of myself. "I don't know anything about surfing, so I can't tell you about tomorrow's set. If you want a killer breakfast burrito, I think Ernestine's still makes a good one with chorizo. I am morally obligated to also tell you about the Brew for your lunch and dinner needs." I tick off his requests, one by one, on my fingers, before pausing.

"And the number. . .?" he prods me helpfully, still smiling.

"How old are you?" I ask him bluntly.

His grin gets even bigger. "I'm twenty-three," he replies. "Finishing my graduate degree in kinesiology in the spring. I also am the assistant coach of the track-and-field team. One of my athletes had a family emergency, so

I am covering for him. I used to be a mover in my younger days," he adds nonchalantly.

"Right," I murmur. Tatum's watching the two of us like it's a tennis match, her eyes darting back and forth.

"See, Summer, an employed college graduate who helps out his fellow man when needed," she offers.

"Quite a catch, right?" he asks me, waggling his eyebrows up and down.

"Look…" I pause.

"Jacob," he supplies.

"Jacob." I smile at him. He really is cute.

"You're very sweet and so nice to help me move all this stuff today—"

"Kinda what they're getting paid for, Summer," Tatum mutters under her breath.

"But I just got out of a relationship, and I'm not really looking to go out…with anyone. Ever." I smile brightly as Jacob's grin falters a bit.

"I can appreciate that. And if I'm being honest," he continues, "I am not looking for anything serious either. I don't know where I'm going after my master's." He takes a step back. "How about this? I'll leave my number right here—" He indicates to the sheet of paper on the bar counter. "If you change your mind, or even want to grab coffee or something, you can call me. And if you don't, you don't."

"I have a pen!" Tatum nearly shouts, thrusting it at Jacob.

Jacob thanks her and writes on the paper before giving it back. "There."

He returns to the pictures. "Now, where did you want these, Miss Mahoney?"

And he gives me another wink.

⌇⌇⌇⌇⌇

Later, after the movers have gone, Tatum and I relax on my couch in the living room, several varieties of potato chips before us on the coffee table.

I curl my knees up to my chest and gaze out the glass windows in front of me, the Pacific glittering in the distance. There are no clouds or fog in the sky, and the bay is full of slow-moving boats, paddleboarders, and kayakers.

I hear the seals barking up a storm, the foghorn blowing in the distance. The salty, damp ocean air wafts through the open windows and door.

"So. You gonna call him?" Tatum asks with no preamble.

I smile ruefully and shake my head. "Not anytime soon."

"Ah, that's right. You're a bitter divorcée now," Tatum responds dramatically.

"I'm not! I'm not bitter." I shake my head. "It's not in my nature. You know this. Besides—" I smile ruefully "—I think Lucy has the market share of bitter or cynical or whatever you want to call it."

Lucy, Tatum, and I were thick as thieves when we were younger. Tatum was our ringleader, always ready to direct our activities and schemes. In some ways, I think she still is. Tatum and I have stayed close since I left the Bay after high school. She came to visit me on the East Coast plenty of times, and we always saw each other at least a couple times a year. She was privy to my dance injuries and, later, the breakdown of my marriage. She is the one who encouraged me to come back to Estero Bay when I had my doubts.

How many people enjoy coming home with their tail between their legs?

Am I a failure to return to my hometown, down a husband and a job?

Lucy and I are so different; she's hard, unapologetic, and doesn't hesitate to say what she is thinking, no matter how harsh. She is cynical, it's true, but she is fiercely loyal to her friends. During this uncharted time in my life, Lucy hasn't once said "I told you so" or "get over it." She has greeted me with open arms, despite falling out of touch when I married Erik.

I shudder thinking of him now. Then, I shudder again because why should he still have that effect on me? I got what I wanted. We are divorced. The ink is dry; the ties are severed. Why can't I move past it?

"You're thinking of douchelord again, aren't you?" Tatum asks, turning toward me on the couch.

"Not him, exactly. Although I do wish he wouldn't continue to make guest appearances in my brain." Tatum nods. "We were married. We were together a long time, and I am sure, years from now, he won't even be a blip on my radar, but right now… I don't know. I just want to be able to acknowledge that he exists without feeling this overwhelming sense of shame."

"Summer," Tatum says softly. "Do you think you might be acting too hard on yourself? You just said it yourself—you were together a long time. Breakups are hard, by any measure. I know it's clichéd, but it will take some time."

"I know, I know," I murmur. "I know all this, and I know all that stuff, and time heals all wounds, and blah, blah, blah." I gesture with my hands. "This is exactly what I wanted. But I still feel…ashamed that I stayed with him for so long, I guess? Ashamed that I put up with it for so long, even though I knew what kind of person he really was. And then more ashamed that I don't feel happier with the fact that I am getting what I wanted, you know?" Everything comes out in a rush, and I take a deep breath.

"Just because it's right doesn't mean it's easy," Tatum says smartly.

"Thank you, Mel Robbins," I respond, side-eyeing Tatum.

"I'm serious! I just said something similar to my brother recently. Talk about a sad sack."

While I am more than glad to divert my focus from Erik to Nick, I still have barfy feelings. Maybe not barfy exactly, but something in the pit of my stomach stirs when I think back to what he looked like last night. How he smelled. How hard his body was when I hugged him.

I push those thoughts away to respond to Tatum. "Is he…sad? I mean, he looked fine to me."

He looked more than fine, or *foine*, as Lucy would say, but I am not about to have that discussion with Tatum about her brother.

"He is fine. But, you know, he's just *fine*. He mopes around town, does his yoga, works out, plays with Julia's kids. But he's just…existing."

Now *that* I can relate to.

"I get that," I murmur.

"Not that he's ever been an outgoing person, mind you," Tatum continues between shoving potato chips into her mouth. "I just want him to be happy."

"You think he's not?"

"I think…I think he's convinced himself he doesn't deserve to be happy." Tatum side-eyes me. "Actually, you two kind of have that in common, don't you?"

"I don't think that!" I blurt out before I can stop myself.

"Please. You just turned down a potential good time, if you know what I mean, with a hot, younger dude. And I mean sex."

"Tatum," I groan. "I am so not ready for sex, I can't even tell you."

"Well, not that you have to jump on the horse right away," Tatum concedes, "but a word of advice? Don't shut yourself in here like some decrepit old maid, determined to never love again."

"Isn't an old maid someone who never gets married?" I muse aloud.

"Whatever. You know what I mean. I am sorry—really sorry—about Erik," Tatum says honestly. "But you are smart and beautiful and a good person. You deserve to be happy."

"Not to sound conceited, or whatever," I tell her, "but I know. I know I deserve it. And that's kind of why I'm here. To find my new happy."

I reach forward and try one of the other potato chip flavors, nearly gagging when I taste it.

"Ew!" I cough. "Ketchup-flavored—why? This is definitely *not* how I am going to find my new happy, Tatum."

Tatum shrugs. "I don't know. Take the habanero and get that out of your mouth, girl."

"That's what she said," I grumble as I reach for another chip, Tatum snickering.

"Anyway," I tell her. "What about you? Why is there no Mr. Tatum feeding you grapes or these disgusting potato chips?"

Tatum smiles a little but avoids my gaze as she munches on her chips. "I guess," she says slowly, "I am kind of in your camp. The camp of No Dating," she clarifies.

"Okay…like, by choice?"

"Work has been really busy," Tatum concedes. She runs a successful law practice in the county. "But I just…I don't know. Men are so disappointing."

I bark a laugh. "Understatement of the year."

"To be fair, this is a small town, and the dating pool is minimal," Tatum continues. "The decent men are all happily married with children. The not-so-decent men take off their wedding rings when they come to watch sports at the Brew."

"Ew." I shudder.

"I know." Tatum pauses. "There was a guy…kind of recently. He made me excited again, you know? Like it isn't all doom and gloom." Tatum munches on another disgusting ketchup chip.

"But guess what," she deadpans.

"It was very much doom and gloom?" I offer.

"Bingo." Tatum sighs and stretches her arms over her head. "I don't know, I don't want to be so morose or negative or whatever. But men are just…"

"…Disappointing," I finish for her.

"Amen," she mutters. "We can be single together for a while."

"Forever," I remind her.

"Never say never, Summer," Tatum chides me. "But…yeah. Never doesn't seem so long right now."

ᕤᕤᕤᕤ

Of course, there's one man who has never disappointed me.

I had the absolute biggest crush on Nick growing up. A lot of it was just proximity; he was my best friend's older brother, and as far as boys go, he was perfect. Nick was quiet, thoughtful, and protective. He sat with me when I cried because Tatum and I fought over something silly. He got me a Band-Aid when I skinned my knee while riding a bicycle. He put up with the three of us girls—four, if Julia was involved—making him act out parts in my over-the-top original theater productions, where the girls had names like Ashleigh and Arabella, and the boys had names like Buchanan and Westley.

Then, of course, Nick got fuckhot. All those Echeverria kids are blessed with good looks—tons of thick, dark-brown hair, and beautiful hazel eyes that pop against their tanned skin. Tatum is on the shorter, curvier side; she jokes that she developed early and often. Julia and Nick are taller and leaner.

Nick had a crazy growth spurt right around the time he developed this superstrength in his right arm. One summer, I left a skinny fourteen-year-old only a few inches taller than me, went with my parents and sister to visit family in Chicago, and came back six weeks later to a man. Nick's voice had changed, and he'd grown what seemed like a foot taller. Tatum was disgusted by the whole thing. She said Nick had acne and armpit hair, and she wanted to move in with me forever. But from that point on, the girls loved Nick.

Gone were the days of acting in my plays and walking with Tatum, Lucy, and me to get ice cream. The girls wouldn't leave him alone. The only time Nick was alone, it felt like, was when he was playing football. And of course, then he was surrounded by coaches and teammates. The halcyon days of youth were behind us.

Seeing Nick last night was like being thrown back into those old days—before football, before he left for college, before I met Erik and got married, before Nick got married too. Sitting with Nick and Tatum and Lucy at the bar, with Julia and her husband feeding us, pouring us drinks, it felt almost communal, like we were participating in some sort of ritual. We have all gone through Some Shit. Here we all are, back in our hometown, sitting next to each other at the kids table, which is now a lovely refurbished wooden bar, drinking beer instead of apple juice.

And I'd have to be blind not to notice that Nick is still fuckhot. Even more so. He still has wavy chestnut hair that he can't seem to tame. His eyes are still a gorgeous hazel, now with crinkle lines around them. He seems to be all muscle, still cut and lithe. His body radiated heat when I hugged him, and I could feel the hardness from his chest down to the lower half of his body. He smelled absolutely delicious, and it was all I could do last night not to climb him like a tree and wrap my legs around all that *man*.

Nick seems even taller and bigger than he was the last time I saw him. I realize that was over ten years ago, when we met up right around the time of the NFL draft in New York City. When I told him I had met and was going to marry Erik. I even got to introduce Erik to Nick that weekend.

To say it did not go well would be the understatement of the year.

And then I never saw Nick again. Not until last night.

I didn't even watch his football games because it was too painful.

My memories didn't do him justice. I didn't remember the brightness of his eyes, the firmness of his body, until he hugged me last night. I know he was only hugging me back, but for the first time in a long time, I felt content. Safe. Protected.

I also felt something I hadn't genuinely felt in a long time. Horny. Or at the very least, sexually attracted to another human.

During the end of our marriage, when things got really bad, Erik refused to touch me, let alone have sex with me. Not that I wanted to. After years of living with someone who belittled me every chance he got and made it clear in no uncertain terms that there was nothing I could do to change the vast number of things wrong with me, the last thing I wanted to do was sleep with Erik. And I mean that both literally and in the biblical sense.

Of course, I had other ways of seeing to my needs, but the thought of touching another male in a sexual way really made me apprehensive. It still does. I don't know if I'm ready to be with a man that way.

Or at least, I didn't know until last night. Because the minute I wrapped my arms around Nick's hard body, I felt something snap to life inside me, like someone flipped an "off" switch to "on." His masculine scent, the sharp jut of his chin, the light in his eyes, and the feel of his body pressed to mine had everything in my body screaming *Yes! Please, more of this!* I felt a throbbing deep in the pit of my stomach that quickly made its way down to my core.

Thankfully, I was able to make a really intelligent comment about his soup and dashed over to Lucy and Tatum.

While Nick has always been fuckhot, he's also always had a harem of girls around him. In high school, in college, and I am sure the NFL was just like those days, only with more—more women, more beautiful women, more beautiful women willing to do anything he wanted.

And me? I was always his kid sister's best friend. Nick certainly never saw me as anything more than a dorky, freckled kid with skinned knees and a penchant for messy art projects. And because he is older than me, I knew he would eventually go off to college and do great things in the football world. Even after he did, he was still a presence in my life; I'd see him when he came home to visit. By that time, I was living with Tatum—and Nick's—family after my own parents died.

While I'm a dreamer, I'm also a realist. Nick is not here on his white horse to restore my faith in love. My plan in returning to Estero Bay was to work on me, devote time to myself, and figure out, frankly, what I am going to do with my life.

That Nick is also here, apparently figuring out the same thing with his own life, has nothing to do with me.

But if there was ever a guy to break my "never" promise…

He'd definitely be the one to do it.

Chapter Nine

Nick

I**T'S BEEN A WEEK SINCE** I **SAW** S**UMMER AT THE BAR, AND** I **AM MORE** anxious than normal.

Given the level of anxiety I currently live with, this is saying something.

Summer is coming over today to lead me through a yoga session, and I have checked to make sure the toilet seats are down no fewer than four times. I've made sure the kitchen has an abundant supply of both coffee and tea, as I remember her loving those herbal teas with the inspirational messages on the tags. I don't know if she still does, though.

I really don't know a lot of things about her anymore, other than that she's divorced and living back home. Just like me.

What a pair we are.

The doorbell rings, and I open the door to see Summer standing on the doorstep, wrapped up in a cozy white sweater that looks big enough for both of us. A few wisps of copper hair escape the dark purple knit beanie she's got pulled over her head.

"Hi!" she chirps at me, giving me a big smile, her dimple popping in her left cheek.

"Hi," I mumble back, shuffling my feet a bit before opening the door wider to let her in. I step back to allow her to pass me and get a whiff of something sweet, like she's been baking cookies. She smells delicious.

"Just head on upstairs. There's the big living room we can work in, or I have a smaller home gym where Luther and I practice." Summer starts up the stairs, leaving me to follow behind her. I'm doing my best not to focus on her ass as she bounds up the stairs, but it's impossible—whoever invented yoga pants sure knew what they were doing.

Summer is small but mighty, and her round cheeks are just beyond my eye level, flexing with each step she takes. I nearly salivate at the thought of getting my hands on her bottom, over her thighs, feeling her skin, kneading my fingers into her curves as she sighs—

"—you move in here?" Summer interrupts my horny inner monologue as she reaches the top of stairs, turning toward me and pulling off her beanie. Her hair is intricately braided along the crown of her head, like a St. Pauli Girl. Her freckled cheeks are ruddy, probably from her walk to my place on the edge of our little town.

"I'm sorry, what's that?"

"I said, when did you move in here?" Summer doesn't allow me to answer before saying, "I don't even remember what this place looked like before. You must have done a lot to it."

"Yeah, it was owned by an out-of-town family. They used it to vacation for decades, I guess, and when the older family members passed away, the younger generation sold it rather than hold on to it. Some people don't think Estero Bay is as cool as we do apparently."

Summer smiles again. "Well, it's not for everyone. I wouldn't want to live here if I were twenty-one and single." She shakes her head. "I mean. Not that I am either of those things. Shit. I mean, I am not twenty-one. I am single. As are you. Both of us. We. We're single." Her cheeks have flushed as she continues her rambling. "Shit."

I smile. "Summer. It's okay, and I know what you mean." I walk her into the living area. "It's not like there's a lot happening, which I think surprises some people."

"Yes, that's exactly right," she says as she follows me. "Not really a nightlife. Not that it matters to me, but it might matter to someone who wanted to go out all the time. Erik would hate it. Did hate it. Does hate it." She gasps and puts her hands over her mouth.

"Are you okay?"

"I just—*shit*." Summer looks miserable. "Here I am, supposed to be the one making you feel all zenned out or whatever. And I manage to bring up my ex." She shakes her head. "I'm sorry."

"Stop apologizing." My voice comes out a little harsher than I intended, and Summer raises her eyebrows, but I'm not about to turn this into a contest of who is sorrier. "I mean it." I lean against the counter and regard her carefully. "If I'm being honest…"

She nods quickly, and I smile a little at her eagerness. Yes, honesty has never been a struggle for her.

"Well, if I'm being honest, I think that's normal. You were with Erik"—I manage to get his name out without growling—"for a long time. I think it's normal to think of him, refer to him, even, in certain situations. It's like your brain hasn't caught up to your new reality."

"Whoa," Summer says softly. "That's really good."

"I learned it in therapy," I admit. "And besides…I found myself doing that too, when I moved back. Like what Gretchen, my ex, would like or wouldn't like." I take a pause here. "It goes away anyway, after a while."

"After my brain catches up to my new reality?" Summer asks ruefully.

"Exactly."

"And my new reality is…" Summer's voice trails off, and I decide to be blunt again.

"That you kicked that asshole to the curb," I say confidently. It doesn't give her the ego boost I envisioned, though, as she visibly blanches.

She recovers quickly. "Anyway. Thanks for the pep talk, Nick." She takes her eyes off me to look around. "Can I start over? I promise my yoga classes don't usually begin this way," she adds with a little smile.

"Yes." I clear my throat. "Welcome to my home."

"It's lovely," she says, moving toward the long bar separating the kitchen from the living room. "Can I put my stuff in here? Do you have any hot water?" She walks into the kitchen to investigate before I can respond.

"Kettle's over there."

"This is really beautiful, Nick."

Summer runs her fingers along the bar's counter, a pearly off-white Julia told me was "gorgeous but so impractical. You'll be wiping it down three times a day." Seeing as how it's just me in the house, however, I haven't had those issues.

"Thanks. I pretty much gutted the place when I bought it. It was an ode to wood paneling, for sure." I lean over the counter to observe her, distracted again by those damn yoga pants. "I think I have some tea in the cupboard, if you want to check," I add nonchalantly.

Summer puts the kettle on and rummages through the cupboard above the coffeemaker, squealing when she finds the herbal tea I picked up. "My favorite!"

It's all I can do not to fist-pump the air.

"You want the tour while you're warming that up?" I offer.

"I would love one. This view is amazing." Summer darts over to the floor-to-ceiling windows alongside the living room's edge, where the sliding door to the wraparound balcony is partially open. The cool, salty breeze of the bay drifts into the room, along with the off-kilter harmony of someone's wind chimes.

"Yeah, the view pretty much sold me on the place," I respond, once again doing my best not to look at Summer's ass in those pants, once again failing miserably.

Summer turns back to me quickly, and my eyes dart up to meet hers. "Show me the rest before we start?"

I'll show you anything you want.

I nod, beckoning her to follow me down the hallway.

She smiles and moves toward me, linking her arm through mine unexpectedly. My senses perk up at this, our first touch since we hugged at the Brew last weekend. She is small next to me, barely coming up to my shoulder. If I wanted to, I could rest my head on top of hers.

And I do. Want to, that is.

But I concentrate on not being so inappropriate and give her the tour as requested.

~~~~~

"I think a little discomfort is good, so long as you are not truly in pain." Summer gives me a little side-eye. "This would be the point where I would ask my class, 'Do you know the difference between discomfort and pain?'"

I feel the corners of my mouth turn up. "I think I'm familiar with the distinction between the two."

"I figured you would be," she responds. "So, I do want to push you a little bit. I want you to be sweating."

I can think of a number of positions I'd like to be in with Summer where we could both be sweating, and I try to redirect my focus. "That's fine. I want to be pushed." Summer's eyebrows raise at that. "I mean, I will tell you if there's something I can't do or it doesn't feel right or whatever."

"Good. So, let's just start with some basic sun salutations. And I hope you don't mind, but I'd like to practice next to you instead of right in front of you. It's a little more cooperative that way, don't you think?"

The jerk in me weeps at the realization that I won't have the opportunity to look down Summer's tight tank top if she's not bending over in front of me. The gentleman in me is grateful I won't have that chance.

The realist in me understands that it doesn't matter either way. As Summer unrolls her yoga mat and stretches out next to me, all long limbs and sweet smells, I know I am fucked no matter where she is standing, as long as she is in the room with me.

~~~~~

Our yoga session is less of an exercise in stretching and more of an exercise in torture. The only things being stretched are my sanity—as I watch Summer gracefully glide from pose to pose like the dancer she is—and my cock—as it protests against its confines in my underwear.

I am holding a downward dog when one of my hamstrings cramps up. It's a common ailment, given my injury. I had to really build up my hamstrings again to compensate for the weakness in my quads.

"Does that feel better?" Summer asks quietly, applying pressure to the small of my back as I stretch throughout the backs of my legs.

"Yeah," I answer gruffly, willing my erection to go down before Summer sees. At least in this position, with my shorts tenting my front and my T-shirt covering the shorts, I do an effective job covering up the goods. Thank god I didn't put on sweatpants this morning.

"Good." I feel both despair and relief as Summer's hand leaves my back, and she moves back to my side on her own mat, mimicking my pose. "Let's do ten deep breaths here."

I close my eyes and breathe deeply. I can hear Summer doing the same less than three feet from me. We are silent and still, sharing breath. I make sure I am not clenching my jaw, and that my shoulders aren't bunched up around my ears, and let my thoughts flow. I smell the ocean air and something else—something that's distinctively Summer. It dawns on me that we are engaging in an intimate act, this sharing of breath in a sacred space.

I turn my head slightly and risk a glance at Summer. Her eyes are closed. As she exhales, her mouth opens slightly, her pink lips pushing out oxygen as she stretches her arms overhead to her purple mat. This woman is all colors, all the time—no muted grays or blacks for her. Purple hat, dark-pink tank, maroon yoga pants, purple mat. Even her cheeks are full of red color, the movements of our practice reflected in her face.

I stare longer than is appropriate, watching her breathe in and out. Wanting to put that serene look on her face myself, wondering what it would be like to have her be mine, all to my very own. What it would be like to nibble at her bottom lip. What it would be like to lick my way down her warm neck, biting at the juncture where her shoulder begins.

Summer sighs softly as she deepens her stretch, that ass that I love so much directly in the air, her strong shoulders supporting her weight. I can picture her sighing for another reason as I run my hands over her warm skin. I can picture her holding that pose for another reason as I come up behind her and grip those luscious hips, squeezing tightly as she wiggles her rear in the air, offering herself to me, moaning when I take my time, caressing, rubbing, smelling the scent of her as I press my body toward hers, my chest to her back, both of us heaving with the anticipation of what comes next…

I jerk my gaze away from Summer's as I find myself heaving—my chest, not from the exertion of our practice but with arousal, and my cock, nearly weeping from the scene I've drawn up inside my head.

Fuck.

Luther cannot come back soon enough.

Chapter Ten

THIS WAS IT.

This was the moment I had been waiting for—my chance to tell Summer how I felt about her, that I wanted to be with her. I liked her as more than a friend, and I wanted my future with her in it.

We were in my Manhattan hotel suite the week of the draft. Central Park and the city beyond sparkled outside my floor-to-ceiling windows. I felt like a king. I was about to sign my first NFL contract. I felt good. Healthy, mentally and physically. And having Summer here with me—her copper hair curling in waves around her shoulders, her lithe body clothed in a hip-hugging emerald dress—only reaffirmed my decision.

It was now or never. I was ready to tell her. Fuck it, the world was my oyster, carpe diem, and all those other assorted clichés. I wanted Summer, and there was nothing stopping me.

"You look beautiful," I told her, and she raised her eyebrows in…surprise? Surely she couldn't be surprised to know that I thought she was beautiful.

"You think so? Thank you," she replied.

"Do you want something to drink?" I asked her, gesturing for her to sit on the couch. "They stock the hotel with everything, I swear—champagne, beer, wine…" My voice trailed off.

"Nick." Summer interrupted me a little forcefully, taking a seat on the white couch. "I am fine. I just want to sit and catch up before"—she gestured with her hands—"things get all crazy. After all," she continued with a small smile, "this is it, right? After tomorrow, you won't remember all us little people," she said, referring to tomorrow's draft.

"Jesus. No way, Summer."

This was my in.

I moved to sit on the couch beside her, angling my legs toward hers. The sunlight streaming in from the window framed her face, highlighting the russet tones in her hair. She looked like an angel, smiling at me so honestly.

There was nothing in the world that could hold me back now.

"Nick, I met someone."

Except that.

"What? You met—who? What?" *I refocused my eyes on Summer, still bright-eyed and beautiful before me. But I realized…her excited demeanor was not because we were meeting up. It was because she was excited over someone else.*

A male someone.

A male someone who was not me.

"His name is Erik. We met in the city—his parents have season tickets to the ballet, can you believe that?! Erik came to one of the after-party type things the company holds, which I usually never go to. But apparently, he was taken by my performance, and so he sent me these beautiful flowers and asked me to meet him at the party, which I did, even though I was exhausted from the performance and still had my makeup on. Anyway, you don't care about all that. But the important thing is, we are totally in love, and we are getting married!" *Summer rambled a mile a minute the way she did when she got carried away, either in anger or happiness.*

This was happiness—her smile beamed, and she looked absolutely ecstatic.

But this is insane, I thought to myself.

"You—you're what? You're getting married? But Summer, you're only nineteen years old!"

Summer looked at me sharply. "I think you mean to say—congratulations?"

I exhaled quickly and rubbed the back of my neck. "I'm sorry. You just… you just caught me off guard, okay? I thought we were going to catch up, go to dinner… I wasn't expecting a marriage announcement."

She smiled tentatively. "Oh, we are totally doing all those things! We are taking the city by storm. Well, maybe more of a light sprinkle, given that tomorrow is the big day."

I already knew I was going in the first round. Papers were drawn up, my agent had confirmed everything, and my family was in town to celebrate with me.

But I didn't give a dusty fuck about any of that as I caught sight of the giant rock on Summer's left ring finger. How had I missed that before? All I could think of was that Summer's hands were tiny and delicate—wasn't that ring uncomfortable?

"Jesus," I said as I took in her ring.

"I know," she said, looking slightly embarrassed. "It's a little over the top, but that's kind of Erik's way. You'll see when you meet him. You don't mind, do you? He's going to meet us at the restaurant a little later. He had some board meeting to attend."

"Yeah, sure, of course, but… I mean, who is this guy? How did this happen?"

"Well, I told you, he came to one of the shows—"

"How long have you guys been dating?" I interrupted Summer. I had no knowledge of her dating anyone. I mean, it wasn't like we talked every week, or even every month. But Tatum hadn't said anything. Surely she would tell me if Summer were in a serious relationship, right?

"We've been dating a couple months," Summer replied, her voice a little softer now, as if she knew I would not be pleased with this information.

"A couple months?" I asked incredulously. This had to be a joke, I thought to myself. Who gets engaged at nineteen after dating a dude for a couple months?

"I know, I know it's fast, but he's just so wonderful. So wonderful, Nick. I'm happy! And I would appreciate it if you, one of my oldest friends…could be happy too?" Summer looked at me with equal parts uncertainty and hope, twirling the giant rock on her finger with her other hand.

I sighed, looking down at my hands, clenched on the top of my thighs. This was definitely not how I anticipated the night would go. But Summer was too important to me to push her away.

I glanced back up at Summer, where she was looking at me with such anticipation, I couldn't help but smile a little. "Yeah, Summer. I can be happy for you."

Surely if this guy was good enough for Summer, he was good enough for me.

ᔕᔕᔕᔕᔕ

We weren't even finished with dinner when it became apparent this guy was in no way good enough for me, and certainly not for Summer.

Erik Johnstone was rich, smarmy, and entitled. I didn't like a thing about him.

I didn't like the way he casually suggested that Summer forgo the steak and garlic mashed potatoes for "lighter fare." I didn't like the way he kept his fucking arm across the back of Summer's chair the entire dinner, even while he was eating. I didn't like that he was rude to the waitress.

My mom always told me: it's not always about how someone treats you; it's about how they treat other people.

And this guy Erik did not treat other people well.

I didn't like his hair, his face, his entire being.

I didn't like that he was breathing the same air as Summer.

"So, Nick. Pretty exciting time for you, huh?"

"What?" I had been staring at Summer, trying to send her messages telepathically, while she pushed leaves around her plate.

Erik smirked at me as if he knew how uncomfortable this was for me. "The draft, man. You've got to be stoked about that, right?"

"Uh, yeah. Yeah, I'm excited." I took a deep breath and addressed him directly. "It's pretty unbelievable—but I've put in the work, and I am excited to see how things turn out." That was the stock answer I gave to anyone who wasn't my family about the draft. I knew I was going to San Diego, barring something crazy happening.

"That sounds like a bullshit answer if I've ever heard one!" Erik guffawed, tossing back his scotch. "Come on, Nick, how about a clue? San Diego looks good. Cleveland? New York?"

I didn't miss the way Summer's eyes darted to me when Erik mentioned New York, the city where she lived.

"I'll be happy no matter where I end up," I answered, another stock response, but the truth.

"Mmm-hmmm. More bullshit. No way do you want to end up in Cleveland." He laughed like he'd just said the funniest thing ever.

So Erik was also one of those people who considered himself better-than because he was from the East Coast instead of the Midwest. I wonder what he would think of our small town.

I loathed him.

"New York would be cool, wouldn't it, Nick?" Summer asked me, sounding a little wistful. "We could totally hang out!"

Erik chuckled. "Nick's not going to have any time for his old friends, Summer. Once he's in the pros"—what a douche; no one called it "the pros"—"he's going to be on to bigger and better things. And anyway, you're so busy with your career, Sum." He moved his arm from the back of her seat to wrap around her shoulder. I noticed that he gripped her shoulder tightly as he spoke.

Sum? What the hell kind of stupid nickname was that?

～～～～～

The rest of the dinner was more or less like that, with plenty of passive-aggressive bullshit from Erik, and an uncharacteristically quiet Summer. I said good-bye to them after dinner and went back to my hotel room, but I couldn't sleep a wink.

I was greeted in the morning with banging on my door. I shrugged on a T-shirt and ambled to the door, not surprised when it was Summer on the other side, smiling as if she hadn't a care in the world.

"Happy Draft Day, my soon-to-be-professional-athlete friend!" Summer barged in, the smell of sugar trailing in her wake. She had a huge box of baked goods and, more importantly, coffee.

"What's all this?" I asked her, my voice raspy.

"Just a little something to get your day started. We can't have you passing out from lack of calories when they call your name." She walked over to the kitchenette area and started unpacking items from the box.

"You know I am not technically supposed to be eating any of that, right? My chances in this game depend on me having a certain body type." I was practically salivating at whatever pastries she had just put on the counter. My stomach grumbled loudly, causing Summer to eye me skeptically.

"Well, one last hurrah isn't going to hurt you," she said knowingly. "Here." She handed me a large cardboard cup of coffee. "Nothing added, just the way you like it."

I closed my eyes and inhaled as I took my first few sips of coffee, letting the elixir work its magic on me. "That's some good shit," I mumbled, taking another sip.

"You are welcome," Summer responded. Having set up our impromptu breakfast, she wrung her hands the way she did when she was nervous.

I eyed her cautiously and set down my coffee. Was she going to bring up last night? The dinner that, as far as I was concerned, revealed that Erik was absolutely no good for her?

"About last night," I began.

"So, what did you think of Erik?" Summer blurted out at the same time.

Summer smiled a little hesitantly at me. "You go first," I said, gesturing to her.

"Well, I just wanted to know. What did you think? Of, you know, my affianced?" Summer said it with a faux French accent.

He is awful. He's no good for you. He doesn't deserve you.

Those were all potential responses as I looked down at my coffee.

"Summer, I…I mean, he's nice enough. I just didn't really, you know, I didn't spend a lot of time with him," I hedged.

"Nick. Be honest." Summer still had her hands together, and she looked at me with such hope in her eyes that I felt like the biggest ass.

We'd known each other for years. She was trusting me to give her an honest answer, wasn't she? I owed it to myself to trust her in return and believe that she would understand where I was coming from.

"It's just…" I took a deep breath. "Isn't it a little soon for you to be getting married?"

Summer's eyes widened, her light-brown gaze wounded. "What?" Her voice was quiet.

"It's just…" I repeated, pausing. "You are here in New York, doing your thing—your career is just taking off. Do you really want to jump into forever right away?"

Summer cocked her head, her gaze narrowing. "Un-fucking-believable," she muttered. Followed by, "You sound just like her," under her breath.

"Just like who? I thought we were talking about Erik?"

"Just like Alexis!" Summer spat out. "You guys are reading from the same script. 'You're too young.' 'He's too old for you.' 'Don't you want to live life a bit?'" She scoffed. "As if I don't know my own mind. As if I need permission!"

I hadn't seen Summer's older sister in years, and while we were certainly never close, if she didn't like this guy either, then sign me the fuck up for Team Alexis.

"How old is he, Summer?" I demanded, raising my own voice to match her volume.

I was being an asshole; I knew it. I had no right, no claim to Summer. We'd seen each other occasionally over the past several years, but I'd never given her any indication I saw her as anything more than my little sister's best friend. And putting my feelings for her aside, she was right. She could make her own decisions.

"What does that matter?" Summer asked exasperatedly, throwing up both of her hands.

"It matters, Summer, because…because this is a mistake! You are too young, he is too old!" I was exasperated that she didn't see the reasons why Erik was all wrong for her.

Because you haven't told her the real reason, *a little voice in my head told me.*

"If the only thing wrong with my relationship is the age difference between me and Erik, then I don't see the problem!" Summer was yelling now. "He treats me well. He loves me. Do you know how happy I am? No! Because we hardly ever talk, Nick." I opened my mouth to respond, but she waved her hand to continue speaking. "And I'm not mad or anything, Nick. It's a normal part of life—that we will grow apart as we get older." She paused and then smiled at me, a little sadly, letting out a big exhale.

"We're grown-ups now, you know?"

"Yeah, well, sometimes being a grown-up fucking sucks," I muttered, pressing my hands to my eyes.

If this was what being a grown-up felt like, then count me out. And I sure as hell didn't feel like a grown-up as Summer continued ripping my heart out of my chest.

"Summer." I tried to begin again. "He is not good enough for you."

"Please. You know that after one dinner?" Summer took a deep breath. "For the first time in my adult life, I have a partner. Someone in my corner. I've been alone for so long. So long, Nick," Summer choked up a little, and it killed me to hear the sadness in her voice.

"My parents are dead. I have a sister I see maybe once a year. I have no one, Nick. Do you know what that's like, to be alone in the world? And I know my parents didn't leave this world by choice. But Alexis's decisions are all her own. And Erik… I finally have someone to depend on. I am happy," Summer concluded fiercely.

Her statement was directly at odds with the tears in her eyes.

"You don't look happy," I muttered.

That pissed her off—her eyes flashed at me, and she raised both her hands in disbelief. She was so beautiful like that, fiery and pissed off.

She was so full of life, she made me feel alive.

But deep down, I knew that wasn't a good thing. I shouldn't rely on someone else to make me happy, to make me feel like life was worth living.

Who wouldn't feel that way around Summer?

And now, she would be someone else's. I'd missed my chance, and she was going to marry this fucker Erik.

I couldn't let that happen.

"Summer. Believe me. I am absolutely not trying to ruin your happiness." I ran my fingers through my hair before rubbing the back of my neck. "I want you to be happy."

I can make you happy, I thought to myself, but like a chickenshit, I didn't say it.

Because I knew I couldn't make her happy. Not then. Not with all the shit I was figuring out.

"I just-I just think this is a mistake."

Summer's chin trembled, and her eyes continued to spit fire at me. "Give me a reason—a real *reason—why I shouldn't marry Erik." She raised her chin and met my gaze head on. "Tell me exactly why he's no good for me or why I shouldn't marry him."*

Her eyes drilled into mine, and I saw the challenge in them, daring me to rise to the occasion. It would be so easy.

You shouldn't be with him because you should be with me.

But I just stared right back at her, willing her to see the truth in my eyes.

After a few seconds, Summer's gaze softened, her mood resigned. "That's what I thought," she said softly.

Chapter Eleven

"THANK YOU FOR YOUR PRACTICE, AND YOUR PRESENCE, TODAY," I say to my class, bowing slightly to them from my position in the front of the room where I sit in my lotus pose.

I've officially been an Estero Bay resident for two whole weeks. I've been drinking plenty of water, unpacking my life in my new home, getting a full eight hours of sleep, teaching yoga.

I am truly adulting with the best of them.

Of course, during those eight hours of sleep, I am having totally inappropriate and impure thoughts about a certain six-foot-four ex-NFL quarterback with hypnotic eyes and a chiseled torso.

Our one-on-one session certainly left me with several impressions.

First, despite his injuries and his obvious pain at times, Nick still has an ass you can bounce a quarter off. Maybe even a half-dollar. When he answered the door in his old T-shirt with the sleeves cut off, his golden, hard chest visible through the large armholes, it was all I could do not to drool. The last time I spent much time with Nick, he was in arguably the best physical shape of his life—playing college ball, preparing for the draft. Time has, of course, changed him. But in an annoyingly good, sexy way. He's got those little crinkles at the corners of his eyes and not an ounce of fat on that hard body. I don't know what his recovery period was like, and I am sure it took some time to redevelop the muscles that had been neglected during his convalescence. He is lean, firm, and carved to perfection.

Second, he's quieter. Not that Nick has ever been a chatterbox—he's always been thoughtful about speaking when he has something to say, rather than as the default rule. And with sisters like his, it wasn't as if he had much peace and quiet anyway. Perhaps he's the classic middle child. But there's something different now, a slightly troubled expression in his eyes that wasn't there before. I want to soothe his muscles and his mind, take away whatever put that there.

But.

I am adulting. I am working on myself. Nick certainly had no interest in me panting after him when I was younger. There's no way he wants the newly divorced friend of his little sister to lick his wounds now.

Although I think I wouldn't mind doing some actual licking…

"Summer, thank you so much for the class." I am distracted by Leticia Abernathy, who waves to me as she rolls up her mat. Letty was a couple years ahead of me in high school. She still lives in the Bay, running the local art gallery. Like a lot of funky, small beach towns that time forgot, Estero Bay has a pretty vibrant art scene, with classes for the young and old, the experienced and the non-experienced.

"No problem, Letty," I reply, standing up from my position. "I am so glad to see you."

"That was a really good class," Letty says, stretching her head from side to side. She has box braids piled atop her head with a beautiful purple headscarf wrapped around them.

"I am loving your scarf," I tell her as I roll up my mat. Our class was pretty full, about twenty students, and most of the others are making their way to the exit at the back of the room.

"Thank you! It's from the gallery. We have a lot of this kind of stuff for sale—headbands, scarves, jewelry. All that Etsy stuff, you know? Have you been by?"

"No, I have only been back a couple weeks. I will make it a point this week."

"For sure," Letty says, taking a drink from her bottle. "How long have you been teaching these classes?"

"I did my teacher training about a year ago."

"In New York, right?" I have no idea how Letty knows that I was on the

East Coast, but it's par for the course in a small town. Everybody knows what so-and-so is doing, where they are doing it, and who they are doing it with.

"How cool. Last I heard, you were dancing on the stage on Broadway." Letty's dark eyes are sparkling at me. "It sounded so glamorous."

I shift uncomfortably, doing my best to smile at her enthusiasm. "Not Broadway—trust me, you don't want to hear me sing," I joke. "I was dancing with a ballet company, for several years in the city." I pause, Letty watching me expectantly. "I had an injury, though, so no more ballet for me. The yoga is something I took up in recovery."

Letty nods, a sympathetic look on her face. "Damn. I didn't know that. You're okay now, though? I mean, you must be, if you can lead us through this class."

I give her what I hope is a reassuring look. "Absolutely. I had a pretty bad knee injury—it's actually the same injury that ended Patrick Swayze's professional ballet career before he decided to try acting."

"No shit?" Letty raises her eyebrows, and I nod. People love the Swayze factoid.

"Damn. Now that was a great loss. He was one good-looking dude."

"Amen." We both take a moment to acknowledge the fineness of Mr. Swayze.

"Anyway. I will definitely be back for more of this torture." Letty smiles at me as she turns to leave.

"See ya," I respond, bending to pick up my mat and water bottle.

"Hey, Amber," I hear Letty say as she exits the room.

Ugh.

Amber Bracamonte is another Estero Bay local, and she works here at Luther's studio too. She was in my grade growing up. She is busty, bright, and beautiful—and also used to date Nick in high school.

I would hate her if she weren't so damn nice all the time.

"Summer, your class was so great!" Amber stops in front of me, looking like she just stepped off the Lululemon home page. Her ample chest is on display in a mint-green tank top with intricate straps across the back. She wears matching mint leggings that hug every inch of her curves. She has long eyelashes, pouty pink lips, and tons of long, dark hair braided over her shoulder. She is, frankly, stunning, and I am sure next to her I look like an overgrown six-year-old, with my flat chest and freckles.

Erik had wondered on more than one occasion if I would ever consider breast implants. One of our acquaintances in the city—the wife of one of Erik's colleagues—got breast implants, and Erik went so far as to make an initial consult for me after asking for the surgeon's name.

I've long made peace with my "lack of a rack," but it was still strange to hear my husband voice his discomfort with my body. I mean, I had these breasts when we got married—it wasn't like I tricked him with Wonderbras, only to say "Ha-ha! Gotcha, sucker!" on our wedding night.

Somewhere along the way, Erik began to make me feel like I was not worth any effort. Like everything I did was unimportant, every opinion I had could be disregarded. I didn't know what I was talking about; I wasn't educated enough or cultured enough or *good* enough. Every hope I had was juvenile and silly.

And somewhere along the way, I started to believe him. Or at least accepted that This Is The Way It Is.

My lack of a rack, of course, was just one of the many things that Erik found fault with over the course of our marriage. And I don't know or care if Amber's breasts are real or not—whatever floats her boat—but it's hard to shake off years of passive-aggressive comments from the guy who promised to love you for better or worse. Maybe we should have changed the vows to "for better or worse, but only if you increase that A cup to a full C by the time you're thirty."

"Thanks, Amber," I respond wanly.

"You make it look so effortless!" Amber continues in an excited voice. "And you're so flexible!" Amber really does talk like every sentence ends in an exclamation point. "I guess the years of dancing have really helped, huh?"

She goes on before I can answer her. "How are you settling in? Good, I hope?" Amber's face changes, from bubbly to concerned. "I was sorry to hear about your divorce. But it's really nice to have you back here in our little town!" She giggles then, her expression changing yet again.

"Thanks, Amber." I swing my yoga mat holder over my shoulder, moving toward the door, hoping she will take the hint.

"Well, I guess we'll be seeing a lot of each other with Luther being away for a bit, right?"

"I guess we will."

"And if you ever need me to cover for anything—the classes or the private clients—let me know that too!"

I pause at that and turn to her. I don't know what, if any, kind of relationship she has with Nick, other than as an old high school flame. And maybe she's just being nice—she may not even know that I am having the one-on-one sessions with Nick.

Amber continues smiling at me brightly, ever the cheerleader.

"O…kay," I tell her slowly.

The thought of Nick being with anyone else kind of makes me gag, even though I've no right to him. And Jesus, at this point, we've been married to other people.

But I never met Nick's ex-wife; I didn't attend his wedding, and we didn't exchange Christmas cards or anything. Nick's ex-wife is more of an abstract idea to me. I know he was married to a blond lady in San Diego, but I have no face to put with the blond hair. Because I am mature and adulting, I choose to give her the face of Angelica Huston in *The Witches*. After she takes off her mask.

Seeing Amber in front of me, in all her sweet-smelling glory, and knowing that she's had a part of Nick that I haven't? Even though it was a million years ago, it still sucks.

It just sucks to be seen as the friend, the kid sister, never the sexy one.

I push those thoughts from my head as I debate my response to Amber. She hasn't mentioned Nick by name yet, and I don't want to either. And my self-esteem issues are definitely not her problem.

"Thanks, Amber. I think I've got it under control for now, but I will definitely let you know if anything changes."

Amber's expression doesn't change a bit. "Great! That would be great!" Her eyes dart suddenly to a point over my shoulder. "Hi, Nick!"

Out of my head and into the yoga studio, there is Nick, in all his football-god glory, taking up all the damn space in the doorway like a mountain. He's casually dressed in a T-shirt—with sleeves, and more's the pity—shorts, and flip-flops.

Shit, is he here for Amber's class?

Does he *hate* yoga with me?

Does he hate being around me?

Before my mind can take one of several detours it's currently contemplating, Nick speaks.

"Hi, Amber." Nick briefly looks at her and nods before turning his eyes to me. "Summer." His deep voice deepens when he says my name.

"Hi," I reply softly. His hair is tousled and shiny, still looking damp from a shower, maybe.

"It's so nice to see you!" Amber continues, apparently unaware of my inner turmoil. "Are you here for my class?"

Nick doesn't take his eyes off mine. "I didn't come for a class." He moves into the space, and I notice that he's holding something in his hand—a yellow box of tea.

"Here," he says gruffly, thrusting it toward me. "I got this for you." He blinks for a second and then says, "I mean, I had some extra. I thought you might want it. You know. Since you just moved back, and I don't know what you have been able to get from the store or whatever."

It's my favorite ginger blend, the kind I had the other day at his house. It's such a thoughtful gesture, and I am touched. I smile and take it from him, the brief touch of our fingertips creating a buzzing sensation along my skin.

"That's so sweet, Nick," I tell him honestly. "Really, you didn't have to do that."

"Yeah. Well." He puts his hands in his pockets and kind of rocks back and forth. "I know moving sucks when you don't have all the normal creature comforts, and uh, I know you like tea, so…" His voice trails off, and he glances down a minute before looking up at me, his gaze intense. "I wanted you to have it." His eyes are so clear and bright, and his smell reaches me— minty toothpaste and freshly showered man.

"Thank you," I respond, beaming at him. He seems to relax a bit as his shoulders drop, and I think I see the corners of his mouth almost turn up into a smile.

I'd kill to get a real smile from him.

"Oh my gosh, that is so sweet of you!" Amber squeals from behind us. Her high-pitched voice makes me jump a bit; I'd almost forgotten she was there.

"Nick, you are such a good brother to take care of Tatum's friends," Amber continues as she walks closer to us.

Nick finally turns his gaze toward Amber, as if he's seeing her for the first time. "Summer's not my sister," he says softly but firmly.

Amber's eyes widen and her smile falls. "Of course not! Of course not," she says quickly. "I only meant—well, she used to live with your family af- ter…" Amber's eyes widen even more, and her face is turning bright red. "Oh shit," she whispers. "I'm sorry, I just—"

I've got to help a girl out. "Amber, it's totally fine," I reassure her.

My parents have been dead for fourteen years now. I miss them, and while I cherish the memories of the time we had together, I don't burst into tears every time someone brings them up or every time I am reminded of them.

Nick stares at Amber for a beat longer. "It was nice to see you, Amber." His voice is kind but dismissive. Amber's gaze darts between me and Nick, and she gathers her wits before turning that million-dollar smile on us once again.

"It was so nice to see you too! Summer, I'll see you soon! I'm just going to go and see if anyone is here to check in!" She bounces out of the room, her long braid flailing down her back.

Nick turns back to me.

"This is nice," I gesture to the tea. "Really, thank you. Again."

He assesses me for a minute, I suppose to make sure I am not going to burst into tears, before nodding. "You're welcome."

He doesn't make any move to leave, still standing with his hands in his pockets. "Well…" I begin to speak, indicating the door as I move to leave the room.

"Come with me."

"What?" I look up at Nick.

"It's boat day. Me, my pops, my buddy Brock." Nick clears his throat. "We're taking the boat out on the bay. Maybe farther, depending on the wind today." He rubs the back of his neck with one hand, regarding me a little… nervously? "We might catch something, have some beers. Pops would love to see you," he adds with a chuckle.

"I don't want to intrude," I respond, although the day he describes sounds like paradise.

"No, no, you won't be. Trust me, Pops will be mad if he finds out I ran into you and didn't invite you," Nick says ruefully.

That's not exactly an indication that Nick wants me there. And not that I don't love his grandfather, but you know what? I'll take it.

"I probably need to run home to get some warmer clothes," I tell him, gesturing to my yoga ensemble.

"I'll walk with you. Although Tatum keeps extra clothes under the seats, if you want to use her sweatshirt or whatever."

"Okay," I respond, smiling at him. "I would love to join you," I add before I can change my mind.

And then I see the full Nick smile—his bright white teeth set against his tanned, chiseled face. I mean, *Jesus*. It's a smile people pen novels about.

I know Nick is going through Some Stuff, but I aim to get that smile again before the end of the day.

Chapter Twelve

Nick

I AM HALFWAY TO THE DOCK WITH SUMMER. I'VE SECOND-GUESSED MY decision to ask her to join me no fewer than half a dozen times.

She is still in her yoga clothes, and I am still grateful to the person who invented yoga pants. She's got her purple beanie covering her hair again and a dark, striped poncho-thing covering her shoulders. She looks cozy as always, and I want to wrap my arm around her as we walk.

Estero Bay is a beach town, of course, but it's not a warm-weather locale. The running joke is that you can tell all the tourists who come here from the inland Central Valley because they're all wearing brand-new, bright-red "Estero Bay Lifeguard" sweatshirts, walking around in flip-flops with chattering teeth. The middle part of our state gets brutally hot in the summertime, though, so sixty-five degrees and overcast probably feels like a different kind of vacation, one from the blistering heat.

This time of year, it's pretty quiet as we meander toward the water. The fog is thick, and you can just make out the base of the Rock across the bay. The ever-present noise of sea gulls and seals battles for our attention, and the briny ocean smell is thick in the air.

"Thanks again for inviting me," Summer comments, tucking some loose hair back under her beanie. "I haven't seen your grandfather in forever. He's liking retirement, Tatum says?"

"He likes it enough. He's not really a sit-back-and-watch-TV kind of guy, though. He's found enough things to do to not drive my mom crazy."

Summer smiles. "Like the boat."

I nod. "Yeah, like the boat. He still has his old dinghy, but I got him one that's a little nicer—I told him it was a retirement present for both of us. Otherwise, he would have refused."

"That's sweet, Nick." Summer looks at me approvingly, and I can feel my cheeks heating a bit with her praise.

"Mom's not a big ocean person, but he gets a ton of use out of it. Julia's kids love it too—we bring them out and fish, or just cruise so they can jump off out into the open water." The bay is beautiful, but it's not exactly clean.

"And your friend, is he a local too?"

"Brock. No, he's not. You, uh, you probably know him—Brock Donovan?"

Summer looks at me blankly.

"Big guy? Professional football player?"

Summer looks a little embarrassed. "So, honestly…I am not a huge football fan. I mean, I was a fan of yours, of course," she says quickly. "Am. I am a fan. I mean, of you generally, but also when you were playing. I just didn't—" Summer exhales briefly. "I, ah, really didn't catch your games too much, let alone games, generally." She gives me a guilty look. "Sorry?"

I chuckle and shake my head. "Please. No apology necessary. I am just surprised, I guess. I mean, Brock was the guy who caused my injury."

Summer looks taken aback at this revelation, stumbling a bit. I reach out my hand to steady her, placing it on her poncho. I feel the same electric tingles from this simple touch as I did during our yoga class.

"Whoa. Sorry, I was not expecting to receive that information!" Summer looks at me a little disbelievingly. "So…you guys are what, besties? After that?"

"Yeah, it is a little weird. We really didn't know each other before the hit, before my injury," I explain. "He actually came to visit me when I was in the hospital, and then he kind of kept coming back. He's like that," I add. "He is one of those people who will force you to be his friend."

"Like a barnacle," Summer says with a nod.

I bark a laugh. It feels different, untried. "Yeah, I guess so."

She smiles back at me. "It's an appropriate metaphor for the beach, huh?"

It's not difficult for Brock to make friends wherever he goes. He was notorious in the League for being the life of the party. He's huge, bigger than me, and built like a brick shithouse. He's from Wisconsin and has pretty much been a football star since he was ten years old.

Is it strange that the guy who essentially ended my professional career—which, incidentally, led to the end of my marriage—is now one of my best and, frankly, only friends? I don't think so. Like I told Summer, Brock came to visit me in the hospital, which was decent. And I thought it was just a one-time visit, but then he kept coming back. He eventually met my parents, my sisters, Lincoln, and of course, Gretchen.

We've never talked about the end of my marriage; he's never asked. I just told him one day that it hadn't worked out, he said he was sorry, and that was it.

Brock is retired now, too, and has some ridiculous villa in Malibu. He laughed his ass off when I told him I was going to move back to the town I grew up in—some rinky-dink beach town where half of the stores and restaurants are closed from October through March. But when he was done laughing, he looked at me and said, with all seriousness, "Good for you, dude."

I am pretty sure Brock is the type of guy who, if I called him in the middle of the night and told him I needed help, he'd be there—no questions asked.

I don't know for sure, because I have yet to ask anyone for help in the middle of the night. But I am fairly certain he's that guy.

"Well, then I am excited to meet him," Summer says, bringing me back to the present.

"I should warn you. He can come on, ah, a little strong."

Summer laughs a little and rolls her eyes. "I am sure I can handle your little friend, Nick," she says. And I am not going to lie—I get a little flustered when she says my name. I want her to say it again, preferably in a low-lit room, both of us a little sweaty and out of breath. I want to hear her whimper my name as I trace my hands down her warm skin. I want to figure out all the different parts of her—the soft and the hard, the smooth and the rough, the loud and the quiet, and have all those parts coalesce into something more than the sum of our parts.

But right now, I will settle for a boat ride.

∼∼∼∼∼

We reach the dock, and I use my key to open one of the pedestrian gates leading out to the slips. "We're the last one out there—the white boat with the navy trim."

"*Izarra*," Summer reads the name of the boat aloud.

"Pops picked it out. It means 'star' in Euskara," I explain.

"That's beautiful," Summer replies. "Is he going to yell at us in Basque like when we were kids?"

"Hopefully not today," I tell her jokingly. "But he still does that with Julia and Linc's kids—he's taught them all sorts of colorful words. Although, I will say that neither Julia nor Lincoln seems to mind as much as my mom did when we were growing up. I mean," I continue as we make our way closer to the boat, "with Julia for a mother, both girls knew what the f-word was by the time they started elementary school."

Summer laughs at that. "No surprise there."

I hear an old Garth Brooks song playing from the deck, and I step over the gangplank onto the boat. "Need a hand?" I turn back to Summer, and she slips her hand into mine to step onto the deck through the little swinging door. Her skin feels soft and warm, and I want to keep holding her hand as I show her around.

She removes her hand from mine before I can do that, though, and turns around to take in the boat. "So…wow, you are a liar," she tells me cheekily. "This is *not* just a step up from the old dinghy."

"Yeah, it's not bad, huh?" I respond, rubbing the back of my neck with my hand.

"It's lovely," she responds. "*I* want to retire on this boat."

I immediately picture Summer and me on the catamaran, sailing on the open water, jumping off the side when the weather is warm and sunny, snuggling in the cabin when the weather is cold and foggy. I want this viscerally, so badly I can almost taste it, and decide this is my new goal. I stare at Summer as she moves around the deck, running her hand over the seats and the side, her cheeks rosy and her lips pink. I can see it all so clearly now.

If I want to do all the things to Summer that I am thinking, though, I should probably get my own boat and get my grandfather to admit that this one was a retirement gift, just for him.

"What. Is. Up, My Dude!" I am suddenly enveloped by a hulking mass of a person. Brock wraps his arms around me and squeezes.

The guy is not one to fly under the radar.

"What's up, buddy? Oof," I respond, giving him a couple quick slaps on the back before stepping back. Brock is still huge but is no longer a mass of veins and muscle like he was when we were playing. I mean, if there was ever a guy who was built to cause a career-ending injury, Brock is That Guy.

"Nicky, looking good, looking good," he responds, rubbing his chin and eyeing the petite redhead beside me. "I didn't know you were bringing a friend," he says with an easy smile, immediately turning on the charm.

Brock's blue eyes twinkle as he looks to me briefly, then to Summer, then back to me. I stifle the urge to roll my eyes. "Brock, this is Summer Mahoney. We grew up together. Summer, this is Brock Donovan."

"Hi." Summer steps forward and offers her hand to Brock. "It's nice to meet you. Full disclosure, I don't know anything about professional football."

Brock places his hand over his chest dramatically. "Straight through the heart, Summer." She laughs as he takes her hand in his.

Which I don't like. He doesn't need to be touching her like that, right?

"So, you grew up together, huh? Was this guy always so grumpy?" Brock asks as he flips her palm over to peck the back of her hand.

He definitely doesn't need to be kissing her. Any part of her.

Summer, however, giggles like it's the funniest thing on the planet.

I am fairly certain I have never had a girl giggle over something I did in my life.

"All right, all right, introductions are over," I bark, briefly bumping Brock on the shoulder as I move past him. Not that it does much; the guy is a damn oak tree. "Pops around?"

"He's in the cabin, unloading some of the stuff your mom sent with him."

"Food?" Summer perks up as she looks at Brock. "I haven't eaten since breakfast," she adds a little sheepishly. "I was going to grab a bite after my last class, but then Nick invited me along. I hope that's okay? I don't want to intrude on your outing."

Brock tsks at her as he offers her his arm. "Summer, Summer, a summer breeze on a cool day. You are just what us old, retired guys need." He gestures to the fog around us and then looks at me. "Seriously, dude. This fog is unnecessary and offensive. It's seventy-five and sunny in the 'Bu."

"I am happy for you, and nobody calls Malibu 'the 'Bu,'" I respond wryly.

"What can I say? I'm a trendsetter, setting trends. There will be TikToks about it later." Brock links his arm through Summer's. "Now, tell me some embarrassing stories about Nicky growing up. In exchange, I will share some embarrassing stories about Mr. Quarterback's days in the League."

Summer giggles again as I follow them, briefly considering throwing Brock overboard.

Why am I friends with this guy?

Summer

I am even more impressed as we walk toward the main cabin. I assume it's the main cabin—the boat is huge, and I see steps leading down to what might be sleeping quarters. We bypass those steps and enter a kitchen and seating area surrounded by glass.

Nick's grandfather has his back to us as he puts items into the open refrigerator. He turns as we come in, and his dark eyes light up as he sees us.

Nick's grandfather is like a miniature, older version of Nick. He stoops a bit with age, making him about my height. He has the same swarthy skin that all the Echeverrias do. His is aged from his time out on the sea, under the sun. His dark hair is streaked with gray, and he has a gray mustache as well. I smile at the captain's hat tilted on his head—navy with white trim and gold buttons.

He opens his arms for a hug, and before I can go in, Brock beats me to it.

"Mr. Echeverria, good to see you again," Brock says.

"Brock, son, I've told you to call me Antone," Mr. Echeverria—Antone—says, his eyes twinkling.

"I know, I know, Antone," Brock replies, pulling away.

"And you! Young lady, I demand a hug," Antone pushes Brock away playfully.

"It's so good to see you," I say softly as I hug Antone. He pulls away and takes both of my hands in his, searching my face as if to make sure I am all in one piece. "You are good, Summer? Settling in okay?"

Of course he will know that I am here in the Bay, and why. Except for Tatum, I really didn't see any of the Echeverrias in the years I was married to Erik. I never saw Nick after that horrible parting in New York. Nick's mom, Elaine, came to the wedding. So did Julia, and Tatum was a bridesmaid. But over the years, I stopped coming to visit. Erik certainly had no interest in coming to Estero Bay and would find reasons why I shouldn't go home to visit.

Is there really anyone there to see? Your sister lives here.

Why can't Tatum come here? Surely she wants to get out of that dumpy town and come to the city.

I can't imagine spending a week with a bunch of fishermen, but you go ahead.

I find myself blinking back tears suddenly as I try to recall the last time I saw Antone.

I really can't remember, and it's my own fault.

"Hey, hey, none of that," Antone scolds me, patting my hand. "Not on my watch." He stares at me a moment longer and then says earnestly, "I am glad you're here, Summer."

I smile back at him, though I know it's a little wobbly. "I am glad to be here."

"And my Nicky, huh? He is here too!" Antone exclaims as Nick comes into the cabin. Brock has taken a seat in one of the tall bar chairs, a beer in his hand.

"Hey, Pops," Nick says easily, nodding and heading to the sink. "Before you put everything away, can I fix a plate? Summer's hungry."

I blush a little at his statement—I can make my own plate, can't I?—but I can't deny that it's nice having someone take care of me, a little bit.

And Lord knows the Echeverrias love to eat.

"Then I will make our dear Summer a plate, and you children will go to the deck and get us out on the water."

"Aye-aye, Captain." Brock jumps up from his spot at the bar and leads us out to the deck in the rear. The helm and the wheel are in the little covered area, and there is seating behind and to the side of the helm.

"Come on, Summer," Brock says. "Let's get acquainted while Nicky here takes the driver's seat."

I see Nick glare at Brock, but he's not serious. Is he? "Leave her alone a minute. Come help me untie us before we take off."

"Aye-aye, Captain," Brock repeats, winking at me as he follows Nick alongside the boat.

Nick is casually dressed in flip-flops, shorts, and a T-shirt, despite the gloomy day. His legs are dusted with dark hair, and the muscles in his forearms flex and release as he unties several ropes from the dock.

On his way back, Nick lifts up one of the seats to grab a gray hoodie. As he reaches up to pull it over his head, I have a brief glimpse of his tanned, toned stomach and the dark hair curling around his zipper.

I am still staring at his waist—now sadly covered by the gray hoodie—when he says my name. "Summer."

"Hmmm? I mean, yes?" My eyes dart back up to his, and I snap out of my gawking. He gives me a little half smile, as if he knows I've been checking him out. "I said, do you want one of Tatum's sweatshirts?" He gestures to me with another hoodie.

"Oh yes, please." I catch it when he throws it to me, and I take off my poncho to pull the hoodie on. For a moment, I am just wearing my cropped yoga top and leggings, and I now feel Nick's eyes on me as I pull the hoodie over my head.

"So, Summer, what's a girl like you doing hanging out with this grumpy guy?" Brock says as he ambles back over to me. He takes a seat on the bench seat opposite mine, stretching his legs out in front of him. The man is huge—bigger and wider than Nick and built like a sequoia. From what little I know about Nick's injury, I guess that whatever Brock did in the NFL must've involved running hard and knocking people on their asses. It's easy to see that he would be good at it.

"Well." I take a breath and pause. Despite whatever internal turmoil I am feeling for Nick at the moment, I suppose the condensed version is pretty straightforward. "Tatum and I were best friends growing up. Still are. So I've always known Nick"—my gaze darts to him as he turns on the motor and leads us backward out of the slip—"and his family."

"You've always lived here? In Estero Bay?" Brock sounds a little incredulous.

"No, I lived back east for a while, in New York. I…ah, I actually just moved back. I got divorced." I give Brock a little smile, the smile I reserve for situations like these when I tell people I am divorced. The one that I hope says, "Yes, I am divorced and the whole thing sucked, but it's for the best because my ex-husband is a real douchenozzle and I am better off."

Tatum is a fan of the douche terms of endearment—douchenozzle, douchelord. There's really nothing that doesn't sound good with "douche" in front of it.

"Ah shit." Brock looks chagrined. "I'm sorry to hear that."

"Thank you, but don't be." I give a little wave of my hand. "It's honestly for the best."

I am trying to pay attention to Brock, but I keep darting glances to Nick, who is self-assuredly maneuvering this giant boat, very slowly, out onto the bay. This is not San Francisco—our bay is small, and glancing around, I can see there appear to be only a couple of slips that would hold a boat of this size. Once we get out onto the water past the break and the Rock, we'll be fine, but Nick has to navigate around other boats, kayakers, people on stand-up paddleboards, and the occasional seal and otter.

"Can I get you a beer?" Brock asks, making a move to stand.

"No thanks, I'm good," I respond, tucking my legs under me and pulling my beanie over my ears a little bit.

"She likes tea." Nick's voice comes to us a little louder from the wheel, raised to be heard over the motor as we cruise out of the bay.

"Tea, huh?" Brock looks at Nick, then back to me, smiling a little bit. "Well, Summer, who likes tea, I will see what they have in the kitchen."

"That's sweet, thank you." Brock raises his now-empty bottle in salute and moves toward the cabin.

I go back to surveying Nick, who now also has a beanie pulled over his dark hair. I view our surroundings—the buoys, the lighthouse in the distance, the Rock, still covered by a thick layer of fog, our little town getting more miniature as we get out on the open water—but Nick is what pulls my attention. It's no chore to keep my eyes on him as he steers the boat.

And the best part is that because his attention is occupied elsewhere, I can do it surreptitiously.

"You're going to burn a hole through my shirt, Sunshine, if you stare any harder." Nick takes his eyes off the water in front of him for a second, darting his gaze over to mine, using a nickname I haven't heard in…well, over a decade.

Apparently I wasn't *that* surreptitious.

I feel myself blushing furiously to the roots of my hair, and I am rewarded with another Nick grin. Not exactly the way I imagined making him smile, but I'll take it. I quickly avert my eyes back to the coastline. We travel parallel to land, and I make out the golf course on the south side of town.

"Want to steer?"

"What?" I look at Nick, and he's gesturing to the wheel.

"Come on," he says. "You can steer for a minute."

"I've never steered a boat before," I tell him, standing up and moving close to the hull.

"How about when you were little? I remember you and Tatum fighting over whose turn it was to steer on Pops's boat," he replies.

I smile at the memory. "I am pretty sure your grandfather did all the work and gave us all the glory."

He smiles before moving away from the wheel, motioning me to stand in front of him. "I'll help you if you need it. She's got power, but you can control it."

"She?" I move in front of him, my back to his chest, feeling the heat of his body as he takes a position behind me.

"All boats are female," he responds matter-of-factly.

"I didn't know we were gendering our nautical devices." I put my hands on the wheel at ten and two, and Nick places his hands over mine. His are warm and callused, and they feel so good on my skin. I can't imagine how good they would feel on other parts of my body.

Actually, I can imagine, but now is really not the time or the place, as I navigate the vessel alongside the shore.

"I don't make the rules, Sunshine," he responds softly. I feel his warm breath close to the shell of my ear as he helps me steer.

He stands close behind me, his chest to my back, a reversal of how we stood during our yoga session earlier this week. I can feel the heat of his body through our clothes as he surrounds me, enveloping me with his strong arms, steering the wheel with me. Although, if I am honest, there's not much steering to do as we are simply gliding along parallel to the shore-line, beyond the breaking waves.

"Relax," Nick continues, his voice a little deeper than normal. "Push your shoulders down. These are easy waters, and she'll help you along."

I try to do just that, making sure my shoulders aren't tight up by my ears and let myself lean into Nick's hard chest. We are now pressed together, his legs a little wider behind mine, his crotch up against the small of my back. He smells so good and he feels so good and it's all I can do not to rub my back against him and purr like a cat. I want to roll my head back onto his shoul-der and feel his lips on my neck. I want to feel if he's this hard everywhere.

My body decides it is ready for immediate answers to these unknowns, and I push my butt back slightly against him without meaning to. And Nick…grunts? In surprise or approval, I can't tell, but I jerk my body forward a little bit in response.

"Sorry!" I squeak. "I'm sorry. I, ah, just, you're so warm, you smell so good, and I… Um." I heave out a big sigh. "I maybe shouldn't be around people," I mutter this last part to myself.

"Summer." Nick speaks clearly and directly, and I crane my head a little to the side to look at him. His eyes are narrowed, staring at the water before us. His hands still cover mine as we cruise along.

"Yes?" I ask him. I can see the little lines trailing from the corners of his eyes. He has moisture on his long eyelashes from the ocean air.

"I thought I told you to relax."

Now my eyes narrow. "Told me, did you?" I snort and turn my head away. But I am only teasing him.

Honestly, this man can tell me anything he wants.

Nick chuckles. "Fair enough. It was…just a suggestion. I want you to relax." He takes a deep breath. "I didn't ask you out here for any reason other than I thought it would be a nice afternoon. I want to…spend time with you." He begins to steer us farther away from the shoreline, out into the open ocean. "I certainly don't want to make you uncomfortable."

I feel his body creep closer to mine, and he tightens his hands over mine as we steer together.

"I appreciate that." I nod, doing my shoulder check again. "You didn't. Make me uncomfortable, I mean."

We don't say anything for a few minutes as we cruise the boat over the water. It's louder, with the boat moving faster, bounding cleanly through the ocean. We stand like that, Nick behind me, me concentrating on not rubbing my body all over his, keeping my shoulders down. There's gray above and below—the sky streaked with darker clouds in the distance, the fog visible over the mountain peaks inland, the water murky but calm. It's not stormy weather, as far as I can tell. Just a gloomy, lovely California day.

Nick slows the boat down and relaxes his hold on my hands. "It's not always easy for me. To relax."

I'm surprised at his confession and more than a little touched at his vulnerability. After being with Erik for so long—someone who fancied himself a real "man's man" and wouldn't ask for help if he were bleeding to death in a hospital—it's nice to hear Nick confess that he's not perfect.

When will I stop comparing everything to Erik?

It's understandable, I suppose, given that he was a huge part of my life for so long. But I am eager for the day when I no longer am reminded of him.

My brain has to catch up with my reality, I remind myself.

I ease my body back into Nick. I sense that, although he wants to get something off his chest, it's not the easiest for him. So, I listen.

"I, ah, have some anxiety." Nick clears his throat. "I always have, I think. When I was younger, it was easier to let my sisters do all the talking. It was more comfortable that way."

"That's not really a surprise," I can't help but interject with a slight smile. "I am sure they were both more than happy to do all the talking."

I feel, rather than hear, a low rumble from Nick's chest behind me as he hums his agreement. "That's true. Neither of them has ever really been at a loss for words." His grip on my hands is less firm, but he doesn't remove his hands from mine.

"Anyway. You see all sorts of guys in the NFL—some yoga types, some who are convinced that everything must be organic and all-natural, some guys who think if it's not mooing at you, it's not real food. And don't even get me started on the superstitions." Nick takes his right hand off mine to fiddle with some of the controls as we drift slowly through the water before placing it back on top of mine. "There was this one guy who was super into mindfulness and centering yourself and living in the moment, all that stuff. He used to tell me all the time—unclench your jaw, push your shoulders down."

I find myself doing just that, lulled into calmness, listening to Nick's voice and feeling the vibrations from his chest still pressed against my back. It's soothing like a cat's purr.

"It's a little thing. But…it helped me, you know? It helps me check myself."

"I like it," I tell him softly. "It's a simple tool."

But I am rewarded again with the low rumble. "Sunshine." Nick's breath puffs softly against the shell of my ear, making goose bumps rise along my neck. I shiver involuntarily, and I feel Nick's arms caging in tighter around me.

"Cold?" he murmurs.

"Not even a little bit," I whisper, daring myself to turn my head to the right, seeing the sharp angle of his jaw. He darts his gaze down toward mine. I look at him, at his eyes, his lips, full and slightly chapped from what I assume are his frequent boat excursions. It smells like salt and fog and whatever soap Nick must use, a crisp, clean smell that I want to roll around in.

I feel so good here, standing with this big, strong, delicious-smelling man caged behind me, and while I don't want to do anything to ruin the moment, I also don't want to let this opportunity pass by. Because I realize as I see a tic in Nick's jaw that I need to kiss him.

I lick my lips involuntarily, and Nick's eyes drop down to my mouth. I press my body back toward his the way I did earlier, only with more intention this time.

I want him to feel my body press into his. I want him to know that, yes, I am hot for him. I just *want*, and it's been too fucking long since I actually did something I wanted, something just for me, without a care for my career, or "optics," as Erik used to say.

I forcefully shove my ex-husband out of my mind as I angle my mouth toward Nick's and turn my body farther into his. *My past does not define my present*, I remind myself as I move. Preparing to take what I want.

The moment I angle my head toward Nick, his grip on my hands becomes fierce, and I feel his chest expand against my back and hear his sharp intake of breath. I lick my lips and pull back slightly. His eyelids are lowered, and he's looking at my mouth intently.

For all this dude's talk about relaxing, he's wound tight as a guitar string.

"Nick," I whisper, pressing my body back into his and leaning my head against his shoulder. "Relax."

He looks into my eyes, and whatever he sees there causes him to deflate somewhat. He exhales slowly, and I feel his warm breath against the top of my head. "That's better," I tell him, feeling his hands relax over mine on the steering wheel.

"Thank you," he murmurs in my ear, keeping his body pressed firmly against mine. I boldly press back again, feeling him everywhere along my backside. He groans a little before taking my earlobe gently between his teeth and suckling softly. I feel it everywhere—my breasts suddenly feel heavy, my nipples tingling, my core clenching.

It's the most erotic experience of my life, and he hasn't even kissed me.

"I feel you, Sunshine," he whispers as he places featherlight kisses along the shell of my ear. I sigh and lean my head away, tacitly giving him permission to kiss my neck.

"I can feel how needy you are," he whispers again before placing his mouth alongside my neck and sucking.

I whimper, ready to turn around and jump into his arms.

"Got your tea, Miss Summer!"

At Brock's booming voice, Nick's head jerks up, and he takes a step back away from me. I shiver, and he squeezes my hands, still under his.

Goddamn.

Brock is a mood-killer, for sure, but it's probably a good thing he came out when he did. Still, I need a moment to compose myself. I take a deep breath, catching Nick out of the corner of my eye. His hazel eyes are darker than normal, his expression surprisingly calm.

"You good?" he murmurs.

"Yes," I squeak out. He smiles again, blessing me with that bright white against his tanned skin, and I try not to drool.

Before I know what's happening, he gives me a quick peck on my cheek, squeezes my hands again, and lets go. "Go get your tea, Sunshine. Remember to relax," he adds with a wink.

My eyes widen at his apparent ease with what just happened. I want to scream to Brock, to the seals, to anyone who will listen—"*Nick Echeverria just almost kissed me!*"

But I don't do that.

I turn to Brock, and he has a dopey smile on his face. "My lady." He inclines his head, handing me a tumbler with a tea tag hanging out, a plate with sandwiches in his other hand.

"Thank you," I murmur before moving toward my original seat, preparing to ogle Nick some more. My cheeks feel hot, and I am sure that my blush is visible, but I don't care.

Because like I said—Nick Echeverria almost kissed me.

Chapter Thirteen

Nick

"**B**EER ME."

We're back at my place after the boat ride. I managed to get myself—and my dick—under control after nearly mauling Summer with my mouth, and we had a pleasant, albeit distracting, time with my grandfather and Brock. Brock didn't mention anything about what he saw, although he had a really annoying knowing look on his face as he chatted with Summer and me during the afternoon.

He even managed to invite himself—and me, as his "plus-one"—to Summer's night out with Lucy and Tatum at one of the bars later. Brock insisted that we come home and "power nap" before our big night out. I've explained to him that a "big night out" in Estero Bay is probably not what he is used to, but dude apparently needs his beauty rest.

I grab a Hazy IPA from the fridge and move to hand it to Brock over the kitchen counter. He frowns. "Dude. I need something lighter. My Midwestern ass can't handle all these hops."

"What, you need a Pabst?" I ask him.

"No, but I sure as shit wouldn't turn down a Coors Light."

"There might be some in the other fridge. Tatum drinks those things like they're water." Brock ambles off to the fridge in the garage and returns with a Coors Light and a smile, this time taking a seat on a couch in the living room.

He cracks open the beer and takes a long swig. I grab myself a water and go to open the windows on the balcony. It's still foggy, with only the bottom of the Rock visible across the bay. I turn to take a seat and find Brock studying me silently.

It's a little disconcerting. Brock Donovan is usually a mile a minute. I don't like this silent Brock, watching me.

"See something you like, Donovan?"

"You wish." But he keeps staring.

"What."

"What, what?"

"What are you looking at me like that for?"

"Like what?"

"Like you have something you want to say."

Brock raises his eyebrows and looks away, taking a pull from his beer bottle. "So, Summer."

"What about her?" I go for a nonchalant tone.

"She's cute." He takes another swig of his beer and studies me.

"And?"

Brock shrugs. "I'm just making a comment. An observation, if you will. I'm an observer. Like a scientist studying hot girls. And after my study, I can conclude that she's super cute."

I nod but don't respond. Puppies are cute. Little kids in Halloween costumes are cute. My littlest niece telling me I am prettier than Elsa is cute.

Summer's good-looking, to be sure, but in my opinion, that's the least attractive thing about her.

"Surely you think she's cute too, as evidenced by the sweet, sweet cuddles you two were having earlier."

I shrug back at him. "I...don't think she's *not* cute."

Brock booms a laugh. "High praise, Romeo. You catch all the ladies with that charm?"

I flip him off.

Brock is silent for a beat. "She's single, right?"

I snap my gaze to him and feel my shoulders tensing up. "I mean, I don't make it a habit of kissing women who are otherwise in a relationship with someone who is not me."

"Nicky, you don't make it a habit of kissing anyone, period."

I say nothing because...this is true. If I am completely honest—which

I am not, at least not with Brock, not at this moment—I haven't so much as touched a woman since my divorce.

To say I'm a little hard up would be an understatement.

"I'm just saying," Brock replies breezily. "She's cute. She's single. I'm not from here, but I am from a small town, and a woman like that is a diamond in the rough, brother." He gives me a side-eye. "Someone is bound to come along and snatch her up."

I flex and release my hands into fists. "Let me guess. You are that someone?"

Brock closes his eyes and visibly deflates at my question. "No, fucker! Jesus, you are dense."

"But…you think she's cute."

"She is cute."

"You think she's—she's a diamond in the fucking rough."

"She is."

I stare at Brock for a beat longer, refusing to admit out loud what I have conceded inside.

She isn't yours, I remind myself. Summer is entitled to anyone she wants.

But…she could be, right? She almost kissed me. Hell, she initiated it, rubbing her little body back against mine. I can feel my stomach tightening just thinking about it.

"Nicky," Brock says in a quieter tone. "Look, I may be out of line telling you this." He takes a pull of his beer. "And I know we weren't that close—or at all—when you were, ah, with Gretchen."

I nod. While Brock and I had been the type of "Hey, hello, how you doing, going to kick your ass today" acquaintances that are not uncommon in the League, we really weren't buddies until after I was out.

"But I was there for the end of…that. And even during all that, I never saw you as worked up for your ex-wife—the woman whom you had pledged to love and cherish for all eternity—as you are for Summer."

He's not wrong. At the time that Gretchen and I ended things—or should I say, when she unceremoniously dumped me, while I was in a rehabilitation facility, learning how to walk again—I was already pretty numb to any sort of emotion. My career was over; hell, why not my marriage too?

"Summer and I… It's just, we've known each other a long time. Shit, we were kids together. Before the League, before Gretchen, before any of that."

"I am going to go out on a limb and say there's a lot of history there."

"Using your scientific observational skills again, are you?"

Brock shrugs. "There's always one who got away, isn't there?"

It's a rhetorical question, but I respond before thinking better of it. "She was never mine to begin with."

"But you wanted her to be."

I shrug back at him. I take a sip of my water and look out the window at the bay. It's nearly dark now, a few scattered lights on the water, the street-lights bright on the Embarcadero as people head out to dinner, to the bars, to watch whatever ball game is on.

"It doesn't matter now."

"Dude. You are thirty-two years old, not one hundred and two. And Nicky, I am comfortable enough with my masculinity to say that you are a fucking handsome dude. Finish what you started, bro." Brock gets up to deposit his beer bottle in the recycling. "This doesn't have to be rocket science. She'd have you in a heartbeat, for sure."

That gets my attention, and I snap my head up.

He smirks knowingly. "If I hadn't come in when I did, you two would've been banging on the boat, no doubt."

I try not to laugh, but I can't help it. "My grandfather was there. There would be no…boat banging."

"And I am sure, as a boat owner, your sweet grandpa would be the first to tell you—boat banging is a blast." Brock nods with certainty. "Bang the broad on the boat, Nicky."

"She's not a broad, for chrissake."

"I know, I know. I respect and admire all women. I just liked the alliter-ation." Brock sits back, content to let the issue go for now. "And even if your grandpa wasn't there, you wouldn't have made a move."

"It's just—I mean," I sputter, "Of course I think Summer's cute. She's gorgeous. And she's great and kind and smart and always has been all of those things. Obviously."

I mean, I could go on about her smell and her hair and her small waist that I want to wrap both my hands around. I could tell him about how she looked bent over during our yoga session and how I wanted to suck on the little spot where her shoulder meets her neck and how, when she pressed her nimble body into mine today on the boat, it was all I could do not to swing her over my shoulder, stomp down to the bed below deck, and yes, bang her seven ways to Sunday.

I don't tell him any of those things, though.

"She's also freshly divorced," I point out.

"So what? You're divorced too," Brock retorts, waving his hand as if our prior marriages don't matter. "Is there some sort of time limit on when a divorced person can start banging again? Hell," Brock continues, "some people don't even wait until their divorce is final. Some people don't wait at all."

I consider that. While there were no third parties contributing to the demise of my marriage with Gretchen, I really don't know what the hell happened with Summer and her dickbag of an ex, Erik. I am sure Tatum knows, but I've never asked and she's never told me.

"Her ex was a real asshole," I tell Brock, considering.

"All the more reason she deserves a good time aboard the Good Ship Echeverria."

"You're so crass," I mutter, standing up to go shower before we head out.

"I am just trying to help you out, bro!" I hear Brock call as I head upstairs.

"I don't need your help," I call back. "Take your power nap now, old man, before we go to dinner."

Chapter Fourteen

Nick

"**S**O I JUST…TAKE MY BEANS."

"Take the beans."

"And I put them into the soup?"

"Get a big spoonful and put it right into the soup."

"And then add salsa to that?"

"Yeah, but go easy—the salsa is no fucking joke. Especially for your corn-fed Midwestern ass."

"Fuck off," Brock tells me good-naturedly.

But I note that he takes just a small spoonful of the salsa.

That's wise. Lincoln does not fuck around when it comes to peppers.

"And then I take my bread…dude, that bread smells so good."

"I know. It's Pyrenees—the best bread."

"Bless you. Anyway, I take the bread and dip it in the soup?"

"Yeah. And get some salsa on it and some beans and the broth from the soup."

Brock eyes the soup in front of him suspiciously but does what I ask. He chews slowly, and his eyes light up. "Dude!"

I grin back at him. "I told you."

"I mean, cabbage soup doesn't exactly get my mouth watering, you know?" Brock takes another big spoonful. "I am going to need a few hundred loaves of that bread, though," he says around another bite.

We don't say much else for the next half an hour or so as we eat our fill of Lincoln's nightly special—a true Basque setup, it's called, as eaten by the sheepherders who settled in this part of California over one hundred years ago. We eat the aforementioned beans, salsa, soup, and bread, along with

French fries, pickled tongue—don't knock it until you try it—spaghetti with marinara, prime rib, and this amazing garlic fried chicken that Lincoln has perfected. And salad with fresh blue cheese dressing so, you know, we get our greens. By the time we are done, I think we've put away enough food to hibernate for the winter.

"Get. The. Fuck. Out of here with that," Brock nearly growls, and I look to see Julia coming over with a hunk of blue cheese and more bread.

"It's tradition. You don't have to eat it, Tank." Julia chucks Brock on the back of the head.

Julia and Linc got to know Brock after my injury. Although I wasn't there, I was told that Julia greeted Brock with "So you're the uncoordinated fucker who ran into Nicky?" It was all sunshine and roses after that.

"I am. So. Full." Brock takes a swig of ice water.

"If you're unable to communicate in complete sentences, I call that a win."

"Gimme a minute, bro," Brock mutters, taking his napkin to dab his forehead. "That garlic is no fucking joke. I think it's coming out of my pores."

"FYI, we're going to move some of the taller tables out of the way in a bit to make room for a dance floor." Brock and I are currently seated in a booth toward the back of the restaurant. "You guys should still have privacy here, though."

"Such VIP service for us, Mrs. Cruz," Brock says teasingly. "Don't tell me this ex-quarterback over here gets mobbed by the ladies when the party takes over?"

"Well," Julia scoffs, "It's hard to get mobbed by anybody when you are a hermit like this guy. Honestly, I commend you for making him stay out this late."

"It's because we had our power nap," Brock replies confidently. "We're definitely in for the whole night."

I roll my eyes. "Don't get too excited," I tell him. "All night here is probably pregaming for you."

"Nah," Brock replies, wiping his mouth with a napkin. "I've mellowed out in my old age, Nicky. You'll see."

I nibble on the blue cheese but pass on the bread and drain my water. Brock nurses his beer when he suddenly sits up straight.

"Dude. Who. Is. That?" Brock is back to speaking in one-word sentences and gazing out to the front of the restaurant.

I steer my gaze toward the door and immediately see Summer, her dark red hair in a thick braid over one shoulder, clad in a blue dress with tiny straps. She looks gorgeous, and I drink her in from head to toe.

"She changed her clothes," I say dumbly.

"Yes, yes, we all see Summer." Brock can tell where I am staring. "Her friend with the dark hair, who is not Tatum because I definitely don't have a death wish."

I hadn't even realized Tatum and Lucy were there too, but of course they are. Lucy is wearing black from head to toe, no surprise there. She informed us black was her signature color when she was ten years old, and that if she was ever forced to wear another color, she would break out in hives.

"That's Lucy. She's another of Tatum's friends, also grew up here in the Bay."

"Jesus, they grow them right in this foggy town," Brock mutters, staring at Lucy unabashedly. "She's pretty magnificent."

"Yeah, she's something else, all right. Be careful."

"Dude. I am not going to do anything to her."

"I mean, you be careful, Donovan. She'll fuck you up."

Brock scoffs. "Please. She's harmless. What could she do to me?"

∼∼∼∼∼

Three hours later, Brock is several Coors Lights deep, not to mention the shots of god-knows-what he's shared with Tatum, Lucy, Summer, and anyone else who strolled by and recognized the Great Brock Donovan, just partying at the local bar in our small town.

I haven't been able to have much one-on-one time with Summer, given that we're at the most crowded bar on a Saturday night. The inclusion of Brock is not helping matters—he strikes up a conversation with every fan and takes selfies with anyone who asks. He loves the limelight.

Me, not so much.

"Lucy hates me," Brock complains.

"So, we're at the whining portion of the evening," I reply, taking a sip of my now-warm beer. Gross.

"I gave her the handsome eyes, turned on my charm, and she ignored me. Ignored me! Women love me. Men too," Brock confides.

"Good to know."

"I even was ready to bust out the Brock Donovan Dance Moves, but she's totally ignoring me and—Oh."

"Oh?"

"Oh."

I look to where Brock's gaze is aimed and see Lucy and another girl, a brunette I don't recognize, kissing. It's not a full make-out session, but they are into each other, tangled up at the corner of the dance floor on the opposite side of the restaurant. It's kind of that point in the night, though—for those people who are single and looking to mingle, they've had just enough booze to be lubricated and loose and take their chance on another willing body.

I turn away to see Brock's reaction. I am expecting a crude comment from him about scoring with both Lucy and her friend—not that I think Lucy would ever give Brock the time of day—but he looks more disappointed than lascivious.

"Well, damn. I guess she's…not into guys."

I shrug, taking a pull from my bottle. "I mean, I think she's just into whomever she's into. *Maybe*," I continue in an exaggerated tone, "maybe she's just…not that into you." I open my mouth in a faux shocked expression.

Brock glares at me.

"Anyway, my sister told me Lucy's not looking for anything serious. She just got out of a relationship."

"What is it with you people here and your tragic relationships?" Brock muses, then continues before I can answer. "So what you're saying is, she's here for a good time, not a long time."

I shrug.

"Well, I am Mr. Good Time, Nicky!" Brock gestures with his bottle. "I, too, am not looking for a long time."

I raise my eyebrows and tip my beer toward him again. "Well, then go get 'em, tiger."

"Nicky. Nicky. Nick-O-Las." My little sister Tatum stumbles over to me, and I catch her before she knocks over my beer, the table, or anything else in her vicinity.

"Tater Tot." She snorts. She hates it when I call her that. "You okay?"

It's unlike Tatum—Miss President of Everything, who has had her life planned out since she was probably six years old—to be shit-faced.

She snorts again. "I'm great. Fabulous. Just…really, really drunk. Remind me never to drink with Lucy again."

"Bitch, you have free will," Lucy slurs to her, coming over to our table, her make-out partner nowhere in sight.

"Do I? Do I? Do any of us?" Tatum practically shouts to Lucy, although she is looking and gesturing toward the ceiling.

"Okaaaay," I say. "So…are you ladies ready to call it a night?"

"Yeah, big brother. I'm beat to the drum." Tatum rests her body against mine, practically ready to fall over. I get up off my chair and deposit her in it. "You're not going with your friend?" Tatum asks Lucy meaningfully.

"Nah. I told you, I am celibate."

Brock, who has been watching this interaction silently, chokes on his drink at Lucy's statement. She glares at him. Well, since glaring is her de facto expression, I should say that she gives him a stronger glare than normal.

"Whatevs. Water." Tatum waves her hands in the air. "I need water."

"I'll get you some water." I move toward the bar. "But where's Summer?"

Tatum shrugs, nearly toppling herself off the chair in the process. "Dunno. Luce, where's Summer?"

"I don't know either. She was talking to that guy you knew from earlier last I saw her."

"What guy?" I ask quickly before I can think of it, although Tatum is likely way too drunk to pick up on my interest.

"This dude…what's his name? He works at the DA's office. Nice guy.

Boring but nice. That's what I keep telling Summer: she needs a nice, boring guy."

Lucy looks annoyed. "I don't see why she needs a guy at all right now. Let her be single. Especially after her horsefucker of an ex."

"I know, I knowwww. And anyway, she already told me she's not dating anyone."

I perk up with interest.

"*Ever.*"

I deflate.

Tatum snaps her fingers, or at least tries to. "Thad! Thad Toadstool."

"I am sorry, did you say 'Toadstool'?" Brock asks, cracking up. "And… Thad?"

Tatum shrugs again. "He looks like one of the toad characters from *Super Mario World.* But Thad is his real first name."

"And I'm sorry, isn't your name 'Brock'?" Lucy asks Brock in a disparaging tone.

"Ah, so you know my name, huh?" Brock smiles at her, waggling his eyebrows.

"I mean. Whatever. Brock. Brock." Lucy drawls out his name to several syllables. "What kind of name even *is* that?" Lucy rolls her eyes.

"I think it's Scottish or Irish?" Tatum ponders. "Like, you know. Gaelic!" She lifts her beer bottle—which is my beer bottle, if I'm not mistaken—into the air triumphantly.

"Big Gaelic expert, are you?" Lucy asks with an arched brow.

"Don't you watch *Outlander*? It's like a Broch. A *Broch.* With a CH. Like a *brook. A babbling brook!*" Tatum's voice gets louder the longer she speaks.

"Oh yeah, I do like *Outlander*," Lucy concedes.

"Jamie's hot," Tatum hiccups.

"So's Claire," Lucy cackles back. She clinks her bottle—Brock's beer bottle?—together with Tatum's in victory.

"*Anyway.*" I interrupt everyone loudly. "Summer? Thad?" I can't with that name. "Can we focus on where she is?"

Lucy points toward the dance floor. "There they are. Dancing. Or at least, trying to."

I look to see Summer moving her body with grace and style. Even in this meat market, she still moves with the poise of someone who used to dance professionally for a living, even while Prince is crooning about sexy motherfuckers and ass-shaking. Next to her is a dude in khaki pants—at the beach? At a bar, my dude?—who moves with absolutely no grace or style.

I am not going to lie and say I am the best dancer, but it's important to know your strengths, you know?

And yet, I am here on the sidelines, while Thad "Khaki" Toadstool gets to dance with Summer Mahoney.

"Now *that* guy could definitely benefit from the Brock Donovan Dance Moves," Brock muses next to me. Lucy and Tatum both snicker this time.

"I'll go see if she wants to stay with…Mr. Toadstool." Lucy moves with purpose across the restaurant, people scattering out of her way as she marches on the dance floor. I feel my shoulders tensing. Not that it's my business, but…Summer wouldn't go home with a guy like that, would she?

She could have any guy she wants.

For some reason, that doesn't make me feel any better.

Summer

I am in high school all over again, dancing with a guy I don't really care about solely to get the attention of the guy I really want.

While I am tipsy, I stopped drinking the lighter fluid that Brock and Lucy were distributing after one shot—I know my limits, and I've never been great at holding my liquor anyway.

And now I am dancing with Tatum's colleague. Thad, I think his name is, with the khaki pants—khakis? Really? At a nightclub? Or what passes for a nightclub in Estero Bay? Thad is very nice, handsome, and a horrible dancer. But none of that really matters. His most important, or most lacking, quality is that he is Not Nick.

Not Nick doesn't have a light navy flannel shirt with the sleeves rolled up, all the better to show off his ridiculous forearms.

Not Nick doesn't have those arms currently crossed over his chest, causing his biceps to flex underneath his shirt.

Not Nick isn't currently staring right at me and…is angry?

I didn't discuss the almost-kiss with either Tatum or Lucy—Tatum, on account of the fact that she is Nick's sister and I am not sure where things stand with Nick and me, assuming there are "things" at all. And Lucy because, frankly, she scares me a little bit and I am not as close with her as I am with Tatum.

With Nick's gaze on me, I take a breath and use a bit of that liquid courage to move my body to the music, dancing while making sure to avoid any and all physical contact with Not Nick. I mean Thad.

I feel Nick's eyes bore into me as I move my hips from side to side. I run my hands from my hip bones up toward my breasts, and Nick takes a pull from the bottle he is holding, never taking his eyes off me. I move my hands slowly behind my head and give him a wink.

Nick's eyes widen, and he coughs, setting his bottle down and covering his mouth. I laugh and smile at him, and he gives me a slight shake of his head, his mouth saying something, which, of course, I can't hear over the music.

"Summer. *Summer.*" Lucy barrels toward me. "We're off like a prom dress. You gonna stay here with Toadstool, or you gonna hop on St. Nicky?"

There's a lot to unpack in that statement, but all I can think is…

"Toadstool?" I ask her, confused.

Lucy shakes her head. "Never mind." She links our arms together and leads us off the dance floor to the restrooms. Not wanting to be rude, I turn and wave to Thad. He keeps giving me the same goofy grin that's been on his face all night, apparently not offended at our abrupt departure.

"Where are we going?" I yell as we stumble inside the bathroom.

"I'm doing you a solid, sister." Lucy deposits me in front of the sink and scrounges around in her purse, black and studded all over with silver tips. They look like bullets, I realize. "Here." She hands me some gum. "And here." She hands me…a condom?

"What the hell?" I say out loud.

"You should go pee first. Do you have to pee?"

"What the… No, I'm good, but…what are you doing?"

"Summer." Lucy sets her bag over her shoulder and narrows her eyes at me. "I've been watching you and Nicky eye-fuck all night. Lord knows that guy's as tight as a drum, and I bet he hasn't bought a condom since high school." Lucy leans toward me and tugs on my braid. "I see that you're hurt, and he is too. And you're both tortured and kind of sad, and while that's all very well and expected, I am just here to speed things along. Think of me like…" Lucy snaps her own gum at me. "Your fairy godmother. The fairy godmother of orgasms."

"I don't know…"

"Don't know what? Don't know if you should ride Nick like a rodeo bull? Don't know what's going to happen tomorrow? Don't know if you shaved in all the right places?"

As to Lucy's last point, I did, but I let her continue.

"None of us *knows*, you know," Lucy drawls with all the wisdom of one who has had several shots of what tasted like hot liquid garbage earlier in the evening. "I am tired of seeing Itchy sad, and you are a beautiful, fiery moon goddess, and, *and*—" Lucy gets louder when I snort laugh "—you deserve this, Summer." She grabs one of my hands with both of hers. "You. Deserve. This."

"Yeah, you do!" Someone yells from one of the bathroom stalls.

Is there a more positive place than a women's restroom full of drunk girls? Probably not.

I find myself nodding along with her. "I…I know."

"You do?" Lucy raises her eyebrows at me.

I nod. "I do. That's why I tried to kiss him earlier. On the boat." I grin at her, my smile getting bigger as Lucy's eyes do the same.

"Summer Mahoney, good for you! Yes! Wait, you guys took out *Sheila*?"

Lucy is hard to follow. "*Sheila?*"

"Yes, *Sheila!* The boat!"

"I thought her name was something Basque?" I ask.

"Nah, I changed it," Lucy says breezily. "I named her for Sheila E., the greatest drummer of all time!" Lucy waves her hands around for emphasis—no, I realize, she's drumming. Or attempting to.

"All boats are females, huh?" I ask, not expecting a response.

"Damn right, they are. So I named her *Sheila*. She's a beauty."

"I didn't realize you were into boats."

"Oh yeah!" Lucy exclaims. "I'm actually a commodore."

Oh Lord. "Like…Lionel Richie?"

She scoffs. "I fucking wish. No, at the yacht club!" At my blank look, she sighs and pats my hand. "The Estero Bay Yacht Club. It's not the most… glamorous place, and most of the members are quite a bit older than you and me." She pauses. "Like, a lot older. Tail end of the Greatest Generation, old. Anyway, my grandma goes to their hall sometimes for mah-jongg, and they mentioned to her they needed someone to do their books because the lady who was doing them died, and my grandma volunteered me, which is great because I actually love Excel. Do you?"

I take a minute to realize Lucy has asked me a question. "Um…I actually don't think I've ever used Excel."

"Oh. Well, anyway, I do their books, and the old guys I met there mentioned they needed 'new blood' in the place, and they made me a commodore, which is really like a fancy, nautical term for board member."

"You…have a boat?"

Lucy rolls her eyes. "Are you kidding me? I own a bakery, and I live in California. I can't afford a boat. In this economy, who can?" She pauses. "Well, maybe you. And Nick. And his stupid big oak tree of a friend. Whatever. I don't know your life." She pauses again and rummages through her purse.

"*Anyway*, what I was going to say before you distracted me with your talk of beautiful *Sheila* was to take this"—she gestures to the condom, which I am still holding dumbly—"and go hop on that dick."

I burst out laughing. "No way."

But do I take the condom and put it in my purse?

Yes. Yes, I do.

"Yeah! Hop on the dick!" another voice rings out from a stall.

Lucy's determination is infectious. Drunk ladies' determination is infectious. "I…haven't exactly done that. Or anything close to that…in a really, really long time," I confess to Lucy.

"Yeah, I am going to take a wild guess and assume douchelord was *not* exactly sexing you up, right?"

I smile tightly. "That's kind of an understatement."

Lucy gives me what I think is supposed to be a sympathetic look. But it just looks a little less scary than her normal look.

"That sucks," she says frankly before remembering what I said moments earlier. "Wait a minute—you tried to kiss him? What happened? I mean, you remember how kissing works, right?"

"Of course I know how kissing works," I huff. Never mind that I haven't kissed anyone in what seems like years, but that's neither here nor there. "But it wasn't just us on the boat. His grandpa was there, and Brock kinda interrupted me—unintentionally, of course, but…" My voice trails off.

"But you took initiative," Lucy tells me. "That's a good thing. Nick could use a little *initiative* in his life, if you know what I mean. And if you don't know what I mean, I am talking about a horny lady who knows what she wants."

If that doesn't describe me to a tee, I don't know what does.

"It feels…kinda good, you know?" I ask Lucy, who frowns in confusion. "I mean, with Erik—" she pulls a face, which makes me laugh; they really do treat his name like Voldemort "—it was, like, frowned upon if I wanted to *initiate* anything. That whole stereotypical bullshit about being sexy, but not too sexy, and looking sexy, but not slutty, you know? And sometimes I just—I just want to *take*, you know?"

"Yes, girl! Take it!" another voice yells from a stall.

"I do know," Lucy murmurs, eyeing me understandingly. "And that is why you need to *take* that—" she gestures toward the condom "—and exercise some *initiative*."

"I will! I will," I tell her quickly. "I will hop on...oh Lord," I mutter. "I will do my best to...exercise initiative."

"And don't you worry about the others. I will handle Ms. Echeverria and that giant, big, lumbering oaf of a man." She moves to exit the bathroom. "You just need to handle Nick's giant—"

"Yes, yes, I got it," I respond hurriedly, rushing out of the restroom. "I will handle...that thing you just said."

"Get that dick!" comes another yell from the stall as we leave the bathroom.

Chapter Fifteen

Summer

I WAKE UP WITH A DRY MOUTH, A MARCHING BAND IN MY HEAD, AND the sound of…seals, I think? Ringing in my ears.

"Ugh." I open my eyes a fraction to see that I am lying on a couch, still in last night's clothes, with a giant hoodie over them. I had the where-withal to remove my shoes apparently. I am also covered in a soft blanket, my purple-painted toes peeking at me from underneath.

It's daytime, but—unsurprisingly—foggy weather that I view through the sliding glass door. The seals have woken me up with their barking, reminding everyone to get up and carpe diem.

"Ughhhh." I open my eyes bigger. I take a deep breath and am rewarded with Nick's woodsy, comforting scent. It's his hoodie I am wearing. The thought brings a dopey grin to my face.

I didn't handle his dick—or any other part of his body—last night, as it turns out. But I recall him handling me, for lack of a better phrase, as our crew made its way from the bar to our various destinations last night.

Brock is around somewhere, because he's staying here with Nick. Lucy and Tatum went to Lucy's house, I recall. And Nick helped me climb the approximately forty-two million stairs to his house in my heels last night before plying me with water and Advil.

And then apparently deposited me on the couch in his hoodie.

I take another breath and close my eyes, when suddenly I hear jostling behind me. The couch is a big, L-shaped piece of furniture, and I turn my head to my right to see…someone else's feet at the foot of the other L.

Someone's big feet. No purple toenails.

"Morning, Sunshine." Nick's voice is…directly behind me? I turn my head farther to the right to see his head less than a foot from mine.

I am in his hoodie, and we totally slept together, high school style. I would laugh out loud if my head didn't hurt so badly.

"Hi," I grunt out. I wince slightly as I maneuver my body to a sitting position, taking in the full specimen that is Nicholas Echeverria, from head to toe, laid out on the couch before me.

He's covered in a blanket too, resting low on his hips. I guess not everyone likes to sleep with the blanket covering literally every part of their body except for their head. Weird.

He gives me a soft smile, his eyes bright against his bronzed skin. He has dark stubble covering the lower half of his face, making him look like a pirate. A sexy pirate.

He brings one of his arms up behind his head, causing his tricep muscles to flex in a horseshoe, which is ridiculous and hot and totally unfair to all other triceps. I must be staring a moment too long, because his smile gets a little bigger and he clears his throat.

I dart my eyes to his, not even the tiniest bit sorry about checking him out. He's here, he's hot, and I'm a human, red-blooded, heteronormative woman.

I clear my own throat. God, I need water.

"I didn't do anything too embarrassing last night, did I?"

He shakes his head. "Not at all. You are a friendly drunk. Not like Tatum and Lucy." He pretends to shudder. "Those girls are mean."

"Hey." I mock him. "Those girls are my friends, and they are definitely not mean." I pause at Nick's raised eyebrow. "Well, Tatum's not mean."

Nick chuckles. "Honestly, everyone was well-behaved." He stretches his arm straight above his head, and I try my best not to drool at all those muscles on display. I'd kill to take a peek under the blanket right now.

"You feeling okay?"

I nod. "I'm fine. Nothing a little water and some grease won't fix." I yawn and immediately cover my mouth. "I could…use a toothbrush, though, if you have an extra."

"The guest bathroom down here probably has one. Tatum keeps a ton of stuff here for when she stays over." Nick sits up effortlessly and moves the blanket off him. He has dark green and blue plaid pajama pants on and a threadbare Berkeley T-shirt on top. I want to snuggle up to him on this couch all day. All month, even.

I get up too, not as effortlessly. "Thanks. For the toothbrush, and for..." I gesture to the couch where we both slept. Did I snore?

Nick smiles at me. "It's always my pleasure, Summer."

Gah. My heart trips over itself.

"Go brush your teeth, and I'll start breakfast."

I make quick work of myself in the bathroom—thank you, Tatum Echeverria, for keeping this bathroom stocked with quality face wash and moisturizer—and return to the kitchen to see Nick handling eggs on the stove. I smell bacon, and my stomach growls like a semitruck.

"Hungry, Sunshine?" Nick asks without turning to face me.

"Cooking for me, huh?" I take a seat at the bar, enjoying the view of Nick's rear end in those pajama pants. "A girl's going to get ideas."

He turns his head sharply, a glint in his eyes. "Oh yeah?"

I nod.

We obviously got interrupted on the boat yesterday. And I was way too Drunky McDrunkerson to make any sort of move on last night. But make no mistake—I want Nick. And I am not going to be shy about letting him know it.

"Maybe I want you to have ideas." He holds my gaze for a minute before moving from his eggs to the cupboard. A minute later, he's placed a glass of water in front of me. "Drink."

I shiver a little at the heat in his gaze and push up the sleeves of the big hoodie over my wrists. "Bossy." But I drink.

The corner of his mouth turns up a bit. "Not so bossy." His eyes drop down before rising again to meet mine, his look intense. "I like you in my hoodie."

"I like being in your hoodie." *In your house, in your pants, in your bed...*

Nick nods at this, as if I've confirmed something for him. But instead of continuing our flirting, he goes back to the eggs before pulling a tray of bacon from the oven.

Layne Staley immediately bounds into the room, tail wagging behind him, before sitting down and watching Nick with the tray. Nick blots one piece with a paper towel before tossing it into the air, Layne Staley catching it with ease.

"Oh my gosh, that smells amazing." I am definitely drooling now.

"Linc swears by baking it in the oven. Don't tell him, but I think he's right." Nick moves to the refrigerator to get other supplies—tortillas, cheese, what appears to be fresh salsa.

"Breakfast burritos!" I squeal. What can I say, I am a basic girl who likes to cure a hangover with a burrito as big as my head.

"Not just any breakfast burrito, Summer," Nick tells me. "A California burrito." He turns off the heat on the eggs and goes to his mise en place—tortillas, cheese, bacon, salsa, all his products lined up. It's pretty impressive. "No more for you, buddy," he adds to Layne Staley, who has been sitting patiently, waiting for more bacon. He snuffs, walks around in a circle a few times, and lays down near the dining room table.

"You had one?" Nick asks me.

"A California burrito?" I sip my water. "I mean, I've had a burrito obviously. In the state of California. But I can't say I am specifically acquainted with a burrito from California."

"Summer. Sunshine. Listen," he tells me seriously. My chest feels tight and my stomach light at his use of the endearment. "It's not that the burrito is from California. It is the type of burrito—the California burrito." Nick clears his throat and straightens importantly.

"Is this your TED Talk?"

Nick ignores me and continues his speech. "The California burrito is legendary. And lots of people do it differently. It *will* have carne asada—that's nonnegotiable. It *will* have cheese—also a must. It's got to have fresh pico. Some do rice, which is disgusting, and I don't talk to those people. And some do guacamole, which I suppose is fine. But the absolute best. Fucking. Part?"

Nick steps closer to me, leaning over the countertop where I watch him.

"Yes?" I squeak.

"French fries." His eyes bore into me. He apparently feels very, very serious about those French fries. "The California burrito must have French fries. If not, it's not a California burrito."

I can smell his breath as he leans closer to me—coffee and mint, warring for supremacy. I'll take both, please.

"French fries…French fries are good," I mumble.

"French fries are *great*," Nick corrects, sharpening his gaze.

"Great," I echo, apparently content to parrot whatever this guy tells me.

He nods again and abruptly turns back to the oven to pull out another tray, with French fries. Jesus, God, Mary, and all the Saints. I am never leaving this house.

This feeling is confirmed a moment later when Nick plates before me a giant tortilla—definitely as big as my head—with a mixture of bacon and carne, eggs, cheese, fresh salsa, and, of course, French fries. "I didn't know how spicy you want it, but there's hot sauce too."

"Hit me." He gives my meal a healthy dose of sauce and wraps it up tightly.

"*Oh my god, Nick,*" I moan around my bite a second later. "This is fucking unreal." I don't look up from my food for several bites, pausing to drink my water. I catch his eyes from across the counter.

He's not eating. He's not drinking the coffee cup he's gripped tightly in his hand. He's just…staring. At me, at my food, as if it's done something to offend him. A muscle ticks in his jaw.

I take another bite. "What?"

I have manners, I swear. It's the combination of being hungover and horny that has me eating like a slob.

"You…you're just really…enthusiastic with your food." Nick's voice is low, and he sips his coffee.

I shrug. I finish chewing and swallow. "Why not? Food's meant to be eaten, life's meant to be lived."

Nick's eyes crinkle a bit at the corners. "Truer words."

We go on like this, him sipping his coffee and me eating my burrito "enthusiastically," although I try to tone down the porny sounds. I can't help it; the thing is just so damn good.

I wipe my mouth. "You have got to talk to Lincoln and Jules about putting this on the breakfast menu."

"They actually don't do breakfast." Nick shrugs. "There are a million spots in town for it, and it's already hard enough running a restaurant with two little ones. Sometimes Sunday brunch, though."

"I can appreciate that." I take my last bites and another sip of water. "I will just count on you to be my own personal California breakfast burrito chef."

"As you wish," Nick responds with a flourish, before taking my plate and starting to clean up.

Did he…did he just *Princess Bride* me?

He definitely did.

I hop up and move to the kitchen. "Let me." I roll up the sleeves of my, *Nick's,* hoodie and move to the sink. "It's the least I can do."

"I don't mind."

"Then at least let me help you." I act before he can respond, soaping up the dishes in the sink.

We work in tandem for a time, silently, and it's not uncomfortable.

"Do you miss it?" I ask him suddenly.

"Miss what?"

"San Diego. I mean, other than the California burritos, which, I am not going to lie, I don't blame you even a little bit."

He gives me a lopsided smile before throwing my words back. "You know…not even a little bit." He pauses, loading the last dish in the dishwasher before closing it and leaning against the counter. "I enjoyed my time there," he continues, speaking carefully. "But it was time to go."

"Because you were no longer with the team?" I fill up the electric kettle with water. When I turn to plug it in, I see that my favorite tea is already sitting to the side. I give a side glance to Nick, and he meets my eyes quickly before shifting his gaze down.

"Not just that…" His voice trails off in response to my last question.

"You definitely don't have to talk about it if you don't want to," I tell him in a rush.

"No, it's fine." He squares his shoulders and meets my gaze. "I mean, I knew my career was over, for sure. I was strangely fine with that. I did what I wanted, I played hard. I gave it my all, everything." His voice gets firmer the more he talks.

"But my…Gretchen, my ex." He pauses. "She was not fine with that. Not even a little bit." He laughs, but there's no humor in it.

"But I mean…there's no way you could have played again, right? I read somewhere that you had to have fourteen surgeries or something like that."

"Something like that." He winces, shifting his stance. "Yeah, there were a lot of surgeries. As to whether I could play…it depends on who you asked." He hands me a mug from the cupboard when the water is hot enough. "My mom, Julia, Tatum—no. Hell no," he adds with a little smile.

I can envision those women fighting hard for Nick. It makes me glad he had such warriors on his side.

"My doctors, they were straight shooters. Could I play again? Sure. Would it increase the chance of an even worse injury? Sure." He pauses.

"Gretchen, though…not to mention my fucking agent." His gaze becomes unfocused as he continues. "They thought for sure, *for sure*, if I just worked hard enough, I could play again. I could be the same quarterback I was. 'Think of it, Nicky! What a comeback!'"

It's unusual to hear the venom in his voice—Nick, always so calm. I can't really remember a time I have ever seen him mad.

"That must have been hard," I say, for lack of anything better to say. What do you say? I know how it feels to have the one person who you thought was in your corner turn against you.

"The thing is—" Nick meets my eyes again, his eyes flashing. "I *did* work hard. I did everything I set out to do. I played hard. I was focused. We won the fucking Super Bowl…" He runs a hand through his hair. "I had everything I wanted, and so did she."

His shoulders deflate a little bit, and he shuffles one of his feet. "I guess she didn't, though, huh?" He looks back at me, the bleakness in his eyes breaking my heart just a little more. "Apparently I am not all that exciting if I am not in the League."

It's my turn to get angry. "That's bullshit, and you know it."

Nick scoffs. "I can't say that I blame her. I mean, come on, Summer. I am not exactly Mr. Excitement." The corners of my mouth turn up a little because, yeah, he's right. "I don't party, I don't like crowds," Nick continues. "Shit, my best friend is my grandfather." He smiles back at me sadly before continuing.

"Before we got together, it was wild. People always wanting a piece of you. No one really cares about you, who you are inside. Then I met Gretchen, and I thought how fucking lucky I was that I had found someone who saw me for me, you know?"

I nod, because…yeah. I do know.

"But once that life was over…turns out she didn't. She didn't see me for me."

The kettle is now steaming, and I move to Nick's side to pour the water and dump my teabag. He shifts to continue facing me.

"I am sure you have your family…your friends…your therapist?"—I ask it as a question, and Nick nods affirmatively—"to tell you this, but you know none of that is your fault."

"I know. I mean, yeah, I do know that. And honestly, hindsight being what it is, it makes sense." I blow on my tea and see Nick watching my lips move. "Gretchen liked the attention. She liked the fast-paced life. When it became clear I wasn't going to be that guy in retirement, she found someone who was."

"She did?" I blurt out, surprised. I can't imagine anyone who could replace Nick Echeverria. I mean, why are you buying ground beef when there's a prime rib right in front of you?

"Yeah. We were already over before she began with him, but not by much," he adds wryly.

"Jesus. That must have made you furious." I blow on my tea.

Nick pauses at that, eyeing me carefully. "Not as furious as you might think," he murmurs, taking a last slug of his coffee before setting his mug down.

He doesn't explain any further, and I don't ask, instead choosing to blurt out, "You're totally worth it." It's out of my mouth before I can stop to think.

Nick raises his eyebrows at me.

"I mean, you said you weren't all that exciting, you know, if you're not a professional athlete, and blah, blah, blah." I rush on hurriedly, because why stop now? "But I don't think that's true."

Lord knows I was into Nick way before he was the star of College GameDay, let alone the NFL.

"When I told Gretchen I wanted to move back here, she about fell out of her chair," Nick adds with a shake of his head.

"It's not for everyone," I concede.

"You came back," Nick points out.

"I love it here. I couldn't think of a better place to…"

"Lick your wounds?" Nick asks with a lopsided smile.

"Yeah, I guess so. But it's more than that. I thought…I thought this place would heal me. The quiet, the salty air…something about it, it's like a big, warm blanket. It's comforting. I don't know, I can't explain it."

"No, I understand," Nick says softly. "I think that's why I wanted to come back. Maybe recapture some of…my life before, you know?"

We stand there silently for a minute, pondering the decisions and the past events that led us to where we are now. At least, that's what I am pondering as Nick's gaze lands on my lips.

I blow softly again on my tea.

"Thanks for my tea. And my burrito."

"You're welcome." Nick's voice is gravelly again as he watches me. He's leaning against the big kitchen sink, his hands behind him slightly, gripping the lip of the sink tightly.

I wonder what would happen if he let go, literally and figuratively. Let go of the past that seems to be weighing him down in the present, let go of the fucking sink and took what he wanted. I wonder if his hair is as soft as it looks. I wonder if the stubble on his face would irritate my skin. I wonder if he's biting his lip because he's nervous like me. I wonder what he tastes like, and I lick my lips in anticipation of something I don't even know is coming.

I wonder if he knows how desperate I am for a touch—not just any touch and not just because Erik rarely touched me, and certainly never touched me in the last year of our marriage. I am desperate for Nick's touch, for Nick's lips, and for Nick's heat as he moves closer to me.

I wonder, I wonder, and then as Nick leans over and seals his lips over mine, I realize…I don't have to wonder anymore.

Chapter Sixteen

Nick

EVER SINCE MY INJURY—SINCE MY LIFE CHANGED FOREVER—I HAVE been existing in two realms.

One realm is clarity, the kind of sad, bittersweet clarity, where you realize that an act of your life is over, having taught you whatever it was supposed to teach you. I've learned that not all endings need to be sad or tinged with regret.

The other realm is foggy, the fog of uncertainty. Not to sound too introspective, but just what the hell am I supposed to do with the rest of my life? How can I exist in these two spaces—the certainty of two huge endings, my career and my marriage, and the fog of uncertainty regarding my future?

Kissing Summer is feeling those two worlds collide, a beam of light through the fog. The clouds dissipate to reveal her warmth, her smell, her taste. And I feel that moment of clarity I've been missing for so long.

Every inch of me is electrified, on fire, as I feel her soft lips against mine. It feels like someone has shocked me back to life, given me my second wind. My entire body feels worked up, my skin is tight, adrenaline pulsing through my veins. It doesn't escape my notice that it's the same feeling I used to get before taking the field. I feel amped, like I could run fifty miles and not break a sweat.

I haven't felt this rush since before my injury.

And I don't remember ever feeling this way with another woman.

I focus away from that jarring realization and toward the woman in front of me. I slant my lips against hers and lick slightly, testing to see how she will react. She opens her mouth slightly with a gasp, and I move in, tasting her—spicy and minty.

I've closed the space between us, and I place my hands on either side of her, bracing the countertop. I crowd her, dwarfing her with my size, and I don't give a fuck. Our lips slide against each other, our tongues tangling. Summer takes her hands and places them on either side of my face as if trying to pull me closer, trying to deepen the kiss. I let her put her hands on me—of course I do. I am still holding myself back, knowing that the minute I get my hands on her soft, lithe body, it's all over.

I angle my mouth again, taking her bottom lip between my teeth and nipping a bit. Summer gasps again and shivers a little. "Nick," she whispers, drawing her hands from my face, down my neck and shoulders.

"Too much?" I murmur.

"Not enough," she breathes before diving back in, kissing me with abandon. I meet her, nip for nip, lick for lick, all the while gripping the countertop, keeping her caged with my body. She has no hesitation, wrapping her arms around my middle, pulling me close to her body. I run hot as a furnace, and so does she. She whimpers and sighs as we continue like this, rubbing up on me, greedy with her touches, unabashed in her exploration. Every part of me is hard, every inch of me primed to pounce on her.

"Nick," she pants my name again. "Please." She rolls her head back slightly as I kiss down her face, along her long, graceful neck. I can feel her pulse pounding under my lips.

"You taste so good," I mutter, kissing back up to her jawline.

"Please. God." Summer continues writhing against me, running her hands up and down my back, my shoulders, my arms. It feels fucking fantastic.

"Put your hands on me, Nick," Summer demands, a note of frustration entering her voice as she brings her head up to meet my gaze.

I grip the countertop tighter and pause. I take in Summer's bright eyes, determination in her gaze. Her cheeks are flushed, and she has some of last night's eye makeup—sparkly purple and silver—under her eyes.

She is the most beautiful thing I have ever seen.

Summer raises her eyebrows slightly in a challenge. I take a deep breath in response, before pushing myself back from the counter. She keeps her hands on my chest, and I take them in mine before bending down to kiss her again, softly, gently, in contrast to our frenzied kisses a moment ago.

My chest tightens, and I feel it again—that ray of light breaking through the fog.

I want to do this right.

I am jumping into this with my eyes wide open. No distractions, no rushing.

And so it is with a heavy heart, and a heavier dick, that I pull back from Summer.

"Nick…" Summer looks worried as she tries to pull her hands away from mine, but I grip her tight.

"No." I interrupt her, wanting to get this out before I throw caution to the wind and take her down the hall to my bedroom. "No," I repeat in a calmer voice.

I look her directly in the eye and decide that in this instance, honesty is the best policy.

"You have no idea how long I've wanted to do that," I tell her, stroking her hands with my fingers. Summer lights up like a Christmas tree, smiling slightly.

"Oh, I am sure I have you beat there, buddy," she responds softly.

I give her a quizzical look, but I move on. If I don't get this out now, I might never.

"I want this." I use our hands to gesture between the two of us. "Whatever this is, I want it. I want…you, Summer." I clear my throat. "But I want to do this right."

Summer's gaze doesn't waver from mine.

"I don't have the best track record when it comes to relationships," I tell her wryly, and she gives me a hint of a smile. "You…you're special to me. You always have been." I pull her hands, still linked with mine, to my chest. "I don't want to fuck this up."

So, I might not be the best with words, but at least I am honest.

"I can't imagine that you would do anything to 'fuck this up,'" Summer responds with a little smile. She takes a breath.

"But…I can appreciate where you're coming from. As someone who also does not have the best track record with relationships. Well, really just the one, I suppose. You know. Erik. Anyone else before that was fine, I suppose, but it doesn't help that the only serious relationship I have had was with someone who turned out to be a sociopath, huh?" Summer stops and takes a breath. "Sorry. I ramble sometimes." She looks down at the floor but steps in a little closer to me.

Fuck that Erik guy, so hard.

"Yeah, I've noticed." I remove her hands from mine and take her chin in my hand, tilting it up so I can look into her amber eyes. "Let's do this together, okay?" I ask her softly.

"Together," she responds. "I really want to kiss you again," she blurts out, not looking even the least bit embarrassed.

"Who am I to deny a pretty girl?" I tilt her chin some more and dip my head to hers. The ray of clarity runs through me again, as I seal our deal with a kiss.

Chapter Seventeen

I APPRECIATE NICK'S SENTIMENTS.

I understand them, even.

We are two adults, doing adult-type, consensual things.

God knows I harbored a crush on Nick before I even knew what that really meant. I can wait a little longer, can't I?

Sure I can.

But at the same time, damn if I don't want to throw caution to the wind, run straight back to Nick's fortress of solitude, take off all my clothes, and ask him to ravish me in the manner of a historical romance novel.

We are taught to have no regrets. Everything happens for a reason. God/your angels/insert chosen deity here never throws more at you than you can handle.

But again. Damn, if I don't have some regrets about my time with Erik.

After the death of my parents, I felt lost. Understandable for anyone who suffers a loss like that, I suppose. But I didn't really have any other family to lean on. Alexis had made it clear that she was not capable of giving me whatever it is that someone needs after going through what we did. At the very least, she wasn't moving back to Estero Bay, and I certainly wasn't going to join her in Chicago, at least not until I finished high school.

Where Alexis is cold, I am hot. Where she is reserved, I am outgoing. Where she shies from touch, I am tactile. I always have been. I like touch, I like feeling, like dancing, movement, of all kinds. In dance, we are taught to use the space that surrounds us—use *all* the space. By contrast, Alexis has always been economical in her movement, only using up the space that is absolutely necessary for minimal survival.

I had Tatum and her parents, of course. Her mom and grandfather had no hesitation to bringing me into the fold.

I still wanted my own family.

I wanted my parents back.

I wanted Alexis to be different.

I wanted hugs. Dammit, I just wanted someone to touch me.

And when I met Erik, and he didn't hesitate to touch me—not even in a sexual way, although that certainly followed—I was all in.

I was starved for affection and lonely. Because that bitch hindsight is 20/20, I can see now that Erik recognized my desperation, because that's what it was, and used it against me.

Erik was skillful in many things—manipulation, condescension, being passive-aggressive.

He was also the first—and to this day, only—man I have ever been with.

For someone who was starved for physical affection, I was eager to experience everything with him. I was dickmatized, and I didn't know any better.

It was only as our relationship progressed, only after we married, only after it seemed that no matter what I did, I couldn't please Erik—only then did he begin to use sex as a weapon. Withholding it, indicating I was unworthy of his touch, of anyone's touch. Criticizing my appearance and my weight. Controlling what I ate, what I wore, who I saw, where I could go. I was constantly apologizing, constantly feeling like he was right. I was unworthy.

My parents were dead, my older sister—really, my only living relative that I was close with—had all but cut me out of her life. Erik was all I had.

I always considered myself a strong person with a positive sense of self. Surely I would never allow myself to fall into a relationship with someone who was mean, who didn't have my best interests in mind. To use the word "abuser" was out of the question. That could never happen to me.

You never think it will happen to you until it does. And just like love, it happens gradually and then all at once.

My therapist says it's a "textbook case of emotional abuse." My relationship with Erik moved fast, and things I did under the guise of being madly in love were problematic, to say the least. Moving from a small apartment I shared with two other dancers not long after meeting Erik. Getting engaged shortly thereafter and married less than a year later.

My friendship with Tatum survived, although as the years passed, we communicated less and less. Lucy was too wild, too opinionated, too *Lucy*.

Not that she didn't try to tell me Erik was all wrong for me and that I was jumping the gun, although her words were more in the vein of "he sucks, and you can do better." Being so in love, I didn't listen. And while we never had a true falling-out, Erik forbade me from inviting her to the wedding, and that was that. To her credit, she hasn't blinked an eye since my divorce and return to the Bay, acting as if no time has passed at all.

But time has passed. I am over ten years removed from this place. Being back here, seeing my friends, seeing Nick, makes me feel old and young at the same time. Old, because it's been several years and so much has happened. Young, because I guess that's what memories do to you when you return to the place you grew up—they gently tap you on the shoulder and tell you to *Look. Look at how everything and nothing has changed.*

Like I said, I want rainbows.

I want to walk in the sun. I *deserve* to walk in the sun.

And so, yes, while I understand Nick's hesitation, I am greedy. I am hungry.

And I deserve to feast.

Chapter Eighteen

Nick

I MEANT WHAT I SAID TO SUMMER. I AM ALL IN, AND THEREFORE WE are doing this—whatever "this" is—the right way.

I am determined to do normal, date-like things. And we do.

Over the next few weeks, Summer and I make like tourists and take in all the best parts of the Central Coast. We hike Oats Peak at the state park, taking in spectacular 360-degree views from the Pacific to the interior valleys, lush with green, given all the rain we've had this year. We drive to the San Andreas Fault and see the "superbloom" of wild flowers—again, thank you, rain. We spend a day shopping in St. Bishop's, the college town south of Estero Bay where Tatum lives and works, and see the historic, albeit disgusting, alley wall of used chewing gum, stuck from top to bottom.

We eat our way up and down the coast, too. I've lost count of the bowls of clam chowder we've consumed, each one claiming to be "award-winning."

"I think each restaurant prints out an award for themselves and frames it in the restaurant," Summer muses over dinner one night.

She's not wrong, but for my money, Blue Sky Bistro is the best chowder, hands down.

We eat fish tacos, oysters, tri-tip, and these amazing fried squash blossoms stuffed with fresh mozzarella. We drive north to Big Sur and take a selfie on the famous Bixby Bridge, sun shining, whitecaps visible in the distance. I am not ashamed to tell you that I now have that selfie as my phone's wallpaper. Summer's bright smile, her arm wrapped around me, with her other hand high in the air—it's a perfect moment in time.

We have no agenda and no schedule, other than Summer's yoga

commitments. And of course, both of us keep our standing appointments with our respective therapists.

I like everything we've done. I like her. I like who I am when I am with her. We could be cleaning bathrooms together, and I still would enjoy it.

We also continue to be celibate, which I like a lot less.

We have had what amount to teenage make-out sessions. One particularly memorable session was in the cab of my truck, no less, which truly brought me back to high school. I felt the urge to check the clock to make sure I wasn't blowing curfew.

We have engaged in what my eighth-grade sex education teacher termed "heavy petting." I've felt Summer up, not only over her bra, but over her shirt. What I mean is, there are many layers of clothing, and my dick is extremely displeased about it.

Summer is also a little impatient, if her moans and whimpers when we do make out are any indication. There's also the issue of her repeatedly attempting to cup my crotch when we are kissing. I am hip to her ways now, but she's a sneaky thing.

I know that when she does get her hands on me, it's all over—in a good way. No way can I turn her down. So in the interim, I am turning her down in a different way.

My Catholic schoolteachers would be so proud.

～～～～～

Today, Summer and I are taking the boat out again. For once, there is no fog, no mist—it's the kind of stereotypical, beautiful, sunny day people probably envision when they think of California. It's warmer too, and Summer looks every inch the California girl in her cutoff shorts and tank, having removed her fleece zip-up once I got the boat out to a good spot to anchor and idle for a bit. Her thick red hair is braided down her back, and she's got her Wayfarers and a baseball cap with the Brew logo on it to protect her skin from the sun.

"It's not like I can get any more freckles," she tells me wryly as she applies more sun block to her, yes, freckled shoulders. "But I don't want to chance it, you know?"

I smile back at her and get out the Cubanos I packed us for lunch—ham, Swiss, pickles, shredded lettuce, and this amazing sweet and hot mustard Lincoln makes for the restaurant. I hand half of one to Summer and take the other for myself.

"Thanks," she murmurs, sitting at the high-top bar inside the kitchenette area. We eat in silence, taking in the dark blue water through the open sliding door. The gulls call around the boat, and the waves slosh back and forth gently against the hull. The sun shining through the floor-to-ceiling windows warms the entire interior, and the smells of salt—from our meal, and from the ocean—surround us.

I take a pull of my Corona and sigh.

It's perfection.

"This is the life, huh?" Summer asks between bites, echoing my feelings precisely.

"It is," I agree. I polish off my sandwich and lean back in my chair, pulling my arm across the back of hers. "I thought after we finish, we could head more south, see if the dolphins are jumping."

Summer hums. "That sounds nice," she says before taking a huge bite. She chews thoughtfully for a moment, swallows, wipes her mouth. "Or," she says with a gleam in her eye, "we could make out some more."

I cough, take another pull of my beer, and clear my throat. "That's, ah…" I run my hand from the back of the chair to her shoulders, rubbing across her neck, allowing myself to feel the warmth of her skin through her shirt. "Yeah." My voice is a little lower as Summer looks at me innocently, licking her fingers one by one.

I know for damn sure she doesn't have sandwich remnants on her hands.

She's a temptress.

I also know there is a reason I didn't invite my grandfather to join us on this particular trip.

I clear my throat again, and she smirks at me before leaning forward and standing to grab our plates. "Let me clean up." She leans forward more than necessary, sticking her hips back so that her ass—her beautiful, firm ass—is on full display, her tanned legs so long in her cutoff shorts.

Fucking temptress.

I watch her like a hawk as she cleans up. She's not making eye contact with me, but she's teasing—moving in that graceful way she does, jutting out her hip to display her beautiful body for me. I sip my beer and watch her, one hand clenching my beer bottle, the other on my thigh, trying not to fist both my hands in frustration.

I did this to myself, I know.

I haven't been with a woman in a long time. And who's the moron who decided to be celibate, for all intents and purposes, with Summer Mahoney?

It was me.

Fucking idiot.

Summer wipes down the counters before replacing the towel, washing her hands, and turning to face me, her hands against the sink. It's reminiscent of our position in my house the morning after the Brew, when I made her California burritos. She's watching me now, like a cat ready to pounce on a mouse, determination in her eyes.

"Thanks for lunch," she says with her mouth, not moving from her spot.

I want you, she says with her eyes.

"You're welcome," I respond with my lips.

I want you back, I say with my eyes, eyeing her slowly up and down, resting my eyes on every part of her, from her painted toenails to her flushed cheeks to the baseball cap covering up all that red hair.

I want to make her flush everywhere.

"And for taking me on your boat," Summer says, eye-fucking me right back.

I nod and swallow before placing my beer bottle on the bar and leaning back in my chair.

"It's my pleasure," I tell her, my voice lower than normal.

She starts toward me, but I hold up my hand to signal her to stop.

She pauses, determination warring with uncertainty on her face.

"Can you…" I pause and take a breath. "Just…slow. Come here. Slowly."

She complies, biting her lip. Her eyes sparkle, and her chest rises and falls with her breath.

She's fucking stunning.

I am officially throwing in the celibacy towel.

She comes around the corner of the bar and stands in front of me. I lean back in my chair, allowing her to step between my legs.

She lifts her arms to wrap them around my neck and tilts her head toward mine. I say nothing, just place my hands on her waist and meet her lips with mine. The kiss is soft, a sample, a preview of what's to come.

We move our mouths slowly against each other, in no hurry. At least, I'm not.

We've done this a lot over the past several weeks, and it never gets old. Each time I kiss her, I get that feeling, a rush, an adrenaline spike I thought I would never feel again. I exhale against her mouth and angle my head the other way, moving my tongue past her lips.

I draw my hands up her sides as we kiss. Summer arches toward me, thrusting her chest out as if she's hoping my hands will make a stop there. I smile against her mouth. Instead of going where she wants, I move my hands farther up her body, up her arms, before removing her own hands from around my neck and holding them both in front of me, pulling my mouth away from hers.

"You eager, Sunshine?"

She licks her lips, her gaze darting all over my face, her eyes glazed over with arousal. "You know I am," she says softly.

I lean forward for another brief kiss before leaning back. At this angle, on the higher chair and with her standing in front of me, we are nearly of equal height.

"I know you proposed another make-out session," I murmur before kissing her lightly on her jawline. "But I have some other ideas I think you might like."

"Oh yeah?" Summer tilts her head to the side as I kiss along her jaw, over to her ear, before taking the lobe in my mouth and sucking gently. She moans in response, again thrusting her chest out to me, arching her back.

"Yeah." I kiss my way back to her mouth, and this time, she's fairly ravenous with her tongue against mine, pressing her body toward mine. I keep our hands together between us, trying not to grip her delicate fingers too tightly.

I need to keep some sense of control, because I can tell that if Summer had her way, she'd have us both naked and in bed in the next five minutes.

Not that I don't want that too.

But I want to explore this—explore her—some more before I lose my mind to the heat between us.

Because I know once I do, it's all over.

Decision made, I pull away from her mouth. I keep her hands in one of mine, using my other hand to take the baseball cap off her head and set it on the counter. Her braid is loose, and tendrils of wavy red locks frame her face. I run my hand along her face, tucking her stray hairs behind her ear. Taking care of her.

Her eyes are on me, and it's hard to avoid her gaze. But I want to get this right before we end up fucking on the counter. I think of Brock's comment about boat banging and smile a little.

"What's that about?" Summer asks me wryly, her hands still encased in mine.

"I'm just thinking," I tell her, "about what to do first." I move my other hand from tucking her hair to cradling her jaw. She leans into it and sighs contentedly.

"I want you so much, Nick," she whispers, her lashes fluttering.

This.

This moment of honesty, the fact that Summer doesn't put on airs or play hard to get. She never really has, and she would be the first to tell you she wears her heart on her sleeve. But even after everything—her parents, her shitty ex, starting over—she's still here, still all out, still unrepentant about what she wants.

I love that about her.

It's also slightly terrifying. It makes me want to protect her. If the past several years haven't taught her to build a cage around her heart, it's safe to say that nothing will. Whether that's a blessing or a curse—whether that makes her crazy or a genius—I don't know.

I kiss her once, softly, intending to go slow, but true to form, she's all in, nipping and writhing and kissing me like she's starving and I'm a four-course meal. I manage to pull back and keep her little hands in mine.

"Wanna play with you a little, sweetheart," I grit out. Her thighs snap together like a rubber band, and she sucks in a breath.

"Ok…ay?" She opens her eyes slightly, her lids heavy with arousal.

"I'll take good care of you, Summer," I tell her more seriously now, my eyes meeting hers so she can see I am not fucking around when it comes to her pleasure.

"I believe you," she responds seriously.

"You trust me?" I lift one of her hands to my mouth, kissing the back of her hand softly.

"You know I do," she whispers, her eyes wider now as she watches my mouth on her hand.

"Good. That's good," I whisper back before unfolding her small hand. I kiss the pad of her thumb, before moving to her index finger and doing the same thing. Summer's breath leaves her in a whoosh; she never takes her eyes off my mouth. I watch her right back, not wanting to miss a minute of her reaction.

I kiss the pad of her middle finger, her ring finger, and her pinkie, so softly. I move back to her index finger and kiss my way down her finger from the tip to her palm. Then, I gently lave my tongue against the crease between her index and middle fingers. I watch Summer's face, her breathing heavy and choppy, her mouth open, her chest heaving. I continue to lave her skin, letting her see my tongue lapping against her slowly, gently.

Summer whimpers slightly as I nip at the skin, before removing her hand from my mouth and setting it back down between us.

"Step back, Sunshine," I whisper to her, leaning back and removing my hands so that no part of her is touching me. My skin feels tight, achy at the loss of contact.

Summer looks at me a little uncertainly. I crook up my mouth in a small smile.

"Trust me?"

She nods and steps back, her hands clasped at her navel.

"Take off your shirt," I instruct her.

She raises her eyebrows but does as I ask. Her tank top comes off over her head, revealing a simple black bra and miles of that freckled skin I can't get enough of. I want to spend hours tracing all those freckles, making a map out of her with my tongue.

"You're beautiful," I tell her gruffly, and she smiles at me.

"So are you," she responds without hesitation.

I chuckle and shake my head before leaning forward to run my hands firmly up her arms, across her shoulders and clavicle, before smoothing them down her strong dancer's body, resting them on her hips.

I grip those hips just as firmly, pulling her toward me for a quick kiss on the mouth.

Again, I pull back and remove my hands. At this point, my erection is visible through my shorts, but I really don't care.

"Lose the bra, Sunshine," I tell her softly, looking her directly in the eye.

Summer's cheeks redden, and I see her eyes dart to look out the window briefly before returning to me.

There are no boats around us for miles. We're not close to the actual bay, where boats often dock or anchor. Especially on a nice day like today, I am sure the bay is packed with kayakers, paddleboarders, and folks enjoying the weather.

But I made it a point to come out a bit farther to give us some privacy.

"No one's around, sweetheart," I tell her gently. "But if anyone comes, we can stop."

She opens her mouth as if to say something, then checks herself. Before I know it, she's unhooked her bra behind her back in that magical way women seem to know how to do—I could never figure the damn things out unless they snapped in the front—and she's bare before me, nothing more than her fucking obscene ripped denim shorts covering her body.

Her breasts are small and pert, topped with ruddy nipples that seem to harden under my gaze. "Like little berries," I tell her. I lick my lips, dying to get my mouth around her sweet tits. "So beautiful, sweetheart."

That I am not touching her is a miracle. Every part of her is a damn miracle. Summer raises her chin and eyes me determinedly, but I can tell she's affected. Her chest reddens and her hands dart to her sides, as if she doesn't know where to put them.

I unabashedly rake my eyes over her stomach, over her breasts, before meeting her gaze. She looks at me desperately. "So beautiful," I tell her again. She swallows and waits.

Fucking perfection.

"You need my mouth on you, sweetheart? You want me to suck them for you?"

She nods jerkily, her eyes pleading.

"Can you plump them up for me?" I keep my voice neutral, but I feel desperate myself. I grip the edge of my chair, doing everything in my power to hold myself back from pouncing on her like a madman.

"Wha-what?" she asks, fisting her hands at her sides like she doesn't know where to put them.

"Just bring them up to those sweet tits, honey," I instruct her. "That's it," I grit out as she rubs her hands up her sides. I can see that her hands are a little shaky, her breathing unsteady. "Good girl," I add, and she whimpers at the praise. Fucking hell, she's stunning.

"Nick," she pants, stopping with her hands just below her breasts.

"Oh, Sunshine," I tell her, leaning forward, so close—so close to her skin, I can smell her sun block and whatever perfume she wears—and something else that's just her. I want to lick all over her, absorb every part of her. "You want me to touch you?"

"Yes," Summer sobs without hesitation.

"Impatient," I mutter before putting my lips together and blowing softly, ever so softly, over her right breast. She reacts immediately, her nipple tightening up, a million little goose bumps breaking out over her chest, her collarbone.

"So good," I tell her. "You're perfect." I move to the left breast and—still withholding my touch, by some miracle—blow again. She moans and shivers, her whole body writhing against nothing.

I take my hands and put them right over hers so that we are both cupping her breasts. Her hands are cool and shaking slightly under mine.

"Keep holding them for me," I instruct her with a serious look before I bend forward. I don't hesitate—I take her right breast into my mouth, sucking hard on her nipple. She tastes heavenly, salty and sweet. She cries out and leans back. I wrap my arm around her back and bring her closer to me.

I go all in, nipping and kissing my way around her breast. I raise my eyes to her and find her panting above me, her eyes squeezed shut as she whimpers.

"Summer," I tell her sternly. "Look at me."

She opens her eyes and looks down at me, biting on her bottom lip. "Look at me," I tell her more gently before licking my tongue over her nipple.

She whimpers again, a breathless "oh fuck" drawn from her lips. "Nick," she whispers as I do it again, again, again.

I think I know what she needs, but I want to hear it from her. So instead of giving her what she wants, I move to her left breast before showering it with the same attention—giving little love bites and pecks around the soft flesh. Summer is still holding her breasts for me, as if to display them. It's dirty; she's standing before me at the counter, presenting herself to me, still clothed and squirming up on me, her hair mussed and her eyes unfocused.

I am a lucky fucking man.

I've been focusing all my attention on Summer and trying my damnedest to avoid the raging erection I've got going on in my pants. I continue this way, licking each nipple with the flat of my tongue.

"Nick," Summer pleads. "Please, please. I need more."

"Tell me, sweetheart," I murmur before kissing between her breasts, moving to the next one. "I want to hear it from those pretty lips."

"I need you to… I need it harder." Summer arches her back so sharply I think she'll hurt her spine.

"Mmmmm, you taste so fucking good," I tell her as I lick my way back to her other breast. Her hands are dropping, and I take one mound into my hand, kneading the flesh gently, my other arm still banded around her middle.

"I could lick you all day, Sunshine," I whisper, meeting her eyes again. She sucks in a breath and pushes her breasts back up to me, the warm flesh sitting at the edge of my lips. Fuck.

"Suck on them, please. Please suck on them."

"Good girl," I grunt before taking one nipple into my mouth and sucking. I take the other breast in my hand and pinch her nipple, slight at first, testing to see what she likes. "Oh, fuck yes, Nick," Summer breathes into my hair, and my dick stands up a little higher. I pinch harder, and she whines loudly, dropping her tits and wrapping her arms around my head, holding herself to me like she doesn't want me to escape.

Joke's on her. If I did nothing but suck on her breasts for the rest of my life, I'd die a happy man.

I continue to suckle and pinch her other nipple harder, and she begins bucking her hips, whining and panting. "So good, so good," she babbles incoherently. "Harder. Harder."

I will suck on her breasts until her nipples are red and bruised if that's what she wants.

I moan around her breast, my mouth full of her flesh, my lungs full of her scent, my cock pulsing in my shorts. My dick is screaming at me to do something, anything, and I briefly take my hand off her body to readjust myself. Suddenly, I feel something else on my crotch, and I open my eyes to see one of Summer's hands has moved from around my head to my dick.

Summer starts palming me through my shorts, and I nearly choke at how good it feels. "Summer—*fuck*—wait—"

I rest my head against her chest as she keeps palming me, stroking me firmly through my shorts. I squeeze my eyes shut and forget myself, concentrating on how good she feels.

But this isn't supposed to be about me, this is supposed to be about her, about Summer Mahoney and her sweet smell and her beautiful smile and, yes, she is like fucking summertime, I said it. And then I stop thinking about her and can only think about how nothing, *nothing*, has ever felt so good, and isn't that a bitch? Right now, I think a hand job through my shorts is the height of pleasure, and I don't even care. I truly am a teenager again.

"Nick," Summer gasps, still clutching my head to her chest with one hand. "I want this. I want you. Let me touch you, please, baby." She rubs more firmly against my cock, which is now tenting up obscenely in my shorts.

I huff out a breath at her touch and give a little nip to the side of her breast. She gasps. "You want to touch me, Sunshine?" I growl. "Then take it out."

Chapter Nineteen

I F NICK THINKS I'M GOING TO HAVE SECOND THOUGHTS ABOUT GETTING my hands on him, I'm here to prove him wrong.

That doesn't mean I don't hesitate for a second when he growls his demand.

I am topless, Nick's head against my breasts, his hot breath fanning my skin, his warm tongue laving my nipples. I stand on shaky legs, and there's an orchestra tuning up in my lower abdomen—the woodwinds blow, the bass booms, the drums beat as Nick continues driving me higher, winds me tighter. And I know it's all leading to the ultimate crescendo, one that I haven't experienced with another person in years.

And while a part of me wants to relax and become another instrument for Nick to play with, I also want to take. I want his hands on me, but I want mine on him too.

With that thought solidified, I let go of his head, which I've been clutching to my chest, and move both hands to his zipper. My fingers tremble slightly as I move to unzip him, which is made more difficult by the crowbar he's sporting in his shorts. Our heads are bowed together, him still sitting in that damn chair. I try to catch my breath and move slowly.

"Summer." Nick's voice is deep, and he uses his fingers to lift my chin, so I am staring right into his eyes. His are serious as he speaks slowly. "We don't have to do anything you don't want to. Frankly," he says with a crooked smile, "I planned to focus entirely on you during our little outing today, but I got…distracted."

The orchestra in my lower abdomen tunes a little louder.

"No, I want to. It's just—" I cut myself off.

It's just that I haven't seen a penis in a couple years, and I forgot what to do?

It's just that I've only wanted to do this with you for approximately five thousand years, and I don't know whether to jump for joy or throw up all over your lap?

It's just that I've actually only ever seen one penis, and the owner of said penis left me feeling like I needed a detailed manual to operate it effectively? And then when I had the manual, I kept referring to the wrong section? And when I got to the right section, it was in a different language? And while I know it's probably quality, not quantity, when it comes to dicks, I can't help but feel out of practice?

None of those things sounds great in my head, so I respond with the truth.

"I'm just nervous," I tell him simply, dropping my gaze from Nick's eyes to the very impressive tent in his shorts.

Nervous and horny.

Nick exhales softly and squeezes my chin just a little bit so that I look back to him.

"Sunshine." His voice has gentled. "I promise you that I am grateful for, and will appreciate, anything you do. *Anything*," he repeats emphatically, adjusting himself with a wry grin.

I give him a little smile. "I haven't done this in a really long time. A *really* long time. Like, definitely during the last presidential administration, long. Maybe even before that. Because who really wants to count the last administration anyway?" I bite my lower lip hard to Shut. Myself. Up.

Nick chuckles, leaning forward to tip my chin and kiss me softly on the lips. "It's been a long time for me too, okay?"

I seriously doubt that, former professional football man with a body like Adonis, but okay.

"All right." I pause and eye him again. "Do you promise to tell me…what you like?" Nick raises his eyebrows at me, but I plow on. "Like, if I am doing something you like? Or you don't like? Or you feel ambivalent about…" I take a deep breath. "Just…don't lie. Please tell me, okay?"

I whisper this last part, and Nick's gaze softens. He nods slightly before wrapping his arms around me. He kisses me again, and I respond with fervor. How can I not?

What idiot would turn down this six-foot-something slab of bronzed, chiseled goodness, his cock hard and his lips soft, his piercing eyes taking me in like I'm a goddess and he's a mere mortal?

No one, that's who. No one would turn that down.

And right now, I am no one.

I suck on his bottom lip, moving my hands down to his zipper again. I win that battle and permit myself the luxury of running my hands along the top of his boxers, his skin hard and hot. I feel the crinkly hairs in the center of his stomach. I'm dying to get his shirt off and see if he's hairy everywhere, but I have more pressing needs. As in, the erection that's pressed against his shorts.

I move one hand underneath the elastic of his boxers, and his cock immediately juts out, ruddy and hard, a pearl of fluid glistening at the tip.

I wrap my hand around him. He feels so damn good—warm and smooth, satin over steel. I test him out, squeezing slightly, and he lets out a choked breath.

"*OhmygodSummer*," he groans, and I guess he likes what I'm doing, because when I squeeze him again and glide my hand down his shaft slightly, he bucks his hips.

He lets out another expletive and keeps right on kissing me, his movements getting sloppy. "Those hands. *Christ.* Squeeze—squeeze me tighter at the top. Yeah, like that." Nick pants through his instructions as I follow his commands.

"Like that?" I squeeze him from root to tip, and a little more fluid appears at the top. He huffs in response.

On a whim, I remove my hand briefly, bring it to my mouth, and lick my palm wetly. I don't take my eyes off Nick, who stares at me, mouth agape, as I return my hand to his cock.

"That better?" I murmur, still eyeing him, letting him see how much I want this, how much I want him.

"You. Are. A bad girl," he tells me through clenched teeth, moving back slightly, holding on to my hips as he watches. "Fuck, Summer," he sighs, leaning forward to kiss my chest, the tops of my breasts, my neck, as I stroke him harder and tighter.

"You feel so good," I whisper to the top of his head. I feel his chuckle move through his body.

"I'm supposed to be saying that to you," he tells me, bringing his head to mine so our foreheads are touching. "*You* feel good. Your hand, fuck me…" he pants as his words get choppier.

Again on a whim, I bring my other hand to his cock, using both to stroke him off. Not that I've seen a lot of dicks—something tells me Tumblr isn't the *most* reliable when it comes to average size—but Nick's girthy, and I wrap both hands around him tightly.

"Oh my god," he moans louder, leaning his head back, the muscles in his neck flexing as he moves. "Summer, you're going to make me come…"

"Good," I whisper, leaning forward to kiss his neck softly. "I want it." I suck a little on the tendons where his neck meets his shoulder. He's almost rutting his hips now, a slight sheen of sweat beading his brow.

I squeeze harder at the top and stroke down, up, and down and up.

"Knew it was going to be like this," he slurs incoherently as I stroke him. "Knew if you got your fucking hands on me, it would be like this… I'm gonna go, Summer…"

"Do it," I whisper. "I want your come, Nick."

With a loud groan, he throws his head back again and squeezes my hips hard, arching his own hips up toward me. Every inch of him, from his jaw to his stomach to his hands, is strung tight as he comes, semen spurting from the top of his cock to coat my hands, some landing on my chest. "Oh fuck," he moans, bringing his head up to see where he's spent on me. "So fucking hot, Summer, you're…" Whatever else he was going to say is lost in his groan as he keeps coming, and I keep pumping, his generous seed more than enough to smooth my path, so to speak, up and down his shaft.

"Fuck. *Fuck,*" he drills out, and I slow my hands as I feel him deflate a little. "So good, so good—ahh." He moves one of his hands to cup mine, ceasing my strokes.

"Sorry," I manage to choke out, too captivated by what I just saw to say much more than that.

He smiles ruefully, keeping his hand over mine. "Don't you dare fucking apologize. It gets a little sensitive right after," he mutters.

I smile back at him. He leans forward to kiss me softly on the lips before pulling back. His eyes drift from my eyes to my chest, and his nostrils flare. "Love seeing this on you, Sunshine," he whispers to me, seemingly hypnotized by the dirty deed we've just done. He uses one of his fingers to run through the evidence of his orgasm sitting just above my breasts.

I shiver at his touch. "So hot," Nick murmurs as he continues drawing his finger gently on my skin, his eyes darting from what he's doing to my eyes, gauging my reaction.

Obviously, my reaction is unabashedly wanton, because I am into Dirty Nick. I am into what we did, and, more importantly, when can we do it again?

And how can someone be so sweet, almost shy, and so fucking dirty? I don't know, but I'm definitely not mad about it.

Nick leans forward again to kiss me, his tongue touching mine briefly before he pulls back. "Let's go clean up," he whispers, his clean hand—the one that's not currently circling my own hands, which are still loosely wrapped around his dick—tucking some of the stray hairs of my braid behind my ear.

"Mmmmkay," I mumble.

"Then I want to get you dirty again, Sunshine," he whispers, leaning forward so that I can feel his breath in my ear. "That okay with you?"

I lean to the side to grant him better access to my neck. "Don't threaten me with a good time," I mutter. He chuckles before nipping my earlobe and pulling away.

Nick

It occurs to me as I lead Summer down the short hall to the bathroom that I have severely, severely underestimated my feelings for her.

I feel giddy, like Teenage Nick, infatuated with the first girl to touch my dick. Only, what I feel for Summer is more than infatuation.

I really didn't mean to make a mess on her. Hell, I didn't mean for her to touch me at all. I wanted it to be about her—her body, her pleasure.

I still want that.

I shouldn't be surprised, but as usual, she upended my plans and took the wheel, so to speak.

And by "the wheel," I mean by dick.

Not that I'm complaining.

I knew once she got her hands on me, it would be all over. Her smell, her touch, her honesty. Her lack of hesitancy maybe most of all. It all set me off.

And knowing what I know now about her ex, I want to give her that honesty right back. I want to make her feel good the way she deserves, rather than wielding sex like a weapon, another tool to make her feel bad about herself.

Seriously, fuck that guy.

"Come here," I tell her gruffly, taking her into the bathroom. It's small—we are on a boat, after all—but clean and bright. There are white sconces on the wall alongside a big backlit mirror, a white-and-gray marbled sink, and a shower big enough for two.

Summer washes her hands at the sink, and I lean into the shower to turn it on, the room slowly filling with steam.

As much as I'd love to spend eternity with Summer in the shower, water is a finite resource on the boat.

"Take off your shorts, Sunshine." I catch her gaze in the mirror, and she narrows her eyes at me.

"Take off your shorts, *please.*" I smirk as she moves to comply, but my smile fades as more of her beautiful body is revealed—miles of freckled skin, her small breasts perky, her dusky nipples hard. She steps out of her shorts and stands straight and tall, taking the braid out of her hair to put it up in a bun on top of her head. She hides nothing, raising her chin defiantly as if to say, *Here I am. Take it or leave it.*

I'm taking.

My gaze moves lower, and I see her flush all the way down, from her chest to her stomach to just above her pussy.

My mouth goes dry, and I take a breath, darting my eyes back up to hers and seeing no apprehension there whatsoever. She's a hell of a lot braver than me, that's for damn sure.

"You're beautiful," I manage to croak out, and her shoulders drop a little at that, the muscles in her face easing. Maybe she's not as unflappable as she appears.

"Come here," I tell her again, pulling her flush to me, her bare body pressed against my clothed one. I kiss her wetly, running my hands up and down her back, feeling her flesh quake and shiver as she gives back everything she's got.

I clear my throat, eyeing the evidence of my earlier orgasm on her chest. Goddamn if that doesn't make me feel good, like I've marked her as mine.

"I didn't mean to get you dirty before," I tell her between kisses. "But now that I have…let's clean you up."

I step back and take in Summer's appearance—her flushed skin, her pebbled nipples, her big brown eyes, hiding nothing. I check the water temperature and gesture for her to get in.

She steps in slowly, turning away from me toward the showerhead, closing her eyes and letting the water run over her face, before turning around and facing me again.

"Hi," she whispers with a tiny smile as the water cascades down her back.

"Hi." I lean into the shower, grabbing the soap and putting my hands under the water to work up a lather. Before touching her, I catch her eyes.

"What you said to me before—that goes here too." I rub my hands together purposefully, the clean scent drifting up into my nostrils. "You tell me, Sunshine. What you like. If you don't like something, tell me that too, okay?"

"Okay," she breathes out. Water droplets cling to her brown eyelashes, to her smooth shoulders. She's rosy-cheeked and worked up, and I want it all.

I lose my shirt so I am clad only in my boxers, and I sit on the ledge with my legs in the tub, the perfect angle to get where I want to be the most. My boxers are going to get soaked, but I don't give a dusty fuck about that.

I bring my hands to her chest, rubbing lightly, getting her soapy, never applying too much pressure.

Her skin is warm and soft. She leans into me, arching her back slightly. "That feels good," she tells me softly.

I hum in response, letting my hands map her body. I move them over her chest, around her breasts reverently, in contradiction to my earlier roughness. She sighs contentedly as I shift them down to her center, before brushing the tops of her thighs, my movements tracking the water flowing from above.

Summer huffs, and I glance up at her, seeing her frustrated look as I avoid her center. I place my hands on her hips.

"Turn around, Sunshine," I instruct her, raising my eyebrows when she doesn't comply immediately.

She bites her lip and smirks at me before turning around to face the showerhead. Without a word, she raises her hands, places them on the tiled wall, and arches her back so that—

Fuck.

So that the twin globes of her glorious ass are on display. And given where I am sitting and the angle of her body, I can also see her glistening slit, shiny and pink.

"Fuck." This time, I say it aloud before moving toward her slowly. "Fuck, you are perfect." I place my hands over her ass, squeezing her firm muscles, and she gasps in response. "This ass…goddamn, Summer. Do you know how many times I have thought about your ass?"

"N-no," she stammers, arching farther into my touch.

I lather up again to massage her behind, moving my hands up to her lower back. "Too many to count," I murmur. "You are a fucking wet dream. You and those goddamn yoga pants."

She laughs a little, but it turns to a moan when I slide my hands back down to her ass, massaging her with a firmer touch, each time moving a little closer, closer to her center. She wiggles her hips to drift my hands closer to her pussy.

"You want to ask me for something, Sunshine?" I ask her gruffly.

"Nick," she whispers. "Please."

"I see that pretty pink pussy, Summer," I tell her, trying to keep my voice detached. "You need me to do something about that?"

I rub closer to her center, my thumbs nearly making contact with her folds.

"You know I do. I'm so horny, Nick," she cries pitifully.

A laugh bursts out of me at her blatant honesty. "Me too, Sunshine. Me too."

I let my thumbs make contact then, sliding up and down on either side of her pussy without entering. She cries out and bangs one of her hands on the tile, a soft expletive leaving her lips.

"God, Summer. You're so wet. So beautiful." I rub her down just like this, never entering her, but getting her wetness all over my thumbs, all while I continue to admire the glory that is her ass.

"Nick," she gasps, shimmying her hips quicker. "Please, *please* touch me."

"Poor thing," I murmur, before gripping her hip tightly with one hand, bringing my other between her legs and cupping her pussy. "Let's take care of you, sweetheart."

I feel her clit, puffy and engorged, right at the top of her pussy. I take a deep breath—I'm hard as wood again, despite having a wrecking orgasm not fifteen minutes ago—and rub my index and middle fingers in tiny circles on her clit, determined to make this last for her.

Summer's body has other ideas.

"*Oh fuck,*" she moans, grinding down on my hand to get more friction. "Nick... Nick, I can't stop it. I'm gonna come—"

"Do it," I grit out, rubbing my fingers in firm circles around her clit, the rest of my hand still cupping her pussy. "Do it, Summer. I've got you."

She pops like a rocket, whimpering, her legs shaking as I rub her through her climax, crooning to her about what a good girl she is, how I am going to take such good care of her. I am soaked now—from the shower, from the steam, from her, from my own sweat dotting my skin. Summer whines and moans and grinds, uninhibited in her pleasure, and I want *more*. More of this, more skin, more touching, more tasting, more of this sweetness that I've only let myself dream about.

"Nick," she exhales, her body settling slightly, her legs releasing their hold on my hand. "Oh my god."

"Come here." I lean in to turn off the water before standing outside the tub and pulling her to me, her wet body plastered to mine. Summer regards me lazily, wrapping her arms around my neck and kissing me full on the lips. Her skin is hot, and her hands tremble as we kiss like this, no finesse whatsoever, me angling my head to gain better access to her mouth. I moan when she sucks on my tongue and wiggles her little body up against mine as if she is trying to get closer.

"I got you all wet," she whispers between our kisses.

"Fuckin' right you did," I mutter back, feeling her smile as I continue kissing her.

"That felt so, so good." She has a satisfied smile on her face, and I feel like I hung the moon for her.

"Jump up, Sunshine."

This time, she obeys my command without hesitation, jumping up and allowing me to grab her legs and wrap them around my hips. "Oh—*oh*," she moans, her eyelids drooping a little as she feels my erection, once again tenting my now-soaked boxers.

"Yeah, *oh*." I smirk before regarding her seriously. "You should know by now that a boner is an occupational hazard of hanging out with you."

"Well," she says as she moves her head to kiss the underside of my jaw, "let's go do some more 'hanging out.'" She backs up and waggles her eyebrows mischievously.

"Sunshine," I growl. I grab a fluffy beige towel and wrap it around her, squeezing her tightly.

It's perfection.

Chapter Twenty

Nick

Finally, *finally*, I have Summer right where I want her—in my bed, naked, in between my legs.

Well, it's the bed on the boat, and she's not in between my legs in the way you think. I sit with my back against the headboard, Summer in front of me, her back to my chest, her legs spread as wide as humanly possible—dancers are amazing—as I rub my hands along her inner thighs toward her center.

She's gorgeous here too, all pouty pink lips and creamy skin, lighter than her legs and arms and everywhere the sun hits her.

And yes, her freckles are everywhere.

"Want to feel you, honey," I murmur to her before inserting my finger into her pussy slowly. "God, look at you," I marvel, feeling every inch of her clinging to my finger, warm and wet. "Gonna play with you some more, okay?"

"Okay," she responds, her voice strained. "God, Nick, that feels so good."

"I know, sweetheart," I murmur, fingering her faster. Each time I pull back, a little more moisture is coating my skin, and fuck if that isn't hot.

"Look at you," I tell her again. "Creaming on me like this. You hot for this, Sunshine?"

"*God.* You know I am," she pants in response, writhing her body.

"Gonna fill you up so good," I mutter, adding another finger and stretching her out just a bit.

"I want that so bad," she whines, her tits bouncing as she moves.

"I know you do, Sunshine," I croon to her. "I can tell by the way you're fucking yourself on my fingers."

She moans loudly, her head angling back to rest on my shoulder, her eyes squeezing shut. I want to tell her to open them, to watch what I'm doing, what our bodies can do together, but I can tell she's worked up enough and it won't take long to get her there.

And there will be plenty of time for that in the future…won't there?

"Nick," Summer whispers, and I turn my head away from her center to see her gaze, her head lolling back on my chest, her cheeks pink, and her hair a wildfire around her head. "Kiss me."

I do what the woman says and go for broke, stamping my mouth on hers and demanding entry with my tongue. She meets me stroke for stroke, and my fingers do the same—stroking in and out of her, feeling her tighten and release around me.

"Nick," Summer says brokenly, her eyebrows furrowed. "I think…oh my god, I think I am going to come again…"

"Good girl," I praise her, moving my eyes back to where my fingers enter her body. "You're clenching around me so tight, honey," I mutter, feeling her walls tighten. "I can't wait to get my dick in this sweet spot. But I'm gonna have to work it in slow, though, right? Nice and slow to get it in all this pink." I press my thumb firmly on her clit as I speak.

"Nick, I'm going to come, I'm going to come…" Summer chants it like a mantra, turning her body into me. She grips my forearm with both of her hands, riding my hand furiously.

"Do it," I murmur. "Gush all over my hand. Let me feel you… Yes, Sunshine, that's it." I continue praising her as she climaxes, gripping my forearm so hard her knuckles are white, whimpering and moaning, her hair tickling my shoulders.

"Oh my god," she whines, riding it out on my hand. "Don't stop, don't stop."

"I'm not going to stop, Sunshine." I lean in to kiss her mouth, my tongue mimicking the movement of my fingers as she crests, tightens up her entire body, and releases around me.

I'm never going to stop.

Chapter Twenty-One

Nick

WHEN YOU ARE IN A LEADERSHIP POSITION, PEOPLE HAVE certain expectations of you.

The quarterback is, for better or worse, the leader of a team. The team looks to you for guidance and strategy. Yes, you have a large coaching staff consisting of the best minds in football, but sometimes, those game-time decisions can only be made by the ones playing it.

I love the game. I loved playing the game. I loved the adrenaline, the sweat, performing at my peak. I loved being part of a brotherhood of mostly like-minded individuals who were all dead set on the same thing I was: winning games, and ultimately, winning *the* game.

But over the course of my career, I became two different people. The man I was in the arena is not the man my family knows, the man my friends know.

Playing professional sports isn't just playing the game. In fact, the actual game is, unfortunately, only a small fraction of the obligations that surround you. Promotional appearances. Press conferences. Interviews. Things that, on my best day, make me break out in hives. On my worst day, these are the types of things that keep me in my room, in bed, with the drapes drawn and the door shut.

At the height of my career, people would be genuinely surprised when they met me. How could the man in the arena—the one on TV, the one who yelled and threw and tumbled and fought—be the same guy who couldn't string two words together in public, let alone in front of a camera?

Not only have I always been a quiet guy, but I've been a quiet guy surrounded by women who are…not quiet. My mom never hesitates to say what's on her mind, and Julia and Tatum certainly followed in her footsteps. Anyone who is shy will understand that sometimes it's just easier to let others do the talking. So I never hesitated to let that happen.

But Julia and Tatum obviously didn't come with me to the League.

I ultimately learned some tools from a therapist to get through those dreaded public appearances and press conferences. And when I could write my own ticket, I had my agent turn down all promotional appearances altogether. No celebrity golf tournaments, no Formula 1 appearances, and definitely no fucking reality dance competitions.

Except for one type of request.

The requests from schools, the requests from after-school programs, the requests from camps—basically, anything with kids, I tried to never turn down.

For some reason, talking and interacting with kids has never brought on the rampant anxiety that I get interacting with unfamiliar adults.

"Uncle Nick!"

Maybe it's because the kids don't have the same expectations as the adults. Most people I met in the League—especially the people I met after I signed my big contract, the one that set me for life—didn't really want to know *me*. They wanted to know Nick Echeverria, all-star San Diego quarterback. They didn't give a shit about the mumbling, stumbling, awkward guy I turned into off the field. And, in fact, they were usually disappointed in that guy.

"Uncle Nick, Violet farted."

But kids? Kids don't give a shit about any of that. They really don't care about what I have to say. They mostly want to talk about themselves—what they've learned, what they like, how far they can throw the ball. And I could listen to that stuff all day. Any conversation where I am not the main topic is a conversation I will gladly participate in.

"My name is *not* Violet. My name is Eyeball."

Kids just don't care about the fame, the glory, all that stuff. And they definitely don't have any preconceived notions about what a quarterback should act like, about what a leader I should be.

"Violet farted *again*, and it *smells*!"

Exhibit A: my nieces.

I am currently hanging out with ten-year-old Sarah and six-year-old Violet while Julia and Lincoln are at an appointment and my mom is helping out at the restaurant.

"Eyeball, huh?" I ask Violet, ruffling her dark hair. "I like it."

"Thank you," she says seriously before puffing out her chest. "*Some* people are still calling me Violet."

"She means me," Sarah says, rolling her eyes with all the cynicism a ten-year-old can muster.

"I mean her," Violet confirms.

"Well, kiddo—er, Eyeball—" I correct myself, and Violet nods approvingly "—a name-change is a big deal. It's going to take time for her to remember that you are now going by…Eyeball."

"Whatever." Another eye roll from Sarah. "Can we go to the beach?"

"I don't want to go to the beach!" Violet shrieks. "I want to play shopping!"

She is decked out in a glittery skirt and a football jersey that she always likes to wear when I come over. It's a hand-me-down from her sister, super threadbare, and entirely adorable. She also has a giant purse slung over her shoulder, which I presume is for the "play shopping."

She's draped a fuzzy pink unicorn blanket across Layne Staley, who lifts his head in interest before going back to his nap.

"I have an even better idea. What if we…."—I pause for dramatic effect—"…go pick up some treats from Lucy's bakery?"

"*Yessss!*" Violet shrieks again and drops the purse, her play shopping forgotten at the promise of sugar. "Uncle Nick, you are the *best*!"

I grin at her, but my smile fades when I turn to see Sarah frowning.

"What's up, buttercup?"

"It's just…" She twirls her long, dark hair around her finger, looking so much like my older sister I almost do a double take. "Never mind."

Julia and Lincoln are not in the habit of forcing their kids to share if they don't want to, so I don't want to press the issue. "You sure?"

She nods quickly, but her face falls when Violet yells—the kid has no concept of inside voice, "She wants to go to the beach because her *boyfriend* is going to be there!"

"Shut *up*, Violet!" Sarah yells back, her face reddening.

"*My name is Eyeball!*"

"Okay, okay, girls. My favorite nieces." I pinch my nose and squint my eyes shut.

"We're your *only* nieces, Uncle Nick," Violet reminds me solemnly.

"And therefore, my favorite." I turn toward Sarah. "We don't say shut up." She nods apologetically. "And Vi—Eyeball," I recover quickly as I turn toward my pigtailed younger niece. "If Sarah doesn't want to share something, you don't need to share it either, *capiche?*"

"*Capiche,*" Violet mutters.

"*Now,*" I tell them both, "get your shoes on so we can walk to the bakery."

<div align="center">~~~~~</div>

"Macaroni and cheese is the best. I like to drink it every day…"

Violet is singing her own compositions as we walk on Main Street's sidewalk. I am about to ask her how it is that one drinks, rather than eats, macaroni and cheese, but think better of it.

Sarah and I trail behind Violet a few paces as she skips along, Layne Staley on a leash between us. Sarah is a quiet kid, and so was I. Walking with her is peaceful.

"School going good?" I ask her after a few moments. Sarah shrugs in her bright-blue school hoodie.

"It's fine."

"Swimming going good?"

I get a nod in response.

"Cool." I put my hands in my pockets as we meander down past the local art studio, the longtime bar that's been here since my parents were kids, and of course…the yoga studio. Anything yoga-related makes me think of Summer, and Summer makes me think of…

The boat.

Her skin.

The shower.

Her lips.

The way she moaned and whimpered and clung to me.

The smell of soap on her skin, the feel of her hair tickling my shoulders as she sat in front of me. Her unabashed response to everything we did, her rush to feel everything without hesitation—it lit a spark in me that's been missing for a long, long time.

I feel alive, like bubbling lava in a long-dormant volcano. And it would be easy to chalk it up to the fact that I had my first orgasm with a woman in a very, very long time, but it's more than that.

It's the clarity I feel when I am with her.

And of course, the orgasms certainly help.

Given that I really do *not* need to be sporting wood while on an outing with my nieces, I clear my throat and focus on our walk, nodding at a few familiar faces as they pass us by.

It's been a few days since the boat trip. Summer's been working non-stop, so I haven't seen as much of her as I would like.

And what I would like is to see her every day, in every way.

I push that thought out of my head as we pass the yoga studio.

One step at a time.

I still want to do this right.

It's the endgame that's murky to me, and I'm still not quite ready to put into words where I see this thing with Summer going. For now, I am going to be the lucky benefactor of her sighs, her smile, her touch.

"Summer!"

I snap my head up to see the object of my thoughts walking ahead of us. And to my surprise, it's Sarah who has greeted her, lighting up for the first time all day, moving quickly towards Summer.

Violet stops short and waits for me to reach her before sliding her tiny, grubby hand in mine. I make a mental note for us to wash up before partaking in whatever Lucy has made at the bakery today.

"Do you know her?" Violet asks as we watch Summer greet Sarah with a bright smile.

"I do," I respond slowly. Violet doesn't remember Gretchen at all—not that Julia and the girls spent a ton of time with her when we were married. But I am still unsure how to introduce the girls to Summer.

"Hi, Nick," Summer greets me warmly when we catch up to her and Sarah.

"Hey," I murmur. I want to go and hug her, but I am not sure of the protocol. Besides, I've still got Violet clinging to me like a barnacle.

"You know my uncle?" Violet asks suspiciously.

"Well, sure," Summer responds. "I know your whole family. Tatum is one of my best friends."

"I don't know you," Violet declares.

"Let's fix that, then, huh?" Summer asks her. "My name is Summer, and I have known your family for a long time. You must be Violet."

"She's actually going by Eyeball these days," I tell Summer.

"No, she can call me Violet. Eyeball is just for my family." Violet examines Summer closely. "How come I've never met you?"

"Well, I moved away for a long time and just recently moved back here," Summer responds.

"What's that thing?" Violet immediately changes topics and points to Summer's purple yoga mat, strapped into some contraption hanging over her shoulder like a harness.

"That is my yoga mat. Do you know what yoga is?"

"Ohhhh *yes*!" Violet leaps into the air with excitement. "I've done Harry Potter yoga and Room on the Broom yoga…"

Summer looks at me quizzically. "It's a YouTube thing," I explain. "There's this woman who tells children's stories and incorporates yoga moves for the kids to do. Like, acting out the story."

Summer raises her eyebrows. "That sounds…pretty awesome, actually."

"Yeah, but the moves are, like, *so* for kids," Sarah interjects with an eye roll. Honestly, I am concerned about the potential long-term damage to her eyes with the number of times she's rolled them this day alone.

"How do *you* know Summer?" I ask Sarah curiously.

"Oh! She came to our school this week to teach yoga," Sarah explains with uncharacteristic excitement. "Our swim coach thought it would be good to incorporate more stretching and yoga into our workouts. Did you know," Sarah continues chattering, "that Summer can wrap her legs around her head while sitting down?! It's this, like, amazing move."

"That so?" I ask with a sly grin directed at Summer. She blushes and clears her throat.

"Yes!" Sarah answers before Summer can say anything. "She's, like, crazy flexible."

"That's…good information to have," I respond, narrowing my eyes at Summer.

"Anyway." Summer cocks her head at me with a look, her cheeks flushed. "What are you all up to today?"

"We're going to Lucy's!" Violet screeches. "You should come, and I can tell you all about my yoga. I'm very flexible too. I can almost do the splits on both sides."

"That sounds impressive," Summer tells Violet, who beams proudly. "But I don't want to intrude…?" She looks at me questioningly.

"No, you should come! Please, Uncle Nick, tell her she should come with us." Sarah looks at me pleadingly.

I clear my throat. "You know you are always more than welcome," I tell her gruffly. "You should definitely come. With us. You should come with us." I rub the back of my neck and offer her a half smile.

She eyes me knowingly and smiles back. "Okay, then. Let's go get some sugar."

"*Yay!*" Violet grabs Summer's hand with her free one, and we're off.

Violet continues chattering about her splits and other moves as we walk, Sarah occasionally offering a comment or question to Summer. I do what I do best and remain silent.

But it's not awkward at all.

I can't imagine anything or anyone nicer as we walk to Lucy's—Sarah on Summer's left, Violet holding her hand on the right, while I hold Violet's other hand.

I feel the bolt of certainty in my chest again.

I can't think of a nicer feeling, actually.

Summer

"All right, let's see if you can move like this!"

After consuming a homemade cinnamon roll from Lucy's, Violet is officially hopped up on sugar. We all are, burning off energy with an impromptu dance party in the living room at Julia and Lincoln's house. Violet jumps up and down like a pogo stick, right on to the beat of "Dance Monkey." She occasionally kicks out one leg, then the other.

Sarah's sitting on the couch, purportedly reading, but taking several breaks to roll her eyes at her little sister.

"Uncle Nick!" Violet shrieks. "Do this!" She tries—and fails—to do a split jump.

"I don't think my knees could handle that, Eyeball." He spins Violet in a circle. "Actually, I am not sure I could do that move even when I was your age."

"'Cause now you're an old man!" Violet exclaims.

"Oooohhh, straight through the heart." Nick faux winces, grabbing his chest. "Where did you hear that?"

"My mom," Violet responds matter-of-factly. "She says you are a grumpy old man."

I burst out laughing. Nick's gaze cuts to me quickly with a feigned look of sadness. "Whose side are you on anyway?"

"I'm sorry," I tell him through my laughter. "But…it's true. You *are* a grumpy old man."

"I'll show you grumpy," he growls, and before I know it, he's grabbed my hips and is tickling my sides. I laugh even harder, gasping and uselessly pushing at his hands. "Oh my god, *Nick!*"

"*Tickle fight!*" Violet screeches and then tries to jump on Nick's back.

He makes an "oof" sound before falling forward to the carpet, catching my back with his strong hands, cushioning our fall.

"Violet, you don't fight fair," he wheezes out as we roll to the side, Nick caging me with his body as Violet tries to get her little fingers on his stomach. Layne Staley barks with excitement.

"My. Name. Is. *Eyeball!*"

I hear even Sarah snort-laughing at that as I hold on to Nick, hugging him from the front while Violet pounds on his back. His warm body is against mine, and I can't help but take a deep breath of him, his pine and minty scent permeated with cinnamon and sugar. It's delectable.

I remind myself not to maul him in front of his nieces.

"Hello?"

The new voice startles us all, and I look toward the kitchen to see Nick's mom, Elaine, taking us all in.

"Hi, Mom. *Umph.*" Nick huffs a breath as Violet uses him to push herself back up, running to greet her grandma with an excited noise.

I scramble to unwrap my arms from around Nick like a teenager caught making out on her parents' couch.

Not that that ever happened to me, but I can imagine how it feels.

Nick gives me a strange look when I move away to stand before smiling at his mom.

"Grammy, we had cinnamon rolls and a dance party, and Summer's going to teach us to do the yoga!"

"It's just 'yoga,'" Sarah corrects her younger sister.

"That sounds very exciting," Elaine says, bending down to kiss Violet on the forehead. She looks toward the living room, where I am standing, suddenly feeling awkward and out of place.

I don't know why. Elaine has never been anything but nice to me.

Maybe it's because you were having carnal thoughts about her son?

I ignore the blush crawling across my skin. "Hi!" I chirp. I even give an awkward little wave before putting my hand back down.

"Summer Anne," Elaine says warmly. "Get over here and give me a hug."

I do what she says and make my way over to the kitchen, letting Elaine wrap her arms around me. She's tall and thin like Julia, her dark hair pulled back into a braid that hangs down her back. She's beautiful, with the bronzed skin all her children have. Unlike her children, Elaine has dark eyes to match her hair. The Echeverria kids clearly got their piercing hazel eyes from their dad. Either way, everyone in this family is all really, annoyingly good-looking.

Nick was only seven years old when his dad died. I was even younger, and I don't recall anything about his death. According to Tatum, Elaine hasn't so much as been on a date since her husband died, let alone had a serious relationship. I suppose it's understandable; she had three kids, all ten years old and younger, to take care of. Elaine is still a striking woman, and I wonder if she ever thought about starting over.

Like me.

"Hi, Elaine," I greet her.

"Look at you," she tells me softly. Her warm brown eyes meet my own, and she pats the side of my head in a motherly way. "I am so glad you are here," she declares.

"Me too," I tell her, realizing that I mean it. I *am* glad I am here.

"And my son, he's not giving you a hard time?" she asks wryly, looking over my shoulder at Nick.

"Mom," he groans as he walks past us into the kitchen to get a glass of water. "Leave Summer alone." He turns back to face me and winks so quickly I almost miss it.

"No!" I exclaim in response to Elaine's question. "No, not at all. He's been, um, we've been…" To my horror, I again feel my cheeks heating up, thinking about what exactly Nick and I have been up to lately.

"It's been nice to spend time together. And with Tatum, obviously. And Lucy. And Pops." I hurriedly tick off all the people I have seen since I've been back, so Elaine will know that there is more to me than wanting to hump her son constantly.

"Mm-hmm, I'm sure," Elaine responds. "Well, I am here to spend time with my two favorite granddaughters until Julia and Lincoln get home."

Violet perks up at that before considering. "But, Grammy," she says slowly, "we are your *only* granddaughters."

"All the more reason you are my favorite, then, huh?"

"You know," I interrupt, "I've got to get back to the yoga studio anyway. I have another class this evening."

"Noooo, don't go Summer!" Violet wails dramatically, throwing herself around my legs as if it's the last time she will see me.

"I'll walk you," Nick offers immediately.

"*Noooooo*, Uncle Nick, don't leave!" Violet forgets about me and throws herself around her uncle's legs.

"No, no, it's all good—it's not too far. Really. But maybe text me, and we can catch up later? Or tomorrow," I continue hurriedly, horrified when I realize that I essentially just invited Nick for a booty call in front of his mom. "Or the next day. Next week. Whenever," I mumble, smiling weakly.

Nick smirks, trying to get Violet to detach herself from his lower half.

"Later sounds good. At least let me walk you out."

"It was nice to see you again," I tell Elaine. Her eyes dart from Nick to me, with a little smile on her lips.

"It was nice to see you too, Summer," she says, coming in to give me another hug.

After being without any physical touch for so long, I have to remind myself that this is normal. Normal friends, friends who are family, hug and express themselves through physical touch.

I hug Elaine back fiercely.

"Thank you," I whisper, not altogether certain what I am thanking her for. But as I pull away and see the softness in her eyes, I think she might know.

Chapter Twenty-Two

Nick

"**S**O, HOW'S SUMMER?"

We've gotten Violet fed, bathed, and conked out after three readings of *Dragons Love Tacos*—hand to God, one of the best books I've read in any genre. Sarah is in her room, supposedly doing her homework.

Mom hasn't had a chance to interrogate me about Summer, but…now's the time.

"She's good."

"She looks good," Mom comments. "She has a spark in her eye, a pep in her step." She glances at me out of the corner of her eye as she opens a bottle of wine. "I am going to guess you have something to do with that?"

"Nah," I demur. "She's good, like you said. I think she's…happy."

"And I am sure you have nothing to do with this sudden happiness?"

I shrug, not certain I want to delve into whatever is going on between Summer and me with my mother.

"Okay, you don't have to tell me. I'm only your mother who knows everything." Mom winks at me and pours herself a glass. "You want one?"

"Nah, I'm good." I sit on one of the barstools at the kitchen countertop across from where my mother stands.

She sips her wine and regards me. "You can ask me, you know."

"Ask you…what?"

"Whatever it is you're working up the courage to ask your wise old mother."

"First of all, you are not old," I tell her. She grins and shrugs. "Second of all…I am just figuring out how to phrase it."

"I'll wait."

I look out the big kitchen window, where the sun has set, the sky painted with orange and pink hues. The fog is starting to thicken around the Rock. "I've been feeling kind of…relieved lately. Like a weight has been lifted off my shoulders."

My mother nods, waiting.

"Summer is just…easy," I say quietly. "Easy to be with. Easy to be around."

"She always was, you know," Mom agrees. "She sure had a lot of strong personalities around her. Alexis for a sister, and Tatum and Lucy as best friends, but she was always the most relaxed, carefree girl. I hate to think of something—or some*one*—dimming that spark in her."

She's undoubtedly referring to Summer's ex, and my jaw clenches involuntarily. "Yeah, her ex was a dick," I say bluntly.

My mom doesn't bat an eye. Cursing never made her angry. "*I care a lot more about whether my children are good people than whether they know the f-word,*" she told us once when we were younger.

"Did you know I saw Summer in New York?" I ask suddenly. "Before she was married to Erik. Actually, I met him that weekend too. The weekend of the draft."

"I didn't know that," Mom responds, her eyebrows raised.

"I should have gotten her out of there," I tell her in a low voice. "I shouldn't have let her marry that guy. I should've—I don't know, but I should've done something."

"Nick," my mom says quietly, setting down her wineglass and moving one of her hands on top of mine. My hand has been fidgeting on the counter, and it stills under her touch.

"Do you think Summer would have listened to you?"

"I would've made her listen," I say stubbornly, but I know what a dumb statement that is.

My mom snickers. "Right. How do you think that would have gone?"

I dip my chin in acknowledgment. *Not well.*

"And from what I understand," Mom continues, "she had other people to tell her that Erik was perhaps not the best choice for her. Her sister. Tatum. Lucy. And what did she do?"

"She got married anyway," I mutter.

"She got married anyway. People need to be free to make their own choices. You did. Summer did. I did. Everyone does."

I scoff. "What choice did you make that was so bad?"

"Well," my mother responds wryly, "not everyone thought it was a great idea for me to get married to your dad at twenty. But, you know, we were in love." She says it nonchalantly, waving her hand in a rolling motion.

We don't really talk about my dad. Not because it's super painful or difficult, although, of course, it's sad. I was seven when he died. Julia was ten; Tatum was four. And all of a sudden, my mom—at the ripe old age of thirty-five—was a widow with three children.

She rarely talks about him, even in passing.

So when she *does* bring him up, I am on high alert.

"We had fifteen good years together. Not everything was good, mind you. But more good than bad. And fifteen years is more than a lot of people get, you know?" Mom sighs and drinks her wine, looking unfocused, maybe thinking of a life before.

"You know," she says suddenly, her focus moving toward me, "when you get a second chance in life, you should take it. Hell, when you get a first chance, you should take that, too. But I think too many people are scared when presented with something they know is going to change the trajectory of their life." Mom sighs, sips her wine, and regards me seriously. "Don't waste time, Nick."

I nod. "I won't."

"I know it's the ultimate cliché, but life really is too short."

"I know."

"I hope you do."

"What about you?"

Mom raises her eyebrows. "Me?"

"What about your life? You're only what...forty?" She huffs a laugh at my joke and rolls her eyes. She is going to be sixty this year, and we both know it. "Are you not wasting time?"

"Well, this conversation is officially over," she tells me sternly, but her eyes are twinkling. "Remember what I said. I am wise, and I—"

"Know everything," I finish for her. "I know, Mom."

Chapter Twenty-Three

Summer

"Your nieces are cute," I tell Nick back at my house later that night.

He did, indeed, return for what I am hoping is a booty call. I was in the middle of painting when he arrived and told me to continue.

"What, are you going to be my model?" I joked.

He gave me a devastating smile in response. "You can pose me however you like," he said, waggling his eyebrows suggestively.

I laughed. "I don't paint people, I paint emotions."

His smile fell fast, his expression surprised.

"What is it?" I asked him.

"I just… I had déjà vu or something," he muttered. He ran his hand over the back of his neck before putting it on his hip. His tell, I was learning, that he had to think about what he was going to say before he said it. "God. I just remember you saying those exact words to someone…maybe my grandfather, or something? When they asked you if you could paint a picture of somebody."

"I don't remember," I told him softly.

"I *do*. I remember." He was firm. "You told them just like you told me—'I don't paint people, I paint feelings.' Something like that." He shook his head and smiled ruefully. "It's weird, the things we remember."

"Sometimes." I paused. "Sometimes, not so much."

Now, I'm in the corner of the living room, where I've laid out a large drop cloth and set up my easel. The sun has long set, but I'm not tired. There's a good energy in the air. I feel energized, alive, hopeful. Yes, part of it is that

Nick is here in my house, and there's some unspoken understanding that we both know what is going to happen.

But I also feel…peaceful. Inspired. Some people have muses, and I believe in all that stuff. Whatever they are, they are definitely talking to me right now.

"They are cute," Nick agrees, referring to his nieces. "Honestly, Julia and Lincoln are good parents. I think that makes a difference."

"No doubt," I murmur, mixing some colors on my palette. Nick is reading on his e-reader—he won't tell me what it is, only that it's "required reading" from his therapist—and I put on my favorite painting playlist. Led Zeppelin's "The Rain Song" is currently filling the room softly, and a cool breeze from the balcony wafts in. Layne Staley is fast asleep on a towel by the balcony door, deep in his doggy dreams.

"You ever want kids?" Nick surprises me by asking.

"Um. Yeah, I think so? It was never a serious conversation I had with Erik," I tell him, noticing his frown at the mention of my ex-husband.

He has that effect on a lot of people.

Erik, not Nick.

"Why not?"

"He thought I should concentrate on my career. A dancer's life is short, you know. I wasn't going to be able to move like this, wasn't going to have my figure forever." I parrot Erik's words to me nearly verbatim.

"That him talking or you?" Nick asks, his jaw ticking.

"Him, for sure." I set down my brush. "He thought that a child might negatively affect my career—who knows if I'd be able to get my body back?" I smile weakly. "Joke's on him, though. My career was cut short for an entirely different reason."

I can hear the bitterness in my voice, no matter how hard I try to keep it out.

"Sorry," I mutter. "Kind of a negative Nancy over here."

"Nah, it's good." Nick goes back to his book for a few moments, and I turn back to my painting, eyeing it cautiously.

"You're allowed to be angry, you know," he says suddenly from his place on the couch.

I give him a small smile. "That from your book?"

"Not this one," he concedes. "Another one from my required reading." He pauses. "But it's true, I think. You aren't doing today what you thought you would be doing a year ago."

I raise my eyebrows.

"Dancing," Nick clarifies. "I don't know how long you thought you would do that for, and it's not fair that you don't get to do it anymore. So… you are allowed to be angry."

"Thanks," I tell him softly. "But to answer your question… Yes. Yes, I think I would like to have a kid one day."

He nods in acceptance.

"What about you?"

"Me?" Nick seems as surprised by the question as I was, even though he asked me first. "I…I guess so. I mean, I don't think anytime soon. Not that I am married or in a serious relationship or whatever." His eyes widen, and he stammers a bit. "Not that—not that I don't take what we are doing seriously. Which, um, I do. I just meant—"

I put the guy out of his misery. "Nick," I tell him with a laugh. "It's okay. Just a hypothetical question."

He smiles at me, a blush high on his cheekbones. "I mean, yeah. Yes, I think I would like to have a kid. Gretchen…" His voice trails off, and he looks down at his feet, his elbows now draped on his knees, those long legs spread wide.

"You don't have to tell me if you don't want to," I remind him.

"No, I want to. She and I talked about it, I mean, even before we got married. We both knew we might have kids one day. But we never talked about it again, and then I got hurt and…" He huffs out a breath.

"And then she asked for a divorce, and that was the end of that."

I blink at him. Nick had already told me that his relationship with Gretchen was in the danger zone around the time he was injured. But it's still shocking to me that someone wouldn't want to be Nick's forever.

"Well, her loss is my gain," I mutter aloud before thinking about it.

Nick narrows his gaze at me. "What was that, Sunshine?"

"Nothing," I stammer, going back to my paints.

He chuckles but doesn't press the issue further. "Honestly," he continues, "it's for the best. If there's one thing to be grateful for, it's that we *didn't* have any children when we split up. Not that there aren't couples out there doing their best at raising kids after divorce, but….it would have made everything a lot harder."

I hear what Nick isn't voicing. I know without a doubt that he could never, ever have left a child of his. He's lived without his dad for well over half his life. Obviously, the circumstances are different, but I can understand that Nick wouldn't want to leave his kid for any reason, including divorce.

I pick up my brush again and lose myself a bit in my painting. I don't think about Nick. I don't think about Erik or Gretchen. I don't think about what I thought I would be doing a year ago or what I think I might be doing a year from now. I just let myself create.

"Who's Jacob?" Nick asks suddenly. I yelp in surprise, nearly dropping my brush.

I turn to see Nick at the kitchen counter, a glass of water in his hand. He's glaring at something on the counter.

"What—who?" I stammer.

"Jacob." Nick jerks his head toward something on the counter, as if it's a bug he doesn't want to touch. "A phone number."

"Oh. *Oh.* That was one of the movers when I first got here." Which now feels like a hundred years ago. "Tatum was playing matchmaker and insinuated—wrongfully, I might add—that I was interested in dating. Which I am not. I mean, which I wasn't. But I am now. But not with Jacob. Dammit," I mutter at my lousy explanation.

"Matchmaking, huh?" Nick asks, tone gruff as he pierces me with his stare.

"I never even wanted the number. Actually, can you throw it away? I forgot it was there to begin with."

I turn back to my painting, but my flow is broken. My senses tell me that

Nick opens and closes the trash can, presumably to dispose of the phone number. I feel his eyes on me, and I wait, trying to keep my breath even as he approaches me stealthily.

I set my brush down, the mood in the room thick with tension as I feel Nick's warmth behind me.

"That looks good, Sunshine."

I exhale a breath, feeling him press his chest to my back, ever so slightly. I wipe my hands on my ratty T-shirt, keeping my eyes fixed on the painting.

"Thanks," I whisper.

Nick hums a little as he presses his chest farther into me. The heat from his body surrounds me, just like when we were at Julia's earlier, and I arch my back before remembering I am covered in paint.

"Wait! Wait," I tell him in a rush. "I've got paint everywhere."

I move away from him, but he grabs my hips firmly, pressing himself into me so I can feel his hard body. I look down to see his forearms flexed, the muscles and veins rippling as he grabs me.

"I don't care," he mutters, breathing into my ear and then gently placing his lips on the side of my neck. I breathe in his smell, that piney, minty scent I love so much.

"But—"

"I. Don't. Care." He nibbles on my earlobe, and I sigh in response, tilting my head to the side. "I've been watching you work for the better part of an hour, and you know what, Sunshine?"

He doesn't wait for a response.

"Watching you paint turns me on. You jut this perfect hip out to one side—" he grips my hips tighter, and I suck in a breath "—and stick out that perfect ass, thinking about…color or light or texture or I don't fucking know what, I'm not an artist." He takes my earlobe in his mouth again and suckles a bit harder.

He sounds almost angry, pissed off at the fact that apparently I can do this to him.

I love it.

"Watching you hold a damn paintbrush turns me on. It's unfair."

And to demonstrate how much I love it, I push my hips back against his crotch, rolling myself against his hardening cock.

"Tell me again how you're not interested in dating, Summer," Nick demands in a low voice.

"That was…that was then," I breathe out, undulating my body against his. "That was before."

"Before what?" Nick nips at my neck before sucking on the tendons there.

"Before you, Nick. Or before…before I knew you wanted me, you know, like this." And to demonstrate, I reach back, wrapping my arms around his neck and grinding down, hard, on his crotch.

"Before I—*Fuck*," Nick grits out. "Before I wanted you? *Before*?"

"But now…" I continue to grind down on Nick, doing my best impression of a cat in heat. "Now I want to date *you*, Nick. Only you."

Nick's hands are so firmly grasped on to my hips, I might have bruise marks.

And I love that, too.

He spins me around, and I gasp at the heat in his eyes. "There is no *before*," he drills out in a low tone. "You get me, Sunshine? There is you and me and now, and *this*." He jerks his hips forward, his erection hitting me in my stomach. "This is more than *dating*," he spits the word out. "You know that, right?"

My skin feels electrified, my heart pounding wildly as I keep my arms around him. "I know," I tell him honestly, looking into his blazing eyes and moving in to kiss him.

And with this kiss, Nick leaves no room for hesitancy, taking my mouth and licking into me with a single-minded focus. I am panting and breathless when he pulls away to look at me again, his hands cupping my jaw.

"Goddammit, Summer." Nick snarls. "You know I've been doing this slowly. You know I've been doing this *right*."

What would be right is if Nick could fuck me right now, I think.

"I know," I whisper, rolling myself against his erection, which—due to our height difference—is much too far from where I want it. "I appreciate your…perseverance."

I do appreciate his dedication to doing this "right," and I understand where he is coming from.

But like I said—I am hungry.

I bite my lip and gaze up at him through my lashes. "Nick," I whine a little. "I need you." I roll my hips again, his cock now a rod against me. "Please?"

Nick looks pissed off and horny, his hazel eyes lit up, his pupils dilated, that muscle in his jaw ticking.

I lean up a little more and let my lips rest against his, just ever so slightly.

I remember all the rules I had to live by before, in my other life. Nice girls don't act slutty. Nice girls don't ask for sex outright. It's okay for a woman to acquiesce to sex with her husband on his timetable and in line with his demands, but don't be so sexual that you initiate sex on your own! Remember to look sexy, but not so sexy that you look like a whore.

Never mind the fact that my ex-husband made it clear I wasn't worth the effort during the last year of our marriage.

I am done with those rules. I am a sexual creature, I want Nick, and we are two adults who should be able to do adult things.

So I put a voice to the one desire I've been holding on to.

"Please fuck me, Nick. I want you to."

Nick

This woman is going to kill me.

"Say it again," I mutter, angling my head lower and looking right into her eyes.

"I want you to…fuck me, Nick," she whispers, angling her chin up. She's blushing, but her eyes flare. She's brave, my Summer.

My Summer.

My cock gets even harder at her declaration, and I have to hold myself back from throwing her down on the canvas tarp, dirty with paint, and beg her to put me out of my misery.

I turn to look out the big doors in the living room. There're other homes in the distance across the street—there's only a slim chance anyone can see in here, but all the same.

I'd rather not have witnesses to what Summer and I are going to do.

I turn back to her, her hips under my firm grip. "Go to your bedroom and take off your clothes," I tell her in a low voice.

"Okay," she whispers.

"And I mean it, Sunshine," I continue, pulling her close so she can feel how hard I am against her stomach. "Naked. No clothing. None."

"Oh—okay."

I check on Layne Staley after Summer bounds down the hallway. He's dead to the world. I shut and lock the sliding glass door, and he doesn't move a muscle.

I pause walking down the hallway, trying to get my rapid pulse under control. I close my eyes and breathe in and out, slowly, counting down from ten.

I'm…nervous.

I've never been nervous with another girl. Not in a conceited way, just…I never needed to be.

I want Summer to feel good. I have no doubt that, no matter what she does, *I* am going to feel good—unless she's into some weird, depraved shit that I know nothing about.

No wasting time.

I shake off my nerves and move to the bedroom door, opening it to find the lights off, the room filled with ambient lighting from the large window. Summer has one of those large salt lamp things, giving the room a glow.

"Hi." Summer's voice is soft, and I turn my head to her.

She sits on the edge of the bed, her legs hanging off the side. And yes, she did comply with my instructions and is completely naked.

"Good girl," I murmur. Her lips part as I move closer, shucking my shirt over my head and standing in front of her. All I see is miles of her freckled skin, her pert breasts ready for my hands, my mouth.

I kneel on the floor, and she sucks in a breath. This is different from our time on the boat. That was bright and frenzied and furious, fucking—or close to it, anyway—in broad daylight.

This is dark, slow, and soft. We have all the time in the world.

"Can I see you?" I whisper, placing my hands on her knees.

She bites her lip, nodding, and I spread her legs open, wide, her aroma filling my senses, salty and Summer.

I don't even look at her center—I keep eye contact on her face, her eyes big and brown as I lean forward, holding her legs open with my hands. She licks her lips and watches me lick right up her center, slowly and purposefully, her taste warm in my mouth.

We both moan, and that's it.

Summer's head drops back, and I grab her sides to pull her forward so she's nearly hanging her whole body off the side of the bed. And I am all in—licking her open, sucking gently on her lips, running my tongue up and down her glistening slit.

"Oh my god," she whines, her legs shaking, her hips thrusting upward. "Oh my god, *Nick*."

"Remember what we said before," I remind her, lifting my head to meet her eyes. "You tell me."

She nods seriously, her eyes almost comically round, every square inch of her flushed.

"So beautiful," I whisper to her, kissing over her mound with a closed mouth, slowly and softly. "Lie back, sweetheart."

"Ungh, Nick," she whines instead, wiggling her lower half.

"You taste so good," I tell her softly between licks. "I could eat you up, Summer."

I proceed to do just that.

By the time I wrap my mouth around her clit and suckle, her legs are shaking harder and her hands are fisted in my hair, her demands alternating between "please" and "don't fucking stop." She hasn't exactly complied with my demand that she tell me what feels good—and while I'm no mind reader, it's clear to me that she's going to come soon.

So I stop, lifting my head and placing soft kisses on her inner thighs, losing track of how many freckles I've counted in some debauched numbers game.

"*Nick!*" I raise my eyes to Summer and see her hair tousled all over her shoulders, her eyes glassy, her mouth agape.

"Hmmm?" I hum, kissing gently over her slit, avoiding her clit.

"Why. Did. You. Stop?" she pants out.

I give her an honest answer.

"I like playing with you, Sunshine," I tell her in a low voice. At the same time, I take my index finger and slide it into her, feeling her wet, warm walls suck the digit inside.

"Remember, I want to get you ready for me, Sunshine." I breathe out the words, fingering her slowly, sliding in and out, my skin shiny with her arousal. "Fucking delicious," I mutter, bending back down to taste her.

"Nick," she whines, "I'm gonna come. I'm so close—please don't stop, please, oh my god—"

"Fuck yes. Let me taste it, Summer." I bend back down and suckle her clit, softly at first, then suction my lips to her, fingering her at the same time. She cries out a long wail, her voice breaking. I am filled with her taste, her scent, *her*, and I never want to stop making her feel this way.

I let her ride it out, feeling her clench and tighten rapidly around my finger. I lap at her flesh, telling her what a good girl she is, resting my head on her thigh and finger-fucking her through her orgasm.

A few moments later, she has stilled her movements and released her death grip on my hair. She huffs a sob, and I raise my eyebrows to see her covering her eyes.

Fuck. Did I do something wrong? Alarmed, I gently remove my finger and squeeze her thigh. "Summer?"

She raises her head, and her eyes are glistening. "That was…very, very much amazing."

"You're okay, though?"

"Yes! Yes, I am good. I just…um, apparently a really good orgasm makes me emotional?" She shrugs, not at all embarrassed.

My shoulders deflate in relief, and I smile. "You feel good?"

"I feel *great*," she responds, lifting herself up on her elbows to assess me. Whatever she sees makes her blush. "Come here," she whispers.

"You see something you like, Sunshine?" I ask with a smirk.

"I see…me. On you," she blurts out.

"You're damn right," I murmur before taking her mouth in a blistering kiss. Summer is languid and limbless, her arms lazily wrapping around my neck.

I, on the other hand, am harder than I have ever been in my life, and I don't mean just my cock—although I definitely do mean that. From the top of my head to the tips of my toes, I feel like a live wire that's been turned to on, revved up and fully charged.

Energy hums through me as we kiss, and I realize it's me making a humming noise.

All pretense leaves me, and I tell Summer:

"I need you. So bad, Sunshine." My voice breaks.

"Poor Nick," she croons, licking into my mouth. "You're all worked up, hmmm?"

I pull back to see a devilish gleam in her eyes. "You know I am, sweetheart."

"Well, in that case…" She removes her hands and nods to the bedside table. "There're condoms in there."

I raise my eyebrows.

"I just have them, you know, in case you came over and ever wanted to…do stuff."

I chuckle at her sudden shyness in the face of her earlier bravery. "Very forward-thinking of you."

I make quick work of the condom, wrapping myself up and rolling back over to Summer, her body relaxed. She opens her arms again and kisses me full on the mouth.

"No more waiting," she whispers.

I position myself right at her center, rubbing through her slick folds. She gasps and cants her hips up, trying to take me in.

"No wasted time," I mutter in response to her earlier statement.

"Wha-what?" she asks jerkily, and before I can respond, I thrust into her—not all the way, but far enough so that I can feel the warm, wet heat of her clenching around me.

Summer moans and tenses up. "*Oh my god.*"

"Relax, Sunshine," I manage to grit out through clenched teeth. "C'mere."

I bend to kiss her, sealing my lips over hers, and she sighs into my mouth. I retreat and thrust, retreat and thrust, letting my tongue mimic the movements of my hips. With every push, Summer sucks me in farther, strangling my dick like a vise. She relaxes, running her hands down my back before placing them on my ass, squeezing firmly.

"*God.* I dreamed of grabbing this ass," she drawls, trying to pull me down into her farther.

I huff a laugh, but it turns into a groan as I bottom out inside her, my dick crammed so tight I can barely move. She gasps and stills her hands on my backside.

This woman is going to kill me.

And it's perfect.

Summer's warm and tight and breathless and everything I ever wanted that I couldn't have.

This is not just a flash in the pan or a hookup. This is home. Summer anchors me to the moment, a safe port in the foggy landscape.

I have never had this feeling before, ever.

And given that I once was married to someone else…isn't that some shit?

I box up those thoughts and shut them in a file cabinet deep in the recesses of my mind. No one else needs to be in this space right now except for me and Summer.

"You okay, Sunshine?" I grit out, my voice hoarse.

"Yeah. I'm good. It feels good," she whispers, her eyes big and trusting as she looks at me. I move a little and catch a small wince on her face.

"Are you sure?"

"Yeah. It's just. Um." She bites her lip and blinks slowly. "It's just… been a long time. For me. Having sex. So. Maybe go slow? I mean, I have heard it's like riding a bicycle, and I know how sore I get the next day after a long ride—"

I bury my head in her neck and chuckle. "Sunshine." I can't say that I've ever been brought to laughter while physically inside a woman, but it's not the worst feeling.

"It's okay. It's been a long time for me too."

"Yeah, but you're not the one with a…with a—"

"Think carefully about what metaphor you are going to use," I warn her.

"Yeah, kinda realized it was a bad analogy in the middle of it."

I lift my head and look into her eyes. Her cheeks are bright red, her freckled skin flushed. She's so fucking pretty it makes my head spin.

I lean down and kiss her softly on the lips, moving my hips just a little at the same time. She gasps and then sighs against my lips.

"We'll go slow, like you said, okay?" I kiss the side of her mouth, her cheek.

"Okay," she agrees.

Instead of retreating and advancing like I did before, I circle my hips a bit, letting our bodies get used to the feel of each other. I keep kissing Summer anywhere my lips can reach—her lips, her jawline, her neck. I suck at the juncture where her shoulder meets her neck, and she swivels her hips back, her body dancing with mine.

"Nick." She breathes rather than says my name. "You feel so good." She keeps swiveling her hips in a figure eight shape, arching her back up to the ceiling.

It's slow and controlled, the movements of our bodies. The room fills with sounds of the two of us—her wetness against my hardness, her breathy sighs, my grunts, our moans. My senses are filled with her—her fiery hair in my vision, her sweet taste in my mouth, her words in my ears. She tells me how good I feel, how much she wants me.

With every rotation of my hips, I bump her clit, and before long, she is grinding against me, harder and harder, moaning in pleasure when I hit that spot and then in frustration when I pull away.

Summer does sex like she does everything else.

All in, no-holds-barred.

"Nick, keep doing that, keep doing that—ugh!" She whines in frustration again when I rotate my hips away from her clit.

"Keep doing what, sweetheart?" I rotate back, rubbing against her. I stay there for a few more beats and let my body press against hers.

"Just like that. Oh my god, Nick—" Summer spreads her legs and thrusts her hips up into me, her eyes glazed over and her lips puffy from our kisses as she tries to grind up against me.

I swivel my hips away again.

"Goddammit, Nick!" She whines and huffs out a breath.

"You're so fucking hot like this, Summer," I intone into her ear. "All pretty and panting and worked up for me." I move my hips faster, hitting that spot, retreating. Hitting that spot, retreating. "We're going to get you there, okay?"

I am barely holding on from spilling everything I have into this woman, but I mean it—she will get there first if I have to die trying.

Which I might.

Summer's hips meet mine, thrust for thrust. Her legs start to shake and her vision is unfocused, and I feel her clenching on me, so fucking tight I have serious concerns she might snap my dick off.

"Nick, I'm close. I'm gonna go, I think I'm gonna—" At her words, I swivel back and grind against her, hard. She rubs her tight pussy against me and grinds right back, all hot and wet and furious. "Ohhhh," she moans, her mouth opening and her shoulders falling back.

I remember what she needs and place a hand between our warm bodies, pinching one nipple, then the other. Gently at first, then tighter. "That's it,"

I breathe out. "Take it, honey." I squeeze a nipple tight, and Summer snaps up quickly, milking me, coming hard.

"Good girl, sweetheart," I murmur, trying to still my movements. "I feel you coming on my dick, Summer. Ride it out… *So fucking good.*"

She whines louder at the filth spewing from my mouth and keeps rubbing on me, her pussy contracting all around me. She opens her eyes to meet mine, nothing but pleasure and lust in her gaze.

"Oh, *oh*," she moans, thrashing her head to the side.

I finally, fucking *finally*, retreat from her, only to plunge right back into her with abandon. Her eyes widen, almost like she is surprised. "Oh fuck, yes, Nick. That feels so good…"

She's still milking me, but her spasms have slowed. I do my best to prolong her orgasm as long as possible, thrusting into her all the way, bottoming out, before pulling out and repeating the motion.

"Faster, faster," Summer gasps, her eyes pleading up at me. "Fuck me faster, Nick."

Well.

I do what the woman wants and go for broke, fucking her hard, bottoming out on each advance. "Fuu-uu-uck," I moan. "This little pussy takes me so good, Summer."

A sheen of sweat covers me, and I lift myself up higher on my hands to angle my dick just right. I look down to see myself disappear into Summer, my dick covered in her wetness on each retreat. It's indecent and filthy and the best thing I've ever seen.

"Ah, Sunshine," I mutter. "I can see you all over my dick. Fuckin' *perfect*."

I thrust back into her quickly, getting lost in her, in her sounds and sighs and scents. And before long, I feel the telltale sensation at the base of my spine that the end is near.

Honestly, I am impressed I made it this long.

"Sunshine. *Goddamn*, I knew it would be this way," I snarl, my movements jerky as I fuck her firmly. She gives as good as she gets, moving her body up to meet mine on each pass.

"Yes, Nick," she breathes, her face flushed, her eyes big and focused on mine as I pump once, twice, and three times.

It's all over for me, my balls tightening up and my entire body tensing. "Summer," I groan, dragging her name out so it's ten syllables instead of two. My release washes over me, and I throw my head back and moan, filling the condom with everything I have. Summer moans with me, widening her legs to take me, to accept me.

This woman is going to kill me.

But what a way to go.

Chapter Twenty-Four

Summer

YOU REALLY HAVEN'T LIVED UNTIL YOU'VE SEEN NICK ECHEVERRIA on top of you in the throes of an orgasm.

I can barely keep my eyes open, but I don't dare shut my lids to take in what should absolutely be a Renaissance painting above me—the tendons in Nick's neck standing out in relief against his tanned skin, his head thrown back, his mouth in a snarl. He's sweaty—we both are—and the muscles in his arms tighten as he thrusts his hips flush with mine, allowing me to feel him everywhere. He keeps his pelvis tight against me, rocking back and forth, moaning and whispering my name or some amalgamation of it.

I never knew I was into dirty talk until that day with Nick on the boat, and holy hell, Nick's words are better than any erotic romance I could ever read. I'd previously been led to believe that sex was something routine, like cooking dinner or turning off the light when you leave a room. But in my previous relationship, it was Erik's needs that dictated when the act would occur. Men had needs, or so I thought. My needs were secondary in everything, up to and including sex. And if I ever wanted anything other than good old-fashioned vanilla, forget about it. Erik came first. Literally and figuratively.

I'll never settle for routine again.

Nick slows his movements, shuddering and utterly vulnerable above me, even though he could easily crush me with his weight. I run my hands up his arms, feeling his warm skin, before moving back down to place my hands atop his alongside my body.

I breathe out a big exhale, not unlike in yoga when I instruct my students to empty their lungs. My lungs certainly feel empty now—my entire being feels empty, and I want nothing more than to snuggle up to Nick like he's a big blanket.

Consciously or not, Nick follows my lead, exhaling slowly and bracing himself on his forearms. His eyes are bright, his lids heavy. He leans forward to place a soft kiss on my lips, exhaling his breath into me.

"You okay?" I whisper.

He grunts in response, kissing me again, pulling out, and rolling on his side beside me, letting me feel the heat of his body. "I'll be right back," he whispers, and he pads to the bathroom. I hear the faucet turn on, and he's back a moment later.

"I, um, brought you this," he tells me softly, and I turn to see him holding a washcloth. "In case you want, you know…"

There goes my heart again, turning somersaults in my chest. "It's warm water, right?" I ask him teasingly.

He scoffs. "I wouldn't do that to you, Sunshine. Come here," he says gruffly, and I obey, letting him wipe through my center reverently. His eyes flare when I spread my legs a little wider.

"Sunshine," he warns.

"What?" I ask innocently.

"I'm going to need like…thirty minutes. Maybe twenty."

I burst out laughing. "I like your stamina, Mr. Echeverria."

"Only around you, Summer," he murmurs before climbing back into my bed. I turn my body to press my backside into him.

"You can be the big spoon." I wiggle against him and feel his chuckle against my back.

"Anytime, Sunshine."

Chapter Twenty-Five

I F I THOUGHT NICK WAS VIGILANT ABOUT THE "NO SEX" RULE BEFORE, he's now even more focused on giving me *all* the sex.

And I am not mad about it one bit.

The next few weeks are a blur of limbs and breaths, tangled sheets and sweaty sighs. I stretch and breathe in yoga; I get stretched by and share breaths with Nick. I relax my sated, sweaty body in my classes *and* after multiple encounters with Nick. Sometimes this even occurs at the same time, as when Nick interrupted a one-on-one session at his house, bending me over the arm of his couch and drilling into me from behind with a single-minded focus.

"I should have known, Sunshine," he gritted out as his hips snapped into me, damn near moving the couch across the floor. "Should have known once I got a taste of your sweetness, I wasn't going to be able to stop."

Nick's ability to maintain a filthy narrative during sex is nothing short of impressive. I am reduced to cries of "ohmygod" and "Nick" and "don't stop." But again…

I am not mad about it one bit.

~~~~~

A few weeks later, I am surprised to get a telephone call from my sister. Not because we don't talk at least once a month, but because 99% of the time, I need to initiate contact with her. Never via text; always via email to tell her to call me, because she usually won't answer the phone if I call her.
~~~~~

"Hi, Alexis," I greet her, knowing immediately what the first question out of her mouth will be.

"Hello. How are you feeling?"

"I'm feeling…really good." I immediately think of the reason *why* I am so good—Nick, duh—and feel my face getting hot. Good thing she's not here to see me blush.

"You sound well," she responds expectantly. "What has changed?"

"You don't miss anything, do you?"

So much for her not seeing me blush.

"I've been told I am preternaturally perceptive."

She makes it sound like a medical diagnosis. Maybe it is.

But in response to her question…what *has* changed? *Nothing and everything*, I think, then snort at how clichéd that sounds.

Nothing has changed, in that I am living in the town I grew up in, with the same friends and the same crush on the same guy.

Everything has changed, in that I think he might like me a little bit too. And my friends and I are smarter and wiser…hopefully.

"I've been…hanging out with someone a lot," I respond carefully, thinking that "hanging out" sounds like something a college kid with a hacky sack collection would say. "Seeing someone" sounds like something from a soap opera.

"'Hanging out'? Is this someone of the opposite sex?"

I am used to Alexis's clinical word choice by now. "Yes, actually. It's…it's Nick Echeverria." There's no point in asking if Alexis remembers him—of course she does; they were in the same grade growing up, and I lived with his family after our parents died.

And anyway, she remembers everything and everyone with that preternatural perception.

"Oh." Alexis pauses, and I know she's thinking about what to say next in the fewest number of words as possible, ever economical in everything, even her word selection.

"You always liked him."

Again, stating the obvious.

"Is it serious?"

"We haven't really…talked about that yet," I demur.

"He's divorced too, right?"

"He is," I confirm.

"Well, I suppose it is a healthy thing to want some sort of physical connection with someone before you leave, especially someone whom you've known for a long time and are comfortable with."

Again, stating the obvious, with the exception of one phrase.

"Before I leave?"

"Before you leave Estero Bay." There's another pause on the line. "You aren't going to be there forever." It's a statement, not a question.

"I haven't really thought about it in a lot of detail."

"I see."

I move from my spot on the couch to the kitchen, getting a tea bag out of the cupboard and plugging in the electric kettle.

"Have you even thought about what you are going to do?"

"Do…when?"

"With your *life*, Summer." For someone who operates on neutral 100% of the time, Alexis sounds unusually emphatic in her response. "I mean, you can't just teach yoga in that sleepy little town for the rest of your life."

I almost push back with a "why not." But the problem is…she is right.

I *don't* want to teach yoga in Estero Bay for the rest of my life. Maybe one day. But not right now, anyway.

"What do you want to do?" Alexis asks me in a more placid tone.

"I want to dance." I don't hesitate in my response.

"You can't do that in Estero Bay," Alexis points out rationally.

"I can't do that anywhere, Alexis," I tell her dryly. "But even if I can't dance like I used to, I want to…I want to create. I want to be a part of something creative, something with other artists who feel the same way."

"You always have been very right-brained that way."

"If you say so." I blow on my tea before taking a sip. "I've been talking with some of my contacts in the dance world about opportunities.

Choreography, consulting, that sort of thing." All of which are quite obviously outside of Estero Bay.

"And what does Nick Echeverria think about this?"

"About…what?"

"About your future. *Your* future, Summer. Do you see a place for him in it?"

I would marry Nick and bear his tanned, tiny children tomorrow if he wanted to.

I don't say that, though.

"We haven't really talked about the future in great detail." Or *any* detail, but Alexis doesn't need to know that.

"You should have that conversation," Alexis says in her tone that reveals not only does she know everything, but she *knows* she knows everything.

"I know, I know," I mutter, flopping back on the couch.

"I am sure he's very handsome and fun"—I have to laugh at that, because "fun" is not a word I would use to describe Nick—"but you really don't want to be making any more life decisions based on another man."

I suck in a breath. I know Alexis means well. At least, she doesn't go for the jugular on purpose.

But her manner of cutting through all amounts of bullshit to get to the real issue can be disarming.

She'd be a horrible therapist.

Or maybe a great one, if you are into that sort of thing.

"Nick is *nothing* like Erik," I tell her firmly.

"I don't doubt it. I apologize if I gave you that impression. Nick's family was always…very good to us." Alexis softens her tone before moving on. "But whatever he is like or unlike is irrelevant. This is your opportunity to do what you want, without having to think about anyone else."

I sip my tea and ponder her words. She doesn't mean them in a selfish way, although this is perhaps the only time in my life I have the ability to be utterly selfish. I have no partner, no children, no job, no long-term commitments. I can rent out my home. The yoga studio can and has thrived without me.

"I called to see how you are doing, and it sounds like you are doing good," Alexis says in a conclusory fashion. "Talk to Nick. Or don't talk to him. I just want to ensure you are making the right decisions for you. For Summer."

"I'm doing my best," I tell her.

"Good. Good-bye." Alexis hangs up without another word.

Again, I know it's not her intention to be cruel or abrupt or whatever. She does things in a linear fashion. In her mind, she called to check up on me. To see how I am doing. Now that she knows I am doing well, what more is there to say?

What more is there to say?

How about:

The way I feel about Nick is different from how I ever felt about Erik.

I think I could let myself need him.

That scares me a bit, but I've never been one to run away from something that scares me. More than anything, it confirms what I've suspected since I saw him in the restaurant that first night.

I think I could love him.

If I don't already.

Chapter Twenty-Six

"I GOT A CALL FROM AN ARTISTIC DIRECTOR I MET IN NEW YORK." Summer and I walk on the beach, the fog curling around the Rock and the jetty in the distance. Summer's bundled up in another one of my old hoodies, the sight of it doing something to my chest. Some loose pieces of hair curl around her face, framing her freckled skin. Her hand is in mine, and I grip her firmly, not wanting to lose the feeling of her touch for even a moment.

I've been a selfish bastard these past few weeks, monopolizing every moment of her time that I can. Seeing her in my sweatshirt is the first time I've seen her fully clothed in a while.

And I am not the least bit sorry about it.

I squeeze her hand lightly and try to focus on her words.

"Artistic director? Sounds fancy."

She gives me a half smile. "He is kind of fancy, actually. He wanted to know if I had—if I *have*—any interest in doing choreography, now that, you know." She gestures to her leg, and I nod, because yes, I do know.

"And…do you?"

"I don't know?" She responds to my question with a question. "I love dancing, obviously. I've always loved dancing. I guess I never really thought about whether I would be interested in putting together my own routines. That's kind of forbidden when you are in a company. It's strictly a do-as-you-are-told kind of gig."

"I think you'd be great at it," I tell her gruffly.

"Really?" She looks at me slyly from the side. "You've had a chance to see my work, huh?"

"No, it's just that… I mean, look at you." I gesture toward her, all bundled up in her yellow beanie, my hoodie, and purple leggings. "You're…colorful." She narrows her gaze a bit, but I continue undeterred. "You just… you have a thing about you. A presence. You dance, you paint, you *are* colorful, and don't give me that look again." She rolls her eyes, but there's no mirth there.

"I'm probably the least qualified to tell you this, but I can just tell—and I bet others can too—that you are an artist. You are meant to create. And whether that's with painting or dancing or telling other people what, like, moves to do—"

"Which is choreography," she informs me.

"—or choreography, then you'll be good at it. I *know* you'll be good at it." I stop and take a breath. I'm not really sure if I got the point across that I most wanted to make, but I'm trying.

"That's sweet of you to say," Summer responds, bending down to pick up a small, smooth stone and attempting to skip it across the flat water.

"I miss that feeling," she continues. "That adrenaline rush I would get before a performance. It's such a high, you know?" She picks up another stone. "Everything else just kind of…fades away. I wonder if I'll have that again."

Now *this* is something I can relate to. "I know that feeling." I pause as she tries skipping another stone. "Here," I bend to pick up a flat rock. "Look." I throw the stone from my side down by my hip. "You gotta snap your wrist a bit." The stone skips three times before sinking.

"They teach you that in the NFL?" she smirks.

I smile back at her. "My grandfather." I clear my throat. "Anyway…I do know the feeling. The rush. I hadn't had it since I played a game. Uh, not until…not until we got together." I mutter the last part. Summer's smile is blinding as she links her arm through mine.

"'Got together'?" she asks. "Is that what the kids are calling it these days?"

"Hell if I know." I shrug.

"Well, I should clarify. I haven't had that feeling *professionally*," she intones. "But perhaps I've felt something similar…you know, personally."

"Personally, huh?" I turn to face her, the water lapping behind her. I spread my legs wide so that we are of a more equal height. "Sounds boring." I lean forward to whisper into her ear, her damp hair tickling my face. "How about…sexually?"

"Mr. Echeverria," she responds mockingly. "Kind of a personal question, don't you think?"

She leans her head to the side, and I take advantage, kissing her neck up to her earlobe. "It is, but…I still want to know." I kiss closer to her ear before taking the lobe in my mouth and suckling slightly. "You get that feeling when I do this?"

She sucks in a breath. "I'm…I'm getting there," she breathes out.

"How about…" I move to kiss her jawline, pulling her a little closer to me. Her slight curves press against me, soft and warm through her clothing. "When I do this? You get that feeling?"

"I'm feeling something, all right," she tells me, pulling me just as tightly against her so that our centers are pressed together.

"Bad girl," I murmur, pulling her in so that she can feel my hardening cock right up against her stomach. I feel the heat of her through her cotton pants.

"How about if I do this?" I widen my stance, letting the ridge of my cock rub just enough against her core, giving her a little friction. Of course, it's not enough, both of us out here in the fog, fully clothed. Her eyes glaze over just a bit, and her lips part slightly.

"That give you that feeling, honey?" I murmur, before bringing my mouth to hers, kissing her gently, sampling the inside of her mouth with my tongue ever so slightly before pulling away.

She gazes at me through half-open lids, her cheeks rosy. "Yeah…I'm beginning to see what you mean. Although," she continues, her tongue darting out to lick her lips slightly, and damn if that doesn't make my cock grow another inch. "Dancing never made me quite this horny."

I laugh at this, and she smiles ruefully. "Poor Summer," I murmur, drawing her toward me again, rubbing against her center. "You need me to do something about it?"

"Yes," she whispers, her eyes darting to mine pleadingly.

"Remember," I tell her firmly, cradling her face in my hands, "I'll always give you what you need."

I punctuate this promise with a stronger drive of my hips, and Summer's lips part slightly again. "I need, Nick," she whispers, gripping my arms tightly as I rub against her.

Maybe I am putting off any discussions about whatever comes next for Summer because I am not sure if they are going to include me. Maybe I am going to use whatever tool I have at my disposal to delay that conversation, and right now, that tool happens to be something I know that only I can give her.

Maybe I am only postponing the inevitable.

Maybe, maybe.

"I *need*," Summer tells me insistently.

It ends up being a short beach walk.

Chapter Twenty-Seven

"No way this doesn't have any dairy in it." Brock takes his third bite of cupcake, polishing the whole thing off.

"I swear!" I take a smaller bite of my own carrot cake cupcake. "It's coconut oil and some sort of nut milk. Right, Tatum?"

"I don't know, and I don't give a dusty fuck. This thing is delicious." Tatum has also demolished her cupcake and is now eyeing a croissant.

Brock came into town to have another day on the boat with Nick and his grandfather, and we all ended up here at Lucy's.

"Lucy." Brock puts his hand over his heart as she approaches us, dressed, as usual, in black, her Doc Martens topped off with ripped fishnets. "This is the best thing I've ever eaten. I need more."

"We're out of those. I think I have some of those Reese's bars you like"—she nods to Nick—"and vanilla and fig scones. They were the special today."

"I'll take them both," Tatum says. When Nick gives her a weird look, she shrugs. "What? I'm riding the crimson wave and need sugar, carbs, the whole enchilada."

Nick blushes and it's adorable. "I'd love a Reese's bar," he tells Lucy.

"Enchiladas sound good too," I muse, and Tatum nods in agreement.

"Anything off-menu? Made for a, I don't know, six-foot-seven block of muscle?" Brock winks at Lucy, and it's her turn to roll her eyes at him.

"I don't see anyone here with that description," she tells him with an arched eyebrow.

"Well, maybe not *all* muscle," Brock concedes, patting his round stomach. "I'm retired now. It's time to eat sugar and all the other good things I've been without for fifteen freaking years."

"I've got a few things in the back," Lucy tells him. "What do you want? I've been up since three, and I am exhausted."

"Baker's hours, huh?"

Lucy's face reflects surprise briefly before returning to her trademark glare. "That's right."

"Not just a pretty face, hmm?" Brock smiles at her, full of dimples and confidence. "My mom is a great baker, used to work part time at a bakery outside Milwaukee when we were—"

"I don't care," Lucy interrupts in a singsong voice.

"You okay?" Tatum asks her.

"I'm fine. Just…" Lucy's voice trails off when she sees us all looking at her expectantly. "Never mind. I just need sleep." But she gives Tatum a quick look that says they'll talk later.

"Sugar, I'll put you to bed, no problem."

I wonder if Brock knows he's in danger of losing a limb.

"Is this the part where you tell me we wouldn't be doing much sleeping?"

Brock looks mock-offended. "I'll have you know, I am a gentleman. And a very good cuddler."

Lucy shudders. "Cuddling. Ew. You know what, I am just going to bring you all out a bit of everything. Stay put."

She turns on her heel and walks back to the kitchen, the silver door swinging back and forth behind her.

Brock whistles after her. "What a woman. Think I'm gonna send her flowers."

Now it's my turn to "ew." "Ew," I exclaim. Tatum, Brock, and Nick all look at me.

"You don't like flowers?" Brock asks.

"I mean, I like the idea of them. They are nice to look at." I pause. "It's just… I don't know, how much do a dozen red roses cost? Thirty dollars? Forty?"

"I honestly have no idea," Tatum responds.

"At least sixty dollars for a decent bouquet. More, depending on what else you are including and where they are being delivered, stuff like that. Inflation is no joke." Brock rattles off the information readily.

"Your mom also a part-time florist?" Nick asks.

"Nah. But I, ah, have my assistant send flowers to women…that I know. Sometimes."

"Ah, you mean like after they stay the night with you!" Tatum exclaims. "Be still my heart, Brock."

He gives a half smile. "What can I say? All happy memories here."

"*Anyway*. I just never got that. The flowers are nice for a couple days and then they start to stink and then they die." I shrug. "Think of how much money people—and, yes, maybe dudes—spend on flowers each year. What if all that money went somewhere else, like…like Planned Parenthood or the Surfrider Foundation or another organization?"

"Ooohhh, I like that," Tatum says.

Brock is just looking at me, mouth agape.

"Sorry that I am not sorry," I tell him. "Is that too angry feminist of me?"

I feel Nick's chuckle where he is pressed to my side. "Ignore him. It's a noble idea. And I don't know where the flowers thing started, but for sure there are other, more useful…uses for sixty dollars."

"Thank you," I murmur, snuggling into Nick's side.

I don't mention that Erik used flowers to express *everything*—his supposedly undying love for me, his pride in my accomplishments, but especially his remorse—after every fight, every argument that left me crying, every comment that left me unsure and uncertain.

And even if I didn't associate flowers with Erik, the next thing they remind me of is my time in the hospital.

Also not a time I recall with a great deal of fondness.

If I never smell another bouquet again, it will be too soon.

"So, you're going home today, right?" Tatum changes the subject, directing her question to Brock. "Do you have plans when you get back?"

"Nothing crazy. I'm still moving in to the new place, so I need to figure out *what* I need, I guess. I've got a call with Mando too," he adds to Nick.

I feel Nick stiffen beside me a bit.

"Mando, he's your agent too?" Tatum asks, sounding surprised.

"He is." Brock pauses carefully. "Says he has some, uh, new business opportunities for me."

"It's no thing to me," Nick says in a low voice.

"You say that, but I still don't like how it ended between you guys," Brock responds. "Which, by the way, I've told him on several occasions," he adds with a pointed look.

Nick shrugs. "It's really no big deal. And…he was a good agent. I'm sure he still is."

Tatum scoffs. "He was good right up until he wanted to play you into a wheelchair," she says sarcastically.

I put two and two together, figuring that Mando is the agent Nick told me about previously. In addition to Gretchen pressuring Nick to return to playing, Mando apparently wanted him to as well.

Hence Tatum's disapproval.

Brock waves a hand dismissively. "He knows he fucked up."

"And to be fair, I am not the most ideal client in retirement." Brock raises his eyebrows, and Nick smiles. "Dude. Come on. I don't do commercials, and can you imagine me on one of the roundtable sports shows?"

"It would be a…quieter affair than normal," Brock offers diplomatically. I laugh because he's right. Nick would be entirely out of place on one of those Sunday NFL pregame shows, full of loud suits and fake jockeying and even louder personalities.

"This guy, however," Nick continues, gesturing toward Brock, "has a face for TV."

Brock smiles again. "Aw, shucks, Nicky. You get me. And you're so right."

"You're so modest," I laugh at Brock.

"An overrated virtue, in my humble opinion," he responds before looking toward the counter, where Lucy is returning with a tray full of goodies. "Oh, hell yes."

"All right, you savages." Lucy unloads blondies, brownies, cookies, scones, and other assorted carb-laden goodies from her tray. "Move over,

I'm joining you." Tatum scoots closer to Brock, and Lucy squeezes onto the booth bench.

"This is amazing," I tell her, taking a bite of the Reese's bar that Nick seems to love so much.

"Not bad, huh?" Lucy demurs.

"Don't be so modest. You know you're a beast in the kitchen," Tatum admonishes before helping herself to what looks like a snickerdoodle.

"A beast, huh?" Brock raises his eyebrows in mischief.

"Dude," both Tatum and Lucy say in unison before laughing at each other. "Jinx," Tatum adds.

"We were just talking about how modesty is the most overrated of virtues," Brock says. "And I've got to agree with Tatum—there's no need to be modest. You've got this prime spot for your bakery, it's always crowded, so you're obviously doing well. Your work—" he pauses to take a bite of a bear claw "—speaks for itself." He lazily wipes away at the crumbs that fall out of his mouth.

"Dude." This time, it's Nick admonishing Brock. "Don't be such a slob."

Brock scoffs. "Cleanliness might be another overrated virtue."

I look to Tatum, correctly predicting that this will get a rise out of her. "Shut your mouth, Donovan," she growls.

"*Anyway*," Nick says in a loud—well, loud for him—voice. "I *am* happy for whatever Mando brings your way. Seriously."

"I appreciate that, bro."

"Anytime, bro."

"Do you want to do one of those shows? The whole Sunday game breakdown thing, I mean?" I ask Brock. I have to agree with Nick; Brock would be really good at that kind of thing. He's animated, he's likable, he's easy on the eyes.

"I don't know. I mean, it would have to be the right fit. I don't want to do it, like, just because it's the expected next step—retire, cohost a football show, film a pharmaceutical commercial," he says, ticking things off his fingers—now covered in powdered sugar—as he speaks.

I nod and take a sip of my tea.

"What about you, Summer?" Brock asks me.

"Me?" I ask in surprise.

"Yeah. You're, like, retired too, right? Is there a roundtable show for ballet?"

I smile at the thought. "Not exactly." I hold my tea mug with both hands, feeling its warmth. "I've been talking to some people."

"Ohhhhh, that's vague and mysterious," Tatum exclaims. "Who are these people?"

"Choreographers, mostly, that I know. I never thought about it while dancing," I go on, echoing what I told Nick earlier, "but there's definitely been some interest from other ballet companies and artistic types." I pause. "I don't even know if I'd be good at that sort of thing."

"Oh please. Summer, you've been making up dances since we were little," Tatum says, Lucy nodding in agreement.

"Doesn't everyone do that?"

Lucy snorts. "I can honestly say, with one hundred percent certainty, that I was never making up dances to anything, ever, at any point in my life."

"Except maybe dancing on the graves of your enemies?" Nick muses. I'm still leaning against him, and I feel the vibration of his deep voice as he speaks.

"Except that," she agrees.

"All I'm saying is, I think it'd be a great thing for you," Tatum says. "I'm guessing this would take you away from here, though, huh?"

"Yeah, definitely. One company is in Chicago, another in Austin."

I sense Nick tensing up next to me at this comment.

"Chicago? Austin?" he asks gruffly.

I turn my head toward his and see a blank expression on his face.

"Well, yes," I respond slowly. "I probably don't have to tell you that there isn't a huge market for choreography of any kind here. I mean, the high school doesn't even have a dance team."

"You don't want to help Amber Bracamonte coach the cheer squad?" Lucy asks sarcastically.

I grimace. "Not even a little bit."

"I just didn't realize…" Nick's voice trails off softly. "I mean, of course. Of course those opportunities are going to be away. Elsewhere. Geographically. Not here."

I cock my head and eye him. "Well, yes, but I haven't even seriously entertained any offers yet."

"But you should. I mean, you don't want to miss out on a good one, right? A good opportunity, I mean?" His words are clipped.

"Noooo," I drawl carefully. "But if and when the right one comes along, I will have to think about it. So far, I haven't had any serious discussions with anyone."

"But you will, though, right? Have those discussions. About these opportunities. That are away." Nick is even more tense beside me, one arm extended along the top of the booth behind us, his other hand gripping the lip of the table.

"I suppose so. But anyway, I'm not thinking about that now, okay?"

And I *really* don't want to be having this conversation at a table surrounded by our friends, but I keep that to myself for now.

"I just don't want you to miss out on anything." Nick blurts it out almost in a panic, his eyes darting back and forth between mine, seemingly encouraging me to understand something he's not voicing.

I turn away from Nick to see Tatum, Brock, and Lucy all eyeing us like we're a pair of monkeys at the zoo. Tatum looks mystified, Brock looks concerned, and Lucy looks…well, like she always does, which is mildly pissed off.

"Anyway." I cut through the awkward silence.

"Yeah," Tatum echoes.

We all sit like this for a moment, taking in the remains of the various baked goods Lucy provided.

Brock clears his throat. "I should be getting out. You want to walk back to the house with me, Nicky? Got to get my suitcase."

"What?" Nick turns to Brock. "Yeah. I mean, yeah, let's go." He gives me a quick, dry kiss on the cheek. "I'll, um, see you later."

And then he darts up and walks toward the exit without even waiting for Brock.

❧❧❧❧❧

Nick

"So, what the fuck."

Brock directs this statement to me. I'm currently on my balcony, nursing a beer that I don't want, staring out at the Rock as if it holds the answers to questions I don't know how to ask.

"What the fuck, indeed." There's really no point in beating around the bush with Brock; he's referring to the incident with Summer at the bakery. I know it, he knows it, the barking otters in the distance know it.

"What are you doing, man?" Brock ambles out onto the balcony with a sparkling water—he's going to be leaving for a three-plus-hour drive down to Malibu, no beer for him—and stands next to me at the railing, leaning against it on his side.

"I…I don't know." I avoid his gaze and swirl the beer in my bottle.

Brock scoffs. "That much is obvious." He pauses, and I can feel his eyes studying me. "You got a nice place here, Nicky."

It's not what I expect him to say. I expect a reaming for the abrupt way I left things earlier. I meet his eyes and reply cautiously. "Uh, thanks."

"You have this nice house. Nice little beach town, even if the nightlife leaves something to be desired." My lips turn up slightly at this. "Nice family. Your mom's great, your pops is hilarious, your nieces are cute. Your little sister is slightly insane, but she has hot friends, so I let that slide."

I frown then, before realizing he's including Lucy as one of Tatum's "hot friends." "Dude. It's never going to happen with Lucy."

"Ah, ye of little faith." Brock turns to lean over the balcony, mimicking my stance. "Fucking fog," he mutters, shivering. "Anyway, this isn't about the tiny, dark-haired, angry baker in combat boots." He looks at me again in a very condescending way.

It's annoying.

"This is about you and your inability to take what you want."

Super annoying. "I don't think—"

"I get why, I do," Brock continues in his superior tone of voice as if I am not even there. "I don't know what the hell happened—or didn't happen—with you and Summer when you were a puny young guy with a rocket arm."

He's not wrong.

"But whatever was holding you back then, Nicky, isn't a variable now."

I digest that for a minute.

Why didn't I make a move on Summer when were in New York, when she told me she was going to marry Erik?

"I thought…we were on different paths." I speak slowly and purposefully. "I was going to be drafted. Summer was going to dance. I thought it was for the best. We were so young, and I didn't think a long-distance thing would have been in our best interests."

"Okay. Sure, I'll buy that." Brock pauses. "But you were also scared." And then he drops the hammer. "Just like you're scared now."

It's my turn to scoff. "I'm not scared."

Brock raises his eyebrows. "Oh yeah? Then what the fuck was all that about 'don't miss any opportunities, don't hesitate to take a job somewhere else, here, I can help you pack' bullshit?"

"I didn't offer to help her pack, you numbnuts," I mutter.

"Don't be so fucking literal."

We both stand in silence, taking in the setting sun, the fog increasing around the Rock, the gulls calling over the water.

"Last time I was here, you were just a mopey guy with a cute dog."

"I am not mopey," I mutter.

"Now," Brock continues, "you are a slightly less mopey guy with a cute dog and a beautiful sweetheart of a woman." He turns away from me, taking a deep breath of the salty air. "You got a nice place here, Nicky," he tells me again.

I don't respond.

"Let's say Summer gets a job in Austin or Toronto or Australia," Brock proposes. "A good job, a great job, her dream job. What would you say?"

My response is immediate. "I would tell her to take it, obviously."

"And she just…sails off into the sunset? Dances off into the wings?"

"I mean, yeah, I guess," I respond, although thinking about that—about her leaving—causes a tightening sensation in my chest.

"Okay, great, and then she meets some jacked, tanned Kiwi surfer guy—"

"I thought we were in Australia," I frown.

"Just go with it, bro. Anyway, Summer meets the Kiwi dude, and he's into her, because he's not blind, he's not stupid, and he's not *scared*—" Brock stares pointedly at me "—and you are just, what? Okay with this?"

No. No, I am not fucking okay with Summer and the Kiwi or Aussie or any other dude from anywhere else, but what can I do?

"I just—"

"You just let her go off with Kiwi guy and keep moping around this foggy town forever?"

"I am not *moping*," I snap.

"Nicky." Brock rolls his eyes. "You loom out here like a bear, hoodie up, glaring at that stupid fucking rock like it insulted your mother. I can smell the emo on you now. We just need some Nine Inch Nails, and you will be the poster child for moping."

I glare at him. "Dude. *The Downward Spiral* got me through some shit."

"I don't doubt it, but don't change the subject. You are the mayor of Mope City."

I shrug my hoodie off my head in defiance and lift my chin up at Brock.

"What's to say you couldn't go with her?"

"With Summer?" I ask.

"No, with Trent Reznor on tour. Yes, dude, with Summer." Brock lays it all out. "You have nothing going on here—no offense, my dude—and you've made it clear your post-football career isn't going to be with you in a role on ESPN."

I shudder at the thought.

"So, it makes sense. You love Summer. Summer loves you—"

"*What?*" I croak.

"She's going to get job offers—you know she is—" Brock again continues as if I am not adding my own commentary to this inane plan "—you go with her, be in love, keep the Kiwi guy away from her, eventually make little emo dancing ginger babies, everyone wins." Brock spreads his hands in a flourish, pleased with himself.

"We are not in love," is all I can think of to say.

Brock gives me a side-eye. "Sure, buddy," he says sarcastically.

"We're not! We haven't even, like, talked about that stuff." I rub my hand over the back of my neck. "We're both fresh out of long-term relationships, dude! We're not ready for that kind of commitment—"

"She tell you that?" Brock asks pointedly.

"And it wouldn't be fair to her!" I exclaim.

Brock pauses at this last statement. "What wouldn't be fair exactly?" he asks calmly.

"You know, I just—I just—I don't know." My thoughts are coming fast, and I can't put them into words. I take a breath.

"The way I see it," Brock says a moment later, "is that nothing is more fair than for us to be with someone who wants us for who we are. In the League, man, you just never know what people are really after. Not only the girls, but everyone around you." Brock shrugs. "I *know* you know what I'm talking about. People just…want a piece."

I nod, because he's not wrong about that.

"Seriously." Brock sucks in a breath. "I mean, do you know how rare it is for you to not only have a second chance with this girl, but that she actually wants you for you? She knew you then, she knows you now, she wants you. She likes you. She's *nice*, man, to you and for you.

"How many of those people," he continues, "were actually *nice* to you? Like, really nice, not because they wanted to be seen with you or wanted access to this person or that endorsement or that commercial?"

"Not many."

"Not *any*," Brock responds emphatically. "And don't give me that bullshit about what's fair. I don't know any details about her marriage, man. Or the whole story about yours either, for that matter—and I don't need to know. Whatever preconceived bullshit notion you have about not being good enough for her is… Well, it's bullshit."

"That your professional opinion?" I snort.

"What would be *fair*," Brock continues, again ignoring me, "would be for Summer to be with someone who wants her, who is nice to her and for her, after being with an unrepentant jackass for so long."

"And you think I can be that guy." It's a statement, not a question.

"My dude, I think you *are* that guy. And I think you do too."

Chapter Twenty-Eight

Summer

"SO, THAT WAS WEIRD."

Lucy makes the assessment as we walk down Main Street after our, yes, weird time at the bakery with Brock and Nick. We've hopped into the art gallery briefly to speak with Letty. Tatum's currently perusing the bookstore while Lucy and I sit on a bench outside, splitting our time between watching a riotous pub crawl at the dive bar across the street and basking in the late-afternoon sun.

We have nowhere to be, really, and no commitments. This town really does move slower than other places, and afternoons like these are one of the reasons I love it so much.

But you can't meander down Main Street forever…

I try to push the nagging feeling outside of my mind as soon as it appears.

Shut up, I'm enjoying myself.

Part of me knows she's right, though, this shadow self of mine. I really can't be strolling down Main Street forever, making idle chitchat and eating cinnamon rolls.

I came back to Estero Bay to recover and lick my wounds. But I suppose I can't do that forever either.

"With Nick at the bakery?" I ask, responding to Lucy's statement.

"Duh."

"Yeah…it was," I respond slowly, watching the pub crawl group stumble down the sidewalk, singing an off-key rendition of "Luci" by Recess Radio.

"Hey, they are singing about you," I offer to Lucy in a horrible attempt to change the subject.

"You know it. And don't try to change the subject," she tells me. "Anyway. I guess you took my advice, huh?"

"What's that?"

"You hopped on that dick."

An older woman in a flowery cardigan and a peacock haircut is walking by and gasps at Lucy's comment. Lucy glares at her.

I feel a blush crawling up my cheeks. "I definitely did."

"Good for you! Listen," Lucy continues abruptly, "the Echeverrias are a moody lot. I know Nick is really putting on this tortured, lonely, no-one-will-love-me angle, and it's working for him." Lucy takes a sip of her boba tea. "But honestly, he wants to be happy, just like everyone else on this crazy rock we're living on."

"And you think I'm the one to make him happy?"

"I mean, I think you'll help. Only Nick can make himself happy."

"You sound like Yoda. Or Oprah."

"I'll take both of those."

I sigh, scuffing my feet on the sidewalk, looking at the chipped purple paint on my toes. "I definitely want Nick to be happy. And I want to be happy. I mean, obviously. It's just that… I don't know, we haven't really talked about 'oh, where is this going,' you know?" I shrug. "I am enjoying our time together."

"I sure as shit bet you are," Lucy drawls. "You have the glow of a well-fucked woman."

I burst out laughing.

She's not wrong.

"Just…force him to be abrupt. He's been in this shell for so long, so convinced he doesn't deserve anything good. Why, I don't know." Lucy shakes her drink and draws on the straw again. "It's kind of like a self-fulfilling prophecy, you know? Like he's been convinced that he doesn't deserve the same kind of happy life others have, so if any one little thing pops up that reinforces that, he runs with it."

"You're very smart," I murmur.

"Who is? Lucy?" Tatum walks quickly over to us, her Stanford Law book bag heavier after her time in the bookstore. "She's all right. Anyway. Guess who I just saw?"

"Oprah?" Lucy guesses.

Tatum scoffs. "This isn't exactly Montecito." She sits down next to us and wraps her long brown hair in a thick coil over her shoulder. "Penny Holder." Tatum references another girl we went to high school with.

"Isn't she married again?" Lucy muses.

"Actually, it sounds like she met husband number three. Which means she needs to divorce husband number two. I referred her to Eddie. At the rate she is going through husbands, she's going to need a good lawyer," Tatum says, referring to Eddie Reyes, her law partner.

"Remember her brother? Marty?" Lucy asks. "Whatever happened to that guy?"

"Marty with the Party!" Tatum exclaims. "I don't know, man. I assume nothing good. You don't do that much cocaine in life and go on to an illustrious future."

Lucy snorts. "True. Remember that time he got us into the Bay Tequila Fest?"

Tatum shudders. "God, don't remind me. I was hungover for a week."

I watch Tatum and Lucy's exchange with humor and maybe a little FOMO. I wasn't here for Marty with the Party or Tequila Fest or cocaine or any of those things. I was married to Erik, in New York, working on being the perfect wife.

Sometimes I let myself wonder *what if*? What if I didn't marry Erik? What would I be doing? Would I still be on the East Coast in a Nick-less state? Would I have come home occasionally and gone out with Lucy and Tatum and gotten mani-pedis and gone wine tasting on the weekends and nursed hangovers with burritos?

Regret is nothing more than self-flagellation, which is why I usually don't choose to let my mind wander to the "what-ifs." But they are there, in the back of my mind, popping up occasionally like an unwanted houseguest.

"Anyway." Tatum's voice brings me out of my thoughts. "I can't imagine getting married three times before turning thirty. Oh well, we all make choices."

Tatum rummages through her purse distractedly, when two women our age exit the bookstore. One is slightly familiar, a short, curvy type with a long trench cardigan, her white-blond hair atop her head in a messy bun. I recognize her as the aforementioned Penny Holder.

I don't recognize the other woman, a brunette dressed head to toe in heather-green athleisure, her feet clad in spotless white athletic shoes with gold accents. She has gigantic diamond studs in her ears and a fierce glare on her face.

A fierce glare directed right at Tatum, who is still rummaging through her book bag.

"Hey, Penny," Lucy offers to the first woman. "How's it going?"

Tatum raises her head, her face paling slightly when she sees the two women.

"Hi, Lucy. It was nice to see you, Tatum," Penny says, her tone a forced kind of cheery. She doesn't pause in her steps, as if she can't wait to get away from us.

But Lucy won't let her off the hook so easily. "You remember Summer Mahoney?" She gestures to me on her right, and I offer an awkward wave.

"Hi," I tell her dumbly, wondering why Penny's friend has made it her life's mission to destroy Tatum with her gaze alone.

"Wow, hi," Penny says, pausing slightly. "Um, been a long time."

"Yup. How've you been?" I ask her.

"Good. You?"

"Good."

Succinct platitudes out of the way, Penny readjusts her purse strap on her shoulder and makes a move to leave.

"Hi, I'm Lucy," my friend in the middle says to Diamond Earrings, who shifts her glare from Tatum to Lucy.

"I'm Beth. And we're late," she announces, offering a last sneer to Tatum—I half expect her to spit at Tatum's feet before departing—and rushing down the sidewalk.

"Nice to see you, Summer. And Tatum. Lucy," Penny mumbles with a forced smile and follows her friend down the road.

All three of us are silent at their departure, turning to watch them hustle away.

"So…what was that about, again?" I ask, confused. "Who is Beth? And Tatum, why did you kill her dog?"

Lucy laughs, and Tatum gives me a look. "That's the only explanation I can come up with as to why she was shooting daggers at you," I explain.

Tatum's shoulders deflate a bit, and she looks toward the ocean in the distance. A cheer rises out of the bar across the street, and a dog barks at a flock of birds on the greenbelt nearby.

Tatum lets out an exhale. "So, remember that guy I told you I was dating?"

I nod. "The disappointing one," I recall.

Lucy snorts at that. "Aren't they all?"

Tatum smiles grimly. "Beth is friends with, um, with his wife."

I raise my eyebrows in shock. "What?! Disappointing guy is married? Did you—did you know? Who is he? How did you—" I am too shocked to continue. Tatum would never knowingly date a married man.

"His name is Trevor," Tatum tells me slowly, and Lucy nearly growls at the name, not unlike her reaction whenever Erik's name comes up. "He didn't grow up here." She pauses, still looking toward the ocean, not making eye contact with either one of us. "He's an ER doctor at the hospital. Crazy hours, his schedule was more chaotic than mine," she rambles on, waving her hand as she talks. "Anyway. He told me he was in the process of getting divorced. I even referred him to Eddie, too," she continues glumly.

"And…he did not get divorced?" I guess.

"To be honest, I don't know what the real status of his marriage was. I obviously never heard her side of the story. But, um, whatever happened, it seems like they must have been trying to work it out, because…because she's pregnant."

"*No!*" I exclaim.

"With his baby," Tatum confirms.

"*No!*"

"That's definitely what I said." Lucy nods.

"With more cursing," Tatum adds.

"How long were you dating for?" I ask Tatum.

"Mmmmm, almost six months." I raise my eyebrows. "I know, I know. I am an idiot for not suspecting anything. Every time he canceled plans, I just figured it was his work schedule at the hospital. Every time we went to dinner in north county, it was because there was some great restaurant he had just heard about. We took weekend trips to Santa Barbara and LA. I mean, all the signs were there!"

Tatum's voice gets progressively louder as she continues, her hand gestures more animated. It's clear she's beating herself up about this whole thing, even though I am certain, based on the limited information I have, that Dr. Trevor is a Grade A asshole.

"Dude's an asshole," Lucy comments, reading my mind.

"I don't disagree, but man. Way for me to *not* read the room," Tatum mutters.

My heart aches for my friend. I definitely know a little something about men who act like someone they are not.

"Tatum, I am so sorry," I tell her honestly. I get up off the bench and head to the side where she is, sitting down on the other side of her and leaning in to give her a hug.

"What are you—oh my gosh, Summer," Tatum chides me, but she smiles at least a little bit.

"Move down, Lucy," I tell my friend on the other side of Tatum, who obliges.

"That sucks," I tell Tatum. Because it does suck, and sometimes you just have to acknowledge the suckiness of it all.

"Yes, it does," she says, her voice muffled a bit by the fact that my arms are still around her and she is probably getting a mouthful of my hair. Oh well.

I pull back to see she still looks rueful, almost embarrassed. I tell her the same thing I told her brother a while back. "You know that it's not your fault, right?"

Tatum scoffs. "Yeah, but I should have been more insistent, more—"

"It sounds like he's a master manipulator," I interrupt her. Again, speaking from experience as someone who has lived with a master manipulator and lived to tell the tale.

"Oh, no doubt," Lucy offers from the other side of us. "Don't think I am getting pulled into this hugfest, by the way," she adds.

Tatum rolls her eyes. "He totally was," she admits begrudgingly.

"Not. Your. Fault." I remind her.

"Yeah, but it doesn't change the fact that I feel like Holly Fucking Home-wrecker over here," she mumbles.

"That sucks," I tell her again. "And you never know what is really going on with a couple behind closed doors," I add. "But screw that guy, Tatum."

"Honestly, I feel bad for the kid," Lucy chimes in.

"Me too," Tatum says slowly. "Although honestly, I hope they really do work it out, if they can."

"And I assume… I assume the wife knows all about you?" I ask, thinking of Beth's demon eyes earlier.

"Oh yes. I mean, I don't know what or when he told her, but she clearly knows about me. God, I had no idea Beth was in that bookstore," she groans, pinching the bridge of her nose.

"And so what? It's a small town. Girl's gotta get books," Lucy says.

"Yeah, I know," Tatum says quietly. She huffs out an exhale and slings her book bag over her shoulder, standing up off the bench.

"Let's get the hell out of here."

∿∿∿∿∿

"Julia. Juuuuliiiiaaa," Tatum calls down to her older sister behind the bar.

After the run-in with Beth and her hairy eyeball, we decided a drink was definitely in order and headed to the Brew.

Where we've definitely indulged in maybe one too many jalapeño margaritas.

"Tatum. I have other customers, you know," Julia says wryly, walking over to where we are holed up at the end of the bar.

"Yeah, yeah, but we are your favorite, right?"

"Actually," Julia responds, her gaze drifting over to several large booths, "there's a bunch of people here for the college rodeo. They are nice, polite, call me ma'am, and tip pretty well."

I turn to where she is looking and see a large group of college-aged kids in Wranglers and boots, several with cowboy hats on.

"You don't mind that they call you 'ma'am'?" Tatum asks.

"Why not? I am probably old enough to be some of those kids' mother," Julia responds. "So long as they stay respectful and keep giving me money, I don't care what they call me."

Tatum grunts in acknowledgment. "I shoulda had a cowboy," she sings in an off-key voice.

"I think it's 'I shoulda *been* a cowboy,'" I tell her.

"I know, I know. But maybe next time I'll go for a rodeo guy," Tatum commiserates into her margarita, now just melting ice.

"I thought you were never dating again?" Lucy asks, taking a big swig from her glass.

"There's that too," Tatum agrees. "God, I am an idiot."

"Enough of that, that's my sister you're talking about," Julia chides Tatum, setting three big glasses of ice water on the bar in front of us. "Now, get hydrated. You're supposed to babysit for me tomorrow." She leaves us to attend to the rodeo folk.

Tatum acquiesces, grabbing the water and sipping dutifully through the straw.

She turns her gaze toward me.

"So, Summer. Summmmeeeeer. You gonna leave us again?"

Tatum and Lucy are definitely not the passive-aggressive types, I'll give them that.

"Oh wow," I mutter. "Okay, we are doing this now? I mean…" I sigh, watching the condensation drip down my neglected beverage. "I mean." I clear my throat. "Eventually? I just…" I sigh. "I don't know. I don't know what my future looks like, but I don't think I can just stay here forever, teaching yoga and eating at Lucy's bakery every day. Not that I don't love your wares," I add to Lucy, who acknowledges me with a nod.

"You don't need the money," Tatum states matter-of-factly.

"True," I concede. "But I need to *do* something. I like yoga. I like Estero Bay."

"You like my brother," Tatum offers blankly.

"I more than *like* your brother," I tell her honestly. "But I need to *do* something. I feel restless. I spent way more time than necessary just like... existing, you know? And I don't want to seem ungrateful because I know, I *know*, how many people would kill for the opportunities I've had. But other than the ballet, what did the last ten years give me?"

Both Tatum and Lucy look at me.

"*Regrets*," I tell them emphatically. "Do you know what it's like to be incandescently happy in one area of your life and miserable in the other?"

Again, just looks from my two friends.

"I do," I affirm. "And now, I have the power and the ability to do what *I* want, without anyone telling me otherwise."

"I didn't realize Nick was holding you back," Tatum says with a raised eyebrow.

"He's not! He's definitely not. I just don't..." I sip my watered-down drink. "Whatever I do, why the heck can't Nick do it *with* me?"

Lucy nods again, as if this makes total sense to her. "He really is just moping around here like a big ol' gloomy Rochester. Without, you know, the crazy wife locked away."

"But Nick lives here," Tatum protests. "You just...expect him to follow you around wherever you go?"

"No! I don't know." I feel helpless, and I am clearly not doing a good job getting my point across. "Look. This is really a conversation I need to have with Nick, but whatever Nick and I are doing—"

"Fucking," Lucy mutters under her breath with a smirk.

"Gross," Tatum mutters back.

"—it's not a casual thing for me. It's not a rebound. I mean, not that I would know what a rebound is, you know. I've only ever really been with one man my whole life. Well, now two since Nick and I—"

Tatum and Lucy are looking at me with open mouths. It would be funny if I weren't so amped up.

"What…?"

"Erik is the only guy you have been with?" Tatum asks me.

"Well, yes. I met Erik when I was nineteen! I never dated. I never went out, like girls do in college. I didn't know any Marty, and I never went to any parties or tequila fests or whatever. And when we got divorced…" I sigh. "I was recovering. Physically, I mean. It wasn't like I was ready to hit the bars or clubs or wherever people go to meet people these days."

"Apparently it's Estero Bay," Lucy muses. "Well damn, Summer. This makes me even gladder that I recommend you hop on Nick's dick—"

"Jesus Christ, Lucy," Tatum growls. "I will pay you cash money if you will stop talking about my brother and his…that."

Lucy smiles evilly. "Anyway, Summer," she says, "you have whatever conversation you need to have with Nicky. It's none of our business," she adds, turning toward Tatum in the middle, kicking her in the shin.

"Lucy! For fuck's sake, you're wearing combat boots." Tatum groans. "And I thought you were never dating again?" She directs this question to me.

Lucy snorts. "Come on, dude," she tells Tatum. "You know there's a history there."

"I guess," Tatum mutters, chewing on the end of her straw. "Um…I know my brother can be…weird. And I'm sorry if I am making things weird."

"You totally are *not*," I reassure her with the certainty only two strong margaritas can provide.

"And who knows, maybe you're right, and you and Nick and Layne Staley can sail off into the sunset together." Tatum pauses. "But please leave the boat. I love that boat."

Tatum's tone reveals her skepticism about whether Nick and I—and the dog—will, in fact, sail off into the sunset.

But like I told her—that's a conversation for me and Nick.

Chapter Twenty-Nine

Nick

S MACK. *SMACK. SMACK.*

My headboard bangs against the wall as I drive my hips deep, feeling every inch of Summer squeeze me. We're both a little sweaty and a lot worked up as I am determined to drag another orgasm from her.

It's been a week since the moment in the bakery. A week with Summer, perfect as ever—a week of beach days, California burritos, morning yoga sessions, sunset beers, and fucking.

But mostly fucking.

If denial is a river in Egypt, then I am happily floating downstream, riding the bumps and curves as the water rushes by.

We've already fucked in the living room, me bending her perfect ass over the couch arm to take her from behind. Her body is beyond flexible, and she currently has her legs spread wide for me, hiding nothing and holding nothing back.

I love her like this—her perfect tits jiggling, her back arching as I drill my cock into her.

"Nick," she moans. "Feels—" *smack* "so—" *smack* "good…"

"So perfect," I tell her, my voice rattling out as I pump in and out of her. I press my hand to her clit firmly, and she nearly shrieks, arching up higher.

She is perfect. Once again, I mentally kick myself for not doing this sooner.

Why did I ever waste a minute without this woman by my side?

I'm not ready to face those questions, but I can't stop some other thoughts as I work her over.

"Should have done this a long time ago," I grit out. "Should have put you on my dick when I saw you in New York."

Summer's eyes widen a bit in response. I start rubbing her clit in slow circles, and her gaze lowers, her mouth open with her pants and little whimpers.

"It's true, isn't it? I should have kept you on my cock all weekend." I rub her clit harder. "Yeah, that's what I should have done. If I had known how greedy this little pussy was, I would've never left the room." I don't lift my gaze from hers, letting her see I mean every fucking word.

"Nick," she gasps.

"Or if we had to leave the room, you know what I would've done?" I clench my jaw as she squeezes my dick tighter. "I would've kept you right where you are now, those legs wrapped around my waist, bouncing like a good girl where you belong. So everyone could see you and know how needy you are."

"*Oh my god.* Nick," she whines, her head thrashing on the pillow, her arms at either side of her body, clenching the sheets. Her entire body clenches—her jaw, her stomach, and her pussy as it strangles me like a vise. "I'm coming…" Summer rambles incoherently, and I don't let up, not for one second, rubbing her clit hard, pumping my hips back and forth.

"You squeeze me so good, Summer," I tell her as she arches up so damn high I think her back might break.

"I can't, I can't…" she moans. Some of the tension leaves Summer's body as her orgasm crests. I don't take a break, though, and immediately flip us over so she is straddling me, my cock hard inside her wetness. She yelps and collapses on me, and all I know is her smell, her skin, her freckles, her hair, surrounding me like the most comforting home I've ever known.

"Can you do it now, sweetheart?" I ask her gruffly, taking in her dazed expression. "Can you bounce on me like a good girl?"

Her eyes widen again, and she whimpers as I rut my groin upward into her. "I can't," she repeats, but she leans back, placing a hand behind her and rotating her hips in a circle, the filthiest cowgirl ride I've ever seen.

"That's it," I croon as she works herself on me. "Give me all of it, Summer."

"I want that," she whimpers. "I want what you said."

"Tell me," I demand, gripping her hips tightly.

She grinds down on my cock, leaning over me. Those perfect breasts are now right in front of my mouth, and I take full advantage, taking one of her nipples into my mouth, giving it a hard suck before laving it with my tongue.

"Oh god. Again, do it again. Please, suck them, anything." Summer babbles, her eyes totally glazed over, beads of sweat on her hairline, her cheeks ruddy. "Nick. Please. I think I'm going to go again—"

"Tell me what you want," I grunt, feeling her squeeze me. She shudders and loses her rhythm slightly, her head lolling back a bit. "Oh, Sunshine. You're fucking hot for it, aren't you?"

She whimpers and brings her head back up, meeting my gaze, her eyes pleading. "Nick," she whines, moving her body back and forth against mine, her clit rubbing me with each pass.

"That's it, sweetheart. You just rub yourself all over me, okay? Good girl. Keep rubbing, honey." We've slowed our rhythm considerably, and my cock is demanding that I bounce her up and down again, rut against her.

But not before she comes again.

"I don't think I can. Nick, I don't think I can come…" Summer keeps rubbing herself on me, both of us panting heavily, slick with arousal and sweat.

"I want to try to get you off one more time," I whisper, before leaning forward again and taking her nipple in my mouth. I suckle it so softly, barely tightening my mouth around her. She arches her back, pushing her breast into my mouth.

"Tell me what you need, and I'll do it, Summer," I murmur to her before taking her nipple back in my mouth.

"Whatever you want, Sunshine, you can tell me." I devote all my attention to holding her steady against me as she continues to rub, rub, hitting that spot that I know she must like, because she tightens up each time her body moves. "No secrets."

"Suck—suck harder," she pants, her expression a little shy even in her arousal. I can feel my cock leaking a little more in the condom at her words.

"Oh fuck." I lean in to give her a sloppy kiss. "Anything you need. You just rub that tight little thing against me, and I'm going to suck on these tits until you cream, okay?"

Summer speeds up her movements at my words.

"You are hard up for it, aren't you, Sunshine? Hard up and horny for this dick."

She whines louder in response. I move my mouth back to her breasts, taking a nipple into my mouth and sucking harder. Summer rubs against me a little faster, and I suck just a little harder, not wanting to hurt her.

"Nick. God, yes. Suck harder. I'm going… God, I'm going to go—" I suck on Summer's nipple until it's red as a berry before taking it slightly between my teeth. That sets her off. She squeezes around me, gripping at my back, announcing to God and the saints and everyone else that she's going to come again.

I grip her bottom with one hand and move the other to her neglected breast, pinching the nipple as I suck, hard.

Summer rubs frantically against me, telling me not to stop, *right there, harder*, and I give her what she wants, what she deserves. Her pussy grips my cock unbearably tight, and her entire body clenches again.

She squeezes her eyes shut and whimpers, her legs shaking as she rubs quicker and more tightly. "I can't—oh, it's happening…"

"Give over, Summer," I pant back, still pinching one nipple tightly with my fingers, removing my lips from her other nipple for just a second. "Let go. I've got you. Ride it out."

I feel her climax rush through her as her pussy milks my cock, pulsing, pulsing, trying to pull everything out of me. I let go too, my orgasm rushing through me like a freight train, pulling everything I have out of me, into her.

I come and I come, groaning as I fill the condom, Summer's little body quaking around mine. "Take it all," I croak out as I continue gripping her hips.

She moans and rubs, her movements jerky, until she clears the crest and drops her head to my shoulder, her body flush with mine. I deflate too a little bit, closing my eyes and breathing her in as I recover.

We lie like this, the only sounds our heavy breathing and the waves in the distance, before I feel Summer go boneless next to me, lost in sleep.

I follow her shortly after, clutching her close to me like she might get away if I release my hold on her.

Chapter Thirty

IT OCCURS TO ME, AS I LEAD MY EVENING YOGA GROUP INTO OUR FINAL poses of the session, that the constant sex I've been having has left me sore in places I didn't even know could be sore.

And I am—or was—a professional dancer, for crying out loud! I stretch, I strengthen, and while I don't move as I did prior to my injury, I consider myself to be in good shape.

That was before my body was introduced to Nicholas Echeverria, sex god.

I've never felt so comfortable in the bedroom—or on the boat, or the living room of his house, or one particularly memorable session in my little laundry room…let's just say the vibration from the washing machine was icing on the sex cake. I've never had so many orgasms with another person.

And yet.

I know Nick is holding back. Not that I expect him to drop everything and confess his undying love for me.

But since that day at Lucy's, he's been more closed off. Quieter.

And he's a quiet guy to begin with.

Initially, I was surprised that *he* was surprised. We live in a small town. Unless you work in hospitality, wine, or education, there are really not a lot of jobs. And certainly not in the arts. So yes, naturally, I am looking for employment outside the Bay.

Then, I wondered…should I have told Nick that I am not here for the long haul? I love Estero Bay, and I wouldn't rule out coming back here permanently one day—but I am thirty years old. I am lucky that I don't have to bust my ass for financial reasons, but frankly, I *want* to work. I want to dance as much as I can for as long as I can, and I am happy to do that anywhere in the world for now, if someone sees something in me they want.

And maybe this is the love-sick teenager in me talking, but…wouldn't Nick want to come with me? *Couldn't* Nick come with me? I've spent hours daydreaming of me, Nick, and Layne Staley setting up in a cute little house in Austin or DC or a cool high-rise condo in Toronto or Tokyo. Admittedly, I haven't asked Nick about any long-term plans he has or "where is this going?" or anything similar. I've been content to be with him, to enjoy him, to live out this little fantasy of mine as long as I possibly can.

But selfishly…why couldn't this be our reality?

Am I not allowed to be selfish?

The music changes to "Poison & Wine" by the Civil Wars. I lead the class through our final pose, shavasana—the best pose, if I'm honest. Who doesn't enjoy lying on their back as part of a therapeutic movement? I feel my students relaxing one by one, and I imitate their shallow breathing. We enjoy the silence together.

I exhale and attempt to let my mind go, acknowledging the thoughts that pop into my head like acquaintances, demanding my attention for a moment and then leaving as abruptly as they came in.

Most of them are about Nick and our future together.

Whatever that might look like.

～～～～～

"Summer! Hey, Summer!"

The last students have trickled out of the studio, and I am getting my phone and mat and everything together when I hear someone call my name. I turn, my smile faltering a bit when I see it's Amber Bracamonte.

It's not that I don't like Amber. She's nice enough.

It's just that I am insanely jealous of Nick's high school girlfriend.

I am woman enough to admit it, as petty as it might be.

"Hi, Amber."

"Hi!" Amber is her perpetually perky self, her long, dark hair done in two immaculate French braids down the back of her head. "How *are* you?"

If I had a quarter for everyone who asked me how I *am*…I would be able to do a lot of laundry.

But Amber means well, and while I think she's overly perky, she's not mean. "I'm good, Amber. How are you?"

"I'm good! So good. I actually have a favor to ask you. I have a couple out-of-town appointments I need to travel to the valley for." She makes a face before continuing. "Do you think you can cover a class or two for me next week?"

"I don't see why not. Can you text me the dates and times, and I'll confirm?"

"Yes, of course! Absolutely!" Amber bobs her head up and down so fast, her generous breasts follow gravity's lead, bouncing in her fuschia top.

"Okay, great," I reply, turning to continue gathering my things. "I'll just be out in a sec."

"Okay!" Amber pauses. "So…you and Nick, huh?"

It's my turn to pause as I sling my yoga strap over my shoulder. "Me and Nick…what?"

"Oh, everyone is talking about it!" Amber gushes, her eyes sparkling. "You know…two broken hearts, returning to their hometown a little lost…" She catches my narrowed gaze and blushes. "Not that—not that *you* are lost. No. That is not what I meant." She takes a deep breath. "Sorry, I…I read a lot of romance novels," she mutters, looking down.

"That's okay," I tell her. "I'm just…not one to talk about my personal life."

Especially with you, person who dated Nick in high school whom I don't really know.

"Especially with me, huh?" Amber says, looking up at me from underneath long lashes. Really long, now that I see them. Definitely salon-applied.

My surprise must show on my face.

"I really don't mean to pry," she says, holding up a hand. "I just… You know, when Nick and I were together back in the day—" she gestures her hand, indicating "—I just always suspected, you know? I guess this is just confirmation bias."

"Suspected…?" I ask slowly.

"You know! Nick is into you!" Amber offers me one of her big smiles.

"Into me?" I repeat.

"Yes! I mean, I know you are Tatum's best friend. Obviously. Everyone knows that. You guys are like sisters." She sounds a little…wistful, I realize. "And then it would follow that you and Nick are siblings too, I suppose, but that's not what I saw."

"What did you see?" I ask quickly before I can stop myself.

I congratulate myself, however, on not going full teenager, like "*What did you see oh my gosh tell me now!*"

"You know. Just that, he would look at you a lot. And it was like I didn't exist when you were in the room." She gasps in surprise as if she's suddenly realized something. "Not that I am bitter about it! No. Not at all. I mean, it was a long time ago, and it's not like we were in love or anything. I've never actually been in love, can you believe that? The girl who is obsessed with romance books doesn't actually know what romance is."

I raise my eyebrows at her, smiling a little bit.

"Sorry," she mutters again, casting her eyes downward. "I kind of have a habit of thinking out loud, I guess."

"You know what?" Amber raises her big Bambi eyes to mine. "I do too, Amber," I tell her with a smile.

I realize that not only is Amber not a threat, not only is she harmless, but she also might be a little lonely.

And *that* is something I can definitely relate to, Nick Echeverria or no Nick Echeverria.

"Would you like to get coffee sometime?" I ask her.

Amber's eyes get so big, she reminds me of a cartoon character. "I would *love* to!"

"Text me those dates you were talking about," I tell her as I move to exit the studio. "And some potential coffee dates too."

"Okay! I will! Have a great day!"

Chapter Thirty-One

Nick

HEMINGWAY ONCE WROTE THAT GOING BANKRUPT HAPPENED "gradually, and then all at once."

Luckily, I don't know anything about bankruptcy. But his description is the most fitting way I can describe my anxiety. It's gradual and then all at once. It's something that builds in my brain, in the recesses of my mind, unbeknownst to me for days, for weeks. Little building blocks that, by themselves, are no big deal. But once they are assembled, it hits me like a freight train, loud and bright and awful, all at once.

It starts small. I wake with a nagging sensation, like I've forgotten to do something. But I haven't. There are no appointments I've neglected, no burner I forgot to turn off, no tap left running. I've been with Summer for weeks now, and we are fine. I'm going to therapy, and that's fine. I'm not avoiding my feelings. I'm not shutting myself out. I respond to Brock's stupid texts.

Everything is fine.

Sure, there is the specter of unresolved issues when it comes to Summer. We haven't had a real discussion about our future, about where we are going. But that's fine too, because it will all work itself out, I am convinced.

Everything is fine.

I even tell my therapist this, and he merely raises his eyebrows at me as if to say "bullshit."

But the most frustrating thing about it is that I don't know it's happening until it happens.

I begin the day with my run. Layne Staley bounds alongside me, happy as ever, constantly looking to me as if to say "See! This is great, man! Can you believe we get to live here!"

I eat. I shower. I do all the things because routines are healing, or so I've been told.

I actually attend one of Summer's yoga classes with other students, something I've been doing more of. I tell myself it's because I like to covertly check her out as she leads the class in their poses. I take some sort of caveman pride in the fact that I know what Summer looks like when she's doing these poses naked, due to an impromptu strip-yoga session we did a few weeks ago.

I tell myself that the reason I am in her class instead of doing a private session is definitely *not* because of the vulnerability I feel during our private sessions.

I do the yoga. I make small talk with Letty Abernathy on the way out without hearing a word she says. I feel the nagging sensation eat at me even more, which is the opposite effect I was hoping to get after a yoga class. My heart rate feels elevated, and my breathing is shallow.

I wait for Summer on the bench outside the studio. I don't have my phone with me—the easiest method to avoid socializing with the locals meandering up and down Main Street. I lean forward, spreading my legs and balancing my elbows on my knees. I look down at the ground. There's a row of ants marching across the sidewalk, quickly and efficiently, creating a shallow vein across the concrete. They move down and over the lip of the curb to parts unknown, some getting trampled on by the passersby. The ants don't stop; they regroup and keep moving.

Sweat dots my brow. I exerted myself in the yoga class, to be sure, but this is more of a nervous sweat rather than from any exercise.

I struggle to catch my breath. I watch the ants and wish I could join them. I wish I had a place like these ants do, a place in their hierarchy, in their social structure. A clearly defined role that no one would question. I wouldn't question it, and therefore, I would have no need to imagine a life other than the one I was given.

"*Nick.*"

I jerk my head up to see Summer standing next to me, a slightly impatient look on her face like she's been calling my name for some time. That look turns to one of concern.

"Nick," she says softly, sitting down on the bench next to me and placing a hand on my knee. "Are you sick? You look really pale." She reaches her hand to touch my forehead, the universal "are you sick" gesture if ever there was one. "You don't feel warm."

"I think…" My voice sounds hoarse. "I think I'm having a panic attack."

Her eyes widen again for a fraction of a second before she recovers, a no-nonsense look on her face. "Okay. Okay. Do you have any water?"

I shake my head slightly.

"Okay. It's quieter in the park across the street—can we walk there?" She strokes my hand softly.

I nod.

"Okay. Let's go."

I have no memory of getting there, but the next thing I know, I am sitting with Summer across the street. I take a deep breath and smell the freshly cut grass, the salty air, and the scent of Summer—something sweet from her lotion, ginger from her tea.

"You know the rule of five?" she murmurs to me.

I give her a jerky nod. "Yeah…I was smelling just now."

"That's good."

I sit there for a moment, trying to get my breathing under control.

"Do you…do you want to put your head in my lap?"

I look at Summer's eyes and try to focus. I see sympathy—no, not sympathy or pity, but understanding. Empathy.

I understand now that I am falling in love with her. I have heard that is also gradual, then all at once.

I suppose it was inevitable for us. At least it was for me.

I nod again and move to lie down. She has the wherewithal to place a blanket under us on the grass. I lie on my back with my head in her lap.

Above me are the leaves of the trees, moving slightly in the wind to create shafts of light around us.

"Close your eyes," Summer says quietly, "and tell me five things you hear."

I follow her commands.

"Um…the leaves blowing. The foghorn. The cars driving by. People talking on the street." I listen carefully. "And…a guitar. An electric guitar, somewhere in the distance. Maybe on one of the outdoor patios."

"Very good," Summer murmurs. "How about smells?"

"The grass. It smells like it's been mowed recently." I take another breath. "The ocean. Something cooking on the grill at one of the restaurants." I open my eyes and see Summer's face above mine. She's biting her lip and regarding me cautiously.

"Sun block. Your lotion. Your tea. It's ginger." My pulse is no longer racing; my breathing is under control.

"I smell you."

She blushes a little bit but doesn't move. Her voice is a whisper. "And how about five things you can see?"

"Your freckles. Your eyes. Your hair. Your lips." I raise my hand to cradle her face, and she leans into it, her skin soft and warm.

"All I see is you."

She turns her head to me to kiss the center of my palm and regards me, her expression calm. Caring.

"Lie with me?" I ask her gruffly.

She nods, and I lift my head to allow her to lie down on her side, angling my body so that we are facing each other.

"Better?" she asks me as I wrap my arms around her.

"I am. But…can we stay like this a little while?" I am suddenly so, so tired. The adrenaline coursing through my veins has now evaporated, leaving me lethargic. I feel like I can sleep for hours, not uncommon after an attack.

"As long as you need to."

How about forever?

But even forever might not be enough. What if whatever cloud I've got hanging over me still follows me around, no matter where Summer goes, no matter if she's with me?

And a little voice nags at me—*who would want to put up with that?*

I don't speak any of those thoughts, though.

Instead, I tighten my embrace around her, kiss her forehead, and feel my body relax into a dreamless sleep.

<h1 style="text-align:center">Chapter Thirty-Two</h1>

"**S**O, I KNOW IT'S NOT THE MOST GLAMOROUS OF SPOTS," LUCY says. "But honestly, there's a clean bathroom with a shower, for those people insane enough to swim in the Pacific, a big bar, and a nice balcony."

She is currently showing me around "the Club," as she refers to the Estero Bay Yacht Club. She's introduced me to Herman, who appears to be approximately one hundred and forty years old, wears a hat like an old sea captain, and a perky windbreaker with "Estero Bay Yacht Club" printed over one breast.

Lucy told us earlier they gave her a windbreaker when she was made commodore, but that it "totally destroyed her vibe." And gave it to her grandma.

I thought I was familiar with yacht clubs, having been to one of the oldest clubs in North America with Erik's family. There's no monarchy in America, but you wouldn't know it from some of the old-money, East Coast clubs, and the one I went to with the Johnstones was no exception. Gold-plated chandeliers, three stories, staff dressed in livery. There was a huge ballroom on the second floor with elegantly draped windows, marbled floors, and candelabras ensconced in the papered walls. People dressed in formal evening attire at night and what Erik's mother called "cocktail reception" attire during the day. And these people actually had yachts, mind you—yachts that make Nick's boat look like a dinghy.

The Estero Bay Yacht Club is…not that.

Sunlight streams through the windows in the hall. The room is huge, with a dais over to one side and four-seater tables and chairs spread on the main floor. A small stage is near the balcony with an abandoned amp and drum kit. And the whole place—the floors, the walls, the ceiling—is covered in shiny mahogany wood paneling.

"I mean, the view can't be beat, for sure." The ocean-facing side has a huge balcony with tables and chairs. It towers over the sand. "Don't people go under this balcony to make out and smoke pot and stuff?"

"Why, Summer Mahoney," Lucy tsks me, "how do you know about such things?"

"Not from personal experience, I assure you."

"Well, yes, you're right. At least, when we were in junior high and high school, that's definitely one of the spots I used to go to." She pauses. "I also fooled around there with Tommy Espinoza after junior prom."

"Good for you." Tommy was fine.

"I know, right? Tommy's a firefighter now. Married to a very nice man who is an accountant. They have twin daughters in Violet's class."

"I thought Tatum mentioned you dated a firefighter too?" I ask her casually.

"Nope. I dated someone in the sheriff's office, and I definitely do not want to talk about her, or that, right now. Do you mind helping me set up for the meeting?"

"Not at all."

I've spent enough time with Lucy over the past several weeks to know that she will move from one topic to another at whim and without giving you a chance to follow.

I open up the bakers' boxes we brought up the stairs. "Dang, Lucy, how much did you make?"

"I made apple cinnamon muffins and peanut butter cookies—dairy free, because if either I or any of these old geezers—" she gestures to Herman, who laughs at her like she said the funniest thing in the world "—have anything that comes from a cow, we will all suffer. And shortbread. They love shortbread. And then I also maybe prepared a baked Brie because I like to live dangerously."

My stomach growls as I take out the cookies, muffins, and crackers for the Brie, all nicely displayed on colorful, nautical-themed plateware.

"Did you buy these things specifically for your life as commodore?"

Lucy shrugs. "HomeGoods was having a sale. Wait to cut the Brie about ten more minutes or so, or it'll ooze out everywhere."

I obey her command and move to display the napkins and plates and cutlery.

"If you write a memoir, you can call this portion of your life 'the Commodore Chronicles,'" I joke.

Lucy snorts a laugh. "As if anyone would want to read a memoir of my life. 'She came, she baked, she disappointed her parents.'"

I raise my eyebrows. I didn't realize Lucy's parents were still in Estero Bay. "They don't live here, though, do they?"

"Nah. They moved to Pasadena a few years back to be closer to my perfect sister and her perfect husband and their two very advanced, very smart, very perfect children."

I laugh at Lucy's description. "Surely they can't be that perfect."

"You're not wrong. But don't tell my parents." Lucy comes over to the table where I have displayed everything and nods in approval.

"Where's that big, moody boyfriend of yours?" she asks, changing the subject quickly yet again.

"I'm not sure."

I haven't seen Nick in a couple days. After his panic attack, he slept a bit in the park and then walked me home. Before he left, he kissed me like it was his last day on earth, thanking me for…for helping him through it, I guess.

I debate on how much to share with Lucy. Nick's business is his business, after all.

I go for vague. "I think Nick is…in his feelings. Not in a bad way," I say hurriedly. "Just…when he needs his space, I want to give it to him, you know?"

"Yeah, I know."

"You do?"

"Yeah." Lucy keeps talking, not looking up from where she is wiping down tables and placing agendas. "I don't know what Nick is going through personally—obviously—but I get like that sometimes. In my feelings, like you said." She raises her eyes to me. She's got a great pair of red cat-eye glasses on, her winged liner on point underneath the lenses. "Sometimes you just need to decompress."

"That's a good way to put it," I murmur. I carefully place the Brie on the table. Lucy's even taken reserved dough to carve out pretty little leaves and berries decorating the top of the puff pastry.

"So how much time do I give him to decompress?" I blurt out.

Lucy raises her eyebrows.

"I just." I huff out a breath. "I don't really have any experience. At all. With men who aren't horrible sociopaths who only think about their own self-interest. And even then, there was just the one," I offer weakly.

"That was a horrible joke," Lucy scolds.

I lift my shoulders in apology.

"*Anyway.*" Lucy regards me sternly, clad, as usual, in all black, except for the red glasses. "If you want to see Nick, go see him. If you want to talk to Nick, text him. Send him nudes. Men are fairly simple creatures."

Herman again laughs at Lucy.

"Oh, he's a smitten kitten," I murmur, smiling at Herman.

"You can speak in a normal voice. He's deaf in one ear and hard of hearing in the other. *You want a muffin?*" Lucy yells this last sentence to Herman.

"Yes, ma'am!" He beams at her.

"Do you think I'm a jerk because I'm entertaining job offers outside of town?"

"Shit, no. Are you kidding me? Look," Lucy says, gesturing to the room we are in. "This is not the life for everyone. It's a small town. Not only that, but *the* small town where you grew up and everyone knows you. It can feel suffocating sometimes."

"I like it here, I just… I don't know if I can stay here *forever*, you know?" Now that I am on a roll with Lucy, my pseudo therapist, I can't stop. "I want to keep my house. I want to come back occasionally. But I want to create,

I want to meet people! I want to travel. And I can't do those things if I am here all the time for the rest of my life."

Lucy nods. "I get that. And Summer, I really don't think that's an unreasonable request or desire."

"But Nick—"

"Do you even know if Nick wants to stay here for all eternity? I mean, he's doing a great job of locking down the Old Town Grump role, but seriously. Talk. To. Him."

"Okay. I will," I tell her determinedly.

"And seriously consider the nudes. Works every time."

Chapter Thirty-Three

Summer

I DID NOT FOLLOW LUCY'S ADVICE ABOUT SENDING NUDES.

Me: Good morning! :)

Nick: Morning, Sunshine.

Me: Tatum and I are talking about going to hike later today—want to come?

Nick: Have you hiked with Tatum before?

Me: No…?

Nick: She's a damn mountain goat. She's insane. I don't know where she got the coordination, but it's basically the worst job ever. It's painful

Me: Sounds like someone got shown up by his little, non-football-playing sister. 😉

Nick: …

Nick: …

Nick: that might have happened

Me: Your secret is safe with me, big guy. So…you in?

Nick: No.

Nick: …

Nick: I have a PT session, and then I'll take Layne Staley for a walk. But you girls have fun.

Me: Okay.

Me: Well, maybe I can come over for dinner or something if you want.

Nick: Sounds good. Good luck—let me know when you're done

Chapter Thirty-Four

Nick

DESPITE DOING ALL THE THINGS I AM SUPPOSED TO DO—STICKING with my routine, exercising, breath work—that nagging little voice hasn't let up the last few days.

It's not that I am ashamed Summer saw me in such a state. I can't change the way my mind works any more than I can change my height or beets being disgusting or the odds of Tatum ever allowing dust to accumulate in her house. Beets are disgusting, and those odds are less than zero.

I am who I am, and Summer apparently likes that person at least a little bit. But I still have work to do. I want to do this right, and ever since the yoga incident, I've been in a funk, a cloud over my head, an inkling that, no, I am *not* doing this right. That we're moving too fast. That I am not ready for this.

Which is why I have taken the mature approach and essentially offered vague replies to all her texts and indications we should get together.

She's smart enough not to ask how I'm doing, probably because she hates that question as much as I do.

How am I doing? Not well, my dude.

I know I can't avoid her forever. I know that anxiety attacks are something I'll have to deal with forever, Summer or no Summer.

But I still can't help but think she's getting a raw deal.

I thought I was out of the fog and ready to feel the sunshine again. Now, I retreat to where I was before—between a painful past and an uncertain future, stuck in the in-between, the unknown.

And that nagging voice tells me to feel ashamed.

Chapter Thirty-Five

Summer

S
O, OBVIOUSLY, LUCY'S ADVICE TO "SEND NUDES" DIDN'T WORK OUT so well for me.

In my defense, I've never taken nudes.

And even if I had, Nick's behavior indicates that random nudes might not go over well.

Of course, he's a guy, so I could be wrong.

Regardless, given that he's still playing things very, very cool, it doesn't seem like nudes are the best way to handle this situation.

The problem is that I am not totally sure what the situation is. Is it that he's embarrassed about his anxiety attack? Because he doesn't seem like the type of guy who would be.

Is this normal, and he just needs some time to come out of his funk? Because if this is the usual routine, then I want to be a part of it. If Nick and I are going to be together, then that means we're going to be together for the good stuff and the bad stuff and all the stuff in between. I don't think he gets to put a hold on everything when he has a bad day.

Unless he doesn't want to be with you long-term anyway…

I sigh, pushing that thought out of my head.

Since Nick and I have *not* been banging like bunnies the past several days—and more's the pity—I've picked up on my adulting with the best of them. My house is clean. My bills are paid. My yoga clients are hopefully satisfied.

But there's a major adulting task I've been putting off. I've been thinking about what Alexis said, what Brock asked me, what Tatum pondered.

What am I going to do with my life?

What is my next chapter?

I love Estero Bay. I am glad I came back here. I don't want to go back to New York.

But I feel the urge to flex my creative muscles, to be a part of something artistic. And I am not sure I can do that here.

I have time to kill before my hike with Tatum, so I open my laptop, checking my email for the first time in…I can't recall how long. *There's really been no one to communicate with.*

But I find an email from Leonard, my artistic director friend in New York, with a message in all caps to "CALL ME!!!!1!!!" followed by about three hundred emojis.

I find Leonard's contact in my phone.

"Babe," he greets me.

"Hi, Leonard."

"It's about time. Summer Mahoney, I sent that email, like, over a week ago."

"I do better via text," I murmur.

"That's what she said," he sings. "That didn't work so well. Anyway, the reason I wanted you to call me over a week ago is because I think I have found your next thing."

"My next…thing?"

"Yes. You know, your next chapter, your next verse, whatever you cis-hetero women who read 'Becoming' are calling it these days. Do you know DeeDee Weaver?"

I pause, racking my brain in an attempt to keep up with Leonard's train of thought. He's as New York as it gets—impatient, fast, and unabashedly himself.

"I don't think so?"

"She's *amaaaazing*. She's doing great things with movement. She's in Austin right now, getting ready to open up a show—an exhibition, really— focused on the history of movement in different cultures. Very hip, very provocative, very avant-garde. Anyway, I think you should contribute."

There's a moment of silence, and I realize Leonard's expecting a response.

"You think I should dance in this thing?"

"No! No, I think you should choreograph. See what they've done, see what speaks to you. So I'll make an intro to DeeDee, okay?"

"Wait! Wait, Leonard."

"Yes?"

Well, shit. Now that he's waiting, I have to remember why I asked him to do so in the first place.

"I am a ballerina," I tell him.

"Okaaaay," he drawls.

"So…why do you think an avant-garde piece of performance art needs something from me? I mean, everything I have done is traditional with a capital T."

"Yeah? And not to sound too much like your therapist, but how did that make you feel?"

"It made me feel…" I think about my dancing days, the dream of being a prima ballerina in my head even as a young child. I think of the hard work and the training. I think of the sweat, the tears, the blood—seriously, Google pointe shoe injuries and get back to me. I think of the diet, the restrictions, the things I didn't do. I think of the people I met, none of whom I talk to anymore.

My dancing days are inextricably intertwined with my marriage to Erik. I think about how his "support" of my career morphed into a totalitarian existence. He was not a home, a place to escape to. And he eventually became a place I needed to escape from.

I think about how my dream ended. I'm not so melancholy that I would say my dream turned into a nightmare, but it's over and done.

I've woken up.

"It made me feel accomplished," I ultimately tell Leonard.

He snorts. "That's boring."

I laugh because…he's right.

"It was good for a while, until it wasn't."

"Jesus Christ, put that on my tombstone," Leonard cackles. "Look, I think this would be good for you. DeeDee's got ambition to take this thing to other cities eventually, depending on how it goes in the Lone Star State. Now that you don't have that asshole as an albatross, you are beholden to no one, right?"

"No, I am not," I tell him truthfully.

"Great. This will be good for you. I'll make the intro. Look for my email by *tomorrow*, Sweet Summer, not next week, 'kay? Love you mucho."

I tell Leonard I love him too and end the call.

Austin. I've never been, but I've heard good things. And Leonard is right, as is my sister, as is Lucy.

I am beholden to no one, and I've already conceded I am not up for staying here and teaching yoga forever.

But this all begs the ultimate question…

What about Nick?

Chapter Thirty-Six

Nick

I'VE DONE PT—MY LEG IS THROBBING—WALKED LAYNE STALEY, AND am currently sitting with all manner of ice packs strategically wrapped around my thigh when the doorbell rings.

Layne Staley bounds to the door, wagging his tail, apparently unaware that we want to be *alone*.

Summer's there on the other side of the door, so pretty it causes a pang in my chest. She's in her regular uniform of yoga pants and a purple sweater, her hair in two long braids down her back. She eyes me cautiously, an uncertain smile on her face. I spy a large takeout bag from Terrific Thai in one of her hands.

"I made it through the hike with the mountain goat and lived to tell the tale," she tells me. "Want to have some noodles with me while I recover?"

"Yeah. Yeah, noodles are good," I tell her dumbly, moving out of the way to let her in the house.

Summer steps in and heads up the stairs to the kitchen, much to the delight of Layne Staley, who attempts to climb her like a tree. She laughs and tells him what a good boy he is.

"Probably should sit at the table for this one. The soup is messy." Summer makes herself at home, ambling over to the kitchen counter and setting up our food.

I wince a bit, my leg twitching, as I move to join her, and Summer notices. "You okay? Oh! Is your leg acting up?" She gestures to the ice pack wrapped around my leg.

"I'm fine. I mean, PT was a little rough today. I think I need to cut back on the running, maybe do more swimming. But it's nothing."

"I can give you a massage later, if you want?"

"No, it's really okay. I got a good rubdown after the session."

"I have some great CBD lotion that you can apply—that is, if you're not against that sort of thing. It's not really, like, marijuana or anything like that, and while the jury is out on the healing properties, I have some clients who swear that it works wonders and—"

"Summer." I interrupt her marathon sentence. "It's totally fine. Let's eat."

"Oh—okay." Summer keeps eyeing me cautiously, taking a seat across from me at the counter.

We don't speak, the room filled with the sounds of our slurping.

"This is good, thank you," I tell her.

"You're welcome."

More silence.

"Did I tell you that Alexis called me a while back?" Summer asks me suddenly.

"Oh yeah?" Summer's barely mentioned her sister since she's been back in the Bay. As far as I know, they've never been super close.

"Anything interesting?" I add more cilantro and hot sauce to my soup—I like that shit spicy—before taking another bite.

"Nothing new. She's just on me to, you know, figure out the rest of my life. No biggie." Summer rolls her eyes.

"She coming to visit you?"

"She mentioned a conference up north, but I doubt it. She hasn't been here in...a long time."

I nod. "So...why is what you do any of her business?"

Summer raises her eyebrows at my bluntness.

"I mean, you're a grown woman. Seems like what you do should be up to you."

"I guess...I guess she always felt like she had to watch me, maybe? After our parents died."

This doesn't jive with my memory of Alexis bolting right after their parents' funeral and my mom taking Summer in, but that's neither here nor there. "Didn't stop you from getting married, though," I say without thinking.

Summer pauses with a bite halfway to her mouth. "No, I suppose not," she says slowly. "But I don't think that it would have made a difference. I was determined to do what I wanted. Still am," she tells me before taking her bite.

"But she doesn't think you should be hanging out here. In Estero Bay," I clarify, "not like, here, in my house. With me."

"To be honest, she's not wild about either of those things," Summer responds carefully.

That comment gives me pause. First, that Summer wanted to—and apparently did—tell her sister about us. Or "us." Or whatever. And second, that Alexis does not approve.

"Well, why not?"

Summer sighs, not meeting my eyes. "I don't know. I guess she feels like I need to be alone for a while or whatever. Spread my wings. Swim in the deep end on my own. Take whatever metaphor you like."

I hum in response.

"Anyway. I told her, just like I had told you, that I've been talking with some people in the industry to see what opportunities might be out there. *And* it just so happens that I found an opportunity that I think is going to be really good, really awesome for me."

"Okay," I respond slowly, not sure I like where this is going.

"It's a performance art piece being put together by this woman DeeDee Weaver. I hadn't heard of her before, but you know, my world was pretty traditional in terms of the movement I was doing, but she's doing amazing things with shape and color and style, and she's working on... I've totally lost you, haven't I?" Summer asks sheepishly.

"I kind of was lost at 'performance art piece,'" I tell her truthfully. "But I think what you are saying is, she's doing something cool with dance, and you want—you want to be a part of it?"

"Yes, exactly!" Summer's eyes sparkle as she speaks, using her hands, chopsticks, and spoon to gesture. It's all pretty impressive.

"Well, that sounds awesome. And it's somewhere here in California?"

The sparkle fades. "No, not exactly. It's in Austin."

I stare at Summer.

"Texas," she clarifies.

"I didn't know there was another one," I mutter, before dropping my eyes and concentrating on my soup.

"Nick." Summer puts down her utensils and folds her hands in her lap primly. "I wasn't sure how I was going to do this, but since we're talking about it, I want you to know—well, that is, I was hoping you might want to come."

I stare at her, my spoon forgotten in my hand.

"To Austin. Texas."

I stare some more.

Summer's eyes dart around my face, her expression pensive. But I am suddenly nonverbal. She squares her shoulders and keeps talking.

"I know we haven't had a talk about, like, what we are. Or where we are going. God, that sounds so junior high," she sighs. "But I want you to know that…I like you, Nick. I really, *really* like you. I don't want this to end, and I don't see why it has to."

"You going to Austin might be a reason," I respond.

Summer continues on undeterred. "But—and at the risk of sounding selfish—why can't you come with me? It's not forever. You can keep your house. You can bring Layne Staley. It's not forever," she repeats herself, her voice getting higher and louder.

"You said that already," I tell her absent-mindedly, glaring at my soup on the table.

It's not forever, I think to myself.

Is she talking about her time in Austin?

Or us?

"What am I going to do in Austin?" I ask her, leaning back in my chair and folding my arms over my chest.

"Same thing you do here, Nick," Summer deadpans. "You can run in Austin. You can hang out with your dog in Austin. You can be *with me* in Austin."

"Don't you think—don't you think it's a little soon for us to be living together?" I ask her, doing my best to ignore the hurt creeping across her face. "I mean, like your sister said—"

"You didn't think so much of what she had to say a minute ago," Summer mutters.

"—that's what I've been saying too, you know, about you finding yourself and figuring it all out or whatever." It's a shitty thing to say, and I know it, but I can't stop the words from coming out.

"Are you *kidding* me?" Summer's eyes flash, her cheeks ruddy. "You haven't said anything at all, Nick, so how the hell would I know what you've been saying? Unless you want to clue me in on what's going on in that big dome of yours."

"I just—I don't know, okay?" I run a hand through my hair, trying to get my bearings. "It just seems—everything is sudden. You are here suddenly. We start doing…whatever it is we are doing suddenly. And now you're going to Austin, *suddenly*!"

"I told you I was going to explore other opportunities!" Summer volleys back, leaning forward in her chair.

I bolt up from my own chair, the legs scraping the floor and startling Layne Staley, who jerks his head up from where he's been dozing on his dog bed.

"Is this—you don't think it's too soon, though?"

Summer doesn't respond, looking equal parts angry and hurt.

"You're recently divorced, I'm recently divorced—we should take our time, shouldn't we?"

"Are you asking me or telling me?"

"I'm just trying to be adult about this."

"Well, thank you so much for being the adult in this relationship," Summer says sarcastically, standing up from her chair and throwing her napkin on the table. "I'll have *you* know I've been adulting just fine!"

"Summer—"

"No! No, you can fuck right off with that, Nick. Who are you to tell me what I am and am not ready for? I was with a guy for ten years who literally dictated where I could go, who I could go with, what I could fucking eat! So if you are here to make some more decisions on my behalf out of some misguided notion that you know what's best for me, you can fuck. Right. Off."

"Of course I don't want to tell you what to do! I just—"

"You know what being a 'recent divorcée' has taught me?"

Fuck, she just used air quotes. Not a good sign.

"I know it's a cliché, but it's taught me to seize the day. Carpe the fuck out of that diem, you know? I wasted how many years of my life with Erik? I am done being afraid, of offending people, of saying the wrong thing, of coming on too strong. This is who I am," she continues, gesturing to her chest, slamming her other hand on the table. Some of her soup sloshes over the side of the bowl. "If you don't want to be with me because of your own insecurity, that's fine. But I am not hiding."

Summer bolts toward the door, grabbing her purple coat.

"I am not hiding anything!" My voice is exasperated as I follow her. I want to grab her, shake her, tell her—

Tell her what? That she's the only one for me, and I can't be without her?

That can't be what I am feeling…can it?

"Oh really?" Summer snaps at me, bringing me back to the moment. "The only time you can truly let go is when we're in the bedroom. Did you ever think of that? Over ten years later and you still won't tell me how you feel about me. If you feel anything at all." Summer spits her words out, her tone disgusted.

And I don't blame her.

I am disgusted with myself.

"You've had one foot out the door this whole time we've been together," Summer continues, gesturing wildly with her hands. "I guess this gives you the perfect excuse, huh? Why bother trying for something lasting when I was only going to leave?"

"That's not true! Summer, I just don't want you to miss out on any-thing, like you said. Like your sister said."

I run my hands through my hair. When did this go so off the rails?

Summer's eyes flash as she moves toward the door. "We could have a great life together, Nick. There is literally nothing and no one standing in our way. Nothing! Do you know how rare that is? The only thing in the way is *you* and whatever"—she gestures wildly again—"bullshit inadequacies you've imagined in your head. I am unashamed to put it out there."

Summer pauses to catch her breath, her chest heaving, her face firm and serious. She seems to be actively controlling her breath, trying to get a hold on her temper. I want to pull her into my arms, calm her, kiss her.

When she speaks again, her voice is low.

"Did you know that I've loved you in some form or another since I was in junior high?"

I stand in disbelief, staring back at her gorgeous face, fiery and sad at the same time.

Summer's shoulders deflate as she once again takes in my lack of response.

"It's my time now," she tells me softly. "I deserve to be happy. And so do you, Nick."

I am slack-jawed and stunned, saying everything by saying nothing.

"What do you think of that? Do you have anything to say to that?" Her voice is almost a whisper.

I just can't.

"That's what I thought."

I don't trust myself.

"Come find me if you're ever ready to get fucking real."

Rather than Summer slamming the door, it clicks softly as she shuts it.

Leaving me alone.

Just like I wanted.

Chapter Thirty-Seven

Summer

I TEXTED TATUM ON MY WAY HOME FROM NICK'S. IT WAS A MIRACLE I didn't see anyone I knew during my walk, but I kept my beanie pulled low and my sweater wrapped around me, tight like armor.

I've made ginger tea and am sitting in lotus on the floor, a cookie-scented candle perfuming the room around me. Yes, I light Christmas candles year-round.

I also love the pine smell, but they remind me a little too much of Nick. Hence my choice for cookie.

I hear Tatum's knock before she enters, stopping short once she sees me on the floor.

"Summer, what's up? I brought some rocky road like you requested." She puts it in the freezer before sitting on the couch.

"Thanks. Um." I pause, a little unsure about how to begin.

Tatum obviously knows that Nick and I have been doing…whatever it is we've been doing, although I haven't told her that I have big-F Feelings for Nick. But she has admittedly been a little weird about the whole thing. And I understand she's going through her own stuff.

I decide, as ever, that honesty is the best policy.

"I got a job offer in Austin," I begin.

Tatum raises her eyebrows. "Okay…so you are leaving, then?" She keeps going before I can respond to that. "You were talking last week about how that was one of the ones you wanted, right? You can help keep Austin weird or whatever," she quips.

"No. I mean, yes, it is great, and yes, I really do want it. The dance director is amazing, her vision is just so unique and inclusive and—" I pause again and take a breath. That's not what I want to talk about at all.

"I told Nick, and he…well, he basically congratulated me and offered to help me pack my stuff," I say, throwing my hands up in exasperation.

"My brother," Tatum repeats. "I mean…I am sure he's happy for you. Isn't he?"

"But he just… I thought we had something here! I thought, yes, he'd be happy for me, but I also thought—why wouldn't he come with me?"

Tatum frowns. "Why would he do that?"

"Because we're together, Tatum! Or at least, I thought we were."

"I see," she responds slowly, examining a whole lot of nothing on her nails. "And you expect him to…what, follow you around wherever you go? Like I said before, you know he's got a life here, Summer."

"A life…doing what? Running emotively through the fog and brooding on his balcony?" I joke before I realize that Tatum is not smiling.

She crosses her arms over her chest, her posture closed off. "He's going through some stuff, you know."

"Yes, Tatum, I *do* know, and I don't mean to make light of that." I am getting exasperated and try to rein it in in the face of Tatum's apparent impassion.

"Look. For the first time in a really, really long time, I am doing things for me. For no one else. I thought Nick was part of that, I thought he got that, but instead…" My voice trails off. Tatum remains stoic.

"Sounds like you might've read more into the 'relationship' with Nick than is really there," she says, taking a tone like I am a freaking toddler.

"Why are you being so mean?" I ask her honestly. This is not the friend I know. And whatever weirdness I expected her to exhibit about Nick and me, I certainly didn't anticipate her to be flat-out mean.

"It's just… I mean, don't you think it's weird that you immediately come here and get things started with Nick? You guys both got out of big relationships. Don't you think it's a little fast?"

My cheeks are hot and my shoulders tight, my voice angry when I respond. "It's Nick, Tatum. You've got to know that he is not just some guy for me!"

Tatum gives me a side-eye. "What, you think the second guy you've ever slept with is suddenly the one?"

I suck in a breath. "What the *hell*, Tatum?!" I can't believe she's throwing that back in my face. "I asked you to come over because I thought you would be sympathetic, not supremely bitchy!"

"Well, I'm sorry I am not living up to your expectations!"

"If you had a problem with me and Nick, why didn't you say something before?"

"You moved so fast that I didn't get a chance to!" Tatum sputters. Her characterization of me as some seductress, aiming to get Nick quickly into my bed, is laughable. But before I can respond to that little nugget, she continues.

"Why can't you be at peace with yourself? You literally just told me, like, a day ago that you never wanted to be in a relationship, ever again! And now you are jumping into something, again, before you are ready."

I feel Tatum's words spread like ice in my veins. Why is everyone important to me—my sister, Nick, and now Tatum—convinced that I can't make decisions for myself?

"What do you mean?" I ask her.

"You married Erik, the first guy in your life who ever paid you any attention." Tatum ticks it off on her fingers like a to-do list. "You are here ostensibly to start over, but you immediately start a new relationship with Nick, the second guy in your life to ever pay you any attention."

My eyes sting, and there is a telltale lump in my throat telling me that tears are imminent. I open my mouth, close it. Open it again. I choke down a sob before responding to her.

"You know what? I think you should leave."

I say it as calmly as I can, but my voice stutters at the end. Tatum's dark eyes flash, and her shoulders jerk as if she's been pushed.

I want to tell her she doesn't know a thing about me, that she doesn't know about what Nick and I have. I want her to comfort me, the way a friend would. I want to tell her that I know she got a raw deal with Dr. Trevor, just like I had a raw deal with Erik, but that it doesn't always have to be that way.

I always thought that during a breakup, girlfriends would eat ice cream, listen to Lana Del Rey, and binge-watch something comforting like *British Bake Off*, all under the safety of a weighted blanket on the couch, a steady supply of potato chips at the ready.

I was wrong about Nick.

I guess I was wrong about that too.

Tatum just stares at me, her hazel eyes wide.

"That was really mean what you said," I tell her in a low tone. "I am sorry that you have had a rough go of it lately. But those issues don't have a goddamn thing to do with me. And so, I think you should leave."

I go to the front door and swing it open.

She leaves without another word.

I go into my bathroom, shut the door, light another candle, and start the shower.

I can listen to Lana Del Rey and eat potato chips by myself.

Chapter Thirty-Eight

Nick

"**N**ICKY."

I ignore my big sister and keep my eyes trained on the college basketball game on television. It started raining on my walk over here. I currently nurse a beer, my ancient Cal baseball cap pulled down low, glaring at anyone who attempts to make eye contact with me. Layne Staley is curled up and content at my feet.

"Little brother."

It doesn't work on Julia. And anyway, she's got the booze and food.

"Here. If you're not going to talk to me, at least eat something."

According to Julia—and my mother, and my grandfather—there is nothing in the world that can't be solved by food. My stomach growls as she sets some chicken and waffle sliders in front of me.

I glare at her some more, before glaring at the plate.

Then I pick up one of the sliders and eat it whole.

I'm mad but not stupid. Julia and Lincoln's food is the best.

Julia glares right back at me, her hand on her hip.

"I'm an asshole," I confess.

"Oh yeah?" Julia rolls her eyes at me. "Martyrs are annoying. What did you do?"

"I'm not a martyr," I snap back immediately. "I'm…I'm a fucking mess, Julia."

To my horror, my voice cracks at the end of the sentence. To her credit, Julia doesn't bat an eye.

She mutters something to herself that sounds an awful lot like "fucking toxic masculinity" before snapping the towel hanging over her shoulder to the bar. She places both hands on the bar and leans over.

"Why are you a 'mess'?"

I take a breath and eye her steadily. "I had a panic attack in front of Summer."

"Okay. So what?"

"So what? So what is… I mean, she doesn't need to be dealing with that. To be dealing with *me*."

"I mean, way to shit on everyone else who gets panic attacks and still thinks themselves deserving of love and a healthy relationship, but please, continue." She points one of her fingers right at me. "Having panic attacks or being in therapy or whatever else has you hung up doesn't make you a mess. It makes you a human being, Nicky."

"I just thought…" I take a deep breath and rub the back of my neck. "I thought this would be easier. I didn't think I would be feeling this way…" Another breath and I exhale, counting to five slowly. "I didn't think I would be feeling these feelings so strongly. I don't like feeling out of control," I add.

"Nicky." Julia gives me a sad smile. "You've been in your feelings since before it was cool." She cocks her head to the side and considers me thoughtfully before continuing. "I wish that this world allowed people—and especially men—to feel the full spectrum of emotion. I wish all the feelings were allowed and encouraged. And I can't imagine what it was like in such a, like, dudebro environment. But there is nothing—" she narrows her eyes at me "—*nothing,* that makes you a mess, other than your total refusal to see that something really good, really special, is right in front of you and that you deserve it."

I stay silent. I know better than to interrupt when Julia Echeverria Cruz is about to drop some wisdom on me.

"And if you want to blame it on your therapy or anxiety or the fact that you take medication or any of that, then that's fine. But I am here to tell you that you are wrong. The blame is entirely with you and your fear. And I am pretty sure that no amount of therapy or medication is going to help you with that."

I chew on that for a moment, but she's on a roll.

"Do you think you're the first person to be apprehensive about the fact that you have such strong feelings for another human being? Especially when it is apparent to me and everyone else around that you've never had these feelings for anyone else?" Julia pauses and eyes me carefully. "Even your ex-wife?"

I narrow my gaze to pin Julia with a glare. "Now, hold the fuck on. I loved Gretchen."

"Sure you did. She was nice, and she was good for you at the time." Julia assesses me. "But not the way you love Summer."

I look down at my hands, which I've folded on the table in front of me.

I can't look at Julia because she's absolutely right.

"Gretchen was safe. Gretchen was your stability in a crazy-as-fuck world where I would imagine that it's hard to know who's really on your side." Julia pauses again. "Actually, that's kind of your MO, isn't it? In high school, you dated Amber, who…while very nice, is also very drama-free and even-keeled. Easy to be with." Julia speaks slowly, like she's putting the pieces of a puzzle together.

"What did you say when Gretchen told you she wanted to get divorced?"

"Say?" I parrot back. I have to think about it a minute. "I mean…I didn't really say anything, I guess. It was apparent that, you know, it was over for a while by that point," I concede.

"Did you challenge her?"

"What?"

"Did you *fight* for her, Nicky? Did you tell her, 'No, woman. You are my wife and we are not getting divorced'? Did you even want to?"

"Want to what?" My question is low, but I am playing dumb. I know what Julia is getting at.

"Did you want to work to save your marriage?"

"It wouldn't have helped."

I am a master at avoiding the real issue that Julia is getting at.

"Did you fight back against Gretchen's demand to get divorced?"

"Never." I answer with no hesitation.

Julia raises her eyebrows at me as if to say *See?*

I laugh, but there's no humor in it. "And what kind of asshole does that make me, then, Jules?" I run my hands through my hair in exasperation. "I fucking married that girl, and I knew it! I knew she wasn't The One, and I did it anyway. Because…because it was easier."

There it is.

That's what's got me tied up.

I married Gretchen knowing that she wasn't my forever.

Summer has all but confessed to similar behavior with Erik—marrying him because she was lonely, because he gave her attention, because he pulled the wool over her eyes, made her think he was worthy of her.

Erik obviously wasn't. And Gretchen obviously wasn't the great love of my life, although I can't dispute that she gave me some stability in a world that was desperately lacking it. And maybe even Amber back in high school, if I'm honest. We weren't in love, but she was nice and sweet, and it kept the other girls away from me.

But what kind of people are we to make these decisions, if we don't know our own minds?

I don't realize I've voiced this last thought aloud until Julia responds. "Do you really think that you are the only person who's made a bad choice when it comes to relationships? Including marriage?"

I raise my eyebrows at her. "You didn't."

She scoffs. "Obviously not." Her face takes on the same faraway look it usually does when she thinks about Lincoln. Which, yes, still grosses me out.

Julia shakes her head. "But this isn't about me. Or Mom or Dad, or any of the other relationships you're thinking of—the ones that are solid and strong. I mean…divorce exists for a reason, Nicky."

I mull that over for a second.

"And I don't think you're a bad guy or less deserving of happiness just because you arguably settled for Gretchen. Just like I don't think Summer is less deserving of happiness just because she married an asshole out of loneliness."

"Of course she's not!" I insist vehemently. If anyone's deserving of happiness, it's Summer.

"Then why the hell are you determined to punish yourself for making a similar choice?"

I mull that over too, pushing away my now-empty plate and wiping my mouth with a napkin.

"Are you really going to spend the rest of your life—and you're young, Nicky—moping around this sleepy little town?"

My lips turn up a little at this. "Brock basically said the same thing."

"Well, listen to him. Listen to me, I know what I'm talking about." I smile a little more at that.

I nod in acknowledgment.

"So…what are you waiting for?" Julia lifts her chin in challenge.

It's a good question. And I don't know the answer.

～～～～～

I am momentarily distracted from answering Julia's million-dollar question when she looks over my shoulder. "Hey!" she says in a surprised tone. "What're you doing here?"

Tatum dramatically seats herself at the barstool next to me. "I need a Bloody Maria, please."

Julia raises her eyebrows but gets to work. When she's done, she sets a Bloody Maria—made with tequila instead of vodka—with a toothpick the size of a ruler in it, speared through a couple giant tater tots, olives, a spicy pickle, and a huge slice of candied bacon.

"Jesus H., Julia," I tell her. "That's a damn meal."

"I know!" she responds gleefully. "It's nineteen dollars, and people will pay for the thing happily. Unbelievable." At Tatum's side-eye, she tells her, "For you, ten dollars."

Tatum rolls her eyes and starts drinking. Julia and I watch our younger sister, waiting for the inevitable reveal.

"I'm an asshole," Tatum mutters after five minutes, half of her drink gone.

"Join the club," Julia says casually. "So's this guy." She gestures to me, and I wave at Tatum.

She huffs a laugh, but it dies quickly.

"You want to tell us, or should we guess?"

"I said some…not so nice things to Summer."

"Good Lord, you two!" Julia barks. Tatum winces. "Give the poor girl a break."

"I know, I know," Tatum moans, regret evident in her voice.

"Did you guys have a fight? Wait, I don't want to know. What did you say? Is she okay?" I can't get my questions out quick enough.

"I may have accused her of…I don't even know. Rushing into a relationship with you, not being mature enough to know her own feelings, that sort of thing."

Julia laughs cryptically. "Just like this guy over here. You were right, Nicky, only it's you two who are a mess."

"Both of you are assholes," Tatum mutters.

"It's a club of three! Mom will be so proud." Julia smiles. "You can be the president," she adds to Tatum.

"I mean, obviously," Tatum responds.

"*Anyway*," I interrupt to get these ladies back on track. "Julia is…not wrong."

Tatum raises her eyebrows at me in question.

"About what I said to her—about rushing in."

Julia scoffs. "So basically, Summer has had two people—two people whom she really loves and respects, no less—question her judgment over the course of a few hours."

"Three people," I correct her unhappily.

"Who's three?" Tatum asks, slurping her drink.

"Her sister," I respond. "Not today, but she said they spoke recently."

"Oh, that woman," Julia mutters darkly. "Not helpful."

"Yeah, I get that impression," I agree.

"Anyway. That's fucked up, Tatum. What you said." Julia uses her best "I'm not mad, I'm disappointed" voice.

"I'm not mad, I'm disappointed" voice.

"*I know!*" Tatum screeches. "Summer basically told me as much."

"She did?"

Tatum looks chagrined. "Yeah. And then she told me to get out of her house."

"Good for her," Julia says firmly. Meanwhile, my heart is breaking—not only did I potentially screw up any chance I ever had being with the woman I love, but my sister might have destroyed whatever good will Summer had toward Team Echeverria.

"Fuck."

"Pretty much," Tatum agrees.

"Look," Julia interjects. "If I may? As 'sudden' as you both think this is—" my big sister dodges the French fry thrown by my little sister "—you gotta know it's not like that."

"What do you mean?" I asked dumbly.

Tatum scoffs now. "Come on, man. You know Summer had a crush on you. All the girls had a crush on you."

"Once you became Nick Echeverria, football god, Mom had to beat them off with a broom." Julia picks up the narrative, nabbing a French fry and popping it into her mouth.

I make the connection. "Yeah, but I don't think Summer... I mean, she wasn't one of those. Back then? She didn't like me that way...did she?"

She did say that, didn't she?

I have loved you in some form or another since junior high.

Both of my sisters look at me as if I am, again, the dumbest person in the room.

"Little brother, Summer's had a crush on you since the boy band era. Maybe even before then too," Julia offers.

I process that for a moment when Tatum pipes in. "I also may have insinuated that Summer has an...inability to be single."

"Like J.Lo," Julia offers.

"Hey, the woman is in love with being in love," Tatum responds diplomatically. "But basically, I may have insinuated that she is uncomfortable being alone."

"Insinuated?" I grit out.

Tatum glares at me.

"What were your exact words?" I ask her.

"They were actually pretty shitty, and I already feel bad enough, so no, I am not sharing them with you right now." Tatum sighs in defeat. "Suffice to say I am definitely the reigning president of the asshole club."

"Tatum," Julia admonishes her.

"Look, I know! I was mad and frustrated and new to the reality that is the Nick and Summer Love Story, okay?"

"But why?" Julia asks.

"Why what?"

"Why are you mad?"

That pulls Tatum up short. She eats a French fry and takes a sip of her Bloody Maria. "I don't want to talk about it," she says quietly. She goes back to eating, and that's the end of that.

Whatever. That's an issue for her to deal with. "Tatum, I love Summer."

She coughs and coughs and takes another sip of her drink. "Jesus Christ, Julia, this is going to put hair on my chest." She sips her water. "Okay. Okay, that's good. Because I think she loves you too."

"She does," I respond affirmatively.

"How do you know?" Julia asks.

"She implied as much…"

"What were the exact words?" Tatum asks me mockingly.

"'I love you.'" I avoid both of my sisters' direct gazes and fiddle with my water. "She may have also told me I need to grow the fuck up, or something to that effect."

"Dude. You are an asshole." Tatum holds up her drink to cheers me.

"Takes one to know one," I respond as we clink our glasses together.

I sip my iced tea and think about how I left things with Summer. "She, ah…she thinks I should move with her. To Austin."

"Yeah, she told me that too," Tatum says.

"So, why don't you?" Julia asks.

"But—I mean—I live here! I have a house here." I sputter. "Layne Staley likes it here."

"Wow, great reasons, Nick," Julia says sarcastically. "Look, Layne Staley would go to the moon so long as you were there. And if that's your reason for staying, then you really have no reason at all other than the fact that you're being a big scaredy-cat."

"I am not. Being. A scaredy-cat," I growl.

"Meow!" Tatum cackles and takes a huge sip of her Bloody Maria. I hope she chokes on an olive.

I really don't, though. I love my sisters.

"You can get a house anywhere, and you know it. Hell, you can keep this house and get a damn subdivision if you want, Nicky." Julia moves down the bar to take an order from a new customer.

"Why is everyone so goddamn *nonchalant* about this?" I try not to sound stressed, but I can hear my voice cracking.

"Aw, Nicky, are you sad that no one is going to miss you?" Tatum asks me, fiddling with the pickle on her toothpick. "Gross," she mutters, putting it on the plate.

"Look." She turns her body toward me. "You love Summer."

I nod.

"Summer apparently loves you."

I shrug.

"Don't discount her feelings. She told you she loves you, so she does." Tatum chews on her candied bacon.

"Now, I may have had a similar reaction to the whole Austin thing when Summer told me. *I* was a dick. Don't be a dick like me."

I nod begrudgingly.

"So! This is an easy fix. Summer accepts the new job, she goes to Austin, you and Layne Staley go with her, voilà! Everyone is happy." Tatum spreads her hands with a flourish and goes back to the salad on the toothpick.

"I guess," I mutter.

I hate it when not one, but both of my sisters are right.

"I know you hate it when I am right," Tatum tells me, reading my mind. "But honestly, Nick. Get over yourself."

"That's what I told him too!" Julia says, returning to us and hearing Tatum's last statement.

"Kind of an asshole thing to say," I tell them.

"Well, as you know, we are card-carrying members of the Asshole Society," Julia tells me with mock pride.

"And it's time for you to renounce your membership," Tatum says.

"You too," I tell my little sister.

"Don't I know it," she mumbles, before taking another gulp of her drink.

Chapter Thirty-Nine

Nick

AFTER RENOUNCING MY MEMBERSHIP IN THE ASSHOLE SOCIETY and "getting over myself," I had to plan.

Not really my strongest skill, but I had to do it quickly.

I didn't want to run after Summer without a plan in place.

Tatum is normally who I would go to with any planning needs. But she's still being a little weird about the whole Summer-and-me thing. She says she's happy for me as her brother and for Summer as her friend—this, of course, assumes there is a Summer-and-me to be had—but there's something under the surface that she's not saying.

So I go to another person who, while I don't know anything about his planning skills, I do know he'll give it to me straight.

Brock.

"Nick, you poor, grumpy bastard," is his response when I tell him how elaborately and conclusively I fucked things up with Summer. "Of course I will help you."

"Thanks, man."

"But before I do, I want to know one thing."

"Shoot."

"Do you deserve Summer?"

That pulls me up short.

"Because," Brock continues in his know-it-all manner, "I know that before, you were operating under this misguided theory that perhaps you did not deserve a woman as stunning and delightful as Summer. Which is bullshit, to be clear."

"Right," I mutter.

"So yes, Nicky, I will help you. But only if you concede that you deserve Summer, she deserves you, and you will ride off in the Texas sunset and have brooding, athletic, graceful dancing babies together, so that in six months or a year or whenever, you aren't bitching to me about being less than or not good enough or whatever."

I wait a few seconds to make sure Brock is done with his monologue.

"Okay," I tell him.

"Okay…?"

"Okay. I deserve…I deserve Summer. I am good enough for her, and she is good enough for me." I parrot his words back to him, feeling like I am doing a group therapy exercise.

Maybe I am.

"I'm so proud of you, brother. Seriously. Tearing up over here."

"Fuck off."

"You kiss your mother with that mouth, Nicholas? Now, let's talk about what we're going to do to get your girl back."

Chapter Forty

Summer

I AM TRULY ADULTING WITH THE BEST OF THEM.

I have a cute apartment in a funky neighborhood.

There are approximately forty billion eclectic restaurants, cozy coffee shops, and hipster dive bars for me to check out in my spare time.

My colleagues are diverse and friendly, and the level of talent is unreal. Sometimes I have to pinch myself to remind myself that I get to do what I love—create—for a living.

Put on "Unwritten" by Natasha Bedingfield, because I can feel the rain on my skin.

I've been so busy running around Austin that I've barely had time to think about Nick.

In fact, I mentally pat myself on the back for how actively I am *not* thinking about him.

I push his stupid, beautiful face out of my head when I do my morning sun salutations.

I shut the door on all the sweet, sexy words he said to me when I am getting ready for the day.

I ignore the pang of loneliness that hits me when I am eating at a taqueria near the rehearsal space and see "California burrito" on the menu. I want to laugh and cry when I see that this particular burrito has French fries (good), but also rice (sacrilege).

I definitely don't think of Nick and his magnificent ability to be both soft-spoken and the dirtiest talker I have ever known, late at night when I am lying in my bed.

Every dog I see doesn't remind me of Layne Staley, and anything related to football—of which there is a *lot; Texas loves football, maybe you've heard—doesn't remind me of Nicholas Echeverria and that one time we almost had it all.

I try to remember to be grateful that I got to have him for even a brief moment in time.

I try to remember what my mother used to tell me. "Your superpower is your ability to love. But not everyone has that ability."

I know, I *know* Nick is hurting. And I'm not so self-centered to imagine that there aren't other things going on in his life—in his head, in his heart—that have nothing to do with me.

It doesn't make it hurt any less, though.

Because one thing has become apparent in all this actively-not-thinking-about-Nick I have been doing.

I love Nick, and maybe I always have, in a way.

And I'm not apologizing for it.

But I do have to live with it.

༄༄༄༄༄

"Summer, are you trying to butter us up?"

DeeDee is just as I found her to be in our conversations before I moved to Austin—big, brash, and bossy. She wears loud colors all over her body—her tattoos, her lipstick, her clothes, her hair. Today, her hair is a cerulean color and is styled in pin curls, like Marilyn Monroe. She's wearing thick black cat-eye glasses and pale-pink lipstick, and her voluptuous figure is clad in a navy wrap dress.

I look up from the laptop where I am watching film from our last rehearsal and see her balancing three big bakers' boxes in her hands.

"What are those?"

"OMG, are those from the Sweet Society?" José asks from behind me. My new colleague is deep in his own film review.

"I didn't order anything," I protest.

"Well, do you have a man friend we don't know about? Woman

friend? Other…friend?" DeeDee winks at me and puts a hand on her hip expectantly.

"There's a card," José informs us as he grabs a purple-frosted donut.

"Thank you," I murmur uncertainly, reaching for the card. DeeDee smiles at me before walking away.

Summer, I know receiving flowers isn't your favorite. So, I decided donuts would be better. I hope you like them. They are apparently really popular in Austin. Plus, they are purple (at least I hope they are purple…that's what I ordered).

I remember what you said about money for flowers would be better spent elsewhere. I remember everything you said, actually. Anyway, you should know that in addition to the donuts, I made a donation to the Public Arts Performance Center in Austin. It looks like they are doing great things for children who want to dance and sing and all that other stuff.

I miss you.

Nick

"Are they…are they from him?" José whispers loudly. I glance up at him where he's trying to be nonchalant, but I can tell it's killing him.

"They are, actually," I respond, folding up the note.

"Donuts of apology? Donuts declaring his undying love for you? Donuts admitting he's a moron?"

I smile ruefully. "No apology, no declarations of love. But…he did say he misses me," I add carefully.

"Hmph." José sniffs. "Not really a grand gesture, is it?"

"No, not really. But…I don't think Nick's a grand gesture type of dude. Actually, I know he's not. He's actually really shy, if you can believe that. I know most people probably assume that he's all outgoing and chatty, but he's pretty quiet and reserved…" My voice trails off when I see José giving me a knowing look.

"Do you miss him?"

"Of course I miss him." There's really no point in arguing otherwise. "Yes. I miss him. But these…" I gesture to the boxes. "They don't mean anything. And it's nice of him to make a donation, but…" I shrug. "Maybe it's a way of saying good-bye."

"Maybe," José agrees reluctantly, but his eyes are telling me he doesn't believe that for a second.

My ability to love doesn't feel like so much of a superpower right now.

Chapter Forty-One

NICK'S MESSAGES DON'T STOP WITH DONUTS.

Over the next few weeks, my best-laid plans to actively *not* think about Nick go up in flames.

A few days after his first delivery, I receive an email from the local YMCA, thanking me for the generous donation made on my behalf for their after-school programs, including sports, swimming, and dancing.

I don't receive a message like I did with the donuts, but the email from the Y says the donation was made "by N.E. in honor of Summer Mahoney."

To say that didn't make the butterflies in my stomach rise up and take flight again would be a lie.

The next week, I get a phone call from a woman who introduces herself to me as the donations coordinator for a local food bank. In the thickest Southern accent I have ever heard, she thanks me profusely for another generous donation made in my name. I let her speak and confirm that the donation was made a "Mr. L. Staley."

The butterflies fly higher.

And the next week, I receive another email from a local shelter for LGBTQIA+ youth, again thanking me for the generous donation, which will enable them to purchase clothes, toiletries, and other essentials for those at their shelter. This, of course, leads me to browse their website and read some of the stories of the young people who have visited this shelter, which, of course, makes me bawl like a baby. I immediately sign up to make a recurring donation.

The butterflies flap their wings faster.

I want to call someone. I want to go knock on the door of my neighbors, an older lesbian couple named—I kid you not—Ethel and Lucy, and show them the things Nick has done. I want to call a radio station—do people do that anymore?—and ask them what it all *means!*

I want to call Tatum. But we haven't spoken since our fight. And while I know it's petty, I don't want to be the one to break that silence.

I am not so self-involved that I think Tatum's anger and the hurtful words she spewed were all about me, or all about me and Nick. I know Tatum's got her own issues to deal with. She's a strong woman with a strong personality, and I have no doubt Dr. Douchebag did a number on her.

But I also know that right now, it seems like she's not ready to deal with the fallout from that.

So, I don't call anyone, and I leave Ethel and Lucy alone. Instead, I wipe my eyes and get my phone.

Before I can chicken out, I go with simple.

> *Me:* Hi.

I get a response immediately.

I can't help it; I squeal like a teenage girl. Picture me holed up in the pantry on the landline, the phone cord pulled tight as I talk with the guy I like on the phone into the wee hours of the morning.

> *Nick:* Hi.

And then…

> *Nick:* I was hoping to hear from you.

OHMYGOD YOU WERE?! …is not what I respond with.

> *Me:* Well, you certainly got my attention with all the things you've been doing. Seriously, that is so, so amazing. Thank you so much. It means a lot.

> *Nick:* I remembered what you said about flowers being pointless and dying and being stinky or something like that

I laugh out loud. Yes, it was something like that.

> *Me:* You got the gist of what I was saying, that's for damn sure.

And now…what do I say? "What does this mean?" "Are you sorry?" "Are we friends now?"

Ew. I do not want to be Nick's friend.

I am saved when Nick sends another text.

Nick: There's a lot of stuff I want to tell you that isn't really appropriate for texting. Can I ask you a huge favor?

Me: Sure

Nick: Can you be at West Cedar High School this Friday, around 2:30 p.m.?

That is…not what I was expecting.

Me: Okay…?

Nick: Heads up that there's a huge exhibition game that night between West Cedar and their big rival. I don't know how early people get there for the game, but make sure you are on time.

Me: Okay…

Nick: Okay, thanks

Nick: I miss you.

Well, fuck me. The butterflies are now doing somersaults, on the roller coaster, bungee jumping. I want to tell them to stop, to relax. We don't know why the hell I am supposed to be at a high school in Austin, Texas, on a Friday afternoon; we don't know anything at all.

But Nick misses you!

I sigh, flopping down on my bed and clutching my phone to my chest like it's a love letter.

And maybe it is.

Chapter Forty-Two

AUSTIN IN LATE SPRING ON A FRIDAY AFTERNOON IS HOT AND humid, but you wouldn't know it from the hundreds of people milling about West Cedar High School on this day.

I snag a parking spot and make my way to the football field. The stadium is huge—it must hold thousands of spectators, not less than five hundred like at my old high school football stadium. People are decked out in their respective team gear, some with face paint already sliding down their skin in the heat.

I enter the stadium and nearly get bowled over by two little boys in matching jerseys, chatting excitedly with each other.

"Sorry, ma'am!" one of the boys chirps to me, and yes, I am "ma'am" here. God bless Texas.

The little boy goes back to chatting with his friend before running off. "Brock autographed mine! I can't wait to show Mikey! He's going to be so jealous!"

At the mention of Brock, my interest is piqued. Turning my attention toward the field, I see lines upon lines of kids—girls and boys—in football jerseys, team T-shirts, and other sports apparel.

My eyes immediately leap to a familiar name on the back of a jersey. *Echeverria.*

My heart drops, and I jerk my head to the field. In the center, you can't miss Brock Donovan—he's huge, his smile clear to me even across a football field. I can imagine this is kind of his thing, being surrounded by fans. Although, when the fans are children, I can also imagine that is an enjoyable perk of being famous.

Brock is signing everything being handed to him—shirts, jerseys, papers, hats. And to his side, only slightly smaller but no less intimidating in size, is Nick.

My heart drops again, and I stop short.

Nick is *here?* In Texas? Because…he is signing things?

Reminding my feet to work, I walk toward the chain link fence surrounding the turf. There are a ton of people leaning on the fence, fanning themselves with programs in the hot sun. I squeeze through and rest my arms over the fence. I am greedy—I want to watch Nick for a moment before he sees me.

"God, I would climb him like a tree," a woman a few feet to my left mutters to her friend. She has on pink lipstick to match a pink visor placed over her perfectly styled blond hair.

"Which one?" the friend on her other side asks.

"Does it matter?" she replies. The corner of my mouth turns up because she's right. That's two good-looking men out there.

But only one of them whom I want.

"Hey, Brock!" the friend calls out. "I've got something for you to sign!"

I hear some chuckles, some hooting, and some gasps—I guess this is a family-friendly event, after all—but Brock looks up with a smile and catches the woman's eye, gesturing toward the line.

"Not what I hoped for," the woman mutters.

Brock is about to go back to signing items when he does a double take, catching my eye. I sheepishly raise my hand in a little wave, and he grins like the Cheshire cat. He turns to Nick, elbowing him, and gestures toward me.

Nick's eyes meet mine.

And even though we are a good thirty yards from each other, I feel the force of his gaze everywhere.

I really fucking missed him, my best-laid plans to push him out of my head notwithstanding.

There's a man in a light blue suit with a navy tie—he must be sweating his ass off—standing near Brock and Nick. Nick says something to the man, speaks briefly to the next people in line waiting to get his autograph, and then turns and starts jogging toward me.

"Shoot, he's coming over here," Pink Visor whispers.

"Shit," I mutter to myself.

Nick has on a navy T-shirt and black athletic shorts. As he makes his way over to me, I take in the muscles in his legs, the tendons in his golden arms, flexing even during this moderate activity.

He is Nick Echeverria, football god, and I am fucked.

His hazel eyes swallow me whole as he gets closer. I suck in a breath and bite my lip, leaving my hands dangling over the side of the fence, willing my heart not to climb up and out of my chest.

Nick slows down, walking and stopping right in front of me, the fence the only thing separating us. He reaches his hands forward as if to grab mine, then checks himself, putting his hands on his hips. There's a hum of voices around us, reminding me that to all these people, he's a Super Bowl-winning quarterback.

I guess he's kind of a big deal.

"Hi," he says, his voice low.

"*Hi*," I squeak out.

He smiles, white teeth flashing, before stepping closer.

"Thanks for coming," he tells me. "Sorry, I know it's hot."

"You can't control the weather," I tell him. "And…what have I come to exactly?"

"I can explain it all later," he responds. "But for now…do you want to come with me? There's a pop-up with some shade over there. And water. And Gatorade if you are into that. But you can hang out there, if you want? Until Brock and I are done? I mean—only if you want to. If you aren't busy or doing something else?"

Nick rambling is about the most adorable thing I have ever seen. He runs a hand over the back of his neck, waiting for me to respond.

But honestly, I stopped listening after his question of "do you want to come with me?"

I guess he still doesn't get that I would go with him anywhere.

"Yeah," I tell him with a smile, enjoying the sparkle in his eyes and the relief on his face. "Yeah, I'd like that."

"Great. There's the entrance down that way—I'll meet you there."

I push myself off the fence and walk toward the entrance he indicated. I see Pink Visor and her friend watching me with envy and admiration. I give them a wink and a smile; Pink Visor elbows her friend and smiles back.

"You go, girl," she says.

"I will," I promise.

Nick

Brock has made all the jokes and kissed all the babies, I have mumbled my way through a hundred introductions, and we've both signed all the things.

Summer's been patiently waiting for the better part of an hour under the pop-up, and now we have to get the hell off the field so that teams can do their warm-ups before tonight's game.

I make my way over to the shade, where Summer is currently charming the pants off Mando, my former agent, of all people. Yes, it did not end well with him at the conclusion of my career, but he's been instrumental in getting all this set up.

"Hey. All done," I tell him, grabbing a Gatorade from the cooler.

"Good, Nicky, good. Summer here has been telling me stories about what shenanigans you got up to when you were little."

I scoff before downing the drink in three gulps. "That's nonsense," I tell them, wiping my upper lip. "Now, Summer? And my sisters? Those girls were hellions."

I see Summer's smile crack a little at the mention of my sisters. I assume Tatum hasn't patched things up with her yet.

But one plan at a time.

"I believe it, I believe it," Mando says, his megawatt veneers present through his wide smile. "Well, Nicky, I am glad we got to get together and let bygones be bygones, you know?"

I nod. "Me too. And thank you for helping us do…all this."

"What is 'all this'?" Summer asks, not without a little exasperation. "I tried to get it out of Mando here, but he's like Fort Knox."

I look to Mando, who shrugs. "I figured you went to all this trouble, you want to tell her yourself."

"Thank you," I tell him, strangely touched. "And Sunshine, to answer your question—'this' is the Austin Junior Football Camp."

"Spearheaded and led by none other than Nicky over there," Mando jumps in. I am sure it was killing him not to shill the camp to anyone who asked.

"Football camp?" Summer asks.

"Yeah, you know, for anyone under high school age—girls or boys— who want to play, but maybe aren't good enough to be on the school team or who attend a school that doesn't have a football team. Nicky is going to be coaching them, with special guests as scheduling permits." Mando spreads his hands in a flourish. I know that he's doing his sports agent thing to get some of those "special guests."

"I wanted him," Mando continues, "to call it the Nick Echeverria Camp for Kids. The acronym would have been NECK. But," he sighs dramatically, "I was shot down on that recommendation."

I roll my eyes at his antics. "No one wants to go to Camp NECK."

"That's not what your mom said last night," Brock chimes in, joining us in the shade. "Good show, Mando." They clasp hands.

"That doesn't even make sense, dude," I tell him.

"In my twisted brain, it does. Summer, always a pleasure." Brock gives a little wave before turning to go.

"Wait, you're leaving?" Summer responds.

"I've got a date with some air conditioning and a cold beer," Brock responds. Probably also with one of the women he was flirting with earlier, but he doesn't mention that. He turns to me and gives me a side hug, leaning in so I can hear him whisper, *"Seal. The. Deal."*

Mando pipes up. "And I'm out too, Nicky. Summer, it was good to meet you."

And they take off before I can say anything, leaving both Summer and me standing under the tent.

I watch them walk away and then turn back to Summer. She's got her purse slung over her shoulder, her red hair pulled back off her face in a braid. Her brown eyes are searching me, wondering.

"You're—you're going to have a football camp here? In Austin?"

"Texas," I confirm.

"But…how long is the camp for? A week? A weekend?"

"Nah, longer than that," I tell her, wiping my brow. "I mean, at least a few months, until the traditional football season officially starts…" My voice trails off.

"But you're going to be here, in Austin, and I am here too, and—where's Layne Staley?"

I smile. "He's currently at the home I'm renting, in a beautiful, air-conditioned room with all his toys and his dog bed. He's very happy."

"The house—the house you're renting? But—"

That's enough questioning.

I toss my empty Gatorade bottle in the recycle bin, move toward Summer, and place my hands on her cheeks. I pull her into me, her body flush to mine. I am sure I am sweaty and might smell bad; I don't care. Because if I don't kiss this woman right now, I am not sure I can take another breath.

So, I do.

Summer squeaks at my sudden movement, and I place my lips on hers. Her squeak turns to a sigh as her eyes flutter closed, and we just stand like that for a moment—pressed together, her slight curves against my body, sharing each other's breath.

And I know in this moment that everyone was right—regardless of what happened in our past, it's over now. It doesn't matter, and what does matter is the woman in front of me, the woman in my arms, drawing her own around my neck and sighing again as I lick into her mouth to kiss her deeper.

"Nick," she whispers. "I missed you so much."

"I missed you too," I whisper back, kissing her again, letting her tongue meet mine, her mouth warm and inviting.

"I love you so much," I add, surprised at how fucking *good* it feels to say that. It feels right.

It feels freeing, because it's the truth.

Summer gasps and pulls away, her eyes wide and searching, her freckles popping against her skin. "You do?"

"I do," I murmur, bending my head to kiss her softly. "I love you, Summer. And I am sorry I was such an idiot before." I kiss her again, letting my hand drift up her neck to feel her hair. "I'll go anywhere you go."

"Really?" she whispers, her eyes shiny.

"Really. We have nothing and no one holding us back," I remind her, and she smiles widely.

"I only ever wanted to be with you," she tells me, resting her head against my chest and circling her arms around my middle.

"I still have a hard time believing that," I murmur, dropping my head to sniff her hair.

She pulls back and looks at me incredulously. "Seriously? Have you seen yourself?"

My skin heats up, and it's got nothing to do with the heat. "I should have—I should have told you. Before. *Way* before, in New York. Before you got—"

Summer jerks her hand up in a motion to cut me off. "None of that." She shakes her head, her expression fierce. This is the woman I love, her cheeks pink, her eyes flashing.

"When I tell you I want you, I want you as is—your past, present, and future," she says seriously. "Maybe we made mistakes before. But you know, we'll probably make mistakes again. And although it pains me to say this," she continues with a wince, "I'd make those same mistakes all over again if it means we can be together."

I pause, considering her words. What if I *had* had enough courage to tell Summer how I felt all those years ago? Who's to say it would have worked out anyway? Who's to say I was ready, or that she was?

"We have a lifetime to figure out our lifetime," she tells me softly, squeezing her arms around my middle.

I smile, leaning down to kiss her forehead before tucking her head under my chin.

"You're right, Sunshine," I respond, wrapping my arms around her. We stand like that in the heat, shaded by the pop-up.

If I have any say in it, we absolutely have a lifetime together. And I realize something that has previously escaped me: I *do* have a say. This is my life, my future undeterred by anything but my own insecurities.

I squeeze Summer tighter, breathing her in.

"Let's go home, Nick," she tells me.

Nothing sounds better.

Epilogue

Nick

One Year Later

SMACK. SMACK. SMACK.

My feet hit the wet sand alongside Layne Staley's paws. His tongue hangs out of his mouth as he trots happily beside me, returning to Estero Bay from our lengthy run.

Returning home to Summer.

The corners of my mouth turn up a little and my heart skips a beat when I think of her, in my—no, *our*—house, doing yoga or making tea or whatever the hell she is doing. I left her in our bed, warm and drowsy with sleep, when it became clear that Layne Staley was not going to be denied a lengthy run.

Warm, sleepy, and very satisfied after our night together.

It is warm and muggy on this September day, no fog or clouds in the sky, the Rock clear in the distance. The strand along Highway 1 is already full of beachgoers at this early hour, folks seeking respite from the heat. It's the kind of day where the cold waters of the Pacific are actually refreshing instead of just freezing.

Summer, Layne Staley, and I returned to Estero Bay a little over a month ago. We stayed in Austin just over six months, Summer doing choreography for the dance company, and me busy with the football camp. I had help from Brock and other players, thanks in no small part to Mando, who has apparently made it his life's mission to see that I am professionally satisfied in my retirement.

And I am.

Professionally satisfied, that is.

After Austin, we headed to Seattle, where Summer followed DeeDee on another artistic endeavor. Seattle in the winter and early spring is, to the surprise of no one, wet and rainy, and I spent the few months there relaxing, reading, and generally enjoying my time with Summer.

What I am saying is there was a lot of sex.

And I am not mad about it in the least.

After Seattle, we traveled a bit, spending time in the Basque country, France, and Spain, before returning home. To *our* home.

To say that I am personally satisfied would be the understatement of the year. Summer was right; I would live the same past ten times over if it means I can have Summer with me, in my arms, every day for the rest of my life. I have made peace with my past, and Summer with hers. I have made peace with the fact that my future—our future—might be uncertain, but it's still ours to live together.

"Today is another day you are alive, Nicky!"

I remember my father's words and feel grateful, not regretful.

I don't want to waste a minute.

∿∿∿∿∿

I grab a towel from a hook in the laundry room, doing my best to mop up my sweaty face. Layne Staley takes off toward his water bowl as soon as I unclip his leash.

"Sunshine?" I call, heading up the stairs to the living area.

"In here," she responds.

I huff up the last stair and drape the towel across my shoulder, moving to grab a water from the fridge. Summer stands at the sink, looking out the window at the bay, seemingly distracted as she sips her ginger tea, the steam wafting up from her purple mug.

Her hair is still mussed from sleep, and she has a pillow mark on one cheek. She's thrown one of my T-shirts over her body—never get tired of seeing her in my clothes—and gives me a half smile.

"What's up?" I move to kiss her cheek, trying not to sweat all over her.

"Hi, you," she responds, turning to kiss me full on the mouth, apparently not caring that I am sweaty.

"Hi, Sunshine," I murmur before closing my eyes and tasting her, the tangy ginger flavor intoxicating and familiar. "Tell me you're naked under that shirt."

She giggles a little and smacks me in the chest. "Ew," she says, waving her hand.

"It's humid out there," I acknowledge. "What's up?" I ask again, because she still looks distracted.

"I just got off the phone with Tatum," she responds, turning toward me, leaning against the countertop. I am struck by the memory of one of the first times she was in this exact same spot, sipping the same tea, while I cooked breakfast for her. She's just as beautiful now as she was then, and now I have the luxury of being able to touch her, kiss her.

She's mine, and I'm hers.

I smile as I move to run my hand up her smooth, freckled leg, seeking to test my theory about her underwear—or, God willing, her lack thereof.

"Okay?" That's nothing new. Tatum handled her shit, relinquishing her Asshole Society membership and fixing things with Summer.

"She, um, she has some news," Summer continues, her breath hitching a bit as my hand makes its way up, up, higher on her thigh, encountering more warm skin where ordinarily I would find her underwear.

I swallow and start estimating how quickly I can take an absolutely freezing-cold shower before getting sweaty with Summer in a different way.

"Okay," I repeat gruffly.

Summer puts a stop to my exploration, placing a hand on mine. "Nick."

I dart my eyes up to hers at her tone, which sounds serious.

"Tatum's pregnant."

THE END

Thank you so much for reading *The Second Wind!*

I hoped you liked Nick and Summer's story. If you have a moment and can leave a review, I would appreciate it so very much. Reviews are the best way for other readers to discover new authors like me! You can leave a review on Amazon.

Sign-up for my mailing list to receive information on my next release! You may already have an idea of who is going to be featured in Book Two…

www.samanthabensonauthor.com

Acknowledgements

In 2018, I was out to dinner with my husband, and told him I wanted to write a romance novel.

"That's great," he said. "You should totally do it."

So I went home, immediately plotted and drafted a compelling, interesting book, and released it into the wild.

Given that this book—my first book—is not seeing the light of day until August 2023, that is obviously *not* what happened. Nothing like a little global upheaval to get in the way!

BUT. I did it, and I hope you enjoyed it.

While writing is a solitary endeavor, this book would not be possible without the following people:

Thank you, first and foremost, to my husband, who encouraged me every step of the way. He understands time is currency and gave me the space necessary to go to my favorite coffee shop and get the words out. He also gets a huge thank you for coming up with the title, brainstorming the cover with me, and generally picking me up (metaphorically) when I would collapse into a heap of drama and snot (metaphorically), crying about how I was never going to be an author. Joke's on me!

Even though she won't read this (for a long time and maybe never), thank you to my daughter, my soulmate. She inspires me every day and I am so lucky to be her mother.

Thank you to Melinda Skye for reading my work, brainstorming with me, and just generally being a badass friend, mother, and writer. I will forever appreciate your encouragement and knowledge. Thank you also for the cinnamon rolls.

Thank you to Brent Burchett, editor, orator, and reader extraordinaire. I still have the first draft of this book printed in a folder labeled "Climate Issues," which is where I think I'll keep the working draft of whatever book I happen to be writing at the moment. Imagine someone looking to read about global warming's impacts on viticulture and instead finding some dirty romance! HA. I appreciate your intelligence and honesty. Now get up off your ass and write your own book!

Thank you to Allison for reading the dumpster fire of a first draft, and for talking about this book with me ad nauseam. If you ask me, the perfect day is you and I sitting on the beach with our notebooks and bubbly waters while our husbands chase after the children. There are also snacks involved. Let's make it happen.

Thank you to Kiah Twisselman Burchett for being the best hype-woman. You are wise beyond your years and such a badass. I could talk to you for hours about anything, and I feel so lucky to be your friend. Thank you also for helping me (dare I say coaching me?) about all things social media and websites. I don't feel like *so* much of a boomer now! (That's a lie, please never leave me)

Thank you to my family and friends for listening to me drone on about the mechanics of writing, publishing, marketing, advertising…and some other stuff I forgot. I promise to talk about other stuff now. Maybe. We'll see. Special shout-out to TeeTee and her many levels of soul, and my Moms Dinner Group.

Thank you to Lisa Hollett for your edits. I am so grateful I found you and I promise to buy a better thesaurus and sleep with the rules regarding em-dashes under my pillow.

Thank you to Mida for the Basque translations.

Thank you to Stacey for the flawless formatting.

Thank you to Sarah for the beautiful cover.

Thank you to Sarra Cannon for being such a selfless leader in the author community. You have helped me more than you will ever know.

And thanks to you, reader, for taking a chance on a new author. You probably know this but the best way for new authors like me to succeed is to get reviews, which you can leave at www.amazon.com/author/samanthabenson.. I know how busy you are, and I truly appreciate even a short review to let others know about my book.

Until next time,
Samantha

About the Author

Samantha Benson lives on California's central coast, the perfect setting for real life romance stories. Sam loves dirty-talking heroes, intelligent heroines, the ocean, Lay's potato chips, Las Vegas, and 90's music of nearly every genre. When not writing, she is reading, watching Law & Order reruns, or enjoying a bicycle ride with her family.

The Second Wind is Sam's first book, but it won't be the last! Sign up for her newsletter to be informed about her upcoming releases, and visit her website at www.samanthabensonauthor.com.